THE LOCATION SCOUT

a novel

Michael Jarvis

Brown Badger Books
Miami, Florida

Cover photo and design by the author
Cover layout by Vortex Communications
Author photo by Beverly Visitacion

For invaluable editorial assistance, the author
thanks Annie Smith

For Peter – friend, scout, traveler, photographer
And for Beverly, as ever

It was about that time I realized that searching was my symbol, the emblem of those who go out at night with nothing in mind, the motives of a destroyer of compasses.
—Julio Cortazar

We're always attracted to the edges of what we are, out by the edges where it's a little raw and nervy.
—E.L. Doctorow

Ah, good taste, what a dreadful thing! Taste is the enemy of creativeness.
—Pablo Picasso

What I like best is a book that's at least funny once in a while. What really knocks me out is a book that, when you're all done reading it, you wish the author that wrote it was a terrific friend of yours and you could call him up on the phone whenever you felt like it. That doesn't happen much, though.
—J.D. Salinger

CONTENTS

1. Mr Scout

Lucas Sloan remembered telling a friend of a friend, a marine carpenter working on a sailboat moored on the Miami River, that he was there to take some pictures of the boatyard because maybe it would be used in a television show, and the friend of a friend had stared at him for a minute and then laughed and said in a tone somewhere between incredulous and skeptical, "You're telling me that's an actual job?"

And now here Sloan was, walking down to the beach in front of a house in Nassau. All the clichés seemed proven true. The endless blue sky, the gin-clear water, the balmy tropical breeze, all of it calling the visitor to enter the water and relax. No wonder their advertising slogan—It's Better in the Bahamas—was working. It could just as easily have been: You Won't Be Bloody Sorry in the Bahamas.

But Sloan was carrying his backpack over his shoulder and was not dressed for swimming. Nassau was a quick jump over from Miami and he had landed that morning and hit the ground running. He found an available realtor, a friendly, wide-smiling guy named Clinton Pinder, who seemed eager, probably prompted by dreams of a finder's fee, to show him a house that the owner was willing to rent for short-term use in a television commercial.

"If the price is sufficient," he had added.

The main element, of course, was beachfront, that legendary Bahamian ocean beauty, the kind of imagery used again and again to sell whatever you wanted to sell. Just link your product to a proven, moneymaking scene that the viewer could mentally plant himself in with ease. The product hardly mattered. A brand of beer, a boat, a cleaning agent, sunglasses, baby powder, hair gel, underwear, toothpicks, a laxative, whatever you were hired to present and sell to the masses. They all mingled together in a vast market of beautiful images, catchy jingles and clever, irresistible pitches to the gluttonous consumer.

Sloan walked down a path sloping seaward behind the house, stepped onto the sand and crossed the expanse of beach toward the water. He needed to shoot this location and move on. This was no vacation and people were waiting for results. No matter the beauty and the beckoning call for enjoyment, the clock was ticking and the underlying tension of the job—the pressure to produce what you had been sent to do, to successfully complete your mission—was always present. Sure, you took it in stride, paused here and there to explore and appreciate the novelty of the situation, but the bedrock fact remained that you were there because someone was paying you to perform the job to the best of your ability.

He surveyed the long white beach, the tranquil surf rolling in and flattening into liquid sheets over the sandy surface, the bathers down the way frolicking in the clear warm water, the fishing boat crossing the horizon, the other beachfront houses that might be worth investigating. He took out his camera and slung the bag over his shoulder. Maybe he would walk for a while and check out the neighboring properties before it got even hotter.

But he'd been escorted here by Clinton Pinder. How much time did the realtor have? And what was he doing now? Airing out the house? Taking a shower? Making a sandwich? Was he napping?

Sloan looked back toward the house and his heart jolted. Frozen in disbelief, his feet melded with the wet sand. Three large black dogs were running down the slope at full speed, galloping right toward him. He saw instantly that they were Dobermans. Guard dogs. What the fuck?

His mind raced into calculations and survival vision. He glanced away, saw the sea, and tried to judge how far out he would need to go—waist deep at least—if the dogs pursued him into the water. He saw himself with the upper hand when they came dog-paddling at him. He could push the lead dog's head down if it came to it, holding the animal underwater until it gave up the chase or drowned. Surely the others would react to that threat, their legs waving rapidly through salt water, their feet no longer on solid ground, their long noses lifted above the glittering surface.

He turned to see the dogs quickly closing the distance to him. He could not understand why he was still standing in the same stationary position, why he had not dropped his gear on the beach a long time ago and begun to sprint, why he was not already splashing wildly through the surf. Was he suicidal and, only just now, in this fraught moment of indecision, able to recognize it? Did he think that by remaining perfectly still he might be mistaken for a piece of driftwood? Did he think that he would be so coated in the sweat of fear that gnashing teeth would slide right off his skin?

In his distress he must have wanted to seem nonthreatening and his hands lifted above his head. His midsection—groin and belly—were exposed. Wasn't this like a wolf surrendering to the more dominant members of the pack?

The Dobermans braked, three parts of one fearsome muscular beast, a terrifying vision of Cerberus. They nosed him and sniffed and gathered whatever information they needed. He saw a blur of animal movement as their heads circled his motionless form. In a matter of seconds they regrouped and tore off up the beach, eager to run and gather more information and scare the hell out of other unsuspecting beachgoers.

Clinton was coming down the pathway to the sand. He waved as he approached, then frowned when he was close enough to read the expression on his visitor's face. A second later his dark shiny face transformed back into the features of a beaming salesman and he extended his arms as if presenting his personal version of island paradise to a lucky foreigner.

"How about all this, mahn? Just what you ask for." When he got no answer, he said, "Why you looking cross, Mr Scout?"

"The dogs, Clinton. Somehow you neglected to mention the dogs."

"Ahh," Clinton said, shaking his head in apparent disbelief, then chuckling a little. "Them dogs is friendly, mahn. So friendly. Big lovable puppies."

Sloan smiled back. "That's great to hear, man. The only little problem is that I had no fucking idea what those dogs were about. You know, never having *seen* them before."

Clinton frowned comically, exaggerating the downward movement of his lips to make a face he might use with friends later over drinks to illustrate how his visitor had appeared.

"Seriously mahn," he said. "Seriously. You got to relax mahn. You not stressing back home now."

"I don't stress at home, Clinton. I don't have big dogs running right at my balls."

Clinton clapped his long hands together and laughed. "That's good, mahn. I see you coming around to the humor of the situation." He reached out and put his fingers on Sloan's shoulder. "You alright, Mr Scout," he said.

Sloan looked down the beach and saw the dogs playing, chasing each other in the shallow surf.

"It's fine," he said. "I enjoy wildly elevated heart rates from time to time. Let me take some shots here at the beach and we'll go up to the house so I can get the interior."

Clinton's face formed a lightweight frown, his shorthand signal of any slight problem on the immediate horizon. "Well, that's the thing, mahn. Mr Clancy don't authorize interiors. Everything else on the property. And all this," he said, sweeping his arm to indicate the view of as much of the world as could be seen from this spot.

Sloan looked askance at his host. "But I thought you understood," he said. "The commercial has a man stepping out of his house onto the porch with the beverage in his hand and then taking in the view."

Continuing the motion of his sweeping arm, Clinton's directional indicator now pointed at the house. "No porch Mr Scout," he said.

"Yes, I see that. All the more reason for the talent to step out with the beverage he just got from his kitchen. Sometimes we have to improvise with the real-world location. Maybe we trade the porch for the island kitchen, a cool relaxing place to start the action. Maybe there's a window to the beach."

"Ahh," Clinton said. He squinted up at the house

as if visualizing the kitchen and his own vision of the commercial. "The camera can catch him right by that oceanside door," he suggested. "The man, he just admiring the day, feeling pretty good, but not quite perfect." Clinton smiled the broad smile he may have seen himself using with ad agency execs in New York City as he made his pitch. "Just then this fine young island lady come round the corner and hand him his beverage, sweat running down the can but her face cool and sexy. Now things getting a whole lot better."

Lucas Sloan looked down at the wet sand, the paw prints and the toenail trenches, the chaos of thrown sand trails. He looked up at Clinton again. "Here's the thing," he said. "I'm not hired to rewrite the commercial. I'm hired to find the places to shoot it."

"Of course, mahn," Clinton said. "But I got just the girl in mind. Very fine."

"Well goddamn, my friend," Sloan said. "Why don't you call her up and let's go get some lunch."

Clinton squinted at the American. "You joking, right?"

"Yes, I'm joking," Sloan said. "Let's get this work done, perhaps look at another couple of houses, then grab a cold Kalik later in the day with your lovely niece."

Clinton smirked. "How you know she's my niece?"

"Just a lucky guess," Sloan said.

2. The Producer and the Pinders

The Regal Bahamian Hotel was wasted on Lucas Sloan. It totally sufficed, especially for a late reservation, and had plenty of amenities and comforts. But it was essentially too big for his needs, its bureaucracy geared to dealing with groups booking outdoor activities and long leisurely meals. He didn't have the time to wait in line with people drifting through their days in pursuit of recreation. Or to get caught up in the great creaking morass of the place with its valet parking, bottomless breakfast buffets, diving and snorkeling trips, fishing excursions, rounds of golf, tennis lessons and court reservations, croquet, shuffleboard, extravagant lunches, solar alignment of pool chairs and umbrellas, rolled-towel pyramids, snack and drink orders, bocce, billiards, kayaks, Jet Skis, and cocktails delivered by costumed waiters in matching hibiscus print shirts and white slacks who rotated nearby like a fractured Vegas revue, quietly omnipresent and completely accustomed to the demands of everyone from track-suited rappers to dysfunctional families.

Sloan had just gotten to his third-floor room and removed his sandals on the balcony when his phone rang. He saw the New York number of the producer who had hired him the day before.

"Hello," he said, imbuing this single word with focused energy and purpose.

"Luke, how goes it?" Trevor said, not actually inquiring about Sloan himself, but about the job.

Sloan pictured the man: leaning back in an ergonomic chair, running shoes up on the desk, the metropolitan skyline in view, eyes scanning his computer screen, one hand squeezing a relaxation ball, the other on a mouse opening emails while in reach of a steaming chai latte.

"Yeah, pretty good," Sloan said. "Shot three beach houses. Couple more lined up for tomorrow."

"What's that noise?" Trevor said.

Sloan stepped inside and closed the sliding door behind him. "A conga line at the pool."

"A what?" Trevor said.

"You know, tourists having a good time."

"Couldn't you find a more corporate place—less distractions and with a production rate?"

"It was last-minute," Sloan said, mentally rolling his eyes. "I was lucky to get anything decent."

"When will I see some pics?" Trevor said.

"I'll upload as soon as I can," Sloan said, lying back on the bed under the ceiling fan. "Front desk said there was a temporary internet issue."

"Are you fucking kidding me?"

Sloan imagined the man jerking forward, spilling warm chai on his pants. "Probably too many people using it," he said. "They'll get it fixed soon to avoid complaints."

"You should go out and find another source," Trevor said. "A café or something."

"I'll just grab a quick bite," Sloan said, "and by

then I should be good to go."

"Make it quick, my man," Trevor said. "The agency is all over me on this."

"Absolutely," Sloan said. "I'll text you when the upload's done."

"Ciao," Trevor said.

Sloan showered and went down to the lounge, a large dark room with a three-sided bar and heavy wood tables and rattan chairs. From his barstool he perused the menu and the scene, downing a cold draft beer and then a rum on the rocks. The room was fairly lively for a weeknight, the music a steady pump of calypso and reggae for the casually well-dressed crowd of young couples, businessmen, and local players. The job pressure he carried in his chest began to dissipate and he thought about the dogs of that morning and how long ago it seemed and he laughed under his breath. The fun surprises of the trade.

He ordered grilled grouper with rice and pigeon peas and another rum and then took another look around the room. The door from the lobby opened and an attractive woman in a slinky, form-fitting dress entered and stood waiting as a man joined her. Clinton nodded toward the bar and escorted the woman over. She wore a ponytail afro and her dark skin was as smooth as lychee flesh.

"Well, well, Mr Scout," Clinton said. "I see you relaxing after a hard day producing."

Sloan stood and shook the offered hand. "Yes indeed, Mr Pinder. Good to see you."

"May I present my lovely and talented Brenda," Clinton said, gesturing at the woman with open palms.

Niece, cousin, or girlfriend, Lucas Sloan did not care. He was pleased to meet her and extended his hand. "My pleasure, Brenda Pinder," he said. "Clinton's description of you did not go far enough."

"Just Brenda," she said, smiling at him as their palms bonded. "Pleased to meet you too. Clinton has been praising your nerves of steel, Mr Sloan."

Clinton let out a laugh and slapped Sloan on the shoulder, reminding him to release the woman's hand.

Sloan suggested they grab a corner table that had just opened. Clinton and Brenda headed over while Sloan presented his credit card to the bartender, asking the man to separate the food and the alcohol, putting the food on his room and the drinks on the card and keeping the tab open for the three of them.

At the table Sloan's meal arrived and Clinton ordered a burger and fries, along with a rum and soda. "To wash it down," he said. Brenda abstained from food but opted for a white wine, which she sipped only occasionally and in such a way that the volume line hardly lowered.

"I told her you might be considering the hiring of some local talent," Clinton said.

Sloan laughed involuntarily, then straightened his face and looked seriously at Brenda. "If it was in my power," he said, "you would be at the very front of the line."

"I'm studying to be an actress," she said, her large dark eyes pooling moisture as she blinked demurely, on the verge of tears and auditioning for a part.

"That's great," he said. "Where are you studying?"

"With my cousin," she said, and a single tear ran down her left cheek like an exclamation point.

Clinton swirled the ice in his glass. "Mr Lucas Sloan knows many people," he said.

"You are the producer," Brenda said.

"No, I'm the location scout," Sloan said.

"But he has the ear of the producer," Clinton said. "And the director. And all the rest. He's the only one right here mixing with the locals. Meeting people and making *con-nec-tions*," he said, drawing out the last word and adding volume. "He's the trailblazer."

Sloan smiled at this and let the assessment rest. His phone vibrated in his pocket. The waiter appeared with food and the men ordered more drinks and ate their meals.

"Who you working for?" Brenda said, slowly turning her full glass around by its stem, a semi-sophisticated gesture to counter her lonely abstinence. Two men at the bar were looking at her.

The lounge noise had fallen off a bit, and Sloan leaned toward her as if in conspiratorial confidence. "I'm a freelance agent," he said, "so I get hired by different companies. Case by case, like a detective. Or a mercenary." He was feeling the rum, growing more poetic, more romantic. "Battle by battle," he said.

"So serious," she said, smiling. "Life and death struggles. But which is the current employer of your deadly soldiers?"

He leaned back and took another sip. They were both watching him. "It's a production company called Wiseman, Torrance, and Ferragamo," he said, "commonly known in the industry as WTF."

Clinton laughed. "For real," he said.

Sloan nodded. "The order of the names was based on seniority and neither of the first two was willing to change it," he said. "Three directors with big egos whose collective attitude turned out to be the same as their initials. They could have chosen something generic like Circus Act or Team Bro but I guess they wanted to sound subversive, edgier than their work could ever be."

Brenda squelched a little giggle, deciding she did not want to appear frivolous. "You don't sound like a big fan," she said.

"I don't need to love their work to work for them," he said. "Last year I did a job with Ferragamo. It went well and they called me back. That's how it goes.

You're only as good as your last job."

"They make movies?" she asked.

"Just commercials," he said. "They develop an idea they get from an ad agency who is hired by the client."

"And this client is a beverage," she said.

"This client is a top secret new beverage," he said. "Super Berry Soda, aka SBS. Don't tell anyone or I might be killed."

She laughed. "Secret?" she said, glancing around the lounge. "Are there spies following you?"

"You would think so," Sloan said. "Maybe you've heard of corporate espionage. Funny, right?"

Clinton leaned forward and spoke in a low voice. "Some fella at the bar been watching us and listening," he said. "Real close."

"I would expect that," Sloan said, "with Brenda sitting here." His phone buzzed again.

"Excuse me for a second," he said, pushing back his chair. "I just want to answer a text." He crossed to the door to the patio and stepped outside.

Trevor's text was short. *Shoot me an update.*

Another text arrived, from a number he didn't know. *Hey Luke, it's Amanda from WTF. Director will call you at 8am to go over new brief. Thanks.*

He answered Amanda. *Got it, thanks.*

Then Trevor. *Standby, soon come.*

There was one couple in the pool, hugging the ladder in the deep end while hugging each other closely. Sloan imagined he heard sounds of moaning and lifted his eyes beyond the pool to the swaying beach palms, the pier with its huddled watercraft, the ocean, and the soft dark sky.

He turned to see Brenda standing beside him. "Hey," she said, her hand touching his arm.

"Hey," he said. "You're quite stealthy."

"I'm a corporate spy," she said, smiling mischievously. "I'm not disturbing you, am I?"

"Not at all," he said. "Where's Clinton?"

"He's fine," she said, her hand still on his arm. "Saw somebody he knows."

"Cool," Sloan said. "You want to walk out to the pier?"

"Sure," she said.

Since she inquired, he explained that he'd been in the film business for at least fifteen years—probably closer to twenty if he did the math—and had worked on movies, television shows, commercials, and to a lesser extent, print campaigns for magazine ads, and to an even lesser extent (and hopefully never again) music videos. He was divorced. No kids. No pets (though he was fond of petting and speaking to most of the dogs he encountered). There were no responsibilities that prevented him from taking off on a job with hardly any notice. As to what attracted him to the work, he paused and reflected as they stood at the pier's railing and looked out to sea, the reflection of starlight tumbling through the surf beyond the offshore islands, the glittering shoreline lights stretching to the east where Atlantis rose like the fabled holiday kingdom it was rumored to be.

"I like working alone and I like exploring," he said. "Seeing new places, meeting new people, figuring out what has to be done to complete the mission."

"What about the crew?" she said.

"When someone else shows up," he said, "that's another story. A whole different ballgame."

"That must be hard on someone special left at home," she said.

"It was," he said. "A relationship can get pulled apart by the distance and time away."

She stood listening beside him, then pulled back and touched his cheek and turned his face to look at her. "You let me know if you need any help here," she said. "In a foreign place you may need a friend you can call on."

"Thanks," he said, suddenly noticing other people to his right. "I appreciate that."

Another couple had noiselessly materialized at the opposite railing. "Where'd they come from?" he said. "Did they approach by sea?"

"The night is full of spies," she said, smiling at his look of feigned shock. "And you are naturally suspicious, I imagine."

The other couple did not look at them but began to act as if they had the pier to themselves, the man pushing his partner against the railing with his body and bending her backward with an onslaught of sloppy kisses, her head twisting to counter him, the sounds of their passion soon filling the air with wet noises easily heard over the sea breeze bending the nearby palm fronds in apparent solidarity.

"Sounds like they're shoveling mud over there," Sloan said.

Brenda squeezed a hand over her mouth and suppressed an urge to laugh.

"Digging for clams," he said. "I think they were in the pool earlier and needed to get wetter."

"Why don't they just go to their room?" she said.

"Well, aren't you the practical sort?" he said. "They could be stuck in foreplay. Or getting turned on by being seen. They might be members of a tongue-sucking society."

Now it sounded like fish were breaking the surface on the other side of the pier.

Brenda was gazing at him. "You like that too?" she said.

"What, the sound of mullet jumping?" He gave her his skeptical look. "I'm the secretive type," he said. "I like spycraft. I could go into greater detail on our next meeting," he said, "but I still have to get some work done tonight."

"A meeting or a date?" she said, cocking her head slightly.

"I don't think we even have to name it," he said.

3. The Brief

In the morning Sloan made a cup of watery room coffee and sat on the balcony drinking it as the pool was being cleaned below. A few early risers were walking on the beach and there was activity on the pier as the ferry was readied for the first wave of guests going out to the resort's private island, an idyllic-looking strip of sand and palms a quarter mile offshore. It was both an auxiliary beach and a fantasy island. From its oceanside perspective imaginative guests could pretend, depending on literary preferences and family dynamics, that they were castaways like Robinson Crusoe and his man Friday, the Swiss Family Robinson, or Prospero, Miranda, and Caliban, should Shakespearean dreams prevail. For the less historically minded, there were the shipwrecked characters of recent motion pictures.

His phone rang at 7:35. He put down a packet of crackers and finished crunching before he answered.

"How's the weather?" Trevor said.

"In a word, perfect," Sloan said.

"Good. Keep it that way," Trevor said, only partly

joking. "Wiseman will be calling you shortly. The client is rethinking everything. Apparently ripped the creative a new asshole last night for the lackluster concept."

Trevor was drinking a thick energy smoothie with too much protein powder and as he tilted it vertically a sizable mass broke its cohesive seal with the side of the cup and, like an iceberg calving, slid into his mouth. He swallowed too much, too fast, and the resulting gurgle rippled into Sloan's ear like a tiny tsunami.

After a dramatic choking fit, Trevor continued at a higher pitch. "I'm hearing something about an island," he said, the last word sounding like "Ireland," due to the overflow occurring at the corners of his mouth. He coughed. "Don't they have one where you're staying? An offshore island."

"I'm looking at it," Sloan said. "The first of many boatloads is filling up to head over."

"Is there a time when no one is there?" Trevor said.

"Yeah, at night," Sloan said.

"I'm thinking buyout," Trevor said.

"It's part of the hotel," Sloan said. "They're not going to tell paying guests that Fantasy Island is closed for the day."

"Give it a shot," Trevor said. "You never know how their financial picture actually looks. Word is, the client is ready to throw more money at this. They want a real wow factor when this beverage rolls out."

"Okay, I'll ask the question," Sloan said.

"Feel it out," Trevor said. "Don't mention any specific sum. Let them tell you."

"Sure," Sloan said. "I need to get moving."

"Your houses look decent," Trevor said. "Follow up, get some prices in case we have to pivot back to that. Ciao."

Sloan was stepping out of the shower when his

phone rang again. He wrapped a towel around his waist, went out to the balcony and stood dripping. "Hello," he said.

"Good morning Luke. This is Amanda from WTF. Hold for Alan Wiseman please."

"Holding," Sloan said, watching a woman in a black bikini doing laps.

"Sloan," a loud New Yorker's voice said. "We need a fantastic fucking island, a place that shouts at the viewer "YOU NEED TO BE RIGHT HERE, RIGHT FUCKING NOW." You get me? I don't even care how we get the fucking gear there. I just want a place that blows your mind. Brilliant white sand, crystal blue water, idyllic in every sense of the word. Nothing but paradise."

"Yeah," Sloan said, "I get it. What's the action?"

"Our guy," Wiseman said, sounding like he was shouting from Queens, "steps off a boat with his SBS in hand and can't fucking believe where he is. But doesn't show it. He's cool with the whole scene. Accepts it as natural, the place he's been heading his whole fucking life."

"So we see the boat," Sloan said. "Do we need a landing spot?"

"There is no fucking infrastructure at all," Wiseman said. "The boat will back up into the shallows to unload our single passenger, who will step off the stern like they do in The Virgins and Costa Rica. We'll see the boat approach from open water. Then I'll cheat the reverse if necessary so we still see open ocean. I'll use a chopper to establish the wide— the boat pulling away, leaving our man in paradise. It would be great to see coral heads juxtaposed with powder white sand. Textures, rough and smooth, like life's journey. Then I'm close-up on our man, serenity on his face as he drinks in his reward. Background is majestic—coconut palms, not sea grapes and a bunch of scrub shit. Then the horizon, open sea, infinity, optimism, wordless pleasure. You get me? Our man does not utter one fucking word."

"Understood," Sloan said. "I'll start researching a boat scout right now."

"This is happening fast," Wiseman said.

"And this client is a motherfucker," he added.

4. The Hero Island

Of course, what else would he be doing except looking for a desert island? Sloan had done this before and was familiar with the region.

Over to the north of Andros were the Berry Islands. Stringy, rocky, topped with low scrub, bordered by shallow water and other islands. Neither the director nor the audience would yearn to be there.

Around Nassau there were only so many choices and only one that could actually work. How many ways can you pitch a desert island? No point in getting too philosophical. How many original ways can you scout the same brief?

He got Clinton on the phone and explained the change.

"What about the houses I been setting up?"

"We have to leave those behind for now," Sloan said. "I need a boat to Sandy Island and I need to get in touch with the owner."

The pause seemed like a dead line. "Clinton?"

"I can't be jackin around, mahn," he said. "I got deals happening."

"No one's jacking around. Things change. Right now I need to get a boat."

"Weather comin in," Clinton said. "Better tomorrow."

Sloan exhaled with the phone lifted away from his mouth. "Can you give me a name?"

"I got no contract," Clinton said. "I got nothing for my time."

"It's not over," Sloan said. "We just need results that work for the current brief."

"Let me check around, call you back later," Clinton said. Then he hung up.

"Fuck," Sloan said.

He walked down to Bay Street, past the circle to the market, and bought a cheese sandwich and a strong black coffee and stood outside at the wall sweating through his shirt. Cars and scooters and golf carts moved back and forth through the heat. He tracked a parasail out over the water, two tourists hanging in straps like meat cabled to the boat pulling them above shark level.

Back at the hotel's front desk he waited in line and inquired. "No rental boats we can recommend, I'm afraid, sir," the clerk said. "You may wish to check down under the bridge by Potters Cay."

Taxis hovered out front. He hopped in one with his backpack. He was light—sandals, shades, fast-drying shorts—and carried cash, camera, and water. They drove along the waterfront, past the wharf, through downtown, to the docks under the bridge.

A carnival market of boats, conch sellers, seafood shacks. The smell of smoke and seawater. The air layered and tarnished with fuel and fish and sun.

A conch seller told Sloan the place was all working boats. "No help for island hopping," he said.

"Someone must know someone who wants some extra money," Sloan said.

"Maybe in the afternoon," the man said. "But a storm coming over by Andros then."

"I need to get out to Sandy Island before that," Sloan said.

"Got a marina down the road and a seaplane office over there," the conch man said, gesturing toward the base of the bridge.

Sloan nodded. "I'll check those out," he said, moving away. "Thanks man."

"Better weather tomorrow," the man said. "Clear skies."

Overhead, the bridge thumped with the rumble of tires and horns blared, a stream of vehicles rocketing to and from Paradise Island. The seaplane office was closed and the sky was clear. Sloan took a photo of the door with its contact info, then went into the office supply store next door.

"Clive's out on a trip," the shopkeeper said. "One man, one plane. Leave him a message."

Sloan asked for and received two short strips of tape with which he stuck his business card on the seaplane office's door, along with a written message.

PLEASE CALL ASAP. Need early trip to Sandy Island. Tomorrow. Thanks, LS

He added the date and time to the message.

Then he called the number on the door and left a voice message saying that he was leaving a note on the door and then relayed the note's content in calm, well-measured words, adding more detail to explain the urgency. He returned to the office supply store and informed the man that he had left the two messages and would appreciate it if the shopkeeper could have a personal word with the pilot or his wife or assistant or girlfriend if he happened to cross paths with any of them later that day or in the morning. He thanked the man and bought a roll of tape to show his gratitude, and in case he found himself in a similar note-leaving scenario again.

To loosen his mind and engage his shooting eye, he took photos of the scene at Potters Cay. Boats and vendors, sunlight sparkling off the water on either side of the lane of shade the bridge threw down, and the floating arc it drew through the blue above. General coverage of light and color. Some days his eye was on—shapes clicked into form, compositions rolled out in fluid sheets, balance and torsion married and bore fruit, giving birth to more than themselves, fully formed images that cried out and then breathed on their own. Other days, he stumbled in a fog, shooting wildly to disturb and waken his sleeping eye. Today he squinted, half-blind behind polarized eyes.

He moved east along Bay Street and found the marina.

The trip out to Sandy Island was only four miles. The hot May sun blasted the world into pixels of blue, green, and white, and the waves threw knives of light in their faces. They were in a Whaler 17 Montauk, the young captain Niven at the console, the blue breeze-inflated Bimini top offering a slice of shade for Sloan to stand under and take their general bearings. The other passenger, a shirtless Brian Mouvance from Louisiana, lounged in the sun across the bow seat and tried to keep his plastic beer mug from spilling whenever he took a drink. He said he was catching up with his vacation buddies and the thought of a fraternity party on the beach gave Sloan a bout of psychic nausea.

Still, he was surprised to see what amounted to a marine invasion of the small island. With the tide falling a long west-reaching sandbar extended like an inviting tentacle that doubled the length of the land and provided a narrow white beach where a lone serious man might contemplate the universe while ingesting his newly discovered miracle beverage.

Wouldn't a normal person, Sloan thought, be having a cup of coffee? Was Super Berry Soda loaded with caffeine?

But now, in the heated doldrums of a sunny afternoon, a string of anchored boats lined up along the beach like remoras attached to a shark. Various sources of music—heavy metal, ska, Top 40—blasted and intersected over the water and made Sloan think of the crossed wires in a maniac's brain.

Brian Mouvance stood up and waved as they approached the sandbar but none of the prancing partiers in the water acknowledged him. On the lee side Niven slowly brought the vessel parallel to the sandbar to drop off his first passenger. Sloan stood, examining the rest of the island, its small but fairly perfect castaway size, the open ocean to the north, the palms at the other end.

Brian Mouvance crouched on the bow seat in preparation to disembark.

"Hey," someone shouted. "It's BM. He found us." Several guys about Brian's age pointed and laughed, one of them flinging himself backwards in the water as if he had passed out with shock or dismay. A chorus was taken up. "BM is here. BM is here."

Niven idled and motioned to Brian Mouvance, who gave him a thumbs-up and leapt overboard with one hand on the rail and the other holding his mug. He caught his right foot and his body turned and splashed sideways into the water. He came up laughing with his thumb raised again. His friends howled as he swam to retrieve his mug. Someone shouted, "Our BM boy is chasing a floater."

There were a couple of other boats positioned at the island's central beach and Sloan could see people among the trees. Niven eased into the shallows, nudged the Whaler's bow up onto the sand and cut the engine. Sloan sat on the gunwale and hopped down into thigh-deep water.

"This sucks," he said, looking up at Niven. "All these boats. I need to shoot this place with no one around, maybe at sunset. Does it clear out by then?"

The young Bahamian shrugged. "People come and go as they feel. Cloudy day better for you."

"But not for photos," Sloan said. "I'll be back in a bit." He shifted his backpack, trailing his hand along the boat's hull for balance as he moved toward shore, and then stepped up onto the beach.

To the south the expanse of Rose Island and its long eastward tail filled the view. Nassau and New Providence Island loomed across the southwest. He walked over to the north side. Small waves lapped at the rocks lining the windward shore after they broke on the reef some forty yards out. He spotted two snorkels and the corresponding appearance of fins breaking the surface. The view out there was uninterrupted ocean, pristine castaway background. He continued eastward to the palms and the picnic occurring outside the ruins of an old stone cottage. A half dozen men and women stood or sat talking and laughing around a blanket with coolers and beach bags. One of them waved as Sloan passed through the shadows of fronds.

At the eastern point Sloan looked back to consider the angles and shot sequence. He would have to show all the boats, all the reverses with their other land masses, everything that was not in the brief. But he didn't have to emphasize those elements. The story started right here, among the palms, fronds and sky, the remote feeling conjured in the viewer's mind when the eye saw nothing but sand and coconuts and the blue horizon.

He lay on the ground and shot up through palms to the sky, then moved between the trunks, shooting the shifting blue view of ocean stretching away forever.

He moved along the southside beach looking back at the palms, a broader view. The light wasn't great but so far the location looked deserted. The cottage ruins were mostly hidden and a few extra greens could cover any angle desired. He turned around to show the reverse, the other islands and all the yahoo boaters. He heard a whistle.

Niven was waving at him. Motioning him over. Then pointing to the west where a vast gray veil of moisture hung in the air like an entrance to upheaval. Anchors were being pulled, boats were backing out, voices were shouting and laughing on top of the music.

Walking to the Whaler, Sloan slid his camera into a plastic bag and stuffed it into his backpack.

"Push the bow off," Niven said.

"Can't we wait it out?" Sloan said.

"No mahn, we got to go now."

"Everyone will leave and I can shoot the late light," Sloan said.

Niven shook his head. "Push her off and get aboard," he said.

The rain came hissing toward them, the surface jumping like electricity.

"What if I stayed and you picked me up later?" Sloan said.

Niven started the engine. "Not in the contract, mahn," he said. "They will charge your card for default."

Sloan pushed them off and pulled himself up the side and climbed into the boat as it turned away. The picnickers had run out of the trees and were loading up quickly. The Whaler got up on plane and slashed into the wall of stinging rain. Sloan squinted back at the misty island, a mirage now, and saw it and the last beached boat erased into nothing.

5. Circumstantial Tension

At Sailor's Haven, a boater's dive near the marina, Sloan dried out and drank rum while rain pounded on the metal roof. In the loud semi-darkness he consumed a fish sandwich with fries and slaw in record time. He shared the bar with several nearly invisible locals but couldn't identify anyone he would unmistakenly label a boater, or even a deckhand.

As soon as the rain ceased he called Clinton Pinder, got his voicemail, and left a message.

"Mr Pinder, Mr Sloan here. I'm calling about those properties we appraised. Let's discuss terms at your earliest convenience."

He called the Bahamas Film and Television Commission and a woman answered.

"Good afternoon. Film Commission. Roberta Albury speaking," she said.

"Good afternoon Roberta Albury. This is Lucas Sloan from Miami. I'm scouting locations over here for a commercial from New York. I'd like to reach the owner of Sandy Island as soon as possible."

"I see," she said. "Mr Sloan, please hold the line for

a moment." He heard the receiver clank as it was set down on a hard surface, then what sounded like a metal chair scraping over what he imagined was a standard government linoleum floor. He heard voices in the background, an indecipherable conversation occurring between two or more people. It turned out to be a lengthy discussion and he began to wonder if the conversation had moved to a topic that did not involve him at all. He found himself listening with intent, imagining he heard something about a bridge tournament, then part of a recipe for hot sauce. He used the time to order another drink and then stood up and headed back to the restroom carrying his damp backpack and holding his phone to his ear.

The restroom's narrow door was pushed inward to reveal a broom-closet-sized space, which in fact held an assortment of brooms and mops leaning as a battered cleaning gang in a back corner of the toilet stall, plainly visible due to the stall's missing door. A high tiny window let in some modicum of air but not nearly enough to combat the accumulated odors emitted by the bacterial colony in residence.

Sloan hung his backpack on the window's handle and faced the urinal holding his phone up near his ear. It was on speaker now and as he peed he heard some coughing, then a shout.

"Hello," he said, but there was no reply.

He heard someone scrape past the restroom and then the back door creak open and slam softly, as if brought to close by the weakened elasticity of an elderly spring. A miniscule wafting of weed soon entered the window and he alternated this small olfactory pleasure with periods of holding his breath.

He flushed the toilet with his elbow, lifted his pack and exited without touching the sink. He pushed open the rear door and stuck his head out squinting like a mole rat into the steaming sunset. Two guys sitting on upturned buckets were in the process of passing a joint between them and they paused as they saw Sloan holding his phone up like he was about to pass them a call.

"I'm on hold," he said. "For like twenty minutes."

One of the guys, wearing a stained, formerly white apron, held up the burning joint and Sloan reached down and took it. He drew a significant toke and handed the joint to the other guy just as his phone let out the profound *thunk* of what could have been a three-hole punch and then shuffling and thumping sounds, like pieces of paper being organized into a tight stack by slamming the held ends together on the surface of a table or desk. The three backdoor smokers burst into laughter for no reason other than the perceived humor found in mundane office tasks.

"Mr Sloan," a voice said. "Mr Sloan, are you there?"

"Yes," he said. "Yes, Roberta, I'm still here."

"Mrs Albury," she said.

"Of course," he said, stepping out into the rising steam. "I descended into limbo and lost my way."

"I beg your pardon," she said.

"That was a record hold for me," he said.

"My apologies, Mr Sloan," she said. "We have other requests in addition to yours."

"No problem," he said. "We're here for each other."

"In a manner of speaking," she said. "Pursuant to your request, I was able to reach the assistant of Mrs Sweeting, the property owner's representative."

"Outstanding," he said, dancing a few steps and pumping his free arm in the air.

"She said they have some photo shoots coming up and availability is an issue."

He came to a complete standstill while the alleyway and the adjacent buildings seemed to pulsate around him. The backdoor man in the splattered apron—which at this moment reminded Sloan of a Jackson

Pollock painting—offered the joint again in what appeared to be such a supremely sympathetic gesture of support that Sloan stepped over and took it.

"You see, Mrs Albury," he said, inhaling sharply, "we only need the island for a single day and I would be honored to meet with Mrs Sweeting at her earliest convenience and figure out a mutually beneficial arrangement." He exhaled and coughed away from the phone. "I can assure you and Mrs Sweeting that we are seriously interested in the island and I think a face-to-face would be mutually beneficial." Fuck, didn't he just use that phrase?

The apronman stood and went back inside. Sloan returned the joint to the other man and gave him the universal OK hand signal, a thumb and index circle with three standing fingers, meaning yes, that was plenty for the three of us and thank you for sharing.

Out there in the slanting light and gelatin shadows and pauses, Sloan felt he may have slipped into another hold and he listened again for the sounds of office life. Seagulls were passing overhead.

He jumped when Mrs Albury spoke. "I'll see what I can do, Mr Sloan. Let me have your number."

He said his number twice and thanked Mrs Roberta Albury. He told her he loved the Bahamas.

6. Freelance Gambling

As Sloan wandered the bustling street in search of a taxi, Clive Dorsey, the sole pilot and owner of Island Seaplane Adventures, returned his call in a jaunty British accent.

"I just got back to my office and saw your note," he said. "Had to dodge that storm but no worse for the wear. Are you still in need of an early flight to Sandy then?"

"I am," Sloan said. "I want to shoot sunrise by air and ground before anyone else shows up."

"Roger that," Dorsey said. "If we depart at zero six thirty you should be good."

"Great," Sloan said. "I just need an hour. What will that run me?"

"That will run you fifteen hundred," Dorsey said.

"No shit," Sloan said. "Seems high for an hour."

"Yeah," Dorsey said. "Half-day rate, mate. If I'm out with you I'm missing someone else."

"I have no problem," Sloan said. "But it's not my money so I'll have to get it cleared."

"Yeah, sure," Dorsey said. "I'll put you down and if

you confirm within the hour, we're on. If not, it'll have to wait a few days until I get back from the Abacos."

Sloan agreed and realized he had stopped walking directly in front of a liquor store. He popped in for a quart of rum, then stepped out and hailed a passing taxi. Things are falling into place, he thought. Trust your instincts. He called Trevor from the back seat, got his voicemail, then sent a text.

Call me asap. Time sensitive. Thanks.

He got an immediate reply. *On the phone. Call you soon.*

Sloan was back in his room in thirty minutes. He ran his head under the shower and toweled his hair vigorously, picturing himself drying a thick-coated dog. A chow chow came to mind.

He texted Trevor again. *Time sensitive, as in very soon.*

The phone rang six minutes later. Nine minutes left on Dorcey's deadline.

"Budget meeting," Trevor Welch said. "What's up?"

"I want to book a seaplane to get an early look at this island," Sloan said.

"Why don't you get a boat?"

"I did that today but the place was mobbed."

"Are you posting up?"

"I didn't get the shots I want yet."

"What's the plane cost?"

"Fifteen."

"No fucking way. Just post what you have. We'll take it from there."

"Look," Sloan said. "I want to sell this location and I can't do it yet."

"Focus on some other options," Trevor said. "We can't have one fucking choice."

"Don't you think I've thought of that?" Sloan said. "Other islands are unsuitable or off-limits. The one in front of this hotel looks like something used by cruise ships. It's not *Robinson Crusoe*, it's *Night of the Living Dead*."

"Get the boat again."

"They don't open early enough. I can get sunrise with the seaplane."

"Here's what you do," Trevor said. "Post what you have, mention the seaplane in your notes, scout another choice so there's something else on the table, and let's regroup after that."

"Look, Trevor, this place can work if it's shot right. The seaplane offers aerial and sea level. Wiseman told me he wants to do aerials on this shoot."

"You're not hearing me. We just had a fucking budget meeting. Everyone's looking at the money now. You don't need to do aerials just because *he* wants to do aerials."

"You're not hearing me," Sloan said. "I'm trying to deliver the location on a silver fucking platter."

"What the fuck, dude?" Trevor said. "Have you been drinking?"

"You know what, producer Welch?" Sloan said. "You're totally fucking blowing this chance."

"You're completely out of line, Sloan. You need to take a chill pill and process the fact that you're hired help. You're the fucking location scout. You're not driving the ship."

"Who's driving it? You?" Sloan said. "If so, why don't I see a wire transfer to cover my expenses?"

"I told you we're bidding this thing," Trevor said. "Accounting is not set up."

"Anyone can make a transfer," Sloan said. "Do I need to call Wiseman?"

"Are you out of your fucking mind?" Trevor said. "Don't bother him with money stuff."

"I have to go," Sloan said. "I'll figure this out on my own."

"Sloan!" Trevor was trying to control his voice. "You

run this through me. Is that clear?"

"There's a toga party at the pool," Sloan said. "I need to get down there." He hung up.

It was now past the booking deadline given by Dorsey but they were operating on island time and Sloan needed a few minutes to think. He walked barefoot down the hall with his ice bucket and his phone, expecting it to ring at any second. The chaotic rattling of the dropping ice was a brief waterfall of peace. No call came and he carried the bucket back like a trophy of momentary triumph.

He sat sipping rum on the rocks on his balcony with his feet up, weighing his options. String lights stretched across the beach and around the dock. The ferry was down for the night and the distant island of dreams was barely discernable. He dialed the seaplane pilot and said he was good to go.

"Splendid," Dorsey said. "Drop in at zero six fifteen to sign the waiver and get yourself ready."

"The sun waits for no man," Sloan said.

"Precisely," Clive Dorsey said. "Let me get your card number. Normally you have forty-eight hours to cancel but at this late stage a no-show will cost you five hundred."

"Here it is," Sloan said, and read the information to the pilot.

"Cheers," Dorsey said. "See you bright and early. Well, at least early."

7. The Visual Argument

The small plane skimmed and shimmied over the dark surface of the harbor and lifted off like a wobbly whining insect, banking northeast across Athol Island. As it gained altitude the grainy pink glow of the eastern firmament stretched above the plane and the horizon line widened into an orange band.

Sandy Island was revealed as a pale irregular streak in a vast indifferent sea and Sloan was shooting it. It might have been the beginning of land or the beginning of time. A scratch on a page.

As they approached the island from the south its sandbar materialized as a slim finger of beach before the yawning ocean to the north. A grove of palms took form in the early light, the arching fronds offering refuge from all above. The tide was rising.

Directing the path of the flight, Sloan lifted and latched the window and leaned out. He shot the island low and wide, in profile against the endless rolling sea and the granular blue background of the sky. It was the point of view of a rescue that would never come, would never be conceived in the perfect solitude depicted, except perhaps in the form of delivery—chilled cases of Super Berry Soda air-dropped for survival, for pleasure, for life itself.

Dorsey tilted the plane sideways, dipping the wing so Sloan could shoot straight down. As details emerged, as sand lightened and coral shapes appeared in the shallows and palm shadows were cast long and wondrous across the sandbar, abstractions were seen—patterns of paradise, attractive glimpses of isolation and beauty—that became, as he pulled back, the conglomerate whole. *A blissful place where a man might contemplate important things as he stands in the glow of sunrise with a sweating bottle of sweet carbonated froth in his hand. Such profound satisfaction. A line of pink foam runs down his chin. As the pale stripe dries, he decides to leave it, a reminder of this moment.*

Dorsey circled to the west and back around, bringing the plane down into the prevailing wind. He put the pontoons on the water parallel to the sandbar, ocean spray erupting in bursts as the plane skipped lightly over the rippling surface. He left the engine on, the prop turning loudly.

"Where do you want me?" he said through the headset.

Sloan looked behind them. "Back there near the end of the sandbar before it's covered," he said. "I want some shots that feature the plane in the foreground with the island stretching out beyond it. Then I can shoot the island without the plane. After that you could put it up here offshore of the palms so the aircraft is more of a background prop. A story idea."

"Roger that," Dorsey said, turning south to turn the plane around.

When the plane was in position, Sloan gave the pilot a thumbs-up and Dorsey killed the engine.

Sloan popped the door open and stepped down

onto the pontoon and sat on it, judging the water's depth. He slid himself forward and dropped down into the water, holding the pontoon for balance. He got his footing, waded into shallower water, removed his pack, and withdrew his camera.

The blue and white Cessna, the azure sky, the cerulean sea. Compositions of contrasting color and shape. He found his shooting zone and roamed quietly, methodically, instinctively. The climbing sun blazed and grew hotter. He put on hat and sunglasses, drank water, wiped his sweating face, screwed a polarizer on the lens. He crisscrossed the exposed land, lay on the sand as a refugee, his vision tilted, his eyes combing over seaweed, shells, crabs. Overhead, frigate birds, a prehistoric sky. Below, his own bare footprints.

He entered the palm shade and shot the parallel rows of trunks, the vertical symmetry, the texture of bark, a story of coconuts scattered like gifts, the lattice of frond shadows. He lost sight of the product, the production company, the pitch, the stupidity of the concept. He stood steaming in the midst of his own vision.

Stepping into the open, he saw Dorsey standing in the water in the shadow of his plane's wing. The sandbar was almost obliterated by the rising tide. Sloan waved and waited. He cupped his hands and yelled, then jumped up and down waving his arms. Dorsey waved back and climbed up into the aircraft. In a few minutes the engine started and the plane began to move forward on the water.

Sloan changed his lens, put on the wide angle to push the land masses in the southern view deeper into the background, flattening them into the sea. As the plane puttered toward him, he turned to capture the island's eastern end, its clear sandy shallows and dense foliage, presenting the place as a compressed tropical entity, a sovereign outpost of beauty and shelter.

He retreated into the palms to shoot the reverse angle. From inside the lens he watched the plane enter the frame. He shot multiple versions, raising the lowering the horizon, positioning the plane high and low, left, center, and right. As he motioned the pilot to move further out, he saw a powerboat approaching from the west. He waited until it passed and its white wake line subsided. He took a few more shots as he waded out into the water, then beckoned the pilot to retrieve him.

The plane took off into an easterly breeze.

"What about Green Cay?" Sloan said, pointing ahead.

"Not near as pretty," the pilot said. "But you may as well have a look."

He maintained their heading, flying low and south of the island as Sloan shot reference shots.

The island was triangular, its single beach an appendage, an earlobe aiming south at the long shore of Rose Island. Directly behind the beach was an unsightly brown pond, an ugly gaping wound in the center of the island. The north shore, facing the open ocean, was a rough, rocky, irregular line.

"Do you want to land?" Dorsey said.

"No," Sloan said. "Just swing around to the north so I can get some angles from that side."

He kept shooting as the plane banked and straightened.

"Got it?" the pilot said.

"Yeah, we're good," Sloan said.

As the aircraft gained altitude and passed Sandy Island again, heading over the sparkling ocean toward Nassau, Dorsey spoke philosophically.

"Was it worth it?" he said.

Sloan looked at the pilot. "Well, you won't know

until you fly over and see a barge down there loaded with gear, and a bunch of crew scurrying around the island gesticulating."

Dorsey smiled. "So it might not happen?"

"You don't know it's real until you're on set eating your breakfast burrito."

The pilot laughed. "What about boat traffic? You want a man on a desert island."

"In Miami we'd use police support. Here, our marine department will have to have boats delegated to enforcing the perimeter."

"And what will you do when someone ignores them?"

Sloan grimaced involuntarily. "Then I'll have to work it out, persuade them somehow, or make some kind of deal."

"You mean financially?"

"We'll have a permit. I'll try that, but whatever it takes."

Dorsey nodded. He spoke to the airport tower inland and began to drop into the mouth of Nassau Harbor. "All that for a man drinking a soda," he said.

"Totally absurd," Sloan said. "Complete bullshit. But with a lot of money on the line."

"You're contributing to commerce," Clive Dorsey said. "Helping gullible consumers decide how to part with their hard-earned money."

Sloan saw a distorted mask of his face reflected in the window. "It haunts me sometimes," he said.

He went straight to the hotel, ordered room service, and spent the next two hours editing his photos, eating eggs and potatoes and toast and fruit, sipping coffee, organizing his pictorial story. He uploaded his files, sent out the link by email, took a shower, and waited for the reaction to his visual argument, his explanation for unauthorized behavior.

The ringing phone startled him, woke him out of a

dream in which a sudden wind vibration had shaken the plane violently and caused him to drop his camera out of the window. He watched in disbelief as it plummeted toward the ocean like a bomb. Why hadn't he had the strap around his neck? His phone was vibrating on his chest and fell to the bed as he sat up to see the clock radio. He saw his camera lens staring at him from the desk as if it had been watching him sleep. He felt a great sense of relief even as its round eye reminded him of HAL, the malfunctioning, sentient computer in *2001: A Space Odyssey*.

Sloan picked up his phone and looked at the screen. WTF was calling.

When he answered, he heard Amanda's now-familiar voice. "Hello Luke. It's Amanda. Hold for Alan Wiseman please."

Again, the voice from Queens, almost as if he were yelling up to the room from the pool.

"Luke Sloan, what the fuck, hombre?"

The director was laughing so that could be a good sign, right? Or the prelude to an explosion.

"You just take off and shoot some fucking aerials, man," Wiseman said. "Fucking A, dude. Wheels up, motherfuckers. Let's take this to another level. Let's stick our necks out."

"Look," Sloan said. "I just thought—"

"I'm just breaking your balls, Sloan. These photos are brilliant. This is the place. You showed me what I'm looking for."

"Cool," Sloan said.

"But we need something else. Another choice to make this one rock solid. To lock it."

"I'm working on it," Sloan said. "I shot Green Cay as a longshot backup."

"Take that shit down," the director said. "I don't want a reeking brown cesspool in my vision of beauty."

"It was near Sandy," Sloan said, "so I shot it."

"Speaking of beautiful Sandy," Wiseman said. "Is she locked? I don't want the client falling in love with a girl who slips away, who is suddenly unattainable. You feel me?"

"Of course," Sloan said. "I'm working with the Film Commission to set up a meeting with the owner."

"So we don't have this location. You flew out there without clearance."

"I just started on islands yesterday," Sloan said. "If I waited for permission I wouldn't have anything to show you."

"You barely do as it is," Wiseman said. "But this one is fucking killer."

"Good to hear," Sloan said. "I'll get it cleared, no worries. And I'll shoot a reasonable backup, pronto."

"Excellent," Wiseman said. "Clear the fucking plane too. Just in case."

As soon as the call ended, his phone rang again. It was Wiseman's assistant, Amanda.

"Hello Luke," she said. "You probably realize that Trevor's not too thrilled with you."

"Yeah," he said.

There was a pause while she waited for more. "I mean, it's good that Alan likes what you did. But Trevor is the producer."

"Trevor's a pussy," Sloan said.

There was another pause. "Excuse me," she said.

"I said Trevor's fussy."

"It didn't sound like that," she said.

"Tenuous island connection," he said.

She waited, and he added, "I need a wire transfer. Trevor left me hanging."

"Yes, well, you have a point. Send me your expenses and I'll sort it out."

"Great," he said. "I knew there was something I liked about you."

There was no laugh, probably no smile either.

"Don't get too cavalier," she said.

8. A Guy Starts a New Life with a Bottled Beverage

The mellifluous, seductive voice on the phone made the caller want to visit the office in person.

"Film Commission, how may I help you?"

"Good afternoon," Sloan said. "Is Mrs Albury there?"

"Hold the line please," she said.

"Oh Christ," he said.

"I beg your pardon."

"Nothing," he said. "I just remembered something painful."

"I hope you'll remember something cheerier soon," the girl said. "Oh wait, hang on. Mrs Albury does seem to be returning to her station just now."

"Excellent," he said. "You've been total joy. Can we talk again later?"

"Do you mean after you've spoken to Mrs Albury?"

"I mean if I think of a question after this one. What's your name?"

"Roxy. Please hold for one brief second."

The sound in his ear grew muffled as he imagined her shapely hand over the receiver. Voices shifted in and out of range, a conversation being held, then held for a longer duration. Was it just group dynamics? he wondered. Or was everyone in the office working together to subvert his mission?

"This is Mrs Albury. How may we assist you?"

"Hello again Mrs Albury, this is Lucas Sloan following up on our discussion about a meeting with Mrs Sweeting regarding our proposed film shoot on Sandy Island."

"Yes, Mr Sloan, you were on my task list. If you had given me another hour you would have received a call. I did reach Mrs Sweeting's personal assistant and was informed that Mrs Sweeting will be returning from Eleuthera this very afternoon."

"Well, that is most excellent, Mrs Albury. How would you suggest that I set up an appointment?"

"You will need to schedule with Felicia, Mrs Sweeting's assistant. Roxy can help you."

"I'm happy to hear that," Sloan said. "How soon could this happen?"

"Give Roxy a chance to speak to Felicia and ring you back. Shall we say tomorrow morning?"

"Yes, great, that's fine. I will say I'm anxious to move on this. We love the island."

"Mr Sloan," she said with a sigh, "*everyone* loves Sandy. Try to be patient."

"I'll try, Mrs Albury," he said, "but my fate is in your hands."

"Oh my goodness," she said. "I cannot bear the responsibility."

The line went dead. Sloan replayed the conversation in his head and began to feel that Mrs Albury's words held an ominous tone.

He stood on his balcony watching the island ferry returning to the dock, trying to conjure a fully formed woman out of the silky sound of Roxy's voice. He grabbed his hat and backpack and left the room.

The smell of sunscreen was overwhelming. Even on the dock, with its stream of off-loading passengers heading in for a late lunch with more menu options and calories than Adventure Island afforded, Sloan felt as if perfumed lotion was being shot into his nostrils. He realized he possessed a sensitivity to fragrances in general, but c'mon, who doesn't check the smell of a product being purchased? He resolved to discover the most offensive brands—especially the spray varieties that wafted over vast territories as they were being haphazardly applied—and to refuse any commercial work peddling these obnoxious products. Of course in the colossal marketplace of advertising, the odds of being offered such a job were decidedly slim so his militant stand would likely never be challenged. Still, feeling adamant about it at this moment gave him a sense of self-defined justice.

More passengers got off than on but he figured there were still plenty over there, making a day of it. The weather was clear and breezy and the ferry rocked gently through the crossing to its opposite landing. As the island's details came into view Sloan observed the rows and rows of wooden beach chairs, white with blue cushions, lined up facing the lee side's manufactured cove, the blue umbrellas flapping, the waiters coming and going in their white shorts and shirts, carrying trays of drinks and snacks, the open chickee hut with smoke furling up under the edge of the roof, two cooks manning a grill and service table. A few guests stood or swam in the water but the majority lay on white towels on their lounge chairs, drinking, reading, talking, or sleeping. Behind them was a ridge of vegetation—casuarina, bay cedar, sea grape, a few palms—which partitioned the island and separated them from the windward side, the open ocean, so their protected view consisted of the distant hotel, their rooms and belongings over there, the trappings of their real life, close enough but also far away, so they could experience an elemental existence, stripped down to bathing suits, which were modern loincloths really, and primitive food, fish sandwiches and burgers, to make one appreciate the finer points of civilization across the water. Sure, they had alcohol and ice, but this lost world was essentially water and sun for half-baked tribesmen.

Sloan disembarked, took a few more reference shots, then walked wide of the cove area, crunching through the sand in his sandals as he headed to the eastern end beyond the trees and around to the north side.

Rocks. He stood looking at a long irregular—some would say gnarly—pockmarked shoreline. A castaway would be shredded into stripes of exposed meat while being washed up here. Sure, there was sand between the trees and the scabrous shore, and sure, a load of sand could be brought in by barge and spread around to soften the image, to smooth the ragged surface into a proper postcard illusion.

But for Chrissake, why hadn't he taken aerials of this abomination when he had the plane? Why had he not foreseen the need for this while he had the chance? What a royal fuckup! One clean overview could have shown the infeasibility of this location with the utmost clarity.

Hang on, Mr Scout. Refocus. Remember that this is simply fodder, a distant second choice to make the hero island stand alone in its near perfection. He moved along in shooting mode, capturing the open water, the rough shore, the wild vegetation, the bland midafternoon light, the view into the high western sun. Two couples were coming toward him, walking along in wistful lockstep, each couple holding hands with arms swinging together. He captured them too, intrepid white explorers looking for a washed-up case of excellent SBS, or possibly a bale of weed.

He continued his circumnavigation of the island, getting in a good walk, and came to a warped and weatherbeaten dock in a small rocky cove on the western end that had the look of a secret side entrance, but with a black-and-white pirate flag, the Jolly Roger, whipping in the wind above it. What the fuck, Sloan thought. Is this where some kind of game is played?

Should he speak to the hotel's management, have them send the absurd filming request up the corporate flagpole? Nah, fuck it. No director in his right mind would pick this loser location. Yeah, but what if beautiful Sandy fell through? What if Mrs Sweeting was intemperate, unreasonable, insane, or dropped dead tomorrow? A backup was always necessary. Anything could happen, he reminded himself, walking along the wretched windblown beach in the sun, a lone figure hashing things out like Robinson Crusoe must have done. Except Sloan had nothing at stake but his professional reputation. And Crusoe was a fictional character.

Back at the hotel he took a shaded patio table near the pool and ordered a grouper sandwich with fries and slaw. And an iced tea. He withdrew his notebook and pen and wrote.

Call Brenda, Roxy, Dorsey, Clinton
Email Amanda / Shoot date? Expenses
Swim!

In the lobby Sloan saw a miraculous sight—no guests at the front desk.

He asked the clerk, whose name tag identified him as Antoine J, for a printout of his bill as it currently stood. Antoine excused himself to visit the printer in the office behind him. He soon returned with the bill and, when prompted, revealed his surname to be Johnson.

"One more thing, Antoine," Sloan said. "I want to inquire about doing a film shoot on your Adventure Island out there and I need to speak to the manager on duty to get the ball rolling."

"Yes, of course," Antoine said. "Unfortunately, the manager is in a meeting."

Sloan smiled. "It's amazing, isn't it, how often people are in meetings? I've been in meetings myself, probably not as frequently as hotel managers and attorneys, but I understand the difficulty of just grabbing someone on the spot and having an instant conversation."

"It is as you say," Antoine said. "Would you care to leave a message for Mr Pilchin?"

"Mr Pilchin," Sloan said, rolling the name around in his mind.

"Mr Mercury Pilchin," Antoine said.

"In that case I will certainly leave him a message," Sloan said. He seized the pad of stationery on the desk, wrote a quick note to Mercury Pilchin, tore off the page, folded it, and handed the paper to Antoine.

"And one last final thing," Sloan said, "and I mean it this time. What is the meaning of the Jolly Roger flying on Adventure Island?"

"The jolly?" Antoine said.

"The skull and crossbones out on the west end," Sloan said. "The pirate flag."

Antoine looked puzzled. "I'm not aware of any pirates checking in lately."

Presumably then, Sloan thought, they've checked in at other times. "What if they weren't dressed as pirates when they checked in," he said. "How would you know? You don't offer buccaneer discounts, do you? If so, I'll check to see if I brought my plunderer card with me."

"No, no," Antoine said, smiling. "Nothing of the sort, Mr Sloan."

Sloan felt a presence behind him, an impatient shuffling, and turned to see a woman waiting in line. She was an unsmiling brunette in sunglasses and as he took in her general appearance he glanced at her chest, the letters on her t-shirt catching his eye and forcing him to lean back to take in the words displayed in curvature.

ZEN
ASF
UCK

"No doubt," Sloan said to the woman, then turned back to the desk. "Thank you, Mr Johnson," he said. "I'll leave you to your diplomatic work and expect to hear from Mr Pilchin soon."

As he pushed open his door Sloan saw a white envelope on the floor just inside. He leaned back out and looked up and down the hallway. It was quiet. He closed the door, picked up the envelope, and sat on the bed. The envelope was plain, legal size, no hotel logo, nothing written on the front or back. He opened it and slid out a single sheet of plain paper. He unfolded it and saw two lines of computer-printed words, the lines separated by several inches. He read the top line.

A guy starts a new life with a bottled beverage.
Then the lower line.

Another guy can't outrun his past and can't be surprised when his life starts to crumble.

Sloan lay back on the bed and read the words again. He put the letter down and rolled over and lifted the room phone and called the front desk.

When the call was answered, he said, "Antoine, this is Mr Sloan in 343. Has anyone asked for me or left a message?"

"When, Mr Sloan?"

"Anytime. Today, for instance."

"Not since I've been on," Antoine said.

49

"Think carefully," Sloan said. "Did anyone ask about my room number or say they had a letter for me?"

"I've been on since this morning," Antoine said. "Is everything fine?"

"Maybe you could ask your colleagues on the desk today and let me know. Okay?"

"Okay Mr Sloan," Antoine said.

9. The Treatment

The morning felt like limbo. Sloan was in a holding pattern. He went down to the lobby to get a halfway decent cup of coffee and couldn't help surreptitiously glancing around to see if he could spot anyone observing him. Nothing seemed out of the ordinary and he returned to his room and sat on the balcony sipping his coffee.

He got a text from Amanda asking him to check his email. Which he did.

Good morning Lucas, here are the latest boards and Alan's treatment. Give us an update as soon as you can. Thanks, Amanda

He opened the first pdf and saw two pages of storyboard illustrations, apparently telling the simplest story ever told, then opened the director's treatment, nine pages of visual references mixed with paragraphs of his thoughts on style, location, the lone actor, the story, the summation, and his so-called vision for the commercial, presented in a fawning pitch to the client.

Sloan would need fortification to get through this

stuff. He ordered room service—eggs, toast, fruit, yogurt, a pot of coffee—and settled in at the desk.

First he answered Amanda.

Received, will do, thanks, LS

The storyboards were simple black-and-white line drawings, rendered cleanly in a rustic but detailed style. The first page had four images, starting with an overview, as if seen from several hundred feet in the air, of an oblong island with a thin speckled appendage indicating a sandbar. The next frame was a sea level view, some distance away, but close enough to see palm trees at one end. The frame was devoid of anything else except a single cloud. In the next frame the viewer saw the back of a man standing at the edge of land, small waves rippling just beyond his figure and nothing beyond that. The man was barefoot and dressed in capri pants, his loose shirttail catching a breeze, his sleeves rolled up, his longish hair ruffled in the same direction as his shirttail.

The reverse image was filled with the man's face, lightly bearded, serene, contemplative, eyes open and unguarded, staring out to sea without the aid of polarized sunglasses. His mature visage had a few lines and creases that showed mileage, perseverance, and survival. There was no sign of a boat, a plane, or any belongings. Maybe there was a hut among the palms. Maybe a cooler and a hammock. Maybe there were books, an easel and paints, a satellite phone, a mini fridge and a portable generator. The man could have been expecting a delivery.

The second page had four more frames. In the first the man stood holding a bottle as if amazed to find it in his hand. Where did the bottle come from? Is there a waiter just out of frame? In the next image the man is lifting the bottle to his lips and drinking leisurely, with great pleasure in his eyes. In the next he is smiling faintly, holding the bottle as he gazes out to sea again, somehow even more unworried and relaxed than he was on the first page. The final frame shows the bottle alone in the sand, tilted and still sweating perfectly, lines of condensation running down through the crosshatched words proclaiming this life-enhancing beverage to be Super Berry Soda.

Wiseman appeared to be reimagining an old adage. Simplicity is next to godliness.

The subtext could be—Super Berry makes the imbiber a superhero. This character, Sloan thought, looks like he'd be more comfortable with a mezcal cocktail in his hand. But clearly, the dude is so cool he prefers an antioxidant super juice over any kind of alcohol.

Sloan opened the treatment and scrolled down the grid of images. Various small islands—beauty in isolation, sand, sea, sky, and palms. Water and island seen from the air—nothing else around at all. Places on earth where you could still feel geographically lost, in a good way.

Then details. Waves breaking over a reef, a turtle's head breaking the surface, dark coral heads seen under glassy ripples, sun-kissed seashells, fronds spread across the sky, smooth driftwood curves, a macro close-up of a crab, its eye stalks strange and wonderful, its pincers more neighborly than threatening. He read Wiseman's pitch.

Survival comes easily to some. Those who don't worry unnecessarily. Those with confidence in their choices and abilities. Those equipped to handle anything that comes their way—a hostile takeover, a diplomatic emergency, a shipwreck. However these men are tested, we put our trust in them, we have faith that they will prevail. They look capable, physically and mentally, of handling any situation. We admire their calm under fire, their logical reasoning, their actions large and small, how they present themselves to the world. *How they look, and what they drink.*

Our man of the world sees clear sailing in his remoteness. He sees opportunity, a chance to clear his head, which wasn't very cloudy in the first place. He sees a fresh start, even though wherever he was just before this was pretty good too.

Sloan began to imagine his own pitch. *Our dashing pirate treats his men well and sees that they have retirement plans and vegetarian meal options. He cares deeply about his wardrobe, his hair, his body odor, and his meticulous treasure maps that only he can decipher.*

Room service arrived and Sloan took the tray to the desk and ate while he read Wiseman's take on style and location.

Less is more. The elements are stark and vital, the palette blue and white and green. Except for the surprise splash of berry red, which bursts into being and captures the viewer's eye. The location is a place anyone would love to be. The shots are cinematic and hyperrealistic, so we feel we are with the man, dreaming his real-world dream. The location is authentic and also mysterious. Why is this man here? He is a tiny figure in the great wide world and yet he is all he needs to be. Isolation for him is a tonic, what we all need in today's frenetic plugged-in world. He is at ease. He has his SBS to keep him energized and focused. The soundtrack is nature as music. All natural, waves and breeze through the palms, the sounds of a man drinking with extreme pleasure.

Jesus Christ! Sloan stood and went out to the balcony with a piece of toast. It was a wonder these campaigns ever saw the light of day after being buried under such colossal loads of horseshit.

He watched the ferry pulling away and remembered that he needed to post his Adventure Island pics. He decided to forego calling the pilot and, since Clinton hadn't rung him back, to forego calling him too.

While editing his photos, he paused to organize his receipts and tape them on sheets of plain paper. He took pictures of the receipts, then made a spreadsheet to get the total. He emailed the bundle to Amanda with the appropriate subject line.

Sloan petty cash wire transfer

She wrote back almost immediately.

Received

He finished his upload and sent the link to Wiseman, Amanda, and Trevor Welch.

Amanda sent back a thumbs-up.

Sloan put on his swimsuit and went down to the lobby. At the desk, he asked if Mercury Pilchin was in a meeting and was informed by the young lady there that Mr Pilchin was not on property at present. Sloan left another written message and thanked her.

As he passed the pool on his way to the beach, his phone rang. He stopped walking to better appreciate Roxy's voice.

"Mr Sloan," she said, "I have been in contact with Felicia and she has said she has time for you today if you can meet her quickly."

He turned around and headed for the lobby. "Yes, I can," he said. "Can you please give me the address?"

"She will meet you at the front gate," Roxy said, and gave him the address as he sat on a pool chair and wrote it down.

"Excellent," he said. "Will Mrs Sweeting be in attendance?"

"Oh, Mr Sloan," she said, chiding him. "You will have to get past Felicia first."

10. Mrs Sweeting

The cab driver knew where the property was and took Eastern Road to that side of the island. Sloan was dropped at the gate and stood in the sun and mild breeze among nodding pink hibiscus bushes and curly-tailed lizards.

A crushed-shell driveway led up to the house, which was a single-story older concrete dwelling slightly elevated from the yard and set back from the gate. Sloan could see an old Chevy Biscayne, aqua blue with a white top, parked at the side of the house. On the wall above it a green shutter hung askew and a headless royal palm stood behind the house like a demoted guard. He saw no sign of Felicia.

The iron gate was latched but not locked so he let himself in and proceeded toward the house. As he mounted the front steps the door opened and a heavyset young woman in a matching flower-print dress and headscarf stood like a barricade at the entrance.

"Mr Sloan," she said.

"Hello," he said, raising his hand.

"I was just on my way to collect you," she said. She stepped out and closed the door behind her. "People are so impatient these days. Don't you find?"

"I do," he said. "The pace of modern life and all that."

He stepped back on the drive as she descended to his level and walked past him.

"Come along," she said, "and let's start out properly."

He followed and caught up and walked beside her, quietly mystified.

She wore gold leather sandals and took long purposeful strides, crunching the shells underfoot.

At the gate she caught her breath and opened it for him. Lizards watched them from their positions on the stone wall. Sloan paused and then stepped to the outer side. She closed the gate behind him, wiped her forehead, then reopened the gate.

"Felicia Deveaux," she said, extending her hand.

He shook her hand as he stepped back inside, finding her fingers soft and moist.

"A pleasure to meet you," he said. "I appreciate your making time for me."

"We try to accommodate," she said, "and expect a certain decorum in procedures."

"By all means," he said. "If I had your phone number I would have called from here."

"All in good time, Mr Sloan," she said. "All in good time. Now what can I do for you?"

He had imagined that they would converse inside, on fine old chairs under a ceiling fan, with iced tea and shortbread cookies. But no, here they were at the gate, with the lizards.

Sloan explained his proposal in the simplest terms, watching beads of sweat sprout on her cheeks and forehead. In conclusion, he shrugged at the basic scope of the shoot.

She seemed lost in thought. "You know, Mr Sloan, we had a shoot last year with Sardonix."

"I'm not familiar," Sloan said.

"The rapper," she said. "Are you not familiar with rap music?"

"Some of it," he said. "There's a lot of music out there."

"Indeed," she said. "He brought a menagerie to the island."

"How do you mean?" he said.

"I mean he brought a boat and smuggled monkeys onto the island. Plus a parrot."

"Whoa," Sloan said. "I guess that wasn't in the contract." He smiled sympathetically.

"We had a devil of a time catching those monkeys," she said. "Had to pay some trapper boys."

Sloan nodded. "Well, we just have the one actor, no animals of any kind."

"You can't be too careful," she said. "People will try to fool you. Take advantage."

"Of course," he said.

"Another time Def Sleppy threw a big party." She waved her hands in the air. "Giant mess. And there we were again, paying extra for some trash boys to come in."

"I don't know any of the Defs," Sloan said.

"He's a DJ," she said.

"You have to pick and choose," he said.

"Oh yes, my point exactly, Mr Sloan. Don't get me started on the Puffies shoot."

He wished he didn't have to. He didn't need a litany of scandals piled in front of his request.

"Okay, I'll bite," he said. "Is that some kind of Botox lip cream?"

"Oh you can do better than that," she said, the sun reflecting off her wet skin. He was tempted to use his shirttail to wipe her down. And himself. Sweat trails were racing down his arms.

"Okay, was it a commercial for a specially padded bra maybe?"

She suddenly laughed and shook, possibly from heatstroke, and drops fell from her face. "No Mr Sloan, you can remove the undergarment," she said. "This was topless nudity, soft pornography."

For a moment Sloan stood silently, trying to picture puffy models among the palms. "How did you find out what was going on?" he said.

"We had a friend who spent a long time observing the shoot," she said. "From his boat."

"I can imagine he wanted to get sufficient evidence," Sloan said.

"Oh yes he did indeed," she said. "And Mrs Sweeting had to answer for it at the Horticulture Club."

"I wish I could have attended," he said.

She frowned at him. "The meetings are for members only."

"Just as well," he said. "I'm really not much of a club joiner anyway."

She glanced at the sky, perhaps judging the hour from the sun's position, then turned toward the house. "I need to get back," she said. "But I wanted you to appreciate our sensitive position."

"Compared to those examples," he said, "our shoot is simplicity itself. A man drinks a soda on an island."

She looked at him again and from somewhere on her person withdrew a business card and handed it to him. The card was damp and rounded at the corners.

"We must always concern ourselves with the content," she said.

"Like I said," Sloan said, "a man on a beach. No animals, no menageries, nothing improper."

"Is the man wearing clothes?" she said.

"Yes, he's fully dressed. Except for his feet."

"What about the product?" she said.

"What about it?"

"What's in it?" She was squinting up at him, the lower edge of her headscarf dark with sweat.

"It's a soda," he said. "A berry-flavored soda."

She shrugged. "Is it good for kids? Some of these energy drinks have proven quite unhealthy."

He looked at the house, across the yard at a neighbor's place, down the road, into the purgatory of the washed-out sky.

"I'll send you an email with the details," he said as she walked away. "Our shoot is one day, a couple of weeks from now."

"We have several fashion shoots booked," she said, without turning back. She was marching in a wavering line toward the door.

"We just need one day," he said, raising his voice to accommodate the distance between them. "I'll send you an offer."

At the steps she paused and held the railing, facing the front door before the last hurdle. He waited for more but she merely waved to the side in a way that he understood to mean: Show yourself out.

After Felicia entered the house, Sloan went back through the gate and walked down the street and stood in the dappled shade of a poinciana tree. He had neglected to bring water or a hat. And the meeting had left him dizzy with disappointment. Fuck! He needed a swim to clear his head. He couldn't figure out the problem. Why all the negativity? He was making a simple request with a simple equation. Use of private location equals money for the owner.

He was thinking ten thousand for a day of shooting. Plus a prep day, to bring in greens at least. Wrap out the day of the shoot. So, two days total. Fifteen grand. Would that work? But he hadn't even gotten far enough to discuss actual terms. They might have a standard day rate, or it might vary depending on the job. Maybe it was twenty grand to shoot. It was an island, after all.

After a few more minutes breathing himself calmer in the shade, he was ready to call a taxi.

He heard an engine start and then the crunching of shells. Back at the Sweeting place, a man pushed opened the gate, then got back in the old Chevy Biscayne and drove it out. He got out again to close the gate and Sloan walked toward the car, staying in the middle of the road so the car could not pass him. The car sat idling as he approached it. An elderly woman sat in the passenger seat.

Sloan held up his hand in greeting, then went around to the passenger window and looked in. The old Bahamian woman peered at him from behind dark glasses. She wore an orange hat and red lipstick and looked more like she was leaving the set of a period movie than her own home.

"Good day," Sloan said. "Are you by chance Mrs Sweeting?"

"I am," she said. "Good day. What can I do for you young man?"

"My name's Lucas Sloan," he said. "I just left your place after speaking with Felicia. I'm a location scout looking for an island to shoot a commercial for one day. Our production company thinks Sandy Island would be perfect for this job."

She studied his face for a moment, then said, "Did you encounter a problem with Felicia?"

He was taken aback and hesitated in his reply.

Mrs Sweeting looked stern. "Did you want to smack her chubby cheeks a few times?"

"Nothing quite as theatrical as that," Sloan said.

"Oh, come now Mr Sloan," she said.

"I was mostly perplexed," he said. "She sort of danced around my inquiry."

"Would you care to take a ride Mr Sloan?"

He leaned down to better see the driver, who was appraising him too. The elderly man wore a chauffeur's cap angled rakishly off-center. In his mirrored sunglasses, Sloan saw himself framed in the passenger window as if in an optical tunnel leading to Mrs Sweeting.

"That's Mr Burrows," she said. "You'll be quite safe in his hands."

"I have every faith," Sloan said. "A ride would be great."

He slid into the back seat and they rumbled down the road, the driver glancing at Sloan in the mirror from time to time. The car was in good shape, the seats smoothly wrinkled in a network of ancient creases, and Sloan leaned back, thinking about complimenting the driver and guessing at the car's age—somewhere mid-sixties—but then sinking into the ride and the silence in the car as a cohesive condition momentarily binding them all together in purpose.

Cooled and revived by the air flowing through the car and relaxed by the passing island tableau and the tour by what he believed to be an esteemed member of local society, Sloan began to feel he was on a victory ride. But as soon as the thought appeared he sought to push it from his mind, knowing this kind of thinking was poisonous and liable to backfire as soon as it acquired any credence.

His phone buzzed and he withdrew it to check the text. Brenda Pinder.

How is your spycraft going? I hope well.

He smiled. *Pretty well. I'll know more soon. What are you up to?*

I bought a new swimsuit and want to try it out. Any ideas?

He wrote back. *I think a swim would be a good idea.*

Like this afternoon.

She answered. *I knew you'd be helpful.*

A photo appeared. She was looking over her shoulder, a coy smile showing, while clutching her phone against her shoulder, her back bare except for a red string running across its width, the matching red piece a bikini bottom stretched tight over her posterior, the lower frame line ending at mid-thigh. He liked the composition and its red focal point.

He replied. *Excellent choice. Will call you a bit later.*

He looked up to see Mrs Sweeting looking back over the seat, down at his phone.

He clicked the phone off and nodded slightly. "Making a new friend," he said.

"Mr Hollywood," she said, turning forward again, "should always have a story."

Almost immediately they pulled into a gravel parking lot in front of an old limestone building with a wooden sign mounted over the front door—Pioneers Social Club.

Burrows pulled around to the side and parked in a row marked by several signs designating the area as reserved, then got out and came around and opened the door for Mrs Sweeting. She got out with an orange pocketbook and spoke to Sloan through the open rear window.

"We are having our monthly meeting today," she said. "Perhaps you could say a few entertaining words to our members."

Sloan felt as if the car were parked on a slope and was starting to roll. "A few words?" he said, staring at her. "About what?" He'd been planning to make a few calls while he waited.

She looked at Burrows as if he might explain her guest's reluctance. Then she motioned for Sloan to exit the vehicle. "Come now Mr Sloan," she said. "You must know some Hollywood gossip or some funny movie stories. This is a valuable chance for our members to hear the unexpected. You may wish to consider this little service as part of the location fee. Surely you've spoken to clubs before." She smoothed the front of her black dress and touched the sides of her orange hat as the matching pocketbook dangled from her elbow.

She waved to another woman across the parking lot as Sloan got out. He stood by the car cleaning his sunglasses for a long time. "I'll need a few moments to compose my thoughts," he said.

"Oh, marvelous," she said. "Mr Burrows will escort you inside when you're ready."

She stepped away in a confident strut, a ruling maven resplendent as an oriole.

Sloan said, "What the hell, Burrows. What goes on in there?"

Burrows laughed. "Oh, you'll be on that stage," he said, "looking out at all those women waiting for any kind of mistake, any little screwup from a white man. Anything to make Mrs Sweeting look bad, knock her down a step. They always want a scandal to talk about until the next meeting."

"Ahhh," Sloan said. His mind was tumbling, slipping through space unmoored and unpowered, like a lost satellite without the aid of gravity or substance, destination unknown, the cosmic surroundings unchanging, the long view completely mysterious.

Then he came to earth, saw himself as a puppet dancing on stage, arms and legs jerking here and there, animated by wires lost overhead in the darkness. Out in the audience people were laughing.

"Greetings," he said, and heard another laugh. He sounded like a fucking alien.

"Good start," Burrows said. "Mustn't keep the ladies waiting. Their teeth are sharp and their tummies are growling."

"This is really amusing to you," Sloan said. "I must be a natural entertainer."

"Seize the day," Burrows said. "Start up your Nassau fan club."

"As a guest speaker," Sloan said, "I humbly request a bottle of water." He gripped his throat as he walked away, saying over his shoulder, "I'll be in the shade for a few minutes."

He stood under a stand of casuarina trees and began to walk in a circle, attracting the attention of those entering the parking lot and walking toward the door. He gestured with one hand and rehearsed ideas with his head bowed.

Sidney Poitier. Famous Bahamian, perhaps the most famous, born on Cat Island, rose to international stardom from that poor improbable start. Everyone here knows that, no story at all. What about his movies? Great stuff. Sloan particularly liked *In the Heat of the Night*. But racism? Not a good topic. Poitier was out.

Okay, other great movies? What good are stories and quoted lines without a frame of reference? How can you know what films those in the audience have seen? Or how well they remember your own favorite lines? Have they seen *The Holy Grail*? *Monty Python* was an English troupe, so they could be familiar. But anything from Great Britain could backfire, become a colossal colonial misstep. And there were no Bahamians in the six-man group. All very white.

Apocalypse Now? What if he mentioned Captain Williard? Did any Bahamians even go to Vietnam? And what about the source material, *Heart of Darkness*? Then we're in Africa, treading carefully around slavery, insanity, rogue behavior, termination of command. Nope, can't do it.

How about a western? *Butch Cassidy and the*

Sundance Kid. Who could possibly be offended, other than maybe Bolivians? But what else might be suggested? The romance of manifest destiny, the great western expansion? The trampling of native peoples? On a smaller scale then, how about the glory days of train robbery? The difficulty of going straight?

He looked up to see Burrows motioning from the front steps with a bottle of water.

Sloan trudged toward the building, breathing heavily and sweating. No topic, nothing to say except how happy he'd been to be in the Bahamas. Until this very moment. He made a mental note to track down Mercury Pilcher and secure Adventure Island. He would also come up with a plan to venture further afield and scout even better islands. It wasn't over until it was over.

He followed Burrows inside, passing through a foyer and into the main room. Light streamed in the open windows, but not much air, and the ceiling was higher than he would have guessed. Everyone turned in their folding chairs to look at him as he walked down the center aisle. Mrs Sweeting stood on the stage behind a podium, her orange hat a beacon helping him navigate the undulations he felt in the floor, the old boards seeming to dip and ripple under his feet.

"Here he is," she said. "Our visiting expert in pictures, Mr Sloan from America. Or should I say Mr Hollywood? Eager to entertain us with his movie knowledge and his globe-trotting stories of adventure and luxury. Maybe he'll share with us what he finds so attractive about our islands."

Sloan turned around at the front and looked back into the sea of local faces, maybe twenty-five or thirty, that felt like a stadium crowd. He felt his smile was the sort you might see at a funeral and he waved by lifting his hand shoulder height, as if he were in the back row of a classroom and didn't really want the teacher to see him.

He mounted the steps to the stage and walked to the podium. Mrs Sweeting was clapping and he realized the audience was too. The sound was like wind through a canyon. She stood aside but remained close enough to help him if he collapsed in delirium. His water bottle was misshapen from his grip on it and would not stand on its own. As he placed it on the upper flat portion of the podium it fell off the front and hit the floor loudly. He bent forward and smacked his head on the podium and then leaned back and laughed as he stepped wider. He held one corner of the podium and leaned down to retrieve his water, which was by then rolling toward the front of the stage.

In his peripheral vision he saw Mrs Sweeting's legs and orange heels enter the picture and her hand whisking the bottle up. As he straightened she handed him the bottle and bowed to him and the audience.

He retook his speaking position and said, "Thank you Mrs Sweeting. I was feeling like Charlie Chaplin for a minute there." He heard some chuckles and murmurs and thought he might have conveyed the message that he always started with silent movie pratfalls.

"Louder," someone shouted.

"I'd like to thank Mrs Sweeting," Sloan said loudly. "And Buster Keaton. Can you hear me in the back?"

"Yes, now I can," the same voice shouted again.

"I can hear you too," Sloan said. "We've reached an understanding."

A woman in the front row clapped. He glanced at her and she blew him a kiss. She looked about seventy-five.

He rubbed the knot on his forehead and got a few laughs. Mrs Sweeting was still onstage with him, like his guardian, waiting patiently. Or maybe she was the moderator, running the show. He pressed the cold water bottle against his head and heard more laughter. "You're a great audience," he said. "I'm feeling better now. Thank you Baltimore."

He realized he'd just said what amounted to a closing line. He unscrewed his bottle cap, took a healthy swig, and continued to hold the bottle like a prop. The extra weight was keeping him grounded and he didn't want the heft of it to decrease by much. He wondered if it would be simple to get another one. He looked along the back row and spotted Burrows.

"Everyone knows about the beauty of your waters," Sloan said. "That's one reason I'm here. I haven't had the chance yet for a swim but I'm trying. Sometimes we get in a work mode and forget to enjoy ourselves. I stood in the water taking photographs but I did not swim."

He took another sip of water and wondered what was coming.

"On the other hand," he said, "it's work that got me here. It's just by chance that I'm standing before you today. I guess you could say that about anything. Who we are, where we were born, how we were brought up, the friends and associates we've made." He gestured to his side. "I mean, I just met Mrs Sweeting this morning. And now we are associates on our way to becoming friends. And that occurred because a completely random story brought us together."

The club members were quiet and only the erratic sound of traffic disturbed the silence in the room. Mrs Sweeting took this opportunity to walk behind Sloan and exit the stage, taking a seat at the end of the first row.

"It doesn't matter what the story is," Sloan said. "It could be the most brilliant story ever told. Or it could be a terribly idiotic story, an insult to human intelligence. The content is irrelevant. But what is relevant is the fact that someone is willing to finance the telling of this story. That's why stupid movies get made and moronic commercials are shown on television all the time."

He took another sip of water, looked around the room and made eye contact with Burrows, who nodded at him.

"The story that brings us all together here today is a very tiny story, an infinitesimal dot in the long history of storytelling. It's like a single word or a single syllable or a grunt in the language of story. It may be forgotten even before its first thirty-second airing on television is concluded. Or it may cause viewers to smile or laugh for a minute. Or give them a chance to go get a beer and a sandwich before their program comes back on."

He heard scattered laughter. And then from the back, "Louder!"

"Ah, my old friend," Sloan said. "Perhaps you could hear me if you sat on the edge of the stage."

He saw Mrs Sweeting put her hands together and smile at him.

"Or ..." He paused and scanned the faces in the room. "Or, this simple story could turn out to be incredibly moving, a stark visual statement about the very nature of man, his position in the universe, his bewilderment, his striving for knowledge, for understanding. For sustenance."

Sloan raised his hands and looked skyward in the manner of a preacher.

"Nah," he said. "That's a bit of a stretch."

"When I get a job," he said, "and I get the script or the storyboard and its description, I take a good look and ask myself whether this will be a worthy project, something I will be proud to work on. Then I forget about that and think of the places I'll go and the people I'll meet. I think about getting paid to take pictures and visit cool spots."

"I think about being onstage in other countries and speaking to strangers. Nah, just kidding."

"But actually, this has been an unexpected pleasure. Thank you very much for having me."

There was some clapping as Mrs Sweeting came to the middle aisle in front of the stage.

She raised one arm. "Please feel free to ask Mr Sloan questions," she said. "He's here for you."

Sloan was drinking water as a few hands went up.

Mrs Sweeting pointed to a man a few seats from her and the man stood up.

"Mr Sloan," the man said. "What benefits will we be seeing from your work in Nassau?"

"Well," Sloan said, "there will be hotel rooms and cars rented, food and services—"

"No, I mean us here at the Pioneers Club."

"Oh," Sloan said. "That depends on the location contract, which could include a donation to the club. Just some extra money you could use for maintenance or a Christmas party, for example."

A woman in the front row was next. "Any famous folks coming in?"

"I'm not sure," Sloan said. "There's only one actor and he could be known or unknown. I don't know who is being considered."

"A Black man?" she said. "A true Bahamian?"

"It's possible," he said. "But it doesn't seem likely from the material I got."

"What sort of fella is he then?"

"I guess I would call him some sort of older, modern Robinson Crusoe. Like a shipwrecked entrepreneur who stays clean and doesn't get stressed out."

A man stood quickly and interjected. "The man is English?"

"Probably American," Sloan said. "But could be

French. Or Scandinavian."

Mrs Sweeting pointed to a woman waving insistently in the back row. When she stood, she looked to be the youngest pioneer in the group.

"Mr Sloan," the woman said, "you traffic in fantasies."

He stood looking at her serious, indignant face, her close-cut dark hair, her print dress in reds and yellows, possibly flower shapes. Or explosions. "Is there a question in there, Miss ...?"

"Higgs," she said. "Henrietta Higgs. Would you call yourself a trafficker in fantasies, Mr Sloan?"

"I think that's accurate," Sloan said.

"And you feel that is a helpful endeavor for the average person?"

"Are commercials helpful?" he said. "Or movies or television shows? You could take a survey in this room."

"No, I'm asking you, Mr Sloan, how you feel."

"I like movies," he said. "And I think most people enjoy escaping the trials of their life for a couple of hours. So yes, that's helpful."

"Escaping?" she said, and laughed. "What's your favorite movie?"

He paused and looked around the room, scanned the faces focused on him. He took a few steps to the side and returned to the podium. "I don't have an absolute favorite," he said at last. "But one of them is *Little Big Man*. Another one is *Cool Hand Luke*. Is that really what you want to ask me? Do you have a point to make at all?"

The room had grown quieter as this exchange developed. Mrs Sweeting had seemed on the verge of interjecting but was now just watching and waiting like the rest of the audience.

Henrietta Higgs paused to feed the silence, then said, "I doubt anyone would object to the statement that commercials trick people into buying. Do you, Mr Sloan?"

Without waiting for his answer, she said, "But movies have a price too, don't they?"

Sloan chose to ignore these rhetorical questions. He had the feeling now that she was there for a particular reason, that she had a motive for attending.

"You were involved in a controversial movie," she said. "Would you care to tell us that story?"

He waited for more information, stepping away from the podium again, then heard car tires squealing, followed closely by the bang of metal buckling on impact. Some audience members involuntarily turned toward the streetside windows and it seemed for a moment that the room was somehow trafficking in accidents. Burrows rose and slipped out the door to investigate.

"I'm not following you, Miss Higgs," Sloan said. "What is your purpose here today?"

She smiled. "I'm a person who likes to hear more important stories than the ones you've been telling."

He smiled back and said, "It seems like you have something on your mind that hasn't quite taken shape. Are you even a member of the Pioneers Social Club?"

"I'm an interested party," she said, "trying to set the record straight."

"Is there a record?" he said.

"Not a complete one," she said. "There are holes in it."

"So you see yourself as a designated hole-filler," he said, chuckling. "Is someone paying you for that?"

Mrs Sweeting moved up the center aisle waving her hand. "Now see here, Miss Higgs," she said. "I think we've heard enough of your mysterious accusations." She swirled her hand in the air as she approached the other woman. "You've trespassed among the Pioneers long enough with your vague talk and provocative manners. I'm afraid we must now allow others a chance to speak."

Mrs Sweeting stopped several feet away from the younger woman, imagining that her forthright energy would cast the interloper from the room. But Miss Higgs stood her ground, her posture and expression defiant. She seemed to be gathering her concluding remarks.

She stepped into the aisle to face the older woman, two colorful birds in counterpoint.

"There are things you may wish to know about your guest speaker," Miss Higgs said. Everyone in the room was watching the standoff. Then she turned and walked toward the door, saying over her shoulder, "Ask Mr Sloan about his movie, *Tropical Cavalcade*. Mistakes were made and there were dire consequences." With this final tantalization she exited the building, fluttered down the steps and was gone with the salty breeze.

The attendees turned back to the front and waited for a clarification or whatever the speaker cared to say next. In the center aisle Mrs Sweeting also turned her attention to Sloan.

He walked to the middle of the stage and stood with his hands in his pockets. He didn't hang his head so much as stare at the floor for a few moments. But he couldn't escape exhibiting a trace of the hangdog look.

"As I indicated earlier," he said, "there is a time when you first receive a script when you don't know what to expect. All you have are words on a page. Sometimes it can be obvious that the thing is good or bad right off the bat. Other times, most times, it falls into the mystery category of we'll have to wait and see how it's directed, acted, designed, shot, and so forth."

Sloan looked up to see Burrows reenter the room and take his seat.

"*TropCav*, as we called it, fell into this general category. The thing had action, violence, primitive survival, jungle locations, a wild story, danger, suspense. It was, in a word, edgy."

Sloan paced the stage, rubbing his forehead as if struggling to draw forth his memories.

He shut his eyes tightly and drew several sharp breaths. Then he gazed up at the ceiling with a dreamy look and it appeared he was seeing right through the roof to the sky. "Cool locations," he said. "Real world stuff. A location-heavy picture, no stage, no interiors except primitive huts. And you mix that with stunts, a lapse in security, an unchecked trespasser ..."

He glanced all around the room. "Look, life is dangerous. You work in a cubicle and you still might step on a dropped water bottle, slip and hit your head on the corner of a desk and wind up a quadriplegic." Someone laughed and Sloan grimaced. "I knock on house doors all the time," he said. "Unannounced. That's called cold scouting. One time, I heard a gun being cocked on the other side of the door. Another time an old lady said she couldn't help me because she was getting dressed for church." Laughter erupted like flares. "You just never know," he said.

He stood at the podium and raised his hand. "Thank you very much for the hospitality," he said through scattered applause. He waved at Mrs Sweeting. "Thank you," he said, pointing at her. As he left the stage, she came forward and took his hand. Several other people approached him with handshakes and shoulder pats as he walked to the exit. Mrs Sweeting offered him a ride back to the hotel but he declined, smiling warmly. He told her he would be sending Felicia an email shortly.

Outside, he encountered Burrows.

"Well spoken," the driver said. "Where you film that bad-trouble movie?"

"The Dominican Republic," Sloan said. "Anybody hurt in that accident?"

"No, mahn, just a mash-up."

11. Plan B

After a long decompressive walk, a taxi to finish the journey, the dizzying combination of exhilaration and dehydration, the flush of victory buffeted by the erosion of certainty, the memory of his solid stage performance leaking like a balloon before the pointed sniping of the would-be assassin Higgs, Sloan drank from his bathroom faucet and stuck his head under the shower's cold water.

Who the fuck was that woman and how did she show up there? He hadn't been a booked guest at the Pioneers Social Club. It meant that she had followed him, knew where he was staying, knew things about him, was out to sabotage him. Was she the one who slipped the note under his door?

He grabbed a cold beer from the mini-fridge—breaking his general mini-fridge protocol—popped it open and chugged it as he stood dripping, his phone buzzing with messages.

As arranged, Brenda was down at the pool waiting for their hotel beach date. Amanda was requesting a progress report. A third text was a random shot from an old friend, another location scout. Nothing from the hotel. Nothing more from Trevor.

He changed into his swimsuit and headed out with hat and shades. He was crossing the lobby with his mind on Brenda, gazing again at the provocative shot she'd sent him, when he heard his name called. He looked up to see Antoine at the front desk waving him over.

"Mr Sloan," the desk clerk said, "Mr Mercury Pilchin said to tell you he's in the house."

Sloan had trouble concealing his dismay. He looked over at the north-facing windows, the soft afternoon light, the swaying palms in view, the band of blue water stretching away with undulating optimism. Somewhere out there his companion waited with the promise of personal, sensual ocean frolicking.

"Do you mean right now?" Sloan said. "In this house?"

"Come around," Antoine said. "I'll take you back there."

In his casual tourist attire, his sandals slapping his heels and sending those sounds echoing off the walls like a cheap announcement as they walked the quiet corridor, Sloan followed the clerk to a closed door in the deep recesses of the executive offices.

Antoine knocked gently, heard a response that prompted him to stick his head in, say a few words, then withdraw and hold the door for Sloan, who stepped inside. The door was closed behind him and he stood looking like a disheveled victim of mistaken identity.

Pilchin launched up from behind his desk and became enormous. In his huge and shiny blue sharkskin suit he looked like a former professional football figure about to be televised. His massive misshapen shaved head reminded Sloan of a boulder one might use in the construction of a breakwater jetty. The room had no windows and felt stuffy. Pilchin's breathing was audible and Sloan wondered how much oxygen was left for him.

Pilchin came forward around the desk and Sloan thought he might be tackled. He took the man's offered hand and the grip was firm without causing any noticeable damage.

"My man," Pilchin said. "I hear you been gunning for me." He let out a thunderous laugh, then immediately cocked his head at his guest and pursed his great fleshy lips. He gestured with an open palm at his visitor's casual attire. "You working hard or hardly working?"

Sloan laughed. "I wasn't expecting a meeting and didn't expect you to be American."

"For the most part," Pilchin said, "but I'm a dual citizen here, much smoother that way."

"That's cool," Sloan said. "Where're you from, stateside?"

"DC. Take a seat, my friend," Pilchin said, returning to his own. "What's all this I hear about taking over our little island?"

Sloan sat across from the manager. "Nothing so grand as that," he said, laughing. "We have a one-day shoot with a single actor and could use the outer side, I think, without much interference with your guest services on the lee side. We'd probably need a prep day or two to dress the beach."

"What's that mean?" Pilchin said.

"We'd need to barge in some sand to cover some of the rocks," Sloan said.

"Is that so?" Pilchin said. "Have you cleared this with the Ministry of Coastal Regulations?"

"I haven't cleared anything yet," Sloan said. "We're in the location-scouting phase."

Pilchin nodded. "Have you looked at Sandy Island?"

"I have," Sloan said. "But I need another option."

"Ahh," the big man said. "You need a Plan B." He chuckled. "In case Mrs Sweeting turns on you."

Sloan smiled at Pilchin's shrewd appraisal. His phone was buzzing and he shifted in his chair.

"Let's each take a moment for other business," Pilchin said, pulling out his own phone.

Sloan had a new message from Amanda that was just a question mark. He wrote back.

Standby please, in a meeting.

His other message was from Brenda, also a question mark. Plus a smiley face.

He looked up to see Pilchin texting, then answered her.

Got ambushed by manager. Work stuff. Sorry, be there soon.

Then he answered the earlier text from his fellow scout.

What's up buddy? Will call you later tonight.

He started to compose an email to Felicia in his mind, debating with himself about the pros and cons of mentioning Mrs Sweeting and how much to say. Felicia probably knew he went for a drive with her boss, maybe heard he went to the club and spoke. If Felicia gave him more of the runaround, wouldn't Mrs Sweeting step in, force the issue, and make it happen?

Sloan was startled out of his thoughts when Pilchin suddenly spoke again.

"Where were we, Mr Hollywood? Oh yes, the backup plan," he said, chuckling at his own playfulness. "When we find ourselves facing Plan B, whoa, brotherman, there is trouble afoot. Am I right? The first walls have caved in and now we are up against the last wall standing. Unless there is a Plan C too." He laughed. "People are under pressure and tempers are flaring up." He wiped his forehead theatrically with four thick fingers. "This situation elevates the value of Plan B. Stands to reason." He paused briefly and rotated in his chair, giving Sloan a chance to respond.

Sloan was listening, keeping his face straight and relaxed. The manager was building up to drop the hammer on him. Or he was just having fun, as it seemed, fucking with the whole idea, which he didn't consider a serious request.

"Practically puts it on par with Plan A," Pilchin said, "now that Plan A is gone, collapsed like a house of cards in a sea breeze." He laughed again. Then put his hands together in front of him on the desk, his face assuming a serious cast. "You are asking me to interfere with our valued guests. And you know our first priority has to be our guests. Has. To. Be."

Sloan felt more irritated than nauseous.

"This is a prestigious property, Mr Sloan, a destination. For us to embark on such a disruptive course of action, we would need a good reason. Why would corporate agree to such a thing?"

Sloan played along. "You would need a financial incentive," he said.

"Yes indeed, Mr Sloan. We would need fifty thousand. Otherwise, what's the point?"

Sloan burst out laughing and shook his head. "I hear you, Mercury. Forgive me for finding the humor here. But this is not a Spielberg movie we're talking about. This is a commercial for a new product nobody has ever heard of. Sure, it needs to look good. That's why we're looking at your island. And if your guests go out as usual and business is uninterrupted, then the ten grand you make is total gravy. A gravy bowl landing in your lap."

Mercury Pilchin sat considering this for a minute. "If we could meet in the middle at thirty then I could run that up the flagpole." He raised his huge hands, palms outward. "No promises," he said.

Sloan stood and extended his hand over the desk. "Thank you for your time, Mercury. Let's talk again soon."

Pilchin stood and their palms met and Sloan's hand was nearly swallowed.

"How are you finding the accommodations?" the manager said.

"Good, good," Sloan said. "Very comfortable. Friendly locals."

"I see you're finding some time to relax today," Pilchin said, raising his eyebrows and smiling.

"Yes, I hope to find a relaxing position," Sloan said.

Walking back down the corridor to the lobby, he felt light-headed, like he was in a vacuum, and realized he had not eaten since breakfast. Putting one hand against the wall for stability, he wandered out through the front desk area, glancing over at Antoine, who was engaged with a guest, and stood in the open space thinking about the fastest food option as his vibrating phone indicated a call.

He slumped into a lobby chair, hit the button, and heard some urgency in Amanda's voice.

"Good afternoon Luke," she said. "We have a little situation over here."

"Shoot," he said.

"We're about to have a client meeting and he doesn't want to see any seaplane shots on the site."

"Okay," Sloan said, looking at the closed door to the bar, some motion behind the glass, then wondering about food service hours at the pool, the beach, the locations of vending machines on the property, if pizza could be delivered to the parking lot.

"Alan wants you to remove all the seaplane shots immediately," she said.

The words landed but did not slide into an exact timeframe.

"You mean?"

"I mean the client just dumped this on us minutes before the meeting. How soon can you get to your computer?"

He closed his eyes and exhaled slowly, sliding lower in the chair. *He saw a red bikini floating on the water, heard a girlish laugh, and he was there on the beach holding up a finger to signal a slight delay, just a minute, he promised, and he'd be right back. Hold that wet pose please.*

"How soon?" Amanda said, her voice rising.

"Pretty soon," Sloan said.

"What, like five minutes, thirty, forty-seven?"

"I just got to the lobby," he said. "Give me a few minutes."

"That is so good," she said. "This client is such a diva. He's driving us nuts."

"I'll text you," he said.

"Awesome," she said. "Alan is about to blow a fuse. The agency is having a breakdown."

In his room he went to the snack tray on top of the minifridge and ripped open a bag of chips and stuffed a handful into his mouth, fragments and flakes falling to the carpet as he crunched mindlessly. On the bed his phone lit up with a frowning face emoji from Brenda.

He sat at the desk and opened his laptop and noted the slow connection as he waited for access to his site. He reached over for his phone and texted back.

Work crap. Sorry. Slight delay. Hold tight.

Working with a weak connection he slowly began to execute the requested removals. There were only nine photos showing the seaplane but before he could finish he got a text from Amanda.

Update?

He went to the bathroom and splashed water on his face, then lay back on the bed and looked at his phone. Nothing from Brenda.

He cut the last plane photo and checked the site to confirm the changes. Then texted Amanda.

Good to go.

Sloan was downstairs crossing the lobby again when he got another text from Amanda.

Luke, sorry but client now wants to see a single seaplane shot, the one off in the distance.

"Motherfucker," he said. The female desk clerk looked up at him as he stood staring at his screen. He turned around and headed back to the elevator.

By the time he got outside, clouds had rolled in and there was no sign of Brenda. He checked the pool, the beach, the pier, the water-sports center, and the towel shack, as if she might be hiding back behind the counter, crouched down amid the legs of towel-dispensing personnel.

He stood looking at the darkening water for a minute. Then turned and went inside.

12. The Plug

The remaining light of day was gradually eclipsed by the bar's rubicund illumination. One bourbon followed the previous one and Sloan in his semidarkness was able to relish each rare bite of his dripping burger and every single salty piece of his pile of fries. Each was an object to consider favorably as his hunger was sated and his romantic disappointment anesthetized by increasing degrees.

He cajoled the barman into making him a drink for the road, a double on the rocks in a paper cup. He lurched and followed an imaginary spaghetti line to the elevators, intent on preventing even the smallest drop from escaping the cup and lessening its full and righteous volume.

In the elevator he began the oratory that would grow into an email of concision and finality.

My dear Felicia, on such a day as today—

My kind friend, to meet such a bevy of extraordinary locals—

He continued this practice down the hallway to his room.

My fine glossy gatekeeper, to encounter such a bounty of rotundity—

My plumpest compatriot, were we to meet under different—

My dear spherical princess, how can I express—

Back in the room he washed his face and wove his way around the bed to the balcony with his drink. The illuminated pool radiated waves of electric blue ribbons. A woman was swimming underwater like a seal. Out past the pier lights he could barely discern the dark slinking shape of the island of make-believe isolation. Much closer, somewhere down the beach, a kid was caterwauling as if actual pirates had landed and were presently capturing all of his siblings.

A text came in from Amanda. *Let's talk in the morning.*

He wrote back. *Sure.*

Then he saw the text he'd sent to his film friend, Nico Reed, saying he would call tonight. They'd worked together on *TropCav*. They'd shared women and secrets and bonded through mud and sun and gallons of sweat and rum. About what ... eight years ago? When they were younger and wilder. They hadn't seen each other since, but almost had once, and still kept in touch.

"Scout dog," Nico said, laughter erupting as usual.

"Batten down the hatches," Sloan said, laughing in turn.

"What are you doing right now?" Nico said.

"Island job," Sloan said. "For What the Fuck."

"Good reason," Nico said. "When can you dump those three stooges?"

"Any minute," Sloan said. "What have you got going?"

"Are you sitting down?"

"No," Sloan said. "I'm standing with a drink in my hand."

"What a daredevil. I'm talking about the fucking DR, hombre."

"Whaaaat? Get the fuck out."

"That's right, rounder, I do not shit you lightly."

"Don't say *TropCav2*."

Nico laughed. "I wouldn't do that to you, my dear jaded amigo."

"Is it a portion or the whole enchilada?"

"Depends on the excellent scouting, doesn't it?"

"Studio?" Sloan said.

"Indie," Nico said. Then, into the pause, "Union rate if you can negotiate it."

"How soon?"

"You know. Soon."

"You have the script?"

"I'll send you mine. So you can get the wheels turning in your spare time."

"What's the gist of it?"

"It's all over the fucking map."

"I mean, what's the story?"

Nico made some kind of gagging sound. "Danger, romance, sugar," he said. "Just read it."

"Mr Suspense rides again," Sloan said.

"Saddle up," Nico said. "Talk soon, dragoon. I gotta go."

The blue light beckoned him. He leaned on his balcony rail and drank and stared down and calculated the probability of his actually getting his mind and body into the pool tonight. Now. Soon-like. Soonish. The night-swimming woman was gone. The place was his for the taking, the submersion. Then he could corral those snippets of loose verse and write that email and secure the location. A couple of boisterous jokers entered his field of vision and took pool chairs and carried their conversation into the future at an unpleasant volume. He found himself sitting in a balcony chair laughing.

"Make no mistake," he said. "I will swim. I will definitely swim."

He fell asleep and dropped his cup.

A ringing reached him. He brought his head up out of the burrow of the bedclothes and peered around like a cataracted meerkat. There was light blasting in around the edges of the balcony door's curtain. Someone's phone down at the pool. Answer the fucking thing. Wasn't his sliding door closed? He craned his fogged head toward the desk and saw his own phone perched on his wallet, vibrating and turning like some agitated beetle seeking an escape route. He hand-walked two steps, reached the phone and missed the call. He reversed himself and slumped back into the pillows and rang Amanda back.

"Everything's on hold," she said. "Alan wants you to take a pause. Sit tight for a minute."

"Okay," he said. "Good morning to you, my dear. Is that why Trevor's gone silent on me?"

"Trevor left the project."

"No way! Without even telling me? I thought we were tight."

She paused. "I wouldn't expect a recommendation from him if I were you."

"That hurts me," Sloan said. "I thought he was the sweetest little pussy."

"So you keep saying," she said.

"Did Alan fire him?"

"He left the project," she said. "And we're doing— the client's doing—a reset."

"I guess I'll get a Bloody Mary then."

"You don't need to tell me that."

"A Virgin Mary, I meant to say. Hair of the hairless dog and all that."

He got up and ordered a full pot of coffee from room service, then stood under the shower, the water hot, lukewarm, and cold in turn. He stood dripping on the balcony in his towel, drank a bottle of water, put on shorts and t-shirt.

Once he got caffeine in his system, his email to Felicia flowed like petals on the surface of a stream. Not to say it was flowery, but that it conveyed a certain complimentary indulgence by acknowledging the importance of her position while retaining a firm sense of his mission. He mentioned his pleasure at meeting Mrs Sweeting, attending her event and playing such an unexpected and enriching role in it, an experience he would not soon forget. He would be forever in her debt and hoped, and expected, to remain friends beyond any contractual arrangements.

He walked down the beach and back a few times, got sweaty, read some fiction in a hammock under a palm, nodded off in classic relaxation mode, woke up to the rumbling engine of the ferry. He walked over, boarded, and rode it out to Adventure Island for lunch. While he was eating conch fritters under an umbrella, he received a reply from Felicia. Mrs Sweeting had accepted his offer. The deal was set.

He texted Amanda: *Hero location confirmed. Backup location pending.*

She replied: *Standby please.*

He waded out into the scalloped cove and swam into open water, its clarity amazing and rejuvenating and as dependable as the endless repetition of gin-clear clichés. He floated under—what was it?—gossamer clouds, smiling at thoughts of rainbow fish, palm-fringed tropical islands, white-sand beaches, turquoise waters. Today was good. He could buy all the clichés, and then some. Swimming was a celebration.

Back at his chair the waiter brought him a Bloody Mary and Sloan celebrated his success, alone. He crunched his celery stick, alone. It was a solo job, for the most part.

You needed to appreciate your own company.

You needed to appreciate *Don Quixote*.

You needed to appreciate *Monty Python*.

You needed to appreciate *The Spy Who Came in from the Cold*.

You had to accept the lies and the treachery. The absurdity. All of it.

He was napping in his room when Amanda called.

"The client pulled the plug," she said.

"No way," Sloan said.

"Yes way," she said. "The job is dead."

"Is there a reason?" he said. "That you can share."

"I don't know, maybe a lack of choices. If one were to guess."

"Well, shit," he said. "I can go to Anguilla. Or Puerto Rico. If you want a wider search."

"It's over," she said. "The guy doesn't know what he wants. Or what he wants to spend. Your room will be paid through tonight. Send me your remaining receipts and an invoice. You'll have a ticket waiting for you at American tomorrow. I'll send you the flight info. *C'est la vie*. Good luck, Luke."

"Same to you," he said. "You're great to work with. I mean that."

"Thank you," she said.

He hung up and texted Brenda. *Sorry about yesterday. I'm free tonight if you are.*

He wandered around the property hounded by the empty feeling that lurks at the end of every job. On top of that, though, was the attending incompleteness. The lack of finality as he had conceived it. He felt like he'd taken a train to the wrong town.

He texted Nico and told him he'd be home tomorrow. Fit for duty.

He made some notes at his desk. Nothing came back from Brenda. He knew better than to cancel anything with Felicia yet. A job could easily rise from the dead. You never knew. The ground was shifting all the time. Nothing was solid, nothing was 100 percent.

He read for a while and then headed to the bar for dinner. The bartender greeted him warmly.

He ate a lobster and drank two beers and left. As he passed through the lobby he looked out at the pool but was not drawn there. He would swim in the gin-clear sea again in the morning. Say goodbye to The Bahamas.

And say goodbye to Roxy. Her soothing sensual voice never matched to face or body. It remained pure beauty. He could call the Film Office in the morning, thank them for the help, maybe hear that voice again. Or not.

He would update Felicia. And thank Mrs Sweeting.

In some way this was the perfect ending, the job a diaphanous dream, a mirage at sea.

Just vanish, Mr Scout.

13. The Script

LARIMORE

screenplay

by

Duncan Barlow

1 EXT. JUNGLE (DOMINICAN REPUBLIC) - DAY

Dense greenery fills the frame.

The stillness is staggering, silent, frightening.

We see glimpses of men in camo, a column pushing through the vegetation with guns raised, hard faces half hidden by tropical shadows and jungle hats. Suddenly, birds squawk and scatter, a feathery cloud of panic.

PULL BACK as a man bursts through the green

wall, drenched in sweat, his dirty face red and contorted with the rush of adrenaline, his breathing insane with the intensity of escape. His shirt is in shreds, a shoulder wound leaks blood, his neck, chest, and arms are scratched and mud-streaked. He is brown-haired, sunburnt but clearly not local. He is desperate but not panicked.

Suddenly we hear the tremendous ROAR of falling water, as if the man had been unable to hear anything until this moment. He pauses, looks down at the rushing stream.

HE LEAPS FORWARD.

2 EXT. WATERFALL - DAY

CAMERA TILTS DOWN TO FOLLOW FALLING MAN, arms flailing as he is lost in the spray emitted by the vast volume of water cascading into the pool far below.

3 EXT. WATERFALL POOL - DAY

Massive spray chaotic and deafening. From the pool's surface TRACK the falling man as he hits the water hard and - SWITCH TO UW CAMERA - crashes underwater, down through bubbles as he struggles for control, his feet and legs banging into boulders at the bottom, green moss waving like the arms of demons.

4 EXT. WATERFALL, EDGE OF POOL

The fallen man breaks the surface, gasping,

kicking his legs with relief that they still
work, his relief briefly transforming into
the birth of a grin.

FREEZE FRAME – this is LARIMORE, as the title
reveals.

LARIMORE POV – He looks up through the spray
and thunderous roar in time to see several
rocks falling, slamming into the water around
him.

4A **HE DIVES, SCRAMBLES BEHIND THE FALLING WATER**
out of range of the projectiles.

4B **LARIMORE CLIMBS OUT, CAMERA RISING TO FOLLOW**
stands dripping at the rock wall, surveying
the surrounding jungle. With the dirt washed
off, he's seen to have gone several days
unshaven, to be somewhat gaunt, his chiseled
face crosshatched with natural lines and the
cuts of jungle running, his eyes bloodshot
but still piercingly blue. He is neither
young nor old, his body lean and rangy.
Bleeding from a gash on his right leg, he
rips a strip of cloth from his tattered
shirt, threads it through the tear in his
pants, ties it around the wound. His shoulder
wound is still bleeding but he doesn't try to
wrap it. He has a head start but not much of
one. He's surprised to see that he still has
both shoes.

LARIMORE
(looking up, squinting through
the mist)

Jump, you chickenshits.

5 EXT. JUNGLE TRAIL - DAY

Late light filters through the canopy as
Larimore moves into the green world and
vanishes from sight, the roar of the falls
fading as bird calls come up into his
hearing.

6 EXT. ROAD - DAY

A hot and dusty country road through endless
cane fields. The emptiness is invaded by the
high whine of a motorbike. Camera pans with
the passing bike, two riders flying by as
Larimore emerges from the cane. A girl looks
back and sees the man stumbling at the edge
of the field as she clings to the boy
driving.

6A EXT. ROAD, SHOULDER

The bike has pulled over, the boy leans on
the handlebars as the girl makes a call, the
green cane stalks waving in the background.
She is young, her black hair hanging in front
of her face as she speaks in a murmur. She
pushes her hair behind her ear, looks back,
and we see her beauty.

7 EXT. HIGHWAY, LA ROMANA

A black SUBURBAN rides down the road, Gina La
Vega on the phone in the backseat. She is a
grownup glamorous version of the little girl
on the motorbike, her daughter Penelope. Gina
is in her mid-thirties, has long raven hair
and is dressed in a black dress that hugs her
audacious curves like a bodysuit. Both the
driver and the bodyguard in the passenger
seat are dressed in white linen suits and
hats and wear shoulder holsters under their
jackets.

> GINA LA VEGA
>
> Mi amor, go back and wait in
> sight of the man but not too
> close. Keep an eye on him and
> call me if anyone approaches.
>
> PENELOPE'S VOICE ON THE PHONE
> (over rushing wind)
>
> Mami, we are almost there but I
> don't see the man. Wait, I see
> him now. He's lying on the
> ground.

CUT TO:

8 EXT. ROAD, MOTORBIKE

Penelope holds her phone beside the idling
bike, her friend Eddie Perez with his hands

on the grips, the unconscious man some fifty feet away. She is watching another vehicle far down the road, heading toward them.

> PENELOPE
>
> Come on, help me pull him.

Eddie pulls the bike up on its kickstand and leaves it running. He follows Penelope down to the edge of the field.

9 EXT. CANE FIELD - DAY

The two teenagers run along the wall of cane stalks. Penelope squats beside the man's face and feels his breath. They grab his ankles and drag the heavy body over the ground and into the cover of the cane.

> PENELOPE
>
> Hurry Eddie, distract them
> somehow.

He rushes out of the cane and she remains crouched beside the man's body. She puts the phone to her ear and we realize her mother has been listening.

> GINA LA VEGA'S VOICE
>
> Penny, what are you doing? Go
> with Eddie.

> PENELOPE
>
> Mami, listen. We pulled him out
> of sight. He's bleeding. A car

is coming. If it stops I'll run
into the cane. Don't worry.

10 EXT. ROAD, OPPOSITE CANE FIELD (OVERHEAD)

We see Eddie accelerate into the highway as
the camera rises and the approaching car, a
silver ESCALADE, enters the frame, the two
vehicles heading toward each other.

11 EXT. ROAD, TRACKING EDDIE (CAMERA PANS)

Eddie rides in the wrong lane, playing
chicken with the larger vehicle. He wears no
helmet and his face displays a fierce and
childish determination, his long dark hair
and his clothes whipping wildly in the wind,
the background cane field a green blur flying
by.

12 INT. ESCALADE (POV OF DRIVER AND PASSENGER)

Through the windshield we see the bike
heading for the car.
Camera pans to driver's tense face, his hands
tight on the wheel, and follows his glance to
the backseat and his boss RAMON, whose steely
gaze is focused on the bike. His face is
marked by scars on forehead and left cheek,
and though he is still considered handsome,
no one would call him pretty to his face. He
is the heir to the EXCALIBUR SUGAR fortune,
and all the cane we see belongs to his
family.

RAMON LA VEGA
Look at this little piece of
shit. Don't you fucking avoid
him. He'll move over.

13 INT. ESCALADE (CLOSE-UP OF THE DRIVER)

Jaime Fortuna purses his lips tightly, his
ugly face sweating as the bike continues
straight toward them.

JAIME
Jefe, this could be bad for the
car.

We see the pores in his nose, the moisture on
his sallow skin, his fleshy lips making a
tense little smile, his dark puffy eyes
vacillating between fealty and fear.

RAMON
(laughing from the back seat)
The car? Squash this loco
pissant and I'll get us some
brand new wheels.

14 EXT. ROAD, VIEW OF CANE FIELD – DAY

Camera wide as vehicles are heard approaching
from each side. Road, sky and field, the
whine of the bike, the roar of the car. Cane
stalks waving gently, a peaceful scene of
impending doom as the vehicles blast into
frame on a collision course.

CAMERA picks up the bike as it veers into the lens as if to crash into it, then jerks away to pass the car, camera panning with it.

CUT TO:

15 EXT. ROAD, CAMERA TRACKS BIKE PASSING CAR

Hunched over and flying, Eddie looks at the driver and hurls a rock at the window as he rockets past, one hand tight on the throttle.

16 INT. ESCALADE, POV OF BIKE, THROWN ROCK

The rock smashes against the driver's window with a loud shocking bang. Jaime jerks the wheel away involuntarily and the car runs off the road toward the cane field.

CAMERA bounces with driver trying to control the vehicle.

> RAMON (FROM BACKSEAT)
> Get on the road and run that
> fucker down!

17 EXT. ROAD, ESCALADE SLIDING OFF PAVEMENT

As it turns and finds traction and roars back up on the road heading in the opposite direction, the CAMERA lifting to see the bike receding in the distance. The car follows.

18 EXT. ROAD & CANE FIELD – DAY

The black Suburban pulls over and Gina emerges quickly as Penny peers out from between stalks of cane. Gina runs over and lifts her child, hugs her tightly.

19 EXT. CANE FIELD – LOOKING OUT, GROUND LEVEL
Larimore's POV as he crawls forward. Through
the stalks he sees the girl and the woman,
behind them the parked car and two men
standing beside it. The woman sees him and
puts the girl down, motions to the men and
one of them hurries over.

20 EXT. CANE FIELD & ROAD – DAY
Camera tracks Larimore being dragged out of
the cane by Gina and her bodyguard. The
driver runs to help and takes Gina's place.
At the car the man is propped up against the
rear tire and Gina opens a water bottle and
holds it to his mouth. He drinks, squinting
in turn at her, the two men, the girl. The
sun is beating down. His eyes close as Gina
bandages the bullet hole in his shoulder.

21 INT. MOVING SUBURBAN – DAY
Larimore is passed out across the center row
of seats, his head in Gina's lap, her fingers
stroking his forehead, running through his
hair. Penny is leaning over the rear seat
above the prone figure, phone at her ear.

PENNY
Mami, I can't reach Eddie.

GINA

100

We'll find him, mi amor. He's a
resourceful young man and
probably has his hands full.

CUT TO:

22 EXT. RURAL ROAD

Eddie's POV as he rockets down the road,
passing a road sign, trees, seeing houses up
ahead - a village.

23 INT. ESCALADE FOLLOWING

POV of Eddie getting closer as the car gains.

RAMON

Don't let this little shithead
get away!

24 EXT. VILLAGE ROAD

Eddie slides into an unpaved alley between
houses, dirt flying as he straightens the
bike and keeps going.

25 EXT. VILLAGE – TRACKING, ESCALADE TURNING

The car slides into the corner of the first
house, smashes a porch post, sends shards of
cinder block flying, and continues down the
alley, swerving to the other side.

26 EXT. VILLAGE – POV OF ESCALADE APPROACHING

Behind the adjacent house the car takes out a
cart filled with papayas that explodes in
pieces, a woman in curlers runs behind an
escaping dog as the car continues, its hood

and windshield covered in bits of yellow
fruit.

CUT TO:

27 EXT. ROAD THROUGH CANE FIELD - AERIAL - DUSK

The Suburban is seen from above, like a toy
traveling between vast walls of cane, the
late light golden across the tops of the
stalks and the swirling dust trail left by
the car. All this is Excalibur Sugar, an
empire, and at its center is the human toll.
The car is seen nearing a settlement and the
camera swoops in over the car so we see its
destination. There are small dark huts
connected by plywood trails crossing over
mud, alongside a bare dirt clearing with
puddles of standing water. Barrel fires and
cooking fires are already glowing and smoke
rises in thin plumes. People move about like
shadows. This is the camp where the cane
cutters live, out of sight, tucked away in
their own squalid world. This is Batey #8, a
shantytown for the Haitians who work the
surrounding fields.

Now we hear Gina on the phone in her car.

                    GINA
        I'm taking him somewhere safe.

                MAN ON PHONE
        There is no such place. He must

be crazy to come back here. His
reporting made him an enemy of
the industry and our family.

> GINA

I mean someplace where he won't
be found.

> MAN ON PHONE

Our brother is clever and
diabolical.

> GINA

Don't you think the memory of
my husband reminds me of that
every day?

> MAN ON PHONE

(after a pause) We'll talk
again tomorrow. Good luck. Be
very careful.

28 EXT. BATEY - NIGHT

The black Suburban splashes through a puddle
and stops. Firelight reflects off the
windshield and the hood. Gina steps out and
walks to the figures gathered at the edge of
the clearing. Her bodyguard stands at the
open passenger door. We can hear the whine of
mosquitoes and Gina brushes the side of her
face.

> GINA

> Bonsoir! I'm here to see Madame
> Chery.

The crowd murmurs and soon an elderly woman makes her way forward. She is wrapped in shawl and headscarf, her face is wrinkled and wizened, her eyes sharp, her step steady.

> MADAME CHERY
> Bonsoir, Madame La Vega.

She extends her hands and the women hold each other's hands warmly. Madame Chery nods to the side and the two women walk away and confer privately. Gina discreetly passes an envelope to the camp elder.

29 EXT. BATEY – NIGHT

Madame Chery rejoins her people as Gina walks back to the car. Her bodyguard opens the back door and begins to slide the unconscious man out as two Haitian men bring over a crude stretcher of wood and canvas. Larimore is loaded onto the stretcher and taken away, the crowd leaning over to look at him as he passes. From the car, he is seen to be vanishing into a sea of darkness.

> CUT TO:

30 EXT. MANSION – NIGHT

Elevated camera shows a massive well-lighted home with the glittering sea in the background. This is big money. This is the home of Luis La Vega, the patron of Excalibur Sugar. Off to the side is a security building and several men armed with automatic rifles can be seen in the vicinity. We hear a car as the camera pans to pick up the silver Escalade entering the gates and cruising up the drive to the house.

The camera lowers as the car pulls up to the front. The Escalade's left front fender is dented, the left headlight is cracked, the paint on the hood and the side of the car is badly scratched. Fruit fragments are stuck in the grill.

Ramon La Vega steps out and one of the security men hurries into frame as the patron's son passes sternly and bounds up the steps to the house. There is no sign of young Eddie Perez.

14. Glory is the Reward of Valor

At a shaded metal table on Calle El Conde in Santo Domingo's Colonial Zone, the two scouts were getting reacquainted. It wasn't exactly happy hour but it was close enough and the mojitos were going down easily. They talked about the current project and briefly mentioned the previous one they'd done together, alluding to the scandal mainly to get it out of the way and back in the past where it belonged. Now, they were glad to be there in pure scouting mode, laughing, enjoying the pre-panic time, however long it might last, embracing the movie (no matter its as-yet-undetermined quality) and the work—their own department encompassing the location aspects of the show—before it got into high gear with the higher-ups, the above-the-line contingent, and then the whole chaotic crew, the professionals and the prima donnas, the crazies and the insecure, the beautiful and the warped and the damned.

"From what I gather, it's a midlevel show," Nico said. "Not big, but not too small either. You can't be coming over here without *some* money."

"I meant to finish the script on the plane," Sloan said, "but I fell asleep."

"Not a fan of action melodrama I guess," Nico said, laughing.

"It seems profoundly average," Sloan said, "with a shitload of work for the valiant Locations Department."

"As usual, it's what you do with the material," Nico said. "I just got the word on the director."

"Give me a sec," Sloan said, "to set my expectations as low as possible."

A few tables away their waiter turned to go inside and Nico got his attention with two fingers raised. The waiter nodded. Beyond him, at the next restaurant, some musicians were setting up. Three young dark-haired beauties in matching colorful dresses were with them, which brought about a brief lull in the conversation. The women stood waiting in the dappled light as tourists strolled along in front of them.

"As I was saying," Nico said. "Jonathan Fucking Cragmore."

"What?" Sloan said. "I thought that guy was gone, like off the rails."

"It's only been nine years," Nico said. "I looked it up."

"He went up in flames with the last part of that trilogy," Sloan said. "Unless this is the fourth in a quartet. Whoa! There's a scary thought."

"Everyone loves a comeback story," Nico said. "And everyone loved *Mindblown*."

"True, but then there's a progressive drop in quality. "*Windblown* was light as a tumbleweed."

"But better than the third," Nico said. "Totally forgettable. What was it called?"

"Just *Blown*," Sloan said. "He was down to basics."

"No, there was more than that," Nico said, snapping his fingers. "Yeah, it was *Blown Away*."

"Maybe officially," Sloan said. "But reviewers called it *Blown*, for the missed opportunity. Among other more graphic meanings."

"And he blew it by making it two words, breaking the title formula," Nico said. "Maybe he could have maintained an average quality instead of going completely down the toilet."

"*Blownaway* as one word looks confusing," Sloan said. "Some people might read it as *Blow Naway,* thinking it's some Indonesian dude's name. Then you have a porno-association problem."

Their fresh round of mojitos arrived as the conga drums next-door were warming up, causing the colorful girls to begin to sway in unison.

"Yeah, that name was trouble. No way around it," Nico said. "And now the director will be looking for redemption, seizing this last chance with his teeth. I believe he will want to go large."

They sat drinking and watching the girls as a steady stream of tourists wound slowly through the cobblestone street, drifting like cigar smoke around the lampposts and the vendors.

Sloan pulled out his notebook and pen. "Let's get a game plan together and then grab some dinner."

"Definitely," Nico said. "I'll finish my breakdown tonight and we can divide and conquer tomorrow."

"Right off the bat we have the waterfall, the jungle, the cane field, the village, the batey, the mansion," Sloan said. "Just for starters."

"There's a relatively low number of locations," Nico said. "Which will result in long scenes at some of them."

"We should be doing some of this in Jamaica," Sloan said. "What fucking Dominican sugar company is going to want this story shot on their land?"

"A slight problem," Nico said. "Hopefully we'll have a star who can shift the balance."

"I wonder who's playing Gina," Sloan said.

"No word on actors yet. Hopefully we'll meet with the Film Commissioner this week and get some help setting up a quick sugar meeting," Nico said.

"I'm sure we can sweet-talk them," Sloan said.

"Everyone loves the movies," Nico said.

"Cheers to that," Sloan said, lifting his mojito. "Here's to luck, skill, and the outstanding high points. I hope this isn't the last one."

Nico laughed. "Cheers, brother. What doesn't kill you, makes you stronger."

"Amen, amigo," Sloan said. "We will stay brave and overcome all obstacles. At the end we will dance and sing and laugh like lunatics."

The phone calls placed to the Dominican Film Commissioner, Javier Contreras, were handled by his assistant, a woman named Beatriz Fernandez, who assured Nico that his calls would be returned at some point in the future, the uncertainty due only to the fact that Javier was out of the office on a personal matter. She implied that an email would almost without question produce quicker results.

"Almost?" he said.

"Much faster," she said. "Almost *muy rapido*."

He considered going into the office to meet her personally and communicate the situation and address the gringo urgency that was weighing upon him. For all he knew she might know someone in the Imperial Sugar family or she might be up for a drink after work. In the meantime he emailed Javier and asked for an intro to the Imperial Sugar Public Relations Department or anyone there who would hear their filming request.

Sloan spent time researching sugar producers and came to the unmistakable conclusion that Imperial dominated the local industry. A couple of smaller companies were economically linked and unlikely to go against the wishes of the bigger player.

In the late afternoon Nico and Sloan outlined their priorities and strategy.

"Everything hinges on sugar. We need to build some locations around the cane field and the batey and go from there," Nico said. "We will have to travel but we need this anchor to get going."

"We gotta have the sugar," Sloan said. "And they will ask for script pages. I mean, if we even get to talk to them and if they are even interested. We have to appeal to them in some way that's not strictly money. They're already richer than shit."

"Hold on," Nico said. "Is there any kind of plant we could fake for sugar? It's just a grass."

"Like what," Sloan said. "Corn or cattails? That would look like crap."

"What about elephant grass?" Nico said. "It might pass from a distance."

"Do you think we can find a field of elephant grass?" Sloan said. "Or plant one and wait for it to grow?"

"Yeah, it's all about the cane," Nico said. "Cragmore will insist on authenticity. I can feel that coming."

"What about a mom-and-pop sugar company?" Sloan said. "Are there any? They might need money."

"Now there's an angle," Nico said. "Imperial probably has a monopoly but let's find a local sugar expert."

"You mean other than the Ministry of Agriculture?"

"I mean let's not go down a bureaucratic rabbit hole and never see the light of day again."

"Agreed. What we need is the name of the bar where all the sugar barons hang out."

"Ha," Nico said. "It is time to consult with a knowledgeable local. It's time to add to our team. It is time to confront the production manager with the realities of the Locations Department."

Nico grew up in San Diego surfing the southern coast but was now an Angeleno who traveled wherever movies took him. He possessed neither the classic Californian surfer look nor the expected auburn cast of those with his surname's origin. Due to his Italian mother, he was darker in hair and complexion.

He had surfed with Gene Friedman, the production manager, when they were both starting out as production assistants, and they had worked together several times over the years. Gene had brought Nico onboard *Larimore* and they were generally friendly at the start of a project.

"Absolutely not," Gene said by phone, when Nico requested starting a local location assistant ASAP. "If you two can't figure out what to do then you're on the wrong movie."

"In a foreign country you always need local perspective," Nico said. "With local knowledge."

"I don't disagree," Gene said, "I just don't think you need it this soon. Ask me again in two weeks. In my opinion you need to generate some activity first."

"I'm on the ground here," Nico said. "Your opinion is secondary."

"My opinion is primary," Gene said, voice rising, "on money matters. I let you bring Sloan on right away because I know you guys have experience down there. I also know he has been known to go rogue and I know I can count on you to keep him, and yourself, in bounds. We don't want any kind of replay of that—what should I call it?—incident."

"There's no need to dig up the past," Nico said. "Accidents happen."

"We all know," Gene said, "that conditions can be favorable to accidents. Let's leave it at that. Part of my magical thinking this time around had to do with the low odds of something bizarre like that happening again. Like lightning striking the same place twice."

"You lost me at magical thinking," Nico said.

"Everyone works at some level of superstition," Gene said.

"If you say so," Nico said.

"Let me know when you have some locations," Gene said.

Over breakfast in the courtyard of their small hotel the two scouts broke down the locations and logistics of the next few days.

Foremost, they had to engage in some way with Big Sugar and Little Sugar, the heavy hitters and whatever smaller players they could find as a potentially friendlier location. They needed to shoot some reference shots of cane fields, quickly, without permission, just to put the subject into photographs for discussion. They needed info on the harvesting schedule, the best time to shoot those scenes in the near future, and what specific fields they could control for shooting.

They also needed to peek in on a batey or two. For this, it would be extremely helpful to have a French speaker to communicate with the Haitian immigrants who lived there.

They needed to scout a few waterfalls, see what could really work for the opening scene of Larimore jumping. It was important to get the look as well as the practical access for a film crew, how long it would take to get everyone in. The waterfall scout would include the surrounding jungle as well.

They needed a mansion on the water. For this, as well as for Big Sugar, they needed input from the Film Office. Nico would press the issue and make himself known, and possibly a nuisance, at the office.

Sloan would scout the La Romana region for cane

fields, adjacent roads, and bateyes. He would swing by the southern coast below La Romana to ascertain accessible mansion opportunities, then head north to visit several waterfalls. He would be away from the capital for a couple of nights. Maybe three.

"We really need a local to get below the surface of these locations," Sloan said.

"I know," Nico said. "That little prick Friedman is making us wait. Says it's too soon."

"I don't know the guy," Sloan said.

"He's—let me put this diplomatically—short of stature," Nico said, "so he's always afraid he'll be perceived as an easy little guy to walk over if he grants your request on the first ask."

"Well, fuck that Napoleon," Sloan said. "We should bring someone on when we need them."

"I'm thinking the same," Nico said. "Even if we have to pay them ourselves. Like at a trial period rate, a performance test with the promise of more *dinero* very soon. If that doesn't make us sound like cheap gringo assholes."

"I think it could sound fair," Sloan said. "Sort of an under-the-table, off-the-books deal."

"Yeah," Nico said. "With the chance to get in on a long-running job through the whole show."

Sloan stood on the car's roof and shot a vast polarized panorama of green stalks and the dusty road beside it. He wandered into the field until he was surrounded by the plants and took claustrophobic images there. He lay on his back and saw a world made of cane. Clouds plodded across the sky, and the sun came and went. He crawled to the edge of the field like Larimore and peered out at the road. He pictured Gina running toward him, a union of the real and the imagined.

When the sun broke out the afternoon light was

still too hot but these were only reference shots and he didn't have the luxury of waiting for perfect lighting. He had miles to go and needed to keep his mind attuned to some kind of realistic schedule. Location scouting was an organic process that worked within a loose framework. The images mattered. Logistics mattered.

Out on the perimeter roads he navigated around adjoining fields and found a way to the interior on a potholed dirt track that felt like part of a labyrinth between walls of cane. As he reached a clearing the sky opened with a massive cloudburst and he parked to wait it out. Spurts of mud lifted off the ground in brown jets and rainfall thundered on the car's roof and hood like a drum battle.

He saw blurry figures in the doorways of blurry huts and rainwater ran and pooled as if to transform the community into a swamp. Between the slow swipes of the wipers he shot strange telephoto images that looked vaguely African.

Sitting in his rain-blasted car his eyes closed to the sound and he drifted slowly through a sonic massage. He was breathing deeply and peacefully when his phone jolted him awake.

"Hello," he said. It was a local number. The rain had eased up but he wasn't sure where he was.

"Hi Luke. This is Sonia. Nico said to call you. Beatriz gave him my number. Beatriz from the Film Office."

"Okay," he said, a bit stunned by her fast talking. "Go ahead."

"I can meet you somewhere and help you," she said. "You don't have to pay me at first but Nico said you could pay the expenses. Is that okay?"

"Can you start right now?" he said.

"Yes, I am ready to go," she said.

"Excellent. Are you in the capital?"

"Yes, I live in Santo Domingo."

"Great," he said. "I'm over near Guaymate looking at sugar cane. If I have time I'll look at the coastal area south of here to see if I can spot any potential mansions by the water. At the end of the day I want to finish up near Bayaguana so I can scout two waterfalls around there in the morning before too many people show up."

"Okay," she said. "What do you want me to do?"

"I want you to go to Bayaguana and get two rooms—just basic and clean—and find out anything we need to know about going to the falls, Bayaguana and Socoa. How early we can go, how long it takes, if we need a guide, stuff like that. And find someplace for dinner tonight."

"How can I get the rooms?" she said.

"Just try to reserve them," he said. "Tell them I'll pay when I get there. Or they can call me."

"Okay," she said. "How many days is this scouting? I ask only for packing."

"Of course," he said. "Fair question. Tonight and then tomorrow in Samana. Then we come back to the capital the next day. Okay?"

"Yes," she said. "I will see you in Bayaguana when you get there."

After they hung up Sloan got a text from Nico saying that a girl named Sonia Rivera was going to call and he thought she sounded smart and enthusiastic.

Sloan texted back. *She's on, thanks.*

The rain fell lightly now and figures emerged to investigate the stranger. To see if he needed help or had a purpose for being in this out-of-the-way place. But he did not have anything to say at this time, did not know if he would be back or could explain his presence just then, so he drove forward into the clearing and shot images through the window as discreetly as possible as he turned the car in a loop to exit, covering the dripping shanties in a casual effort to convey their impoverished appearance. He might have been mistaken for a lazy journalist or a real estate agent descending into dementia. Leaving the clearing he shot a small faded sign: *Batey 108.*

As he drove into the corridor of cane to exit the area, movement in the rearview mirror caught his eye, a figure running toward him on the road. His first instinct was to accelerate, then the figure became a small person, a child perhaps. Through windows streaked with moisture he made out a pale green dress—a young girl approaching, a book held out in both hands. He scanned the background for other figures, then looked ahead and checked both sides, wary of a trap of some kind. He did not know what to make of this scene.

He braked the car and waited, watching the girl get closer. About twenty feet from the rear of the car she stopped and held up what she was carrying, which Sloan now saw was a sign, a piece of cardboard with a single word written in black letters. It was backwards in the mirror and he turned to look through the rear window and read the word. *AYUDA.* With her hair braids sticking out in all directions, her young face dark and solemn, her feet bare, her thin dress hanging limply below her knees, she stood holding the sign at chest level.

HELP

He sat for a few minutes with his foot on the brake, watching as the girl held her position, then he put the car in park. He opened the door and stepped out and stood beside the car looking at her.

"What do you need?" he said. Then, "*Que paso?*"

The girl stood still, holding the sign and looking at him. She was maybe ten years old, a stick figure in an old dress too large for her. Suddenly she turned and walked away with the sign under her arm. Sloan hesitated but she did not turn around to look back at him.

He got in his car and left.

15. The Closeness of Colleagues

From the southern coast back up through farmland and the eastern forest and highway villages, and following a text from Sonia, Sloan passed through Bayaguana and continued to Monte Plata and pulled into the yard of the hotel, a circle of cabins around a pool, the western sky beyond the darkened tree line mottled by orange smudges glowing through the soft purple of fig. The cabins were plain and clean, the floors white-tiled, the buildings all connected by gravel paths. A donkey stood peacefully in the grass outside Sloan's room, as still and silent as a statue.

"You should be careful driving at night," Sonia said. "Some Dominicans don't use their lights because they want the bulbs to last longer."

Sloan laughed. "Thank you for the warning," he said. "I've been here before. Another job."

"If we go over to the restaurant we can get something here," she said, "unless you want to drive somewhere in town."

She was warm and alert, had bright teeth and lively dark eyes, a cappuccino complexion, a round face framed by wavy brown hair, a band of freckles across her nose. She was smooth and well-formed, almost as if she'd been poured into her clothes.

"I've had enough driving today," he said. "And I'm glad to be here. Good choice."

In their jeans and t-shirts they looked like a couple and they sat together with Presidente beers in the open-sided building while moths fluttered around the corner flood lights like confetti conferred on a day of promise. The manager brought them chicken and rice and left them alone.

"Did you find any mansions?" Sonia said, smiling like she knew the answer.

Sloan laughed. "It's hard to get a good look when armed guards are blocking the view."

"That's typical," she said. "The rich are difficult to reach. You need help for that."

"This whole thing needs help," Sloan said. "We're dealing with sugar."

"Oh no," she said, shaking her head. "The government needs to help you with that."

"It's a tricky situation," he said.

"What is the story about?" she said.

They ate while he considered a telling, saying the words in his mind, a version of what he had agreed would be non-disclosable.

"I'm telling you this because you're on the team," he said. "And because I already trust you."

"An American freelance writer returns to the DR after writing a sugar story centered around the treatment of cane field workers. He had pretended to be telling a different story, about an industry's progress, while he got acquainted with a sugar family, a father and his sons and daughter. The daughter was sympathetic to the writer and guided him to places he wanted to see. When his real intentions became known, she took his side and they fell in love. But his story, along with other reports, helped propel the changing American policy toward the Dominican sugar industry, which led to a decline in business. In spite of that past, the writer makes an ill-advised and dangerous trip back to the DR under a different identity to see the beautiful sugar princess. He is discovered and his lover must help him survive and further expose the terrible truths of her family's business."

Sonia was quiet for a moment. He figured she was wondering, as he was, how the backstory would be conveyed, if there would be spinning newspapers that came to a stop on bold headlines.

"They will never help you make that story," she said. "You know what you should do?"

"What?" Sloan said.

"You should tell them a different story."

"What do you mean?"

"Pretend you are telling a different story," she said. "Like the writer in the screenplay."

"Oh, you mean give them fake script pages," he said.

"Yes," she said, smiling, her eyes sparkling too.

He laughed and said, "You are making me laugh, I'll give you that. Getting on my good side right away. You have skills."

He called the manager over and got two more beers and the check. He handed the man his credit card and asked for two receipts, one for his room and the food, the other for Sonia's room and the beer.

"Look," Sloan said. "No one above me on this production would ever agree to that. You know why? One word—risk. They would not take the chance that the production could be shut down by someone discovering the subterfuge. The lie. Understand? If the shooting schedule is slowed down or halted, a lot of money goes down the drain. And it's always about the money."

Sonia nodded, watching his face. "I understand," she said. "I have worked on two movies and many other small productions, so I know about the money."

"Okay, good," he said. "Just so we're clear. I like your spirit. We need to be creative and think outside the box. But the job gets done Nico's way. And mine. We have to be unified."

He took care of the billing, the manager bid them goodnight, and they sat back to finish their beers. She watched him in the half-light of the open room and saw that he was watching her too.

"Can I say more?" she said.

"Of course you can," he said. "I always want you to speak your mind, give your ideas, argue if you feel the need. Speak freely."

"Okay, good," she said. "I think sugar is the bad guy in the story and in the real life. This is why the man in the story must lie. He can't tell the truth to the enemy and also tell his story. True?"

Sloan nodded, liking her more and more. "This is true," he said.

"He is fighting alone with his own tools," she said. "Until the woman helps him."

"Yes, he is," Sloan said. "He is also a character in a story."

"And you are a character in your story," she said. "If you lie it must be a secret in your life. Only for you to know. And me. And Nico. This department."

He sat watching her, thinking she might be having some fun, testing his moral fiber.

He could play that game. "Anything to get the job done," he said. "Whatever it takes, right? That's what we always say. And sometimes you have to bend the rules."

"Exactly," she said. "Whatever it takes. But only against the enemy."

Sloan smiled at her. "Once you have a secret," he said, "the list of potential enemies grows much longer."

She looked away, watched the bats maneuvering over the dark pool. Then she met Sloan's eyes again. "You will be okay if you have someone helping you," she said. "Someone who is completely with you."

Somehow she was crawling into him. He was about to get the rum from his room and suggest they sit by the pool drinking. He was about to conspire with her to commit fraud and go wherever it took them. A kind of hot capability was manifesting in his night mind. Did she have some kind of vendetta against the sugar industry? Was diabetes rampant in her family? Did her grandmother have rotten teeth and dental bills she couldn't afford?

Sonia got to her feet. "We should get some sleep," she said. "We need an early start for those cascades."

When they got to the junction of their separate cabin pathways, he decided to walk her to her door. She protested, saying it was such a short distance.

"I can't risk anything happening to a team member," he said.

She turned away and walked and he followed her. At the door she faced him.

"I'm happy to be a team member," she said. "Thank you for hiring me." Then she stepped forward and hugged him around the neck, pressing herself against his body.

She suddenly stepped back away from him. "Sorry," she said. "I grew up hugging everybody."

"It's fine," he said, definitely ready for a shot of rum now. "It's a cultural thing. Sleep well."

"You too," she said. She opened the door and disappeared inside.

Pacing around his spartan room he drank a glass of iceless rum and tried to cage the thoughts flying around in his brain like a flock of birds. Sonia was a stroke of luck, apparently, making him feel good and easing his job tension even as she upended his personal equilibrium. He would manage everything like a professional, to the best of his ability, but he would also write an alternative synopsis. See how it sounded. Like an experiment. A thought exercise. As if deception could become Plan A.

In the morning, after arranging to leave Sonia's car at the hotel until the following day, they backtracked to Bayaguana so that, afterward, the day's route would continue northward. They would stay the night in Las Terranas and be able to hit the third waterfall early the next morning.

The waterfall at Bayaguana was a triple, so not precisely the look Sloan was seeking—also within day trip distance to the capital, which would mean frequent crowds—but the cascades were tall and impressive, and the pool was large and round, its lushness and color splendidly picturesque.

While Sloan photographed the water, Sonia gathered information and took notes. The access road was rough and rocky and there were concrete steps down to the pool. Fifty-peso entrance fee. Adequate parking.

Sloan stood in the shallows of the pool contemplating the scenes. How the jump could be accomplished, the landscape at the top, the vegetation, the potential for shooting from the top of the falls. The jump would be a cheat of some kind. Maybe a stuntman could be swung out from the center falls, the widest one, far enough to avoid the rocks and hit the deepest portion of the pool. What would be needed, a scaffolding of some sort. Permission to assemble equipment at the top of the falls without damaging the landscape. Control of the area, the barring of the public for a day. The idea would be to shoot the wide shots, the beauty and the wonder of this real location, the drama of the scene from above and below. The man on the run at the top, his stark choices, his desperation and bravery, the spectacle of the height and the risk in going over the falls to escape capture and death. Trading one death for the possibility of another.

Sonia came down the forest trail and into the clearing of the pool. Sloan stood in the shallows and there was a guy out near the middle of the water where a rope stretching across the surface dissected the pool, indicating a recommended swimming area and presenting a warning to swimmers about proceeding closer to the spray and the force of the falling water. The guy seemed to be deciding if he should go under the rope and nearer the drama and thunder of the falls.

When Sonia joined him, Sloan said, "Did you bring a bathing suit?"

"Yes, I'm wearing it," she said, and lifted the corner of her shirt.

He glanced at her. "I saw some skin," he said. "No material."

"Because it's a bikini," she said.

"Well, that's perfect," he said. "You're staying in character."

"Who else can I be except myself?"

"Exactly," Sloan said. "It's just a movie term for that. Do you mind seeing how that rope is attached to the wall?"

She placed her shorts and shirt and sandals in a little pile at the side of the blue pool and waded in. As Sloan might have described her actions, at about chest-deep she was abreast of the rope and began to pull on it and feel around the spot where it was secured to the rock wall. She breast-stroked back to the shallows and stood in the sun to dry off, her tawny skin pebbled with drops that clung to her like luminous beads. The bikini was small and orange and attracted the gaze of the other man too. Sloan wondered if he could survive three waterfalls in a row.

"The rope is just tied to a metal ring," she said.

"So it can be untied or has to be cut?" Sloan said.

She frowned slightly. "Probably cut," she said, "but maybe with a tool..." She extended her index finger and flexed her wrist in a prying motion.

"Let's make a note of that," he said. "And then let's get some jungle shots and see how close we can get to the edge up there." He nodded toward the top of the falls.

They followed the river's course and explored the side trails, the tropical fusion of vegetation and scattered light. Sloan crouched and slunk among the vines and ferns, wielding his Canon while keeping Sonia tucked behind him, and then she took a few shots of him as a random man alone in the jungle.

Back at the top of the main trail they circumvented the parking lot and walked to the edge of the riverine woods.

"There is a warning," Sonia said, pointing to a sign:
PROHIBIDO EL PASO
NO TRESPASSING

"That doesn't apply to us," Sloan said. "We have cinematic immunity."

After that single warning there was no further hinderance to pitching oneself over the falls in a daredevil display or comedic performance or an act of tragic bravado.

Sloan walked in the central stream and shot the approach, the surrounding trees and the rushing water progressively pulling him and the anonymous future viewer to the edge as he sought to illustrate that counterintuitive wish to ride along with the current of one's fate, to chance the edge, the blade of a knife, the steep drop into air, to test the very extent of one's own concept of mortality. Sometimes called the unconscious death wish.

There was a major distinction though, between wanting to convey that driving force—to conjure that secretive and sinister inner voice—and wanting to actually experience the physical plunge. Sloan would need an aerial position to get the shot he really wanted. As it was, he got as close as he dared, made sure his footing was secure, not slippery or unstable, and that Sonia was using both hands to hold one end of the belt wrapped around his left hand as she leaned back upon the relatively solid ground of the bank beside him. In this manner he was able to capture with his right hand the panorama of this world's edge—the mist and the churning continuum of water rushing away and falling into the unknown.

The process was much the same at the next stop, Socoa Falls, though by this time of day there were more people enjoying the refreshing pleasures of the pool. Adolescent jokers, mostly. The falls weren't as tall as the previous location but the single cascade looked good erupting out of dense jungle. He was surprised by a skinny young guy who suddenly launched himself out, arms windmilling, and plummeted into the pool. Sloan fired off shots of the next two guys. Sonia was sampling the shallows and finding sharp rocks, so she put her sandals on. The sun was overhead and much of the pool was catching the light, showing its virescent hues.

It was all Sloan could do to keep himself from joining Sonia in the water. Protectively, of course, with these leering jackoffs around, but also for safety, to assist her obvious natural buoyancy, help make sure she got back to the surface, since he asked for a reasonable estimate on the depth at the deepest point.

He wanted more information, and she dove dutifully. Beautifully.

These two locations made a good combo. Both close to the capital, close to each other, so shots could be interchanged, giving the director two looks in the same general area—two pools, two cascades, two points of view from the top, two views upward, two jump options. Sloan was feeling good. As long as he didn't dwell on sugar. Sugar was an unmitigated downer.

What an asset she was. Smart, energetic, up for anything, a busty rule bender. Where was her downside? He hated to think about how bad it might be. There had to be one. If he had to guess, he'd guess explosive temper. When events conspired, when she got mistreated too badly or subjected to some monstrous injustice. He would simply shield her.

At the top, the jungle was perfect. Close, tropical, scriptworthy. She would have jumped too. But he had jump shots and could not bear the thought of an accident, the thought of anything marring her body, knocking her off his team. He could not stomach another incident on his watch.

Overheated and hungry, Sloan got back on the highway and pushed on to Las Terranas on the north coast to secure lodging and find a decent meal. With Sonia's help, he located The Lazy Lagarto, a tranquil bungalow hotel not far from town or the beach. They ate a midafternoon lunch in the garden restaurant under a large chickee hut by the pool, dining on fish sandwiches, fries, and cold beer. Sloan proclaimed the scouting over for the day and they planned to work separately in their rooms and then meet for a sunset beach walk and dinner in town.

He checked in with Nico.

"I'm spending all my time trying to set up

meetings," Nico said. "How is it out in the world?"

"Beautiful," Sloan said. "Good options on the falls. We're up at Las Terranas now."

"Nice," Nico said. "And how about the girl? You know, the one you're working with."

"Oh, her," Sloan said. "She's so quiet you forget she's around."

"Yeah, I know that must be 100 percent false," Nico said.

"So true," Sloan said. "She's a great find, a big plus."

"Then put her local knowledge all over some sugarcane, dude."

"She's on it," Sloan said. "Any other shining stars in the works?"

"I talked to a kid who's recommended," Nico said. "He's checking his busy schedule."

"Cool," Sloan said. "See you tomorrow."

"Roger that, mule skinner."

Sloan spent the next hour editing and organizing his photos, making his folders and files tell visual stories. Then he started a document called Synopsis B.

A stretch of yellow fired the western surface of the bay and the sky joining it. Pink and orange and blue mingled and merged above the yellow, and the tree line of palms darkened into jagged silhouettes that followed the curve of the sand to meet them as they walked. The waves lapped gently and steadily and the air was balmy and calm. On one hand it might have seemed an absurdly romantic scene and, on the other, simply the environment in which they found themselves together.

"I didn't mention this before," Sloan said, "but yesterday when I was leaving the batey a little girl ran up to me and asked for help."

Sonia stopped and touched his arm. "How did she ask you this?"

"She ran up near my car and held up a sign."

"Just her by herself?"

"Yes," he said. "She was maybe about ten years old."

"Wow. That's unbelievable," Sonia said. "They are very private in those places."

"I want to go back there," he said. "With you."

"Why?" she said. "I don't think anyone will talk to you."

He stared out at the changing colors on the water. Up the beach, a couple was leaning against a palm, kissing. "Maybe they'll talk to you. Do you speak any French?"

"Not much," she said. "A few words."

"I just have this strange feeling that I should go back there," he said.

They walked into town and ate at a patio table as the balmy mood continued. Moonlight came filtered through whispering palm fronds. Circling that buoyant mood lurked the ever-present pressure of unsecured locations, for Sloan, a bite into the soft flesh of the night, a toothsome anxiety creeping around his drinks and laughs like a tiger shark that breaks the surface of hedonistic pleasure with surprising ferocity and regularity.

He fought the mental intrusions by ordering more rum. It was self-medication as a way of life.

The booze, though, did nothing to squelch his erotic impulses. Just the opposite. But the team was important and he did not want to disrupt the balance by losing the battle with his salivating id.

For Chrissake, he'd only known her for a day.

She grew up in Santo Domingo and had gone away to school in Philadelphia for a few years. She had traveled to other parts of the Caribbean and to Mexico,

Argentina and Brazil, as well as California and Arizona.

"I want to go to Europe," she said. "Spain, Portugal, Italy, France." She motioned further with her hand.

"Let's go," he said with a drunken smile. "I mean, you know, after all this is over."

"That would be fun," she said, laughing with moist, rum-glazed eyes.

"Assuming we're still on speaking terms," he said.

"We will be," she said. "We're going to be a great team."

This aroused him, but he respected her friendly professionalism as well as every other single thing he thought about her. He signaled for the check.

It was a half hour drive to the Limón falls. This one was perhaps even more impressive, high and wide and spectacular, but the journey was significantly more challenging. It was a long hike down and a rougher one going up. There was also an equine option. At a wooden railing, a row of horses waited like taxis for the lazy, the overweight, or the quasi-cowboy tourist. Sloan had seen some of them at breakfast. Colossal Marlboro men and women.

Most of the horses were chestnuts, with an occasional white or gray mixed in. They wore saddles over cloth pads whose colorful fringe stuck out like homemade throw rugs. They were generally slight or skinny, some with visible ribs. Sonia went down the line, inspecting each one, making note of any cuts or open sores, shaking her head, muttering and cursing in Spanish.

A guide shrugged at Sloan, held up his open hands and gestured at his clothes and his rubber boots to signify his helplessness in the face of poverty.

"This is fucked up cruelty," Sonia said, stroking the long face of a horse.

"I can see that," Sloan said. "And these guys are just trying to make a living. They don't control the situation. They don't have a union."

"We can't use this place as a location," she said, her eyes narrowing, her jaw set hard.

"Well, we certainly will be walking," Sloan said, "and talking about the best course of action."

Her lovely round face turned red. "We have to skip this fucking place," she said.

Sloan walked away and came back. "Sonia, that's not how it works. We can influence the outcome, but we have to scout it. Otherwise, it will become known that we didn't, and the question "why the fuck not" will land on us like a hammer."

She walked around fuming, confronted two guides, one young and one middle-aged, and stood looking at them, then turned away.

She fell in behind Sloan and they began their hike.

The trail was muddy and rocky and only partly shaded. There were long stretches open to the sun. They carried their backpacks and took regular water breaks, about the only time they spoke, the exertion being the best remedy for the lingering tension between them. The jungle was all around but the logistics were a likely deal-breaker for a full company location. A second unit—a small mobile actorless camera team—could go up to get an establishing shot if that was deemed optimal for the story, with the plan that the rest of the scene would be done at an easier location. Sloan could probably make an argument for one of the first two cascades, or a combination of them.

They came to the terminus of the animal trail and saw a small shoddy contingent of beat-up beasts waiting for the return trip. From there the path wound downward in switchbacks, the last section having a railing of boards to aid the walkers under the trees.

The sound of the falls was heard before the cascade came into view. Then the huge pool and the rockface covered in clinging tentacles of water. Rather than falling freely through the air, streams and rivulets gushed down the convex surface of the rock so that the geometry of a jump, unless it was an Olympic-level feat, would finish at the base of the cliff instead of in the water.

There were about a dozen visitors in the pool and on the rock banks around the area, and Sloan began to shoot the location.

A Mitsubishi truck, which had been converted into a tourist bus, arrived from Las Terrenas. The bed had seats for twenty-four and a metal framework that supported a canopy. The crowd assembled at the trailhead and several guides took off to bring over more horses. Typically, a guide walked beside his horse to make sure the animal and the client were in harmony. But with a large group a single guide could lead a string of horses.

This time Sonia declined the swim, already betting that the location was a bust, and Sloan did not press her into any superfluous tasks. Instead, she was focused on the arrival of new visitors, appraising them to be either earth-loving, compassionate walkers or loathsome animal abusers.

Sloan followed the river downstream from the pool's spillover, shooting scenic sections devoid of people as potential locations for Larimore's jungle escape. From there he meandered down a couple of trails. Upon his return to the pool he noted the increased influx of tourists and decided to skip the upper level of the falls and leave the location. He started up the steep return trail, figuring that Sonia was not far ahead of him.

At the lower horse station the number of sweating, mouth-lathered animals was growing. Sonia stood by like an inspector, writing in her notebook. Her legs and boots were muddy, and she wore a ball cap backwards and a black-and-white striped shirt that brought to mind the image of a referee. As Sloan came into view from the lower trail, Sonia was approaching a large man entering the clearing on horseback, the animal slow-moving and staggering. He wore gray spandex shorts and a tight-fitting gray shirt bulged out in so many areas that he resembled badly packaged mozzarella. Around his neck a small towel was tied like a mini-cape, and with his red stretchy headband and mirrored shades he resembled a *lucha libre* wrestler. Maybe one of the little-known *luchadores*.

"*El gran extremo*," she said. "You should be giving the horse a ride."

The man turned on his saddle, his horse shuddered and stopped, front legs trembling, and a young guide stepped forward and held the reins, staring at Sonia.

"What did you say?" the big man said, his face dripping.

"You're crippling that horse," she said, "and you won't be able to make it down to the falls anyway, so your whole trip is pointless."

The man looked at his guide, who was not looking at him, and said, "Little amigo, what is this bitch saying to me?"

Sloan overheard this as he got close to the group. "She appreciates your help with our study," he said to the man. "We're from Animal Supply Source, the A.S.S., and will be recommending the use of Clydesdales for certain members of the public who could benefit from greater mammalian support."

The man's wife, slightly less gargantuan and dressed in a similar manner, perhaps following a family dress code, rode up beside him. "Johnny, we need to unhorse here," she said.

"Lorraine, I need to deal with these assholes," he said. He leaned forward against his horse's neck, his left foot pushing the stirrup back as the animal lowered its long head. Johnny grunted and swung his other leg over the rear of his animal. The guide caught the heavy moving leg around its calf but the big man's momentum carried him off the horse and propelled the guide to the ground with him. They tumbled in the dirt and the guide jumped up quickly and brushed himself off. Johnny lay on his back reaching up, struggling like a beetle with its legs in the air.

Sloan took Sonia's arm and began to walk away. More horses were entering the clearing, as if a stopgap had been removed from the path.

"Come back here, you fuckers," the man on the ground said.

"Let me help you, Johnny," his wife said. She began to dismount, the young guide pressing against her wide descending backside, his hands buried in spandex to keep her stable.

"Roll on," Sonia said.

"I heard that, you fucking bitch," the big man said.

"You pork sandwich," she said. And Sloan pulled her into the trees.

16. Presentations

On the drive back to Monte Plata they brainstormed the alternate synopsis idea and worked on an acceptable narrative.

"Let me reiterate this," Sloan said. "To be crystal clear, this idea is strictly between us and depends on meetings currently being scheduled, so it may never go any further."

"I got it," Sonia said, concluding her notes on their collaborative effort.

Back in his room in Santo Domingo, Sloan wrote the following:

Synopsis B

After reporting on the environmental hazards of phosphate mining in Florida, the resulting toxic algae blooms and dead fish in the Gulf of Mexico, as well as the widespread use of neonic insecticides and their disastrous bee-killing qualities and consequential effect on the pollination of American food sources, Sam Larimore takes on the abysmal treatment of Big Sugar's cane cutters.

He travels to the Dominican Republic to investigate,

then discovers, much to his surprise, that a major player in the industry is recognizing its worker problems and beginning to address them and make much-needed changes.

He plays golf with Luis La Vega, the fun-loving scion of a sugar family, who delights in playing practical jokes, and takes a tour of a cane-worker shantytown that is being upgraded with new buildings complete with running water, a daycare center, plus a game room. There is a heart-warming scene of sweaty workers enjoying Ms. Pac-Man.

Larimore meets La Vega's beautiful daughter, Gina, who is concerned about a shadowy underground group working to slander and demonize her father's company, and she enlists Larimore's aid in exposing the organization, which goes by the name The Bitter Sweet Talkers.

Larimore falls in love with Gina, and they visit some of the country's natural beauty together, swimming at a waterfall and enjoying themselves at a beach resort. Through an old reporter friend, Graham Perry, Larimore discovers that Gina's brother Ramon is funding the group for his own nefarious purposes, to gain control of the company and reverse its new humanitarian policies. Together, the lovers struggle to balance their intense romance with the increasing threat posed by Ramon and his gang of armed subversives.

The dramatic climax takes place outside the amphitheater during a reggaeton concert at Altos de Chavón, the replicated sixteenth-century village and cultural center overlooking the Chavón River. After an intense gun battle, during which Larimore and Gina and her loyal followers defeat Ramon's group, the lovers vow to work for a better future.

Sloan and Nico met for dinner and drinks. Sloan pitched the idea that all of the locations could be found in the southeast of the country between Santo Domingo, La Romana, Punta Cana and the waterfalls at Bayaguana and Socoa. The whole movie could be built within that zone and the production could be based in the capital and La Romana, with only one change of hotels.

"Great," Nico said, "assuming all those locations in that zone are picked."

"We have to center around the sugar," Sloan said, "and there's no getting around that."

"All we can do is present a good plan and hope reason prevails," Nico said.

"That's one giant loophole for mankind," Sloan said.

As if to comment on that statement, the power went out and the restaurant and everything in sight was plunged into darkness. Flashlights poked around and waiters began to carry candles to the occupied tables. The occurrence was regular and no one remarked on it. Corruption and mismanagement were everywhere. Around the area, generators rumbled into action like so many depth charges going off under the surface of the night.

There was no progress on sugar. Nico had not heard from or been able to reach Javier at the Film Office. His calls to Imperial Sugar were unreturned. And the batey would have to follow the sugar so there was no point in pursuing the one Sloan had seen and half-scouted in the rain.

They were nowhere on mansions.

They listed the primary challenges—cane field, batey, mansion, waterfall, resort.

Plus there were two named locations, real places, famous places, that could hardly be faked.

The *Teeth of the Dog* golf course. And the well-known attraction, a replica of a sixteenth-century Italian village with shops and restaurants, artists' workshops, and an amphitheater—*Altos de Chavón*, on the Chavón River, where the climactic scene would occur.

"Stay on Sonia," Nico said. "Push every contact she can think of that leads to sugar or a mansion. Keep digging and something will turn up. I'll stay on the Film Office and hit Punta Cana to scout resorts."

"Roger Wilco, Little Horse," Sloan said.

That night, after he'd given Sonia the game plan and told her to meet him for breakfast in the Colonial Zone, Sloan was sitting in his room reading when he got a text from an unknown number.

Word on the street is you've returned to the scene of the crime.

He immediately pictured Henrietta Higgs but did not reply or delete the message.

Within ten minutes, as he stood at the window drinking another rum, he got a follow-up.

Someone should warn the locals.

Sloan had not mentioned this harassment to Nico and now wondered if his colleague had received anything similar and was also holding it close. If it escalated, something would have to be said.

As Sloan drove, Sonia made calls. She reached out to her ex-boyfriend's ex-business partner and after a few pleasantries and a brief mention of the game-changing movie she was working on, asked if he knew anyone in the sugar business, who preferably lived in a mansion on the water.

"Let me think it over," he said. "Let's have dinner and discuss it. Are you free tonight?"

"I'm working," she said.

"Call me back when you're free," he said. "Let's talk movies while you sit on my lap."

"*Pendejo*," she said, and hung up.

She called two cousins, an uncle, a former employer who did not remember her, a girlfriend who accused her of calling only when she needed something, and a commercial producer she had worked for who said he knew dozens of people in the sugar industry but could not reveal their names.

Sloan drove into sugar country again, seeking any kind of inspiration, direction, or summons, a location he could make his own, letting the rows and rows of green stalks wave at him and taunt him with their sameness, their dual closeness and remoteness. He also wanted to make sure he could readily locate the batey he'd seen before, number 108, though he had absolutely no reason to think it could ever become an actual filming location.

Sonia watched silently as Sloan wound his way deeper into the world of cane, traversing the dusty organic channels to enter the private heart of this world. They passed the Batey 108 sign.

"Is this that place you told me about?" she said. "The one with the girl?"

"Yeah."

Ahead they saw another car, a stationary black Mercedes G-Class. An elderly local man stood at the driver's window, apparently engaged in conversation.

Immediately the man began to walk toward Sloan's car and the Mercedes rolled along beside him. Sloan braked and put his car in park.

"Well, well," he said. "Who could this be?"

As the car got closer the old man positioned himself between the two vehicles and stood near the window as he had been before, as if to protect the driver from intruders. He looked at the visitors as Sloan lowered his window glass. The Mercedes stopped opposite the rental car and the woman driver observed both occupants and then spoke to Sloan in English.

"Are you lost?" she said.

The woman was striking in her features, her intensity, the thickness of her dark lustrous hair.

Sloan was taken aback, momentarily blindsided by her beauty, and the fact that she was here at all, especially here, as if she had stepped out of the screenplay he was using as a blueprint.

"Not geographically," he said.

After the briefest pause, she said, "Then in what way are you lost?"

He could see faint traces of her makeup, a kind of radiant shimmer, the established way she presented herself to the world. Even aside from her fancy jacket and jewelry, she projected an aura of wealth.

"I'm just a little lost in my job," he said.

"And your job has brought you here," she said. "What kind of job is that?"

"I'm a location scout," he said. Then added, "For a movie."

She looked past him at Sonia. "And what do you wish to accomplish here," she said, "besides some hanky-panky?"

This time Sloan was taken back by the incongruity of hearing her use that word. "I didn't expect to hear that from you," he said.

"How could you know what to expect from me," she said, "since we've never met?"

"I just wasn't expecting that sort of slang in this situation," he said. "But you're right, there's no way I can know anything about you." He looked at the old Haitian man who was listening to the conversation without comprehension. "Except..."

"Except what?" she said.

"Except that as soon as I saw you," Sloan said, his eyes meeting hers, "I had the feeling that you stepped out of the screenplay I'm working from." He heard a slight snort behind him but ignored his colleague. "I mean, to my mind, you are almost exactly how I imagined the main female character. Seriously."

The woman stared at him for a moment, then

looked away and smiled as if she'd heard this kind of flattery her whole life. "You are under the illusion that you possess a silver tongue," she said. "Which makes it clear that you want something from me."

"True on both counts," he said.

She nodded at the old man. "This gentleman tells me you were here, or this car was here, a few days ago."

"I was exploring the area late in the day," Sloan said. "My name's Lucas Sloan."

"Mr Sloan, you are not the first to approach," she said. "Others have wanted to tell the story of exploited workers and the evils of the sugar industry."

Sonia chose this moment to interject. "It's a love story," she said.

Sloan looked back at her and frowned, making a little cutting motion with his hand.

"Drama can be made out of anything," the woman said. "But I do not wish to have my employees disturbed without clearance, without prior consent."

"Absolutely understood," Sloan said. "We're in the scouting phase, trying to get information."

"What is the name of the movie?" the woman said.

"*Larimore*," Sloan said. "It's the main character's name."

The woman nodded. "The hero who reveals the bad stuff and gets the girl."

Sloan smiled. "By some chance, did the screenwriter consult with you? I mean, you know, doing research for the story."

"If he had, I could have given him a more original story," she said.

Sloan nodded. "Well, we have to play the hand we're dealt."

She reached over toward the passenger seat, lifted a card from her purse and held it out toward him. "Call me in the morning and I'll meet with you and hear your story," she said.

He reached out and took the card and looked at it. Dulce Medina. Imperial Sugar.

"I will definitely do that," he said. "I appreciate your willingness to meet, Ms Medina."

"I will follow you out, Mr Sloan," she said. "Goodbye."

As he backed up and turned the car around to leave, Sonia said, "What is going on with her?"

Sloan glanced in the rearview, saw the Mercedes pulling forward. "I have no idea," he said.

Cloud cover darkened the day and a breeze hissed through the cane, a harbinger Sloan struggled to cast off. In the dust churned up behind his car, the Mercedes faded in and out of view, a dream of good fortune that switched regularly between corporeal and ethereal. Once they reached the pavement, Sloan turned left and the other car turned right. Sonia was looking back.

"What did she mean by hanky-panky?" she said.

Sloan looked over at her. "That means something improper, like messing around." Off her uncomprehending look, he added, "Sexually."

"Why would she say that?" Sonia said.

"She was trying to put me on my heels," he said. "That's another idiomatic expression. She wanted to knock me off balance, disorient me."

"Oh," Sonia said. "To get some advantage."

"That's right," Sloan said.

They drove down to La Romana and then east to Altos de Chavón, climbing up to the faux Italian village where the vantage point offered views of river and riverbank cliffs and open distant land harking back to a preindustrial era. They walked cobblestone streets among stone buildings and staircases and walls and pillars and plazas. There were courtyards and porticos and colonnades, a church with tower and bells, museums, workshops and studios, bars and restaurants.

At an outdoor café they ordered lunch. Sonia had more questions about the story.

"I don't know how things connect," she said. "I need to read the script."

"You will," Sloan said, "once you're officially onboard."

"You could lend me yours," she said.

"We'll look at the amphitheater and I'll read you the brief," he said. "This is where the climax happens. A night scene. We'll be able to get it on a no-event night. So we need a schedule of upcoming events and an overhead, a diagram of the whole place. And we'll need to come back and scout it at night."

A few tourists were ambling around the amphitheater when Sloan and Sonia climbed up the stone seats to the top level and looked down on the stage. Sloan surveyed the view with his camera. Then a similar view from a lower level, so the vastness of the venue was reduced and fewer extras would be needed to stage a concert. Then lower still. And the reverse angles. The view from the stage, tight shots, sky and stone, the direction of sunset, the palms and poincianas ringing the perimeter.

They walked over to scout the adjacent fountain, the open view behind it, the classical sea monster fish sculptures perched on rocks, the stone seashells, the small parking area. They sat on the fountain's rim and Sloan read the story aloud.

Larimore – Synopsis
Returning to the DR a year after reporting on the conditions of sugarcane workers, Sam Larimore is pursued by Ramon La Vega, the younger son of Luis La Vega, Excalibur Sugar's principal owner. Ramon's paramilitary

unit attempts to apprehend Larimore, who barely escapes by jumping from a waterfall. On the run, wounded, dehydrated, and feverish, he is rescued in a cane field by Ramon's sister, Gina, a reformist who helped him during his first visit, fell in love, and must now protect him. Gina's young daughter, Penelope, and her best friend, Eddie, help in the rescue and are also at risk. On his motorbike, Eddie is chased by Ramon but escapes. Gina takes Larimore to a batey to be hidden and cared for. Ramon goes to his father's mansion and talks with him on the patio about the problem.

Larimore recovers and becomes attached to a young Haitian woman, Fabienne, who took care of him in the batey. During this time the burning of the cane field takes place and the infamous black snow falls upon the batey in a nightmarish scene.

Larimore leaves the batey with Gina, who is locked in conflict with her younger brother and needs Larimore's help to bring him down. Her older brother, Manny, is not in the family business and lends his support to his sister. Gina and Larimore make plans at a beach resort and the flame of their love reignites.

Gina's driver takes Larimore to meet his former colleague, Graham Perry, in Santo Domingo. Perry says he will soon have hard evidence of Ramon's side hustle, illegally procuring young Haitians for sugar cane labor.

Cutaway shot of Ramon's men at the border as Haitian boys are loaded into a van.

Ramon's fixer Montero follows Larimore, who spots the tail and has the driver pull over. Larimore gets out beside a park and walks into it. Montero leaves his driver and follows Larimore. Larimore's car pulls away and drives to the other side of the park to pick up Larimore. Montero's driver has followed but must wait for Montero to catch up and find his car. Larimore escapes.

Hiding out in an apartment arranged by Gina, Larimore only leaves at night to walk and to visit a neighborhood jazz bar where he gets lost in the music.

MONTAGE of Larimore and Gina making love at a beach at night, in a pool at night, in her car in moonlight.

When Larimore leaves the bar, a man follows him down a street of darkness and shadows. Larimore hides behind a car and waits to ambush his follower. Larimore leaps out and tackles the man and they roll on the ground. Larimore pins him and raises his fist and the man identifies himself as Gina's brother Manny, her confidante. It's his apartment Larimore is using. They go inside to talk. Manny gives Larimore damning evidence of his younger brother's misdeeds.

Ramon descends on the batey and, with coercion by Montero, gets the info he wants. He kidnaps Fabienne to use as bait to lure Larimore into view. The batey's matriarch, Madame Chery, notifies Gina and her precocious daughter overhears the call. The next morning Penelope and Eddie follow Ramon from his office and see him meeting with Larimore's American friend, Graham Perry, at a roadside pescado frito stand.

At the famous Teeth of the Dog golf course, Gina and Larimore meet with her father to present evidence that Ramon has been skimming money from the company. When they leave, Luis La Vega calls his son and betrays his daughter. He wants to bury Larimore and continue with business as usual.

Perry sets up a meeting with Larimore at Altos de Chavón, a replica of a sixteenth-century Italian Renaissance village. They agree to meet at the amphitheater where the reggaeton musician Tootski Root is performing.

At the show, Perry tells Larimore that the girl Fabienne is being held in a car nearby. She will be released when Larimore gets in. From within the crowd, Gina watches them. As Perry leads Larimore to the fountain parking lot, he says he's sorry but needs the money. Gina follows from a distance and makes a call to her driver. Perry says Ramon plans to poison Larimore and dump his body in the Chavón River.

As they approach Ramon's car, Montero steps out and holds the rear door open. The girl is in the backseat. In the front are Ramon and his driver Jaime Fortuna. The concert is a loud mask of sound over the night. Larimore withdraws a four-pointed shuriken and flings it into the face of Montero, whose right eye erupts with blood. Ramon steps out, raising a pistol as Larimore ducks behind Perry, who is shot in the chest. Gina appears at the rear of the car, shoots her brother in the leg and Montero in the head. Larimore takes Ramon's gun as Gina's car pulls up. Her bodyguard and driver jump out and get to work. Perry writhes on the ground, dying. The young hostage is put into Gina's car. The wounded Ramon is put in the backseat of his car, along with his driver, and their hands are zip-tied. The bodies of Perry and Montero are loaded into the rear compartment. Gina's bodyguard takes the wheel and drives the car away.

Larimore and Gina sit beside Fabienne and Gina's car pulls away as reggaeton thumps in the background.

The car runs along a desolate road as sugarcane waves under the moonlight. Gina comforts Fabienne, who is looking at Larimore. He sits silently, his eyes on the endless passing fields.

17. The Charity of the Sugar Baby

Dulce Medina was the youngest of four, the baby and the only girl in a wealthy sugar dynasty, and consequently grew up with a silver sugar spoon in her mouth. Two of her brothers, Hector and Francisco, were in the family business with their father and Dulce, after university and considerable personal time spent frolicking in Europe and America, was given an office in the family's modern building. Her eldest brother, Jose, was a restaurateur and raconteur, able to make others laugh, especially his own father, as one restaurant's opening overlapped the previous one's closing. His father affectionately called him *mi pequeño fracaso* (my little failure) or just *Fracaso*. Or sometimes *Defecto*.

"I'm simply trying to make things a little better," Dulce said. She sat behind her glass desk across from Sloan who was in a squeaky black swivel chair. She wore her hair tied up in a casual vertical manner with a thick red ribbon as if she were entertaining girlfriends at home.

The building too, Sloan had thought as he drove

up, did not seem serious enough, not "imperial" enough to represent such a company. It seemed more like an unserious annex, a place where the real bosses would never be found.

Dulce's office was at the end of the front-hall rooms so that no one would ever pass it accidently. She buzzed her secretary for service and the stout woman showed up sweating after the third time.

"Sorry," she said, "I was speaking with your brother." She made a sudden devilish face, as if someone had twisted her undergarments severely. "He's on the warpath today."

"I believe you," Dulce said. "Maria, could you bring us some coffee please? And some water."

After the woman departed, Dulce said, "My brother Francisco, the next youngest after me, equates power with noise." She waved her hand dismissively.

"I was pleasantly surprised to see you out at the batey," Sloan said.

"I'm sure you were shocked," she said. "But there are many bateyes, and they all need help."

"Our main character has the same attitude," he said. "So that's part of our story."

"What are the other parts?" she said.

"As my colleague indicated," he said, "there is the love story between the sugar company reformist, the woman who I said you reminded me of, and the main character, the writer."

"Who is the bad man?" she said.

"That's the woman's brother."

She laughed heartily. "This is turning into an absurdist comedy."

"Weird, right?" Sloan said, smiling. "Either the screenwriter knows something or this is some archetypal story I wasn't aware of."

She looked at her watch. Her secretary had left the office door open but no movement could be heard out there in the hall. "Tell me what you need and for how long."

Sloan pulled out his notebook and opened it to the latest written page. "We need a field nearly ready for harvest. We need a stretch of road beside it. We need a road to a batey and the batey itself. We need a piece of field we can burn. Or we need to shoot one being burned and then fake our batey scene with the falling ash. Or maybe we can build enough of a batey for the tighter scenes when our main character is staying there. This would be about five to seven shooting days. If we need to build the batey I would add another week of construction."

She paused, looking at him, letting the enormity of the request sink in. "The burn is a problem," she said. "The most unpleasant part of our business. The ugliest." She stood and crossed to the door and looked into the hall. She wore gold slacks and a sleek matching jacket, with black heels. As she moved, her upright housekeeper hair stalk swung side to side.

"Maybe there's a less desirable patch of field where we could have a burn and keep that part away from the rest," he said. "I think we could fake some of it with tight shots. We would just need to see it at night, plus the daytime."

She closed the door and came back to her desk and sat. "It's tricky," she said. "It's about image more than money."

Sloan nodded. "I wonder if there is some other kind of field that would work. Not cane."

"I wonder if anyone can explain what happened to the coffee," she said.

Out of the corner of his eye Sloan caught the movement of someone in the hall passing the office window. A man opened the door and stood at the entrance looking at them. He held a small white saucer in one hand and a small white expresso cup in the other. The smell of strong coffee swept into the office. The man was dressed in a beige linen suit, the color of which he would describe as fawn or camel, but not as oatmeal or sand. White shirt, no tie, longish dark hair, smooth puffy face, sharp eyes and nose in collusion with his mouth, the pressed and protruding lips holding a fine line somewhere between smug and amused. His wide mouth opened and his top lip extended as only a prehensile trait would allow, and he slurped the coffee over the edge of the cup.

"That sweet Maria makes a mean café," he said, looking at Dulce. Then he feigned shock at seeing Sloan. "Oh, this must be our secret visitor."

Sloan examined the man and said, "I'm right here in the open."

"This is Mr Sloan," Dulce said. "He's from Far Cry Productions. And this is my—"

"No, no," the man said. "Let me introduce myself. I'm Frank "No Fucking Way" Medina."

Sloan stood and said, "Wow, you're that guy I've heard so much about. This is amazing. I look forward to working together." He put his hand on his heart and then extended it toward the other man. "Privilege," he said.

Frank stared at Sloan for a second, then set his cup in its saucer and smiled. "Dulce, I like this guy," he said. He shook Sloan's hand and said, "He's a real dreamer," then turned and left the office.

Sloan took his seat and said, "I got a great feeling of warmth from your bro."

Dulce shook her head and smiled weakly. "Don't worry about him. I provide the warmth."

"Okay," Sloan said. "I hope he doesn't invade my dreams." His words sounded mechanical to him.

"I'll work out the details with you," Dulce said.

"Will you be the one to sign the contract?" Sloan said.

"Which contract?" she said.

"We always need to have a location agreement," he said, "in writing."

"Then we have another problem," she said.

"We can figure it out," he said. "I'll email you what we discussed and you can think it over and we can talk again. This has been great. I'm very grateful to have met you by accident and then met you again." He stood and reached over the desk and shook her hand.

"Likewise," she said.

At the door, he paused and looked back. "We can meet for coffee," he said. "I'll treat you."

She nodded vigorously, wiggling her hair stalk at him.

In the hall, he met Maria carrying a tray loaded with two small cups of coffee, two glasses and a sweating pitcher of water. She was still sweating too. Sloan stopped and took a coffee and sipped it gently to test its heat, then downed it and thanked her. She bowed her head slightly.

Sloan was unsettled and jittery as he drove, thinking he'd been poisoned. He pulled over outside of La Romana and tilted his seat back. Cars zoomed by and clouds marched across the windshield like manifestations of deceit. His car seemed like it was being shifted by the force of those passing.

He realized his phone was buzzing in his pocket. Nico was calling.

"How was the meeting?" he said.

"Pretty good," Sloan said.

"You sound unsure," Nico said.

"It was good, not perfect."

"Nothing ever is," Nico said. "I finally heard from Javier and we're meeting at his office at two. Can you meet me there?"

"Yeah, I might be a few minutes late."

He stood outside the car and splashed water into

his face until the bottle was empty.

It was a nondescript, single-story building in a residential neighborhood. Sloan parked on the street and peered over the gate and got the guard's attention with a greeting. He showed the man his driver's license and the gate was opened. In the lobby, he showed his ID to the front desk woman. His name was entered into the register and he was directed to an office down the hall. He looked at his watch. He was twenty-nine minutes late.

Javier Contreras was well-dressed, well-mannered, and well-groomed, with a trimmed black goatee, blue silk shirt, and soft brown Italian leather loafers. He shook Sloan's hand and it felt like he'd just had a manicure. His desk and office were immaculate and there were photos of him with various movie stars displayed around the room among posters of locally shot movies.

Sloan's eyes fell on the poster for *Tropical Cavalcade*, colorful and bizarre. It showed an overgrown wilderness from which a procession of primitive misfits emerged, the foreground figures, human and horse, large, fanciful, and somewhat startling, while the rest of the column got smaller as they trailed behind and finally diminished into the background vegetation. The main foreground figure—a cataclysmal Don Quixote—was bearded and wiry astride his roan beast, both man and animal were decorated with garlands of shell and seed pod and feather. The man's arms and feet were wound in strips of fur, and he held a spear upright in one hand as he paraded under a canopy of interwoven fronds.

"That film was before Javier's tenure," Nico said, as Sloan took the empty chair across from the commissioner. "But we want to acknowledge the elephant in the room."

"Shit happens," Javier said. "No movie is immune

from difficulty."

"Quite right," Nico said. "I've brought him up to speed on our current project and he has some great suggestions and insights for us. He knows people at Casa de Campo that could put us in touch with mansions."

"Cool," Sloan said.

"And I've just scouted two resorts in Punta Cana that sound gung ho."

"Outstanding," Sloan said.

"So the big question," Nico said, "is where do we stand with Big Sugar? With Dulce Medina."

Sloan looked at the film commissioner. "She was helpful," he said, "and elusive at the same time."

Javier nodded. "That's her," he said. "She has grand plans that don't go anywhere. She's the baby who wants to do something substantial and prove her value to her father." He let this sink in and pressed his fingertips together. "The eldest son, Jose, dislikes the father and the sugar business. The middle brother, Hector, runs the show and reports to the father, who can only be found at the private rooms of fancy restaurants and the golf course. The youngest brother, Frank, runs around making noise and acting like a big shot." He suddenly leaned forward. "Don't repeat this," he said, raising his eyebrows.

"Totally confidential," Nico said.

"I couldn't figure out why she was at the batey," Sloan said. "But I didn't ask her."

Javier smiled. "Every couple of years she starts an improvement program, presenting herself as a reformist in an industry that definitely needs a better image," he said. "Most of the bateyes don't have good drinking water or electricity. In her last campaign, she wanted the guards to be unarmed."

"I didn't see any guards at the batey I visited," Sloan said. "Are the workers prisoners?"

Javier shrugged. "Even if they want to leave," he said, "they don't have the means to do it. So having guards is not really necessary."

"What's her latest plan?" Sloan said.

"I believe she wants to build some clinics," Javier said. "Especially for the sick children."

Sloan nodded and looked at Nico but didn't mention the child he'd seen.

"Do you know anything about her private life?" Sloan said.

"Ahh," Javier said, smiling and looking at both men. "We all heard stories," he said. "She was wild as a young woman, went abroad, came home married to an American, had twin boys, got divorced." He shrugged. "Now she works. Maybe she tries to atone."

"How old are the boys?" Sloan said.

Javier looked at the ceiling and stroked his goatee. "I think maybe fourteen, fifteen, something like that." His nose wrinkled as if he'd smelled something unpleasant.

"Do they live with her?" Sloan said.

"Mostly her but the father too." Javier said. "How can I say it?" He rolled a pen back and forth on his desk. "They are troublesome boys. Recently I heard them called Satan and Diablo. But I don't know which is which." He chuckled. "Not that it matters."

A young woman stuck her head in the door. "Hello," she said.

"This is Beatriz Fernandez," Javier said. "My assistant."

Nico stood and shook her hand, followed by Sloan, who said, "Pleasure, Beatriz, we were destined to meet."

"Let me know if I can help you," she said. Her black hair fell in long curls and she wore a red dress that matched her lipstick. She looked dressed for casting.

"Thank you," Nico said. "We will."

She turned and left, and Javier said, "She would love to be an extra."

The location scouts nodded. "That shouldn't be a problem," Sloan said.

"Who is the female lead in *Larimore*?" Javier said.

"Margaret Nogales," Nico said. "You know her?"

Javier nodded. "She's Mexican, right? Playing a Dominican."

Nico shrugged. "That's casting," he said. "At least she's a Latina. Maybe the right Dominican wasn't available. Who knows?"

Javier did not hide his disappointment. "Too bad," he said. "You know how these things can smooth the way sometimes."

"I know, I know," Nico said. "Unfortunately, we're not involved in any of that stuff."

"What about the male lead?" Javier said.

"That's Tom Flint," Nico said.

Javier smiled. "Oh great," he said. "I love that guy. He's super rugged. And a good actor."

"Yeah, he'll be perfect," Nico said.

"I know it's not your department," Javier said, "but you may want to try to find some small part for Dulce Medina. It would help you. And she's a good-looking woman."

"Oh, she's definitely that," Sloan said.

Nico laughed. "Luke will do anything to secure the location," he said. "But we definitely need backup sugar. If you have any ideas, we'd appreciate it."

"If she's going to help you she'll need to get her brother Hector to approve," Javier said. He wobbled his open hand to indicate the odds of this happening. "But you never know," he added cheerfully. "Work on her. Sweeten the deal."

"For sure," Nico said. "Any backup ideas come to mind?"

"Imperial owns most of the fields," Javier said.

"There are a couple of smaller companies but they just follow the leader."

The meeting concluded and the scouts thanked the commissioner and made vague future lunch plans and promised to set up a meeting with the film's producer when he arrived in town. On the way out they said goodbye to Beatriz.

Out on the street, they stopped beside Sloan's car.

"How do you feel about this sugar babe?" Nico said.

"I might say anxious if that was a word in my vocabulary," Sloan said. "But I feel fine."

"We need more photos of the batey," Nico said. "And we have to find a backup."

They paused as meringue blasted from a passing car. The sky was gray in three directions and it began to drizzle. They looked up at the clarity in the east.

"I'll meet with her again as soon as possible," Sloan said. "She'll work with me."

"I'm trying to start this kid Wilson Diaz next week," Nico said. "He won't do anything until he's officially onboard. He's supposed to have serious office skills. According to him."

"Sounds good," Sloan said. "Also good on the resorts. I hope you enjoyed yourself."

"Yeah, nothing but a vacation," Nico said, and laughed. "Speaking of which, the designer is coming in for a scout, maybe joined by the director."

"Okay, here we go," Sloan said.

"Strap yourself in," Nico said as he walked away. "Stay safe, Younger Bear."

Sloan laughed. "You too, Old Lodge Skins."

18. In Which Attendant Demands Arise in the Locations Department

They would look back almost fondly on the following week, the last lull so to speak, before the pace of production flamed into being and the mental and physical g-forces stretched their faces into unpleasant caricatures of themselves.

They drank rum and quoted movie lines and called each other by the names of characters in a western they both admired. They inhabited, depending on mood or time of day, the dead space of limbo or a metaphorical river in which they were treading water on their way to the rapids. This was in direct relation to the information coming in or failing to come in and it often seemed as if they had fallen into a parallel dimension and could see what was happening around them but could not affect it.

The production manager requested that they scout production office spaces. Nico had assumed they would use hotel meeting rooms but the production manager wanted options, better prices, a fucking real estate division incorporated into the Locations Department.

Meanwhile, Dulce had gone silent and the reply to their request for permission to scout the Teeth of the

Dog golf course was ambivalent. It appeared that multiple meetings would need to occur. In addition, Little Sugar was nothing more than a concept and had not developed as a backup choice or even as a basic reality.

There wasn't much for Sonia to do except research office space and then set up meetings at these spaces for Nico or Sloan to take photos and make deals. This was the kind of bullshit that drove location scouts mad and made them feel as if they were sliding backwards in the great struggle.

The reactions to the location photographs—by the director, producer, production designer, and production manager—were underwhelming and Gene Friedman had officially okayed the additional team members. On Monday, Sonia and Wilson would submit their paperwork and be put on payroll, and Sloan would bring Wilson up to speed.

This was their team until shooting began, at which point Nico would request two production assistants to help cover time on set and errands that would have to be run. But that seemed far in the future at this moment.

The alcohol was eating into their per diem but Nico and Sloan ordered more shots and neatly tucked this raw fact into the subjective cost of equilibrium. They needed to keep each other afloat.

"Do a quick brief of the locations as they stand now," Nico said, "to show Wilson what we have in mind. Then he can scout or work from the hotel, do the permitting, timecards, uploads, and maps."

"We'll knock off those locations on Monday," Sloan said. "I'll keep pushing a meeting with Dulce to scout the batey with her, and a second one if possible, and we should bug Beatriz about getting a cane field that doesn't belong to Imperial."

Nico downed his shot and looked at his phone.

"Little Big Man wants to talk to me," he said.

"Your heart must be soaring like a hawk," Sloan said.

Nico stepped away and took the call wandering in the vicinity of their regularly scheduled Regroup Meeting, out among somnambulant tourists and local hustlers and strutting pigeons. Sloan could hear a trumpet and occasional guitar chords and he watched a green balloon dollar sign soaring over the courtyard to disappear behind the hotel like a dream of lost income. His seismic anxiety woke him at night, the cavalier stalker, or stalkers, consistently reminding him of long-past transgressions, and now he imagined guards with silver bullet-shaped helmets carrying pikes as they entered the property to arrest him.

Nico came back and sat and squirmed around, as sharp-faced as a ferret.

"What was that all about?" Sloan said.

"Napolean wants workhorses," he said. "Or genuine mules."

"Is that to save money on rental cars?" Sloan said.

"For the falls," Nico said. "The designer is recovering from a foot injury and can't walk far."

"We can carry him in a one of those king chairs and be pole-bearing porters," Sloan said.

"A sedan chair," Nico said.

"Exactly," Sloan said. "Right out of a Tarzan movie."

"He actually mentioned Comtois draft horses," Nico said.

"What?" Sloan said. "Where are we, the French fucking countryside?"

"The portly potentate was serious," Nico said. "He wants us to check Las Terranas because there are lots of French people around there." Nico gave his best insane asylum resident look, a man tormented by demons as he shat in his pants and illustrated it with his face.

"What the fuck is he thinking—we rent a horse trailer and some mules and take them with us?" Sloan started laughing. "We would need a mule tender too."

"He must think we're making a western here," Nico said. "A Fistful of Sugar."

They shook their heads and raised their glasses. "Just fucking roll with it," Sloan said.

"Just fucking roll with it," Nico said, and they clinked their glasses and drank.

"I'll put Sonia on mules first thing Monday," Sloan said.

"Excellent," Nico said. "Ask her if she has a good weed connection."

Sloan drove in the rain, opting to visit one waterfall and pass along the team brief while he and Wilson Diaz got acquainted. Wilson revealed himself to be a major movie fan who had worked on one movie, an independent that went straight to video, plus approximately eleven commercials and maybe eight music videos. He was a major gamer too, a tall gangly twenty-something with curly hair and round wireframe glasses. He was being encouraged to talk, and talk he did. He was excited to be on the project and eager to impart his enthusiasm, his family background, his hobbies, his hygienic habits, his dietary preferences, his general health and intestinal regularity.

"This movie will put a stop to that," Sloan said.

The young man looked alarmed, turning his wide spectacled eyes on his boss.

"Stay loose," Sloan said. "You might be able to rise above the tension."

Wilson smiled, thinking he was being messed with a little bit. "Hey, I wanted to ask you something," he said, his voice rising into a question. "Kinda personal."

Sloan glanced at him. "Go ahead," he said.

The young man gave him a sidelong sheepish look. "Were you guys really on TropCav?"

The wipers whipped back and forth like twin metronomes as Sloan stared at the road.

"Are you a fanboy?" he said.

Wilson opened his mouth wide but didn't actually scream. "Are you kidding me?" he said. "That is one of my all-time fave films. Classic."

"It can't be classic yet," Sloan said. "Way too soon."

"No worries," Wilson said. "Eventually it will be. So awesome, man."

Sloan looked over to see if the kid was serious. "What'd you like about it?"

"Seriously?" Wilson said, bouncing in his seat like a kid. "It was so real. A vision of the future. Insanely primitive. Was the whole show shot here?"

"Yeah, it was all location work," Sloan said. "No stage, no interiors except huts. We had rain delays, a fire, a shutdown." He stopped talking.

"I don't remember any fire scenes," Wilson said. "Except that funeral."

Sloan's next words were barely audible above the rain. "It was arson."

"Oh wow," Wilson said. "That totally sucks."

They drove in silence for a few minutes. A car veered into his lane and Sloan swerved and slid off the wet road a few feet to avoid it. "Fuck!" he said, straightening his wheels and continuing.

"Was that why you had the shutdown?" Wilson said. "Because of the fire?"

"We'll talk about it another time," Sloan said. "Right now we need to focus on this movie."

He drove to the Socoa waterfall, the easier to access of the two within a convenient range of the capital. Parked near the trail, Sloan talked the younger team member through a scenario that could unfold at that location. The details included parking for the entire film company, equipment vehicles and crew cars divided according to priority. They would need a few ATV four-wheelers to get gear as close as possible. They could also use mules for camera gear and certain people who would object to walking, either those less than physically fit or those who considered themselves at a station in the hierarchy where they deserved extra care for their valuable services, much in the way that a monarch and his entourage are catered to and shown to be superior to the average shit-kicking, ass-grabbing, working person. These last might include producers, the director, or actors. And quite possibly Hair and Makeup and Wardrobe.

If the location was selected, they would need a map to it, a parking diagram, monetary deals with anyone whose usual profit would be impacted by the film company's takeover of the attraction. This could include parking vendors, snack sellers, guides, and private property owners whose space might be accessed. They would need security on the vehicles and gear. They would need a catering area. They would need tents on hand for potential weather changes.

The rain continued and they remained in the car drinking water and eating granola bars. Sloan stepped out and relieved himself under the cover of nearby trees.

On the return trip he assigned Wilson a ground mission. There were several Santo Domingo locations that needed to be investigated and scouted. He broke it down for the kid.

"There is a section in the middle of the story when Larimore is lying low in an apartment in town. He only goes out at night when he walks to a jazz bar to eat. So we need the apartment building, the street, the bar. One time he realizes he's being followed from the bar and he jumps the follower, who turns out to be a friend, and they go inside the apartment to talk. The interior could be somewhere else." Sloan paused. "You should be writing all of this down."

"Copy," Wilson said. He produced his phone and opened a note-taking application.

"Don't you have a notebook and pen?" Sloan asked.

"I use this," Wilson said.

"Jesus," Sloan said, shaking his head. "If you use a pen you can make sketches too."

Wilson began typing into his device and Sloan continued.

"Another time Larimore meets an American, a former colleague, at a bar. This will be a different bar. When he leaves, by a car with a driver, he's followed by the bad guy's right-hand man. This is written as a daytime scene." Sloan paused to let the clicking strokes catch up.

"He knows he's being followed so he has the car pull over next to a park. He walks through the park, the car picks him up on the other side, he loses the tail and rolls on." Sloan glanced over and waited.

"So," he said, "we need the bar, the street outside, the park, and streets on different sides of the park. It would be great if the park was nearby, but it doesn't have to be. The park could be split away from the bar because, in all likelihood, they will work on different days. There is quite a bit of dialogue in the bar." He looked at Wilson, who was looking at him. "I'm thinking out loud," Sloan said. "The bar is probably a full day inside."

The rain had stopped, and sunlight was blazing through the wet trees in steamy beams.

"So before you start your office duties," Sloan said, "let's work on these two scenarios. We start with a couple of cool bars, one regular cool, the other one jazz cool. The jazz place is dark, nice decor but not trendy or clubby. No fucking disco balls or any tacky dancehall shit. The other place could be a dive bar." He looked at Wilson. "Do you know what that means?"

Wilson shook his head.

"It means a regular bar, where locals go who don't spend much. Nothing fancy. It's always so dim, even in the daytime, that you wouldn't recognize your own mother. Our two characters in this scene are journalists who have been all over the place. They're comfortable in your basic corner bar. They don't go for tourist places." He made sure Wilson was getting it down. "Look, for all we know, the production designer or the director will change the look but we start with the script, the writing, and how we interpret it."

"Copy that," Wilson said, a subliminal giddy grin on his face.

Sloan wanted to believe him. People who said "Copy that" and "Copy you" when they were nowhere near a film set but already imagined themselves holding a radio and responding to a direct order during the heat of action made Sloan nervous. He hoped the kid was actually a deadly killer at office work.

They started in the Colonial Zone, which was a beneficial area for film locations on multiple levels, the main drawback being the preponderance of tourists, which in large numbers would slow everything down, clog up the byways, make businesses less receptive to outside proposals, less inclined to run the risk of losing a single slow-footed, shuffle-strolling wombat who might be offended if something coveted, such as a shield-sized platter of rice and beans, was temporarily out of reach.

Immediately they found some great exteriors but since the bars were closed during daylight hours they were likely to be too hip inside, too techno, too full of flashy lights and industrial furniture. No honest dive would be closed in the afternoon when pensioners and out-of-work welders got thirsty. To cover the bases though, they would have to scout at night.

Cervantes Park and Enriquillo Park were both solid urban options and they scouted both, imagining angles of story action from one curbside to another, immersed in the city's vibrant energy, seeing Larimore crossing the brick surface amid running children and gangs of pigeons working the dirt and pavement cracks.

In Columbus Park, the mariner's elevated statue pointed ambiguously—as if he did not know where he had landed or where he was going—into the distance while birds lined his arm and sat buffoonishly atop his head, their liquid eliminations streaking the bronze of his cloak and gown. Sloan shot this park too, though he did not like it as much, thinking it was too well-known, looked too colonial, and would be harder to control.

After dark they made their way through a half dozen bars, the majority scratched off at a glance by Sloan. It was clearly the wrong neighborhood for dives but a couple of spots, one in particular, held out promise for a jazz bar. The first place, Alcazar, had a decent lowkey vibe but was a bit too slick in its furnishings, too much chrome and faux leather, and it had a DJ booth in the layout's best position for a piano. The manager was cool though, was interested in the concept, willing to arrange the furniture however necessary to accommodate a piano, allow the electronics console to be hidden from view, and was fine with daytime filming—wherein the production crew would blackout the windows and shoot day for night—before the establishment opened for business.

The second place, Sancho P, was nearly ideal. It looked like an actual piano bar, had a piano in place, although there was a five-piece group on the stage. The band, called Unearthly, ripped through rock and calypso tunes and caused couples to swing and dip and twirl and endanger themselves in the narrow passage between the musicians and the tables— despite the singer's high-pitched disemboweling of the lyrics, which was disturbing a cat on the sidewalk outside.

Sloan's pitch to the owner, a long-haired, middle-aged man of Eastern European origin, was translated into Spanish by Wilson. The man, sitting on a high stool at the back, listened to the entire proposal. Wilson had to wait until the current song ended to begin his delivery, then wait until the next break to finish it, leaving a long dead space in the middle of the request. During this period he and Sloan looked at the band and nodded their feigned approval. The owner understood only part of what they wanted. At the end the owner produced the first in a series of evasions that grew in absurdity and eventually weighed on Sloan like a pile of dirt.

"We are not a jazz bar here," the owner said in English, which to Sloan was vastly overstating the obvious. However, there were green velour chairs in front of book shelves that rose to the ceiling at one end of the room, a dark wooden bar adjacent, and a few scattered and stark landscape paintings that may have depicted the Tabernas Desert of Spain, it was hard to be sure in the gloom.

Sloan was used to explaining the basic concept of designing a location to fit the script. He had also experienced his share of jokers amusing themselves. This guy was named Vukasin.

"Call me Vuk," he said.

When the band took a break Vuk said his piano player only played with the whole group.

Sloan smiled at Wilson, who said they would bring

their own piano player for the scene.

Vuk said he could not be identified with a film whose quality could not be guaranteed.

He said he could not ask his staff to work in the daytime or on their day off.

He said he could not risk damage to his business. And then couldn't feel certain an insurance claim would be honored in the event that damage occurred.

He said he didn't understand why a scene of a man having a drink and listening to music could not be filmed at a food truck in a park. Or in another bar. There were many. He could supply a list as long as his arm. Or his leg.

He said the story did not make sense and didn't seem worth making.

Vuk said he had never heard of the actor Tom Flint and did not care for the sound of his name.

He said he was too busy to watch movies.

He said his life was perfect as it was.

"Okay, you're a lucky man," Sloan said. "We're finished for the night so we'll enjoy your ambiance and have a cocktail."

At the bar Sloan positioned himself with an old-fashioned and his camera nonchalantly resting beside it. While he drank he took long exposures down the bar to the stage and out across the room as Unearthly began their second set. He hated using a flash in general and only resorted to it if the absence of light was on a level with the bottom of the ocean.

Wilson sipped a club soda, leaned over and said, "Too bad about this place."

"We're not giving up yet," Sloan said.

He took a trip to the restroom and when he came out he leaned against the wall and held his breath and shot the bar and several more looks at the room from that angle. Back on this stool at the bar he glanced over at Vuk and saw the man was watching him like he had nothing better to do in his perfect life.

On the way out he shook Vuk's hand and paused at the door with Wilson as a shield between him and the owner, as if taking one last look at the place. He shot a couple of discreet views from the perspective of the entrance, then turned and left.

In the morning Sloan uploaded the parks and bars and met Nico for breakfast.

The big news was that Nico had a meeting with someone in marketing at Casa de Campo, the resort that owned Teeth of the Dog and Altos de Chavón.

"As you know, this place is a major resort," he said, pouring his coffee. "Not only the biggest in the country, but with a high standing on the global resort stage."

"Sounds like trouble," Sloan said. "We should definitely have a backup golf course. If things go south there is no way to replace Altos but we should have something in mind for the climactic scene. Like somewhere else to have the concert."

"That stone amphitheater is impressive," Nico said.

"I know," Sloan said. "We can't just have a concert at the beach."

"Maybe the Cultural Plaza," Nico said. "Something actually historic, not a replica."

"Yeah, or those hospital ruins, the oldest in the New World," Sloan said.

"Saint Nicolas de Bari," Nico said.

"We should apply for it, get the ball rolling," Sloan said. "And scout it for the back pocket. File it under miscellaneous locations."

"Yep," Nico said. "Put Wilson on it. So what about these bars?"

"Oh man," Sloan said. "There is one I really like, but the owner acts like he's not interested."

"But you still scouted it?" Nico said.

"Discreetly," Sloan said. "I want to give it another

shot. Maybe the guy was having an off night. Maybe because he remembered his name is Vuk."

"Fuck?" Nico said.

"Actually, I think he said it like Vook."

"You mean like he's a bad mothervooker?"

"He wants to come across that way."

"Hit him again," Nico said. "Beat him down."

As he was cruising beyond the border of the Colonial Zone, weaving through neighborhoods and streets of small shops and small homes existing within small businesses, trying to feel out the presence of anything that might check the dive bar box, Sloan got a text from Dulce Medina.

Coffee?

He pulled over at the first opportunity, beside bins of brooms and headless manikins in bright dresses.

Sure, he wrote. *When?*

Tomorrow morning, she wrote. *I will send the address and time.*

Outstanding, he typed, then deleted the word and wrote, *Great!*

A car pulled up beside him and stopped, vibrating like a munitions factory and hemming him in. Just ahead, the intersection was blocked by two cars in a perpendicular confrontation, both drivers standing outside their vehicles and engaging in a back-and-forth of gestures and shouts. Sloan could not see any damage to the cars, aside from their overall condition, considerably below the level of showroom. They could have been entries in a scratch-and-Bondo competition.

He got the attention of the driver beside him and made a little tomahawk motion to show that he wanted to leave now. The man made a gigantic shrug accompanied by huge protruding lips.

Sloan stepped out and stood in front of his rental car beside the line of decapitated dummies and struck a pose of patience as he surveyed the scene. Horns were blowing now. The intersection was growing in population and decibels and exhaust. The streets were narrow and crowded. The sheer density of individual properties and pedestrians was frightening. The overhead wires created a web of connecting lines and a wild sense of entanglement. Sloan was waking up to the fact that this spot, this barrio, was a nidus of chaos.

This was the kind of location realization that sprang up on almost any project. He could not subject himself or his team or the production company to this many-pronged killer of efficiency. This was a mental breakdown waiting to happen.

With some gentle urging, using helpful smiles and hand motions, he was able to persuade the driver of the car blocking him to back up enough to give Sloan room to inch out into the street and painstakingly execute the idea of a three-point turn by using eight or nine tiny points.

He went back to the hotel and parked and walked around, determined to find a place that would lend itself to the creation of a cool dive bar with a minimum of dressing. He was also determined to eat lunch. As he sat at a little café table wobbling on cobblestones, he studied the doorway and the waitress emerging and the windows and the darkness within. He stepped inside and observed the tiles on the floor, the long narrow bar, and the high ceiling. The basic elements.

He ordered a couple of empanadas and a salad and took a call from Nico.

"I just got a call from the production designer," he said. "Dominic Larue. You know him?"

"Sounds familiar," Sloan said.

"Turns out he likes a lot of stuff we're putting up," Nico said. "Loves the waterfalls, wants to look at all three of them."

"Cool," Sloan said.

"And," Nico said, "he loves your elusive jazz bar, Sancho P."

"Terrific," Sloan said. "I was wondering when the pressure would kick in."

"I hope you can get it," Nico said.

"Me too," Sloan said. "You'll be the first to know. Or second."

After he hung up, he called Sonia.

"What are you doing tonight?" he said.

"What do you need?" she said.

"Can you meet me for a little scouting?" he said.

"Scouting for what?" she said.

"One bar," he said, "then you're done."

"Why do you need me for that?"

"I want you to wear something..." He paused. "Something nice."

"Do you mean sexy?" she said.

"Something that accents your best asset," he said.

"You mean my brain," she said.

"Yes," he said. "Wear a cool hat."

There was only a brief pause. "For you I will," she said.

They walked from the hotel, weaving their way through people strolling to dinner or taking the night air. The day's heat had waned by a few degrees and Sonia wore a light jacket over her dress. Her top lip was sweating and Sloan was choosing his words as if they were bunched up in a briar patch.

"If I wasn't clear before," he said, "this is only about you stating our case instead of me. I've already been shot down. If you're not comfortable making the pitch, just say it. I'm trying to look at the big location picture but the team is more important than any location. Obviously."

"I know how the world works," she said. "You want

to use my tits to win the game."

"Yes," he said. "Tits are incredibly powerful."

"And sometimes they make men do stupid things," she said.

"Including me," he said. "If you feel the slightest discomfort just walk away."

"Do you want me to talk money?" she said.

"If he mentions a fee, tell him you'll get back to him with details. Get his cell number."

They could hear the music from outside and Sloan thought it sounded like the same band.

"That's weird," he said. A couple of doorways down a gray cat sat licking a front paw.

They stood against the wall, waiting for the band's break. Sloan looked at Sonia and tried to judge her feelings, the look on her face. Her expression made him think of a cat with its ears back. Streetlights cast them in a pale yellow glow of complicity. The music faded away and after another couple of minutes it seemed like it couldn't be the space between songs. Sonia looked up at him and began to unzip her jacket and his eyes followed the zipper down.

Some crazy voice told him he should be more professional and look up and down the street, monitor their surroundings, but that voice was a sound of wind in the desert or a lone prisoner working in a remote mining quarry. Impossible to acknowledge.

She handed him her jacket. "Well," she said. "Is this what you had in mind?"

The dress was low-cut, the material thin and pushed out so that it was tight, formidably eye-catching. She was clearly braless.

"Where do I sign?" he said.

She stared at him as his eyes made their way back to her face.

"If you had this one chance to take them for yourself or show them to a stranger," she said.

He turned away, groaning at the sky. "I did not know you were the torturing type," he said.

She sighed, almost inaudibly. "I'm actually not," she said.

He looked over at the door of the club and she did too. She straightened her back and walked toward it, ran her fingers through her hair, fluffed it out and shook her head.

She paused and turned to look back at him. "He might not even care," she said.

Sloan smiled. "If he doesn't, he'll be the gayest Serbian ever born."

The minutes ticked and stretched as he paced and stopped and talked to the cat and thought of war crimes. He walked to a streetlight and stood beneath it like a character in a movie who'd run out of cigarettes and was dying to cause smoke to lift up and swirl into the glow above.

The club's door creaked open and he started toward it as Sonia emerged whole and intact.

She waited for him on the sidewalk and he reached her, searching her expressionless face.

He held out her jacket and spread it open and she turned and slipped her arms through the sleeves and pulled the lapels over her chest. She turned to face him.

"He will do it," she said, suddenly smiling.

"Unfuckingbelieveable," Sloan said. He laughed victoriously and raised a fist. "As custom dictates, and to show my sincere appreciation of your guts and team skills, I will now buy you a single celebratory drink of your choice at the venue of your choice." She took his arm and led them to a lounge across from the mouth of the Rio Ozama. In his joy, he called the place a possible jazz dive bar.

They had more than one celebratory drink, rum on the rocks in this case, and he looked at her in wonder as she related her interaction with Vuk and spoke of the friendliness he displayed toward her, offering to buy her a drink and suggesting she become a regular and never mentioning the visit by Sloan and Wilson. Sloan laughed and marveled at her power, his vision glassy as she let her jacket fall open, and he said he thought he was either seeing freckles or distant stars and she laughed with him.

"Decent regular people have been smitten by boldness and brains combined with the symmetry and tremendous power of beautiful tits and have lost their way," he said. "There have been all kinds of accidents and wrong turns. Then again, lives have been changed for the better. Fears have been conquered, prizes have been won, children have been fed. Let's get the fuck out of here." He paid the bill, and they stepped out into the feverish air.

In the shadow of a wall corner, he turned her toward him and looked into her dark eyes and held her face and kissed her mouth. She opened her jacket and pressed her body into his and put her arms around him and pulled herself tighter against him as they kissed. The world outside of their bodies and their own generated sounds was nothing more than a rutilant haze of night. They broke apart for more oxygen and baltered forward into the street, still holding each other for balance, which had the opposite effect, so they halted and kissed again, buoyed together, hungry and unleashed from prudent behavior.

19. Acceleration

He remembered the use of the words rabbits and fucking in the same sentence. He remembered her riding him and then her voice pleading to be mounted from behind. Like a lion, she'd said, using the Spanish word, *león*. He remembered a stated agreement of secrecy between them. He did not remember her leaving his room.

In his dream he overslept, a classic stress scenario. His alarm failed for some unknown reason and he scurried into chaotic action, foregoing normal procedures such as showering, changing clothes, even having coffee. He drove like a sweating machine but was late anyway and as he greeted Dulce Medina she told him he smelled like pussy. He was surprised but did not say anything in response. He was more embarrassed by his slovenly appearance, in contrast to her designer splendor. As he struggled to find the words he wanted, he was immensely relieved to awaken.

To meet Dulce Medina at the Rio Dulce coffee shop in La Romana at eleven Sloan had to allow at least an hour and three quarters travel time from Santo Domingo. He left at 8:45am and got to La Romana with enough spare time to drive around the city's central area. He saw the Rio Dulce itself, a Hotel Rio Dulce, a Rio Dulce gas station, a Rio Dulce playground, and a Rio Dulce car wash. He wondered if she'd been named for the river or as a tribute to the sweetness inherent in the family business or due to her newborn expression or a hoped-for childhood disposition.

From a table by the window he saw her approaching. Black pants and long-sleeved black silk shirt, heels, black ballcap, expensive shades that she removed when she entered. She looked like she had been hired to kill someone at the coffee shop.

He stood and she gave him a light hug and a peck on both cheeks.

"Sorry I'm late," she said. "I was dealing with one of my sons."

"No problem," he said. "I just got here. Nice to see you again."

He got them coffee and a plate of *pastelitos*. She said she would take him to an idle section of cane field they could use, a place where they could build a batey and even burn some cane. They would need to rent the field for a large sum and run everything through her.

"What's a large sum?" Sloan said.

Small flakes of pastry clung to her crimson lipstick and she delicately dabbed the corners of her mouth with a napkin. "I need something to make an impression on my brother Hector," she said. "I'll leave that up to you. Also, you must give me something in writing that will convince my brother that the movie is not a hit piece on sugar." She looked at Sloan pointedly. "This can be anything you choose to give me. Just between us."

Sloan nodded. "I think I understand," he said. "You and Hector are not exactly on the same page but you can convince him to let you have this project."

"That's correct," she said. "My brother is more traditional but he will listen to me."

"Okay," Sloan said. "I appreciate your working with me."

She smiled. "There's one more thing," she said. "I want my sons to have some part."

"Some part?" he said.

"Yes," she said. "Like extras or assistants or something."

Sloan rubbed the stubble on his chin. "What can they do?" he said. "What are their names, their ages?"

"Steven and Diego," she said. "They're fifteen, twins. Very smart boys but they need to see some interesting work being done."

Sloan remembered what Javier had called them. Satan and Diablo. He pictured them as shaven-headed, chain-swinging, crack smokers doing cannonballs off the waterfall during the best take of the day.

"I don't see any problem with them being extras," he said. "Like at the resort or in the crowd at the Altos de Chavón concert. You know, either resort guests or music fans. Something like that."

She hummed as she looked at him. "What about staff work this summer, before school starts?"

"There won't be much work until August," he said, "when departments start gearing up for shooting in September."

She nodded, pursing her lips. "Maybe something in your department," she said.

Sloan shrugged. "We're full," he said, "until shooting. Sorry."

She stared at him. "They don't need the money," she said. "Perhaps they could help you out for the experience. Teach them something about the movie business. Behind the scenes."

He stifled the frown that wanted to form. "That's possible," he said. "Let me talk to my partner and see what he thinks."

She smiled and picked up another *pastelito*.

He followed her Mercedes north into cane country. They drove for forty minutes and she turned down a rough dirt road, her speed creating a storm of dust of such magnitude that he was forced to decelerate and fade back to avoid losing all sense of direction in the brownish cloud. When he saw the cloud turn left he followed it and slowed to a stop as the dust settled.

Dulce was standing at the side of the road looking westward into the cane. It was not the best-looking field Sloan had ever seen. It was maybe the twenty-third-best.

He walked out on the muddy ground and stood among green stalks that barely reached the height of his shoulders. He crouched to become more immersed in the cane and moved around taking photos from various angles. He raised his arms above his head and took blind wide shots in all directions.

Back on the road beside Dulce, he said, "This is pretty small but it could work for the batey build and the burn."

"This field is dormant," she said, "and more likely to be approved by Hector."

"I understand," he said, "but I have to show this to other people who have to approve it on our side. I might be able to sell it if we have a bigger field for the establishing shots. That would just be one day of showing where we are, the world of our story. Then the rest is here, for example."

"So you'd still want to shoot something over at 108," she said.

"Or someplace similar," he said. "Just the fields.

But I also need some research shots of the batey so our art department can create a believable look." He took some shots of the road and the field together.

She turned to look out at the cane. "I'm trying to improve things there," she said. "I don't want to present the workers as subjects of interest to an outsider."

"Of course," he said. "I only want to see the dwellings and the layout. I will respect the people and not show any of them. We can go together and you can explain that I'm doing research on bateyes and not on the workers themselves."

Dulce stood conflicted, her thick hair a dark cascade, her silk-enshrouded arms folded, a light coat of dust dulling the luster of her shoes, her appearance misaligned with her surroundings.

Sloan tried again. "Let's call the fee a donation," he said. "So you can build or provide something the people need. A gift from the movies."

She squinted and smirked at him. "What's that expression you Americans use?" she said. "Blowing smoke up someone's ass."

He laughed. "First it was my silver tongue. Now it's smoke blowing where the sun don't shine. I can't imagine what you might say next."

She suppressed a laugh. "We're both risk-takers," she said, glancing at her watch. "Try not to go over the edge. You can have ten minutes at 108. With me watching you."

There were three rough rows of patchwork shacks. These were comprised of foraged tin sheets, sometimes mingled with planks of wood, overlapped and cobbled together with nails and wire into multicolored and rust-tinged dwellings of the most random and basic composition. They were mud-stained around the bottom and propped off the ground with stones and pieces of brick. The doors and windows were wooden constructions or metal sheets that swung outward. It was a scrapyard village erected on a dirt plain. Around a lone spigot standing out of the ground on a thin pipe, water had created a small muddy pond with stones positioned as a bridge. A woman in shorts and rubber sandals was carrying away four plastic jugs. Here and there laundry was strung between poles and trees. Ducks and chickens wandered through the improvised community.

There was a woman on a chair before a firepit, sitting among buckets and pans at her makeshift kitchen. A gray-haired man sat shelling peas from a red plastic basin. A young girl with her hair collected into short braids with pink barrettes stared defiantly at Sloan as he passed. Before a blue wall a young man in yellow sports shorts stood with crutches under his arms, his bandaged lower leg and foot lifted. Nearby, a small naked boy held a long machete vertically, in both hands, as if he'd captured the culprit and had it by the neck.

Through the window of a schoolroom Sloan noticed the day of the week and the date written on the chalkboard in Spanish. He saw two rows of desks and some posters on the walls. Inside a shack he saw a bed, a cooler, and a hanging green blanket that divided the room.

Beyond the village and the surrounding fields, he saw green hills—lush land outside the cane.

Dulce stopped to speak to an elderly woman but kept an eye on Sloan, who was shooting fast, his eye in overdrive, avoiding people but capturing compositions, atmosphere, and details.

He saw two more young males with leg injuries, inexperienced or inattentive cutters, but most of the men were elsewhere. He did not see the young girl with the cardboard sign he'd seen on his first visit. Nor did he see any sign of electricity.

It was confirmed: the production designer was arriving in a few days, anxious to set the tone of the film's look as soon as possible. He was still recuperating from a foot injury, specification unknown. A slice, a sprain, a planter's wart, an ingrown toenail. Nico and Sloan speculated and made a fifty-dollar wager. Nico said skin puncture or cut, Sloan said sprain or dislocation. The point was the man was wearing a protective boot on one of his lower legs and would need help getting to locations. Sloan bet it was his right foot but Nico did not take this second wager.

They received by email a one-page document:

Initial Notes on the Look of *Larimore*, by Dominic Larue

The film's feeling flows from the main character's persona. Tough. Pragmatic. Masculine. Sexy. Thoughtful. A Zen Quiet. Fortitude.

Sugar harvesting is a tough business, basic, brutal, abusive. But there is beauty within its brutality. Elegant green stalks wave in unison, endless as the work that goes on and on, the elements of nature at play regardless of the purpose. The workers are tough. We see their forbearance in their rough dwellings, in their pride, in their dark stoicism. There are touches of bleak style, splashes of color amid downtrodden dignity. We feel the human community. Reminiscent of black and white, color drained partly away, stark beauty, mythic contrast, a world apart shown by its palette. *The Treasure of the Sierra Madre* brought to the vibrant Caribbean. When Larimore is in this world he absorbs it, becomes a part of it.

In contrast to this sugar world, there are modern sensibilities, as personified by Gina La Vega, by the resort, the mansion, and the apartment Larimore uses in town. These will highlight the modernity that coexists alongside the austere colonial labor of the Haitian workers. Even at the park we will be in a super urban environment, full of activity and noise, more contrast to the cane community.

Some of the other locations, the waterfall, the jungle, the beach, showcase the freedom in nature, the open world of beauty and freshness, untarnished by man's governance. The natural beauty of these places will be shown with minimal dressing. For this reason they must be outstanding in their appearance.

The golf course is also outstanding in its appearance but as a colonial construct by man, nature harnessed, created by the wealth of the sugar industry, the rewards reaped by big business at the expense of others.

Concluding with the amphitheater, we have the Old and New Worlds combined in one location. Even as a facsimile, it holds Europe and America in its stone embrace, current music in an ancient style environment. Colonial and modern at once, the conflict we've been witnessing, where the competing parties meet and the climax must occur.

In the closing scene we return to the sight of the cane field, passing and peaceful in the moonlight, but always there, the unseen world that keeps the other one, the modern one, going.

Sonia had located a mule wrangler with a horse trailer and needed to complete the contractual arrangements. Nico guided her in this task and assigned Wilson to accompany her on the physical mission. Sloan contacted Beatriz at the Film Office and obtained a letter stating that a mule could be used at each of the named waterfalls, thus sidestepping the rental of any misbegotten horse at Salto El Limón and assigning written permission for the production to use this solitary mule at the two waterfalls where no animals were normally employed. The rest of the scout team, Nico and Sloan, would walk alongside the mule that carried the injured designer, Dominic Larue.

In the other situations where their scouting might require special transportation, such as the city parks, the cane field, the golf course, and the beach resort, they could rent a golf cart. Presumably, the man would have crutches for short walks.

Dulce Medina had promised she could provide contacts for a mansion or two, and Sloan was now fearing more demands for the unknown talents and shenanigans of Satan and Diablo.

There was no shooting schedule yet so it was not advisable to tie locations together except by educated guess. For instance, in the storyline the dive bar played with the park—Larimore leaves the bar and evades Montero by cutting through the park—but the bar did not necessarily need to be near the park, meaning the locations could be scouted separately. Same with the jazz bar and the apartment.

They needed more bars, more choices, more potential options for the production designer to sift through. They needed some apartments to get the ball rolling on that location.

They would need to create a working schedule for the several days required for the scout.

Interiors would be time-sensitive, arranged in advance. Exteriors could be scouted whenever it made sense, preferably in a reasonable geographic and efficient order.

For the apartment search Sloan wrote a letter that Sonia translated into Spanish so both versions could be delivered to apartments that seemed like good options. The problem with this approach was that the interior furnishings would not be known until access was allowed. They needed a modern look and, in most cases, this could be accomplished with the art department's dressing. As long as the owners were cool with having their personal stuff replaced for the shoot. It was almost always a question of money. The body of the letter, which was dated and had Sonia's number and email at the bottom, was a simple appeal to those interested in the chance to make some unexpected "found" money and those who might also enjoy seeing their home in a movie.

Dear Resident,
We are scouting for locations for an exciting new motion picture being produced by Far Cry Productions, due to begin filming in September. We are searching for an apartment to use as a location for a couple of scenes in the movie. In our story the apartment will be a place for our main character to stay while figuring out his next move.

As you might expect, we will pay a reasonable location fee for the use of the property, and we will be working with a film permit from the Dominican Film Office. We will take good care of any location we use and will always issue a certificate of insurance for any property we access.

Please get in touch with us as soon as possible for more information.

Thank you for your consideration.

With a stack of letters in hand, Sloan and Sonia went out in the afternoon to look at upscale buildings that seemed promising from the exterior. In some cases they were able to gain lobby access and post their letter on a bulletin board or beside the elevators. In other cases they taped the letter to the wall outside the entrance to the building. Since they had no leads to start with, this type of search was like taking shots in the dark, known as "cold" scouting.

One security guard tried to get huffy at their intrusion but was put at ease by Sonia's smooth appeal to help them in their difficult task and in short order he had committed to passing out the letters to residents himself. He now believed he had been deputized into the Locations Department.

At another building, called the Pinos Marinos Apartments, which displayed no discernable association with either pine trees or the sea, they met a young woman entering the building as they were approaching it. After a brief discussion she agreed to let them take a look at her unit on the fourth floor. She led them to the stairs and it became clear that the five-story building did not contain an elevator.

On the plus side, Sloan thought, the staircase was of ample dimensions to support the upward movement of a grand piano. Not only that, the unit was spacious, had high ceilings, was minimally decorated with a few Art Deco pieces—a server, living room chairs, and two wall sconces, all of which leaned toward retro modern—and had pretty decent natural light. In addition, the woman was under the impression that she would have to pay the production company to entice it to use her apartment. When she was informed that she was the one in a position to make money, her face turned red and she beamed and became lightheaded as she confessed her feeling of immense good fortune at having met her guests. She offered them wine. Sloan accepted, then looked at his watch and confirmed his acceptance. At the woman's modest kitchen table they toasted chance meetings and the wide world of entertainment, including the nearly universal love of movies, and, for a moment—despite the treacly sweetness of the pink Moscato which caused Sloan to picture himself and Sonia puking in an alley together—it seemed they would all be friends for life. He took photos of the entire apartment and then the hallway and the stairwell as they descended.

"I'd like a real drink after that honeysuckle peach concoction," Sloan said.

Sonia laughed. "It was a celebration of a potential location, Mister Snob."

Sloan squinted at her. "I was being polite," he said. "In nearly every case the crew prefers some kind of mechanical conveyance that can lift people and gear up to the location."

She made the face she typically made at his displays of experience. "That was a cool apartment," she said, "and she was a cool lady."

"Okay," he said. "Should I just omit the staircase pictures?"

"They might love it anyway," she said.

"Exactly," he said. "The designer and the director could love it and insist on shooting there. Then there's the part where the producer takes me aside and says 'Why did you show us a location without a fucking elevator?' and I tell him I thought we could all use the exercise."

"So you're not going to show it?" she said.

"I'll keep it in my back pocket," he said, "and see what else develops."

As they came out into the sunlight she said, "Are you keeping me in your back pocket too?"

"No," he said. "I prefer you in my front pocket."

Nico called Sloan to cancel their dinner and roundup meeting. He was driving over to Punta Cana so he'd be at a new resort location in the morning to shoot sunrise. Sloan updated him on the apartment scout and said he was heading out to explore the missing village location and hopefully catch some late light.

He took Sonia with him, to translate if necessary and because the time he'd spent with her already that day made him want more. They could even have dinner together.

They drove east out of the city in the direction of San Pedro de Macorís and then turned north into agricultural land. The sun lay across the vast flatness of the grassy plain and was changing moment by moment, splintered into shafts breaking through accumulated clouds above the central mountain range to the west.

On the outskirts of Los Llanos, Sloan began to see possibilities. There were colorful rustic palmwood homes spaciously arranged on dirt roads, basic homesteads with stick fences. That was one look, and there was plenty of space to insert a house façade that could be damaged in the stunt.

He went over the scene with Sonia to bring it in focus for both of them, so they would see the same thing in their imagination and convert the words in the script into real life.

"Eddie is on his motorbike fleeing Ramon in his Escalade," Sloan said. "As he approaches the village he makes a sharp turn between houses. When the Escalade makes the turn it smashes into the corner of a house and then swerves behind another house and hits a cart full of papayas."

"There is so much space around here," Sonia said.

"It's a tricky location," he said. "We could use the space to construct something, but only if we have the cooperation of the neighbors."

"Should we start knocking on some doors?" Sonia said.

"It might be too downscale," Sloan said, "but we have to start somewhere. The problem is that there is no actual road for the bike and the car to continue on. We'd have to create a dirt road that goes on for a little ways."

"Wow," she said.

"Let's keep going," he said. "We can come back after we see more of the village."

They saw a weathered motorcycle with an attached metal bed on two wheels, making it a motorized cart. It was a beautiful custom delivery vehicle and Sloan stopped and shot a photo of it through the window. Then he backed up and shot the license plate.

Further into town the houses were concrete, more substantial and still colorful but without much room between them. They passed the ballfields and cruised the nearby streets.

"These look good," Sloan said. "We'll take some reference shots and if Dominic likes the look we can come back and lock something down."

He pulled over at the corner and they got out. He took some general shots of the street with its houses and the intersection. The shadows were long and there was a vacant lot where a façade could be built. There was no actual alley between houses but the light was golden. At a blue house a woman sweeping the dirt around a hibiscus bush stood in a soft sepia haze of her own creation.

Further up the main street they found dirt side roads running between houses to fields at the edge of town. Sloan shot from the vehicle and turned around to shoot the reverse angles.

"Let's head back to that first area we liked on the other side of town," he said.

On the east side of the street his shadow stretched out tall across the road and into yards and ran flat up against fences and walls but he made sure Sonia's shadow was out of frame.

Driving south in the dusk, he suggested taking her to a fine restaurant back in the city.

"I could make us a nice dinner at my place," she said.

He looked over at her. "I would love that," he said.

She made him the national dish—white rice and red beans with stewed chicken—using her grandmother's recipe and adding a side salad. They drank white wine and sat for a few minutes on her balcony taking the night air. Sloan joked that they might use her apartment for the location. Then he moved to the couch and she cuddled up like a cat and crawled into his lap and his hands were all over her. Her hair fell around his face as they kissed and he began to peel her clothes away. He agreed to stay the night and she made him promise to fuck her again before he left. He raised his hand and spoke the vow and she kissed his palm.

The team prepared for the arrival of the production designer, the first big event to happen since they'd started compiling location options. They were in decent shape, had something to show in most of the categories, but not the mansion or the golf course. The batey was a gray area since they would probably need to build it. It was always a question of quantity, along with quality. And of course, nothing was actually cleared for shooting yet.

"So, Wilson," Sloan said. "What you say about that—quietly, to yourself only—is 'Don't fall in love with anything.' Haha."

"The production designer's of the same vintage as Cragmore," Nico said. "But the guy the director wanted was not available." He shrugged. "So we'll see how that plays out."

Several of the apartment letters yielded calls or emails to Sonia, and they set up meetings to scout the units. The hotel manager put them onto a realtor who specialized in upscale homes on the water. They only needed the drive-up and a terrace, so it wouldn't be as problematic as interiors. There were odds and ends missing, like the roadside food stand and the exterior of Ramon's office. They could possibly pick these up as they drove around.

They could also pick up dengue fever.

20. The Production Designer's Cinematic Discontent

The three-day schedule was presented to Dominic and also to Gene Friedman so he'd be looped in to the latest developments and could monitor the money.

The first day would be devoted to waterfalls. Along with accompanying jungle. The second day would be resorts and cane fields and whatever else could be inserted. Mansion, golf course, village, amphitheater. The third day would be city locations. Bars, streets, parks, apartments.

Wilson would drive the scout car and stay with the vehicle, and Sonia would jump ahead to meet the mule squad and make sure everything was set. The mule wrangler had a backup mule that rode in the trailer with the original, which seemed to be a healthy component of mule morale and would be helpful in the event that the first mule proved to have a bad attitude or expressed a previously undiagnosed case of hydrophobia. In the following days Sonia would continue to leapfrog ahead and make sure locations were ready for the scout team.

The production designer took a red-eye from Los

Angeles, with a stop in Miami. He landed in Santo Domingo around eleven in the morning. By the time he got through customs and met Nico and Sloan, he looked groggy. His eyes were red. In fact, his whole face was red. Sloan thought about describing the color to Sonia. Disgruntled red. Sadistic red. Heat rash red.

Dominic shook Nico's hand and silently waved to Sloan, who was silently thinking the man looked testudinal, with quite a bit of the old tortoise demeanor as he stood leaning forward between his crutches, his bald head and long jaw wagging from side to side, his face slick with moisture, as if he'd just been eating a head of wet lettuce.

His right foot was encased in a black orthopedic boot, visible beneath the slit cuff of black track pants. Above that he wore a black t-shirt under an open long-sleeved pink linen shirt.

They carried his bags outside where Wilson waited at the curb.

Dominic Larue stood looking around at the bustle of people and taxis amid the shouting and car horns, then pulled out a handkerchief and wiped his face.

"Hot as bloody blue blazes," he said, and slipped his crutches into the back seat.

Sloan and Nico exchanged looks and got in.

"Let's get some lunch," Nico said, and they headed into the city.

A glass of wine seemed to restore Dominic Larue to some level of conversation. On the drive in he'd looked wordlessly out the window as if pondering the gravity of his circumstances.

"Let's start with our position of having to overcome the script," he said.

"Okay," Nico said. "We've just been plunging ahead on the locations as they're written."

"As you should," he said. "As you must."

He cut his burger in half and then removed all the

ingredients except the meat. "There are ongoing discussions about rewrites," he said. "This whole trip might be a complete boondoggle."

Sloan looked at the man's plate, the displeasing pile of tomato and lettuce and bacon.

"Any idea about what might change?" he said.

Dominic Larue chewed and swallowed and blinked slowly. "Where to even begin," he said.

"That is the question," Sloan said.

"Our story has a certain simplicity," Larue said. "The locations are few and basic, almost fading into the background. But we need them to connect strongly to the characters. The exception to this is the batey, which I will build. This will be monumental in its imagery, the crux of the film."

Nico and Sloan ate and nodded and let the man roll out his cinematic view.

"I'm pitching this section as black and white," he said. He raised his open hands, thumbs inches apart and pointing at each other, film shorthand for an image in the camera's frame. "Think *The Grapes of Wrath*," he said. "The poverty and squalor, the struggling workers trying to survive. The uncaring world. Everything against them. The shadows, the contrast, day and night, the heat, the fires." He was sweating profusely. The food and drink, the humidity, the excitement, the sudden overheated vision.

They brought him to the hotel where he wanted to rest for a while and go over location photos before they started first thing in the morning after meeting for breakfast.

"We have raw dirt," Larue said. "And our task is to make something meaningful from it."

"An adobe library," Nico said, under his breath.

"Mud dauber nest," Sloan said.

At dusk, Nico got the call from Gene Friedman,

checking in for a progress report.

"Good," Nico said. "He's a bit slow with the bad foot but otherwise we're fine."

"Just give him what he needs," Gene said.

"What he needs is a rewrite," Nico said.

There was a pause, then Gene said, "That's above your pay grade."

"Well I guess I should get a raise because I already know about it."

"Duncan Barlow," Gene said.

"Yeah," Nico said. "The screenwriter."

"The director calls him Drunken Lowbar."

Nico laughed. And simultaneously felt sorry for the guy. "That's harsh," he said.

Gene wasn't finished. "Sometimes he calls him Drunken Barstool."

"The man's in a tough spot," Nico said.

"He might show up down there," Gene said. "Not that it'll affect you. He'll be invisible."

"It's a lonely solitary pursuit," Nico said.

"Keep me posted," Gene said. "And make Dominic happy."

"I'll try to keep him apart from further injury," Nico said.

"Just be your usual professional self," Gene said.

"What happened to his foot?" Nico said.

"What happened to his foot?" Gene said. "He got bit by a Gila monster. How the fuck should I know?"

"I thought your job was to know everything," Nico said.

"Just take care of him," Gene said. "And don't waste any fucking money."

The mule looked sturdy.

Sloan had dreamed that the mule tender brought a donkey instead and the production designer looked like Sancho Panza, his feet grazing the ground as he sat atop the small animal, so that it seemed to Sloan that the man could actually stand and relieve the weight if the animal struggled.

Sonia made the introductions at Salto El Limón and Dominic Larue was assisted into the saddle and looked comfortable enough for the journey. It was decided that the mule tender, whose name was Sanchez—which prompted Sloan to repeat the name silently a half dozen times to get it implanted and avoid calling him Sancho—would pilot the backup mule and lead the expedition. Nico and Sloan would walk behind so they could keep an eye on the designer in case he dropped something or fell out of the saddle.

Wilson waited with the car in case of emergency and Sonia took off to prep other locations.

The group began the downward journey, the mules rocking side to side as they negotiated the uneven terrain. Dominic's protective boot did not fit into the stirrup on that side and without that stabilizing resistance his body listed to the right after a short distance. Nico whistled and got the mule tender's attention. The trail traffic was light and Sanchez faded back alongside the designer and pulled his left arm to vertically align his body again.

They passed through forest shade and full sun, over dirt track and through muddy ruts, meandering downhill beside fenced lots and fruit trees and open pasture. The designer donned a floppy safari hat and tied a bandana around his neck.

"Here we are in a mini-cavalcade," Sloan said.

"There's no escaping it," Nico said. "The cavalcade lives."

They were breathing pretty heavily and after another couple of minutes Sloan said, "How did the man hurt his foot?"

"Still a mystery," Nico said. "Napoleon pretended he didn't know."

"What's the big deal?" Sloan said.

"He operates on the need-to-know basis."

"He's opposed to curiosity and random wagering," Sloan said.

"He doesn't know about the wager," Nico said, "but yeah."

"He's a square peg in a square hole," Sloan said.

"Reaching a stature nearly as high as Yosemite Sam," Nico said.

At the pool Dominic Larue sat on his mule and took photos. He had Sanchez lead the animal around for different angles of view. The designer stared up at the top of the falls where the water did not fall free of the ledge but ran down the rock face in wide clinging sheets. They all watched a couple of young men climb up the wall and jump from attainable positions perhaps a third of the height of the entire face. No one was leaping from the top. Dominic asked the Locations team if they knew if anyone ever jumped from the top—as if they were regular visitors or had taken a survey—and they both said they did not know of any such case.

On the way out a horse guide stood in front of the abbreviated mule train and asked what they were doing there. No other equine animals were at the very bottom by the pool. Sanchez told the guide they were on official business and couldn't say any more about it. The guide looked at the gringos with concern and stepped aside. He may have been worried about an imminent invasion of mules, the establishment of a muleteer union that would lead to the traditional skinny horses being decommissioned and put out to pasture.

"He's wondering why we're walking," Sloan said. "Foreign mule skinners."

"One of those need-to-know situations," Nico said.

Back at the top they stood at the car sweating and

drinking water while the mules were loaded into their trailer. Dominic wiped his head and neck and wrung out his bandana. His shirt was soaking wet and he removed it and wrung it out too, then dried his arms and torso with a towel and took a dry shirt from his pack and put it on. Across the back of his neck were a series of red welts and he rubbed cream on those.

Driving west to head south, Nico and Sloan sat in the rear as before and Nico pointed out the red ridge on the back of the designer's neck, which was now so enlarged and glowing that it resembled a pox of the Middle Ages. Insect bites or botanical reaction? Due to the confines of the vehicle, no wager was made. But they begin to discuss their past personal foot injuries. While snorkeling Nico had sliced his foot on coral in Puerto Rico. Sloan had stepped on a black sea urchin in the Bahamas. Nico had sprained his ankle surfing. Sloan had sprained his playing tennis. They waited for the designer to weigh in with his own recent experience but no response emanated from the front seat. Then his head fell back and they heard the soft serrated rasp of shallow snoring.

They stopped for lunch in Las Terrenas. Fish sandwiches and fries all around. Sloan received a text from Sonia. *Mansion (from realtor) confirmed for tomorrow. Housekeeper will meet you. 2 apts confirmed for following day. Waiting for teeth of dog to call back.*

The designer took Benadryl for his neck eruption, pushing it down with a cold Presidente beer, and slept all the way to the next location, Socoa Falls. When he awoke he thought he was in Surinam. His mule, Samson, was brought to the car but the designer was so disoriented that he started to mount his transportation in the wrong direction, which would have resulted in him throwing his booted foot over into the animal's head. As expected, Sanchez interceded.

In their raw jungle beauty the waterfall and pool

were almost hallucinogenic to the designer's mind and left him speechless, though that parameter was not especially meaningful since he'd hardly spoken, aside from ordering a sandwich, all day. He preferred to absorb locations silently and then process his mental and photographic images after they had been thoroughly digested and compared to other entries in the same category.

By this time the day was at its hottest and the humidity was such that a collective desire to enter the pool was percolating among the filmmakers. But since the designer could not get his boot wet, everyone simply looked at the blue-green water longingly and envied the visitors swimming around emitting sounds of exuberance from their open smiling mouths.

As a minor consolation, the designer asked Nico to wet his bandana and this he delicately draped dripping across the back of his neck, which at a casual glance seemed to be hosting an engorged and feasting red leech.

They had passed through the town of Bayaguana and almost reached the third location, Bayaguana Falls, when Wilson noticed Sanchez's truck and trailer falling behind in the countryside. He pulled over and waited, then turned around and went back. Sanchez was squatting beside a flat tire on the trailer. Everyone except the designer got out to assess the situation.

Each side of the trailer rode on two tires so the forward flat on the left side did not seem like an emergency to the onlookers. But a couple of other things became apparent. The darker gray circular shape on the right side was visible due to the fact that a spare tire no longer occupied that space. And the trailer was, if not exactly vintage, somewhere close to that classification in its well-worn condition. The mules stood side-by-side, facing forward, and tended to look behind them at the open space above the doors whenever someone was back there.

The first concern Sanchez had was that the trailer would ride unevenly and become damaged. He suggested that he and someone else, like Sloan, could ride the mules from there and meet the car at the falls. But then he worried about leaving his trailer unattended, fearing that he would return to find no tires. The others did not like this idea due to the amount of extra time it would take. The designer was watching them with droopy eyes from inside the air-conditioned car.

Finally Sanchez decided to limp forward on three trailer tires and by this he meant that he would proceed at a rate only slightly faster than an agitated box turtle.

The other four waited for him in the Bayaguana Falls parking area and the day stretched on into late afternoon. Visitors came and went like clouds. The sound of crunching granola in the car reminded Sloan of a distant avalanche.

He and Wilson got out for a recon of the area, while Nico stayed in the car in the role of babysitter. The steps that Sloan had taken down to the pool with Sonia on his previous trip were not suitable for mules, the path being too narrow to share with people coming up, not to mention the unnaturalness of the concrete construction and sharp-angled elevation changes as seen from the animals' point of view.

Encountering a boisterous group emerging from the bush, the scouts learned of another forest path that descended to the river below the pool. This would be their route.

Just when the designer had exited the vehicle with cantankerous snorts and was hopping around on his crutches like a huffy puppet, Sanchez appeared. The team assembled and began its jungle journey into a dappled gloom. Before long the whine of mosquitos encircled them and the designer halted to dig into his tropical defense kit. He put on an olive green head net with built-in flexible ribs that kept the mesh away from his skin and gave him the appearance of a large-brained alien with no discernable facial features.

They approached the falls as through a jungle tunnel, Nico and Sloan trudging and stumbling as the river flowed against them. In the clearing, bathers lay about on a rocky beach and others stood in the water or climbed the rocks behind the falls. There were two main streams plunging parallel into the aqua-green depths, with a thin third stream further away across the rock face.

The mules with their riders appeared out of the river and stood on the beach in what bystanders would describe as a startling sight, as if they carried bigshots, one of whom was clearly local and the other a criminal in disguise or a deformed dignitary of unknown origin.

The triple stream of falling water gave the designer pause and made his ultimate choice easier, but he took the requisite photos without moving his mule around among the disturbed bathers. This mysterious sight caused everyone to suspend their activities and focus on the riders.

Nico and Sloan took in the atmosphere, standing half-wet on the beach like foot soldiers. There was a slight feeling in the humid air of building hostility toward the invaders. The easygoing Dominicans might become incensed and revolt with rocks and cans and ripe fruit.

When the designer finally turned his mule around to begin backtracking into the forest, the animal took that opportunity, utilizing the respite and the relaxed feeling of standing on the relatively solid ground of the beach, along with the constant loosening flow of falling water, to lift his tail and dump a staggering load of reeking road apples. Sanchez steered his animal around the steaming blockade and then his mule too, perhaps triggered by the visual and olfactory suggestions—much like the yawning reflex spreads in a group—paused to perform his own satisfying act of sublime elimination.

The bathers were not nearly as satisfied and shouts issued from various spots. The walking Locations team, acting as a rear guard, looked down at the odious parting endowment. There was a moment when wishful images of field shovels and entrenching tools came to mind, some quick and practical way to remedy the situation, but the bad vibes were growing and it seemed advisable to get out of the potential target zone into which brown biscuits could be hurled at the retreating perpetrators.

Not until he was safely seated in the car again did the designer remove his head net, changing his appearance from that of a human fly back into a person, though one who was apparently an object of desire for a majority of biting insects. The backs of his hands, the only skin exposed as he held the reins through the jungle, were pebbled in tiny bumps suggestive of a rash, and he was compelled to pull up the bottom of his track pants to examine and scratch at the red spots encircling his left calf. Wilson glanced over and was startled by the sight. He couldn't help wonder what might have crawled down into the boot.

While the mules grazed at the edge of the lot Sanchez studied his flat tire and checked the others. His mood lifted when Nico presented the cash he was due and Sloan thanked him. He shook their hands and waved at the car. The designer lifted his hand behind the window.

The ride home was uneventful. Wilson put on some low classical music to help filter the front seat snoring. Then he held up a note to the back seat on which was written the word *repellent.*

They were met with rain the next morning but by the time they sat looking at the neglected cane field near Batey 108, the shower had passed. Steam rose off the bent and beaten stalks and the reflected moisture lent a sheen of bedraggled beauty to the location. The designer discussed the building of a batey and was perturbed that they couldn't visit one right then.

"We're here because the burn could happen here," Sloan said. "In general the sugar industry is less than cooperative."

The designer stared at him. "And it's your job to make the locations happen," he said.

"We're working on it," Nico said.

"We'll drive by a bigger field with higher cane where we could establish our location," Sloan said.

"I thought we'd be seeing ten or fifteen fields," the designer said.

Disregarding the fact that the duration of the designer's trip did not allow for so much time spent on any one location category, Sloan did not respond.

The designer put the window down and exhaled into the fresh air. "The problem is," he said, "that we have very few interiors so we have very few cover sets."

They all understood that rain could wreak havoc on the schedule when they began shooting.

"We have the bars and the apartment and the resort room," he said. "And we'll have the batey interiors once they're built. So construction will need to start as soon as my team is here."

"Absolutely," Nico said.

The designer spoke into the view of the field as if daydreaming out loud. "Then we could do these scenes anytime we needed to. Assuming the appropriate actors were lined up—the Haitian girl,

Fabienne, I'm primarily thinking of, and Larimore works nearly every day so he'll be around."

"We'll get as much latitude in the apartment and bar dates as possible," Nico said. "So we can juggle the schedule if the weather demands it."

The designer seemed not to have heard. "I want to do a test burn," he said, "so we know what to expect before we shoot."

"We're hoping a corner of this field could work for that," Sloan said.

The designer raised his window. "Let's go," he said.

On the way up to Altos de Chavón, Sloan got a text from Sonia.

Fernando at teeth of the dog is expecting your call will show you hole #18

She added the phone number and Sloan wanted to send her a kiss. Instead, he sent a thumbs-up.

The stone amphitheater and the adjacent fountain were somehow deemed acceptable, though the designer did not like the idea of a concert taking place in the scene. He wanted a feeling like that in *The Third Man*, a more ominous and deserted atmosphere, but he didn't suggest a Ferris wheel. The Locations Department had not yet presented any alternatives and had not been asked to since this exact, one-of-a-kind place was precisely named in the script.

In a generous universe the lunch choice could've been quite close to a hit with the designer. The view, the river, the clouds, the *sancocho*, a hearty meat stew. Sloan passed on the heavy meat meal because he didn't want to drop into a post-lunch slump with so many miles still to go.

The scout group took the Chavon road down through a winding sea of orange-roofed villas to Central Avenue and over to the golf course. Wilson stayed with the car in the clubhouse lot.

Fernando was a dark man dressed in white. They were cleared to visit and he was friendly, though nowhere close to the final word on their filming request. They boarded his four-seater cart, Nico and Sloan facing backwards, and rambled to the eighteenth tee, then cruised slowly into the long fairway. Two carts, four players were midway out. Fernando stopped so they could take in the open view, the distant clubhouse like a country estate, the expansive green of grass and tropical trees. And not far to the south, the sparkling blue Caribbean.

The designer said, "The water's too far away. There's no reason to be here if we can't clearly see the water. The entire reason we want to be here is to be on the water."

Nico and Sloan got out and stood at the front of the cart. Fernando looked at them but already had his instructions and couldn't contribute.

"This is our starting point," Nico said. "Standard protocol presents the last hole so that when you start at first light you have four hours to get your work done before the first playing group shows up."

"I don't care about standard bloody protocol," the designer said. "We might as well be at a pitch and putt in Cleveland."

Nico looked at their escort. "Look, this is a work in progress," he said. "Fernando can drive us by seventeen, one of the coastline holes, so we can see it. If that one looks right, we can push for it."

The par-four seventeenth hole's entire right side was bordered by the jagged rocky shore of the ocean. Waves rolled in against the edge of the fairway. The designer's silence seemed almost reverent and was taken as a positive sign.

Not far away, still within the Casa de Campo Resort enclave, they drove down Bahia Minitas where various waterfront homes were situated. The amphitheater, the golf course, and the mansion were all close to each other.

The house was new to all of them, unscouted, unseen, untested, unconfirmed, a stone-cold visit. Wilson pulled up to the gate and buzzed the intercom. After a moment, a high-pitched voice answered, the squeak of the housekeeper they assumed, and Wilson confirmed their appointment. The gate began to swing open and they drove inside. The driveway from entrance to house was at least long enough to signify some wealth, though the word mansion was perhaps subjective when applied to the property.

The house was a typical two-story with a red-tiled roof, more of a sizable villa if anyone was inclined to split hairs, but with enough property in front to bump up the prestige a notch. A man with a machete stood at the base of the drive, and a tiny woman appeared on the porch. Wilson parked and got out and introduced himself and shook their hands. The woman wore a smock and pants of the same mauve color, similar to hospital scrubs, and looked to be about fifty.

The porch was not very high off the ground and the designer managed to get himself up there without incident, using his crutches with the scouts on either side of him serving as guardrails. From this slightly elevated vantage point, he looked out at the yard and the entrance, surveying the vegetation and the fragmented view of adjacent properties. He took a few photos and then the yardman led them around the side of the house to the patio.

The pool deck was bordered on three sides by the house and two outbuildings, with a view of a private beach and the ocean. The ocean was more of a bay, a peninsula full of other houses in view along one side, their docks sticking out like tongues aimed at the designer, practically spitting and hissing about their utter lack of exclusivity. We're all villas here, they cried in unison. Nico and Sloan shot their own photos. The housekeeper brought out some water bottles but the designer was already hobbling back toward the front. Wilson took the water and thanked her again, then thanked the yardman, who escorted them to the car. The drive out was marked by a lack of comments.

Wilson had called ahead to each of the three resorts to be scouted with a heads-up of estimated arrival times. In each instance they were met by a manager or assistant manager and given a tour of the property. Bar, beach, pool, room, restaurant. There was a certain conformity noted by the designer. All east-facing, with palms and ocean. Standard Punta Cana.

They saw consistent eating and drinking, water sports, shouting and laughing, holiday revelers enjoying themselves. But it seemed as if the designer were contemplating suicide.

It was more than itching skin and a throbbing foot. Dominic Larue wanted to see his imprint on the film. He'd read the script, as they all had, with an appraising eye for quality. He'd tried to imagine the finished picture being well-received, lauded even, clapped over and spoken about. At the end of the long production road, he wanted to garner praises and glory. And now, in looking for ways to make an imprint, he felt the project would not accept one.

After the third tour, with the afternoon light sinking into golden peacefulness and the music softening, everyone wanted a drink, a good meal, and a comfortable room to fall into.

Instead, they had over two hours of driving, mostly in the dark, a downcast capsule sailing back to the capitol with bottled water, bananas, and crackling bags of cheap snacks.

Back at the hotel the designer opted for room service, unsurprisingly, and the others were happy to get out from under his black cloud. They gathered at a bar down the street.

"This fucking guy is a fucking bummer," Sloan said.

"Obviously going through a personal struggle," Nico said.

"The man's a magnet for plagues and locusts," Sloan said. "I'm worried about comets too."

"If a comet struck the car," Wilson said, "you would not even know what happened."

"Well, thank you, Wilson," Sloan said. "I appreciate the fine-tuned, scientific clarification."

Wilson raised his ginger ale and the others raised their glasses of rum and clinked.

"He wouldn't even disclose the cause of his foot injury," Nico said.

Wilson wiped bubbles from his mouth. "He told me yesterday," he said.

Nico and Sloan turned to look at their colleague.

"Look at this fine young fellow," Nico said. "The secret keeper."

"Wilson," Sloan said. "Even if you're sworn to secrecy, I order you to divulge it."

"It's not a secret," the kid said. "I asked and he told me, in the car."

"Okay, cool," Sloan said. "Let it rip."

"Sure," the kid said. "He was in his shop and he stepped on board with a screw in it. Went through his..."

Nico raised both hands. "Yes," he said. "A puncture wins it."

"When he pulled his foot up, the board came with it," Wilson said, "and he hopped around trying to get the board off but he put his foot down on a skateboard and it turned over and twisted his ankle really bad."

"Christ," Sloan said. "The man is double-cursed. And we have a draw, Mr Merriweather."

The next morning was overcast and the guys started with parks while Sonia confirmed a working schedule for three apartments. The bars would come last.

From the car they explored the perimeters of the city park options—Columbus, Cervantes, and Enriquillo. At each location the designer got out and wobbled to an optimal photographic position, flanked by the obliging scouts. This being the third day, they operated from a heightened awareness of potential disaster and, more importantly, the prevention of such by any means in their power. They wanted to make sure nothing delayed the designer's departure. The accident-evasion clock was ticking and the scouts ran the necessary interference.

The pitfalls were numerous. Chaotic kids on bikes, uneven pavement, tossed balls, slippery mango skins, clusters of erratic pigeons, a surprising phalanx of fluttering nuns.

The designer was satisfactorily protected from these urban onslaughts and driven to the first apartment building. Sonia met the group at the elevator and then introduced them to the owner of the unit, situated on the third floor with a leafy view into shade trees. This umbrageous quality blocked much of the natural light and the city view the designer was seeking, prompting the look of displeasure on his face that brought indigestion to mind.

The other apartments were fine, the owners curious and interested, willing to allow the furnishings to be changed, eager to be a part of a movie. One woman followed the designer around with a small chair in case he needed to sit down quickly.

He was sweating so hard she also brought him a towel. He gave the impression that the fate of their cinematic fame was in his hands.

Outside on the street, Sloan asked Sonia to join them later on the scout of the Serbian bar, Sancho P. In fact, she might as well stay with them for the duration of the scout.

"Sure," she said, but seemed distant to him, beyond the professionalism the occasion required.

Maybe he was imagining it. Everyone was cranky, and they needed a break to eat something.

The designer said they were starving him, trying to kill him on his final scouting day, and everyone laughed, thinking he was being humorous for the first time. No one knew for sure.

It was approaching golden hour, with crowds streaming through the Colonial Zone. They sat for an early dinner outside and had Italian. With wine and pasta the meal had a false feeling of celebration, as if the work had been successfully concluded. Wilson didn't drink, so they adhered to the safety policy with regard to driving the designer around and basic industry protocol.

Sonia barely sipped her wine and drove herself to the next location, apparently not wishing to squeeze in the back seat with her American bosses.

The dive bars were dark, sleazy, and possibly acceptable. The patrons, no matter their level of intoxication, did not fail to notice the three gringos with the younger local woman, who they assumed to be some kind of city guide or adventurous escort. One inquisitive old man even noted their driver double-parked outside.

The bar Alcazar, as surmised by Sloan, was not quite right, not cool enough. But with the best saved for last, Sancho P, was the hit it had promised to be in photos, a positive wrap-up to a difficult scout. The owner, Vuk, was absent during their visit so the departmental triumph was untarnished.

Sonia motioned to Sloan and they left just ahead of the others. Outside she handed him a piece of paper she'd found on her windshield that morning. Sloan glanced down the street where Wilson was parked and then unfolded the paper in the glow of the streetlight. The note was constructed from cut-out magazine words of different sizes and colors pasted onto a sheet of plain paper, the kind of threatening anonymous message sometimes seen in a movie.

Be careful little girl
Your boyfriend can get you hurt
Check the facts

"What is this?" she said.

Sloan stared at the note, read it again.

"Is it about that other movie?" she said.

He scanned the street in both directions and as the other two left the bar, he turned his back to them and handed her the note. "Yes," he said. "They're connected. But nothing's going to happen. I have to hang with Nico tonight or he'll suspect something. In the morning I'll tell you everything I know about this."

She put the note in her bag and they turned to meet the others.

21. The TropCav Incident

Once Wilson deposited Dominic Larue at the Las Américas International Airport and got him into a wheelchair with the accompanying personal assistance and made sure there were no looming delays in the scheduled departure, he called Nico to report the situation.

Nico and Sloan were on their second pot of coffee, mollifying their brain functions to counterbalance the previous night's excessive imbibing. After the call from Wilson, Nico declared the day a working holiday, which translated into nothing more than a proclamation of relief.

They were already in reset mode. Nico expected a blustery call from Gene Friedman that would sound similar to a windstorm. Sloan would review the locations with Sonia.

He texted her and they met at Duarte Park. He brought some pastries and they sat on a bench. Nearby two conga drum players practiced and played off each other, their deep thumps casually reverberating off the stone walls of the surrounding colonial buildings. In a sense, it felt like another version of the amphitheater where Sonia and Sloan had roamed and scouted and discussed *Larimore*.

But now they journeyed into the past, into the telling of a different story and into the current events that reanimated it. The past story itself took place in the future, in a sociological regression, in an inversion of the present set in the same geographical region they now occupied.

"Someone has been reminding me," Sloan said, "of my previous film down here."

"Nico was on it too," Sonia said.

"Yes he was," Sloan said. "But if anyone has reminded him, he hasn't mentioned it."

"Why are they reminding you?" she said.

"There was an accident," he said. "Someone got hurt. Badly. Our department was blamed because we left the set unattended when a security guard failed to show up."

"What happened?" she said.

"A local guy climbed a bamboo tower after dark and it collapsed. Apparently he was drunk. I came back with a new guard and the injured guy's friend was putting him into a car to go to the hospital."

"What happened to the guy?"

"He went into a coma. Head injury."

"Oh my God," she said.

"His sister came back with two friends the next night and they overpowered the guard and burned the tower down."

"Holy Mother Mary," she said.

"That's not all," Sloan said. "As the tower was burning, the guard went to his car and got a gun and started shooting. The vandals were running to where they'd left their car and one of the guys was hit in the ass."

"Wow," she said. "Some of our guards think they're

cowboys."

"No charges were filed by our side," he said. "The family sued the production company and then settled for a large sum of money."

"What happened to the guy who fell?" she said.

"I don't know," Sloan said. "His name was Pablo Cruz."

He told her about the note and texts he'd gotten in Nassau, about his speaking engagement and the accusation delivered by a stranger named Henrietta Higgs. He confessed that he'd gotten similar texts recently. He also mentioned a curious thing about *Tropical Cavalcade.*

"There were dog tags belonging to someone named Pablo Cruz," he said, "but no actual character in the film had that name."

"You mean like a military necklace?" she said. "Why would they leave that name in the movie after what happened?"

"I don't know," he said. "Maybe some kind of bizarre tribute."

"What about the tower?" she said.

"It had to be rebuilt," he said. "Another strange thing about the movie is that the tower in the story collapses and a character dies."

"Wow," she said. "I can't believe that part wasn't rewritten."

"Now it's part of the movie's lore," he said. "It's a weird show but some people love it."

"I don't know why I never saw it," she said.

"The press came down on us like we were the dangerous foreign invaders of old," he said. "The Film Office defended us, and themselves, by saying the injured man was a trespasser and people needed to take responsibility for their own actions. But we were poisoned by then and the box office was bad. Somehow the movie hung on by word of mouth and eventually became a cult favorite."

"I remember some people talking about it," she said. "The controversy. But I wasn't interested back then."

"I have a written description of the story, the setup," he said, "minus the conclusion."

She looked at him, thinking over what he'd said. "What about these threats?"

He looked at the drummers packing up their instruments. The dappled shade rippling over the weathered park stones. The pedestrians and pigeons and passing motorbikes. Normal life. With their unusual work functioning within it. A part of it.

"It looks like harassment," he said. "Mind games."

"Someone followed me home," she said. "Because they saw us together somewhere. Because you're being watched."

"I suppose so," he said, gazing around, wondering if they were being watched now.

"But who?" she said. "The angry sister?"

He shrugged. "Maybe. You can make enemies just doing your job. Sorry to drag you into it."

"You're not dragging me somewhere I don't want to go."

"On top of the increasing job stress," he said, "we have to add this."

"You need to keep me distracted," she said, her mouth curling into a tight smile.

He laughed. "Here's something for that," he said, and handed her several pages.

Tropical Cavalcade
Many years after the pestilence a ragtag tribe of scavengers survives in the wild interior of the island of Hispaniola. They call themselves the *Fortunados* and roam from their settlement on salvaging expeditions, traveling by horseback but avoiding the sea since it is believed to be

the source of the past calamity and of current but unknown dangers. Most have seen its color from mountains and hilltops. There is a common belief that the ocean has been eating the land and will one day devour all of it.

In a guarded pen near the river, the *Fortunados* raise capybaras for their meat and hides. The animals gorge themselves on the carambolas that grow nearby. These and other animals that were released from zoo parks are now wild natives. The *Fortunados* also grow papayas, yams, and yucca, collect wild fruit and spear fish in the river. They construct palm-wood huts with roofs of thatch lashed with vine. They use hammocks and palm-log stools and make fire with flint and steel. They have buckets and clothes scavenged from former sites of civilization or bartered from the trader caravans routinely encountered. These traders tell of other tribes far away.

On their journeys the hunting parties salvage talismanic trinkets and metal tools from the ruins of villages. They burn the dried dung of their horses for cooking fuel. These droppings are collected and transported in the *bizkit kart,* which is last in line and driven by a young man called *Rady Bumo*. The men hunt wild chickens and other birds with the use of bolas and the success rate is approximately 30 percent. They salvage canned foods which no longer have labels. Cans are carried in the *larder kart* and every opening is a surprise. They learned fairly quickly not to eat anything from rusty or swollen cans.

During a scavenging trip a teenage boy called *Alix Jama* disappears overnight. In the morning the hunting party rides off in search of him. His corpse is found before dark, most of its flesh sliced away in strips. Seashells are discovered scattered about the area and *Eco Dermin*, their self-proclaimed *syintis*, deduces that a tribe from the coast has attacked them and is a danger to be confronted. They return to their home with the remains of the boy wrapped in grass matting and call a *Primero* meeting. *Eco Dermin* proposes that they journey to the sea and face their adversaries, whoever they are. Otherwise, he argues, they will be preyed upon again. *Lucy Tiga*, the *prieztez*, agrees with him. The elders argue about the unknown dangers and finally decide to conduct a special ceremony to fortify themselves against the nameless enemy. And to loosen up in the face of adversity.

Dressed in cargo shorts, hides, and guayaberas, the participants drink fermented fruit juice, dance, sing, play bamboo flutes, and cough around a smoky fire. Elders, children and nursemaids sit together to watch and clap. In the morning there is much confusion and vomiting before the start of construction on the *inspyr* tower.

Long wobbly bamboo poles are lashed together by hungover workers and dirt is hauled up a skinny ladder to create the *cielopiso*, the skyfloor, on the platform above. A young couple is selected by *Lucy Tiga* to fornicate on the skyfloor while the tribe below dances and chants to the spirit *Douz Abuv* for eternal unity.

The tower collapses and the falling female fornicator, *Dani Jama*, sister of the flayed teenager, leaps to one of the piles of grass arranged beforehand. The male fornicator, *Chas Duns*, normally one of the capybara guards, misses the grass and is killed on impact. *Dani Jama* is a favored ceremonial fornicator because of her curvaceous dimensions, outsize personality, and wild enthusiasm for the role.

The bodies of *Alix Jama* and *Chas Duns* are taken to a hilltop pyre some two kilometers away and burned in the daylight as a small crowd sings to their souls rising with the smoke.

Because of her bravery through grief, her desire to avenge her brother, and her evident survival skills, *Dani Jama* is asked to join the scouting expedition being organized.

An expedition of forty-one individuals, thirty-four men and seven women, about a fifth of the tribe, leaves the next day, heading north toward the sea to gather more facts, which they call *intelgens*. At night, while most of the group settles down on palm-frond mats under log-and-frond shelters, the defense planners, *Temper Sy* and *Bravo Zulu*, discuss ideas for new weapons and battle strategy, suspecting they are headed into a trap. *Wana Visper*, the animal manager, feeds the horses and comforts them. She is loved by the entire tribe and the horses.

Accidents and hardships are classified as *hapenstans*. Feral dogs are a constant worry and there is a mortal fear of larger animals such as inbred hyenas and lions, descendants of escapees from the personal collection of a mythical figure known as *El Drog Lard*. In recent memory the *Fortunados* have interacted with small nomadic bands and heard tales of distant tribes. None have constituted an actual threat until now but many in the tribe have expected this day to come.

After several days the group arrives at the ruins of the village called *Hatorey* where they meet *Hal Skarpo*, a known traveling man who relates the latest tales of *León*, a fabled male lion who terrorizes the region. In the hills there are many wild cattle but the lion has apparently developed a taste for horses and those who travel with them. *Hal Skarpo* wears seashell earrings and has a dog tag necklace around his neck stamped with the faintly legible name *Pablo Cruz*. *Eco Dermin* interrogates him about the source of the shells, and especially the necklace, which belonged to the murdered *Alix Jama*. *Hal Skarpo* says he got them from another trader who was traveling south three days ago. He presents the necklace to *Eco Dermin* and says the other trader made a point of saying he got the necklace from a man named *Glans Koan* who always wears a large hat like a ruler. *Eco Dermin* writes the name and description in his notebook. He is one of only two notetakers in the tribe. The other one is his apprentice *Flaco Teak*, who remains back at the settlement.

The expedition party camps out near a giant metal crown on the broken overgrown surface of a former park with fires burning at four corners. In the past the park has been cleared of brush for trading fairs. Tonight there is a communal supper that includes *Hal Skarpo*. The fires are manned by sentries with whistles and kept burning through the night. *Wana Visper* is smitten by *Hal Skarpo's* donkey *Zola*.

All the old *mashets* are sharpened. A new homemade weapon, the *cantop mashet*—overlapping sharp round food can lids nailed between the two halves of a split stick—is devised for combat.

The *blaksmit Yany Mendez* strings flat metal washers onto palm-fiber loops to be swung at close range or thrown. He sharpens all the knives, axes, and spears.

Eco Dermin draws a picture of a man with a tall hat and shows it to all the others, informing them that this man is the priority target for destruction.

The *dokter Digo Bok* prepares poultices of folded leaf with mashed seeds and herbs. He has his tools for pulling teeth and stitching wounds.

By firelight *Eco Dermin* studies two of his old drawings, one a crude representation of the estimated regional geography and the other a basic representation of a boat. He carries a rawhide tube with quill pens, old paper salvaged from a bunker, and a small jar of pigment made from palm kernel oil and ash.

In the morning a line of horses and riders and rattling carts leaves the ruins and meanders through the countryside, up and over hills, their colorful garments and jewelry and weapons glinting like decorative warnings in the morning sun. Insects swarm around the procession and beyond its attendant noise are the movements of monkeys, raccoons, parrots, crows, hawks, vultures, rats, and reptiles. There are no more amphibians navigating the riverine moisture, no more bats hanging in the shadows of cliffs or caves.

Even many miles inland, the tribe feels some collective stirring in their brains, some hereditary memories being activated by ocean breezes and the boisterous cries of seabirds they cannot yet physically sense.

22. Drunken Lowbar

According to Gene Friedman—who asked Nico what they had done to the designer, as he was apparently still inflamed in both body and mind—Larue liked the second waterfall, Socoa. Beyond that he was noncommittal.

"He seems like he's on the wrong movie," Nico said.

"Just keep everything alive," Friedman said. "The foundation is rumbling. The walls are shaking. Cragmore wants more action. A lot more."

"What does that mean?"

"It means rewrites are underway. Goddamn, you couldn't even show the man a shantytown?"

"We explained the sugar problem," Nico said.

"Listen to me, Nico. You fuckers have got to crack that wide open."

"And we will," Nico said.

The word went down. Cane. Then more words: mansion, village, apartment, club.

More of everything. Pull out all the stops. Translate that for Sonia and Wilson. We get it, they indicated. Is there anything we can relax about? The resort. Maybe. The waterfall. Maybe.

Where to build the batey? A place of bruises under a bruised sky. A leaking barge in a dusty green sea. The next group scout might require a test burn. Black snow.

"The horror," Sloan said. "The horror."

Nico knew the movie reference well but didn't add anything. Fragmentation was setting in. Discordance was right around the corner, a lurking beast of recriminations and betrayal.

Sonia came through with a pile of potent weed, the cost split by Nico and Sloan. Good news to calm the imbalance.

They had a departmental dinner of solidarity and realignment, a vocalized mission reboot, along with drinks for those who drank. Nico gave a short speech and picked up the food tab on company money, then ordered another round. Wilson drank club soda and acted as buzzed as he could. They broke up in a favorable mood.

After dark Sloan took a solitary walk through the Zone and smoked half a joint, trailing streetlight vapor wisps and the skunk of cannabis. Zoned in the zone.

He breathed deeply and exhaled slowly, trying to banish the spiked tangents of work dread, tunnels into worry. His destination was harmony. Barring that, he'd settle for enduring physical and mental health.

Everything was unfamiliar. Except for those other occasional occasions. He looked up to see a doorway, a distressed yellow wall, a gray cat. Hey buddy. What is that noise? Oh, the unearthly groove of the house band. Do not visit any viable location while highly stoned. He floated onward.

He walked near the black river. Neon squiggles. An effluviant reek. Oil sheen. Bridges. A small sign above a black door. *La Boca del Gato Negro.* The Black Cat's Mouth. He went inside.

Quiet as a closed mouth. His eyes adjusted. All black, the walls, the floor, the bar. A faint halo of light behind the bar drew its borders, its form. A ghost at the bar caught his eye and drew him over. A white guy sat hunched forward, scribbling in the near dark, papers spread like pale reflectors before him, his empty glass a cry for help.

Sloan took a seat and ordered rum on the rocks. The other man glanced over, brushed his long hair aside, pushed his reading glasses up to the bridge of his nose with his middle finger, went back to his task.

Sloan drank, listened to the soothing scratch of the pen, which was suddenly subsumed into a house sound blossoming, as if only one more customer had been needed. Electronic music at the lowest volume he'd ever heard in a public place in this country. It was disorienting. He looked at the motionless bartender, who had almost vanished into the atmosphere.

The man with the disheveled pages stopped writing, rotated his glass, tapped it with his pen like a minimalist chime. "*Por favor, señor,*" he said.

The bartender refilled it, waited in place. The man gestured at Sloan and said, "You?"

It was rum and Sloan said, "*Porque no,*" and slid his glass forward.

The bartender poured.

The writer raised his glass. "To sanctuary," he said.

"Sanctuary," Sloan said. They drank. The bartender set a glass of ice on the bar.

"Barlow," the man said. "And you must be my temporary gringo ally."

"Sloan," Sloan said. "Is this the sort of dive Larimore would frequent?"

Barlow laughed. "Well, shit a brick. Goddamn

skulking location scout in the house."

"I couldn't resist the name," Sloan said.

"Nor could I," Barlow said. "I thought I'd be invisible in the black cat's mouth."

"You still are," Sloan said. "I don't purposely mingle with screenwriters. It just doesn't happen. Why aren't you doing this from your own home?"

Barlow made a solemn face. "It has been said that the writer needed to reimmerse himself in the local culture."

"Rumors are always afoot," Sloan said. "Even our lowly department, the only one yet in town, has heard about the director's dissatisfaction."

Barlow laughed again. "He has a mean streak," he said, tipping his head. "Fair warning."

"Well, c'mon man," Sloan said. "It's not easy to recapture your former glory."

"Or approach your former mediocre pinnacle," Barlow said.

Sloan laughed, drank, took a leap. "I heard he gave you a nickname," he said.

The other man chuckled, rattled his ice. "Good thing screenwriters are not allowed a shred of self-respect." He looked over at Sloan.

"Anything for humor," Sloan said, feeling the knife's edge, feeling carefree and unstable.

"He is actually pretty funny," Barlow said. "But too often in the service of malice." He motioned to the silent background bartender.

"I will follow that up with your new name," Sloan said. "And then the next round is mine."

"Cool," Barlow said. "I'll refrain from steeling myself against any startling originality."

"Drunken Lowbar," Sloan said, laughing because of the telling itself.

"Ah Christ, really?" Barlow said. "What about Drunken Barstool?"

Sloan looked surprised. "He used that one too. You heard it."

"Those are so fucking old," Barlow said. "The guy is simply a middling rehasher."

Sloan laughed with relief and comradery. And bowed to the pouring bartender.

"Here's to great writing," Sloan said, lifting his glass.

"Amen to that," Barlow said. "And here's to screenwriting."

This made Sloan laugh. "Alright," he said. "I hope the sugar's been replaced by bananas."

"There's a new dramatic scene," Barlow said. "Rotten fruit fight on Plantain Ridge."

"It's all fun and games," Sloan said, "until someone gets pulp in their eye."

Barlow drank, looked around the dark room, pushed his glasses up. "To address your departmental concerns," he said, "the script is a work in progress. There'll be more action but not many more locations. And then of course the committee will weigh in for more changes."

"What torture," Sloan said.

"Nothing serious. It's just my bread and butter," Barlow said. "Nothing but a blueprint for someone else."

"Nothing personal," Sloan said.

"Nothing fucking personal," Barlow said.

"How can you write in such darkness?"

Barlow smiled. "After a while, every word is clear."

"Ahhh," Sloan said. "The philosophy of writing according to Barstool."

Barlow laughed. "Is this your first in-country mission?"

"No," Sloan said. "I was here on another picture some years ago."

"No shit," Barlow said. "Which one?"

"*Tropical Cavalcade.*"

"Get the fuck out," Barlow said, turning to face his gringo ally. "I enjoyed that gritty tale. And that last shot—man, woman, and horse on the beach. Beautiful nod to *Planet of the Apes*, man. Just missing the statue in the sand."

Sloan smiled. "It made a few fans."

"Sure it did," Barlow said. "Despite the trouble and notoriety."

"A bad-luck night," Sloan said. "Straight out of the script."

"Construction builds a trap," Barlow said, "and you let some civilian dipshit walk into it."

"That could've been the pitch," Sloan said. "The story within the story."

"Life imitating art," Barlow said. "Because we're in the cliché business."

"Speaking of imitating life," Sloan said, "do you know Dulce Medina?"

Barlow turned slowly and looked at Sloan over his glasses. "Sounds familiar," he said.

"I only ask," Sloan said, "because she reminds me of Gina La Vega."

Barlow closed his eyes and nodded as if in remembrance. "Is she a super-hot Latina mom draped in casual luxury who is knowledgeable about the dirty workings of the sugar business?"

"So, she actually talked to you," Sloan said.

"If she's your contact," Barlow said, "you should be careful."

Sloan set his glass on the bar. "Why do you say that?"

Barlow tilted his glass up and finished its contents. "I spoke to her on the phone and she agreed to meet me in a park in San Pedro," he said. "She was an hour late but we talked on a bench—she professed an interest in labor reform—and after I left, two well-dressed dudes in a Volvo pulled me over and took my notebook and phone at gunpoint. It was an episode of mixed messages."

"That's fucked up," Sloan said. "When she spoke to me, she did not mention you."

The bartender appeared and silently fulfilled his duty. The door opened and a pale orange rectangle of reflected river light flashed on the wall like a warning as a group of three entered the dark room. Barlow and Sloan glanced over at them as they took a table.

"I didn't mention the strongarm to anyone on the show," Barlow said. "I went home and worked on the script."

"Her brother Frank could have been behind that," Sloan said.

"The Volvo dudes were not especially chatty about their orders."

"At least they didn't kill you," Sloan said, and both men laughed.

"It's just a movie," Barlow said. "It's just entertainment. That's the goal, anyway. The names have been changed to protect the guilty. I'm actually surprised it's being made at all."

"It could be funnier," Sloan said. "I mean Ramon's pretty funny, a comical badass. And Larimore has some good lines. He's unflappable."

"He'd rather be a prosateur," Barlow said. "He'd rather write a novel than the hit pieces he does. He wanders through life as a circumstantial hero when he prefers solitude. Beneath his mask he has a bad case of apanthropy."

Along with the rum, the low hum and thump of the music enveloped them and they drank quietly in the shroud of darkness. They seemed to exist in some portal of unreality far removed from the movie. Characters in an unwritten fiction who should never have met. Sloan could smell the tang of the unfinished joint in his shirt pocket.

"Are you carrying weed?" Barlow said, sniffing in the other man's direction.

"I was just wondering if it started smoldering," Sloan said.

"Let's shoot some tequila and go burn that shit," Barlow said.

He requested several bottles to peruse in the poor light, made his selection and had their main man Felix set up a line of shots. No lime, no salt, just down the hatch. It was smooth enough to sip but they were in the throes of akrasia, intent on wayless escape and wreckage.

Outside, they stood at an iron railing facing the river. Across the water a freighter sat high-stacked with metal boxes, a geometrical vision of trading. The water's surface rippled and undulated like a sheet of polyurethane in a breeze, the reflections of random lights glinting in oily iridescence. They wove along a concrete pathway, passing the joint between them as the distant bridge floated in and out of focus.

Duncan Barlow had grown up in a military family, his father an Air Force pilot. He'd lived in Germany as a highschooler and after graduation spent some time based in Berlin while backpacking around Europe. Back in the States he attended the University of California, Berkeley, and then lived in Oakland and Eureka before migrating south to Los Angeles. Once he had some screenwriting success he moved down to Encinitas, where he could easily commute to meetings in LA when necessary.

"Before I get too jaded," Barlow said, "I need to break free of the mediocrity I dwell within."

Sloan smiled at the river. "We're working," he said. "Every project can't be *Chinatown* or *Unforgiven* or *A Clockwork Orange*."

Barlow reached up and waved his hand in the

riverine air, open to catching a star. "Look at *The Wages of Fear*," he said. "Not genius but fucking brilliant all the same."

"If we're going French," Sloan said, "I'll take *The Rules of the Game* for genius."

"And trashed when it first came out," Barlow said. "Just like *TropCav*. Cult status ain't bad. I'm not comparing the two, but all that carnage at the end, a bloodbath of hope. Aside from the amazing fact that you nearly had zero interior locations. Impressive."

"Notoriety helps," Sloan said.

"What will become of *Larimore*?" Barlow said.

"We never know what we're working on," Sloan said. "Too much distance between start and finish. The end product."

Barlow halted and looked at Sloan. "You can't smell any rot? No stench this soon?"

A bubble of silence contained them for a long minute. "It's an okay project," Sloan said. "I like the final scene, the silence, not knowing what he'll do, his resignation to a world of injustice."

"He's going home to write a novel," Barlow said. "Alone."

"He could be your stand-in," Sloan said.

"He could be," Barlow said. "But the mesmerizing movie world sucks us in."

Sloan put his hands on the railing and leaned over like he might vomit. "Woe is us," he said. "The hardship, the changes, the stress, the rancid intestines of glamour. The horror."

Barlow laughed. Sloan laughed. They both leaned over and laughed and coughed until tears streamed from their blurred bloodshot eyes.

They wandered on and told stories. Barlow related his obsession, for a time, with an Olivetti typewriter, a Lettera 22, and how he'd used it for luck at the beginning. And how it had yielded, with his warped mind as a willing accomplice, a specimen so witheringly unworthy, so blisteringly bad, that he had burned the only copy in a stone firepit while he danced drunk and naked and shook a loaded speargun.

Sloan told of an early movie of his where the production company had filmed a series of all-nighters featuring gunfire in a neighborhood, and how an incensed resident had finally come out in confrontation and shined his flashlight into the camera's lens as a scene was underway. And how the off-duty police officers employed by the company had arrested the man because he would not heed their warnings to vacate the area. And how they said that was entertainment, folks. The show must go on.

When asked how he got into the business in the first place, he professed that he hadn't gone to film school at all, but had taken various liberal arts classes and finally gotten a degree in English with no thought toward a career, had knocked around on odd jobs and one day took a scouting assignment because his friend was unable to. Since word of mouth propelled additional work, it was slow going for a while, though natural enough. He found his instincts attuned to the work, to finding places, composing photographs, writing scouting proposals, learning on the fly, weathering slow times. And luck, don't forget the luck, the unexplainable. Pull over exhausted, eyes tired of endless scanning, mind at wit's end, then look up and see across the street the exact location being sought.

As they parted in the grainy depth of night, Barlow said, "You drive yourself to the luck."

Under a dead streetlight Sloan watched the other man moving away, a shape vanishing in the dark. "Go in the direction the car goes," he said.

"Better yet," Barlow said in a whispered shout, "get out of the car."

Sloan smiled to himself. "Got a schedule to keep,"

he said.

Barlow was a two-dimensional form, a voice. "*Solvitur ambulando*," he said. "It is solved by walking."

"So it is said," Sloan said. "And more applicable to writing than scouting."

Barlow lifted a hand high, maybe waved. "Keep yourself grounded, Mr Sloan."

He wasn't sure how he found the hotel. For a moment, as he entered his room, he thought Sonia was in his bed, sleeping, waiting. In the morning, he sat up puzzled, his head a pulsating shell of debris and misgivings. He thought he might have nodded off in the Black Cat's Mouth and dreamed the entire evening.

23. More Larimore

First things first. Dulce. Coffee. Dulce. He needed to reexamine his fake synopsis so she could give her brother Hector something in writing. He needed to state a satisfactory donation figure in writing. He needed to move the ball forward right now. Forget about Frank. He would try to make trouble but he wasn't the power broker in the family. He was the designated asshole.

Room service brought real coffee. He was making a list:

Follow up on mansions Dulce promised.
Have Sonia & Wilson push realtor & scout more.
Scout Black Cat for dive bar.
Get location contract from Friedman.
Meet with Dulce, move forward.
Press Beatriz for sugar option.

He called the Film Office, Beatriz answered, and he reminded her of his last visit.

"Of course," she said. "How is everything going?"

"Good," he said. "We had a very productive scout with our production designer."

"I'm so glad," she said.

"I wanted to mention that we're looking for a spot for you in the movie," he said.

"That would be so wonderful," she said.

"Maybe a club scene," he said. "You looked great in that red dress."

"Oh, you remember?" she said.

"How could I forget?" he said. "It's burned in my mind." He laughed.

She laughed too. "Well, whatever they need," she said. "Wherever you need me."

"Okay, great," he said. "And I still need your help."

"Yes?" she said.

"Yes, I still need another sugar option," he said. "We have something that might work, but I would love to have a small independent field as a backup. Something outside of Imperial."

"I understand," she said, "but I believe most of the small farms sell to Imperial."

"I would be grateful if you could send me a few names," he said. "Could you?"

"I could talk to Javier and get you something," she said.

"That would be great," he said. "I'll call you tomorrow or the day after."

"That would be fine," she said.

"Thank you," he said.

Next, he texted Dulce.

Good morning. I would like to meet at your earliest convenience to go over everything.

How about today or tomorrow morning?

She responded within minutes.

Let's meet for lunch today. I'll bring my boys. They're ready to work.

Sloan stood and paced the room, looked at his face

in the bathroom mirror. Behind his image he saw a mushroom cloud. Then an avalanche and then a tornado. He imagined himself hiring Snidely Whiplash and Wile E. Coyote.

He wrote back.

Great. Name the place and time.

And she replied.

The beach club at Casa de Campo. Good food and view. 1pm. My treat.

He said he would see her there.

He checked in with Nico, then with Wilson, then with Sonia. He asked Sonia what she was planning later.

"I was planning to visit my mom," she said. "Or I could try to get comfortable in your lap. On your lap. Which is correct?"

"Either one works," he said.

"English is tricky," she said. "So many similar variations."

"You should call your mom," he said, "and tell her you'll definitely see her tomorrow."

He showered, went downstairs for breakfast, then, in the business center, printed his Script Synopsis B.

The beach club looked out on a grid of bodies splayed slack and shiny upon lounges broiling between sand and sun. Placed sparingly, square umbrellas cast chunks of shade, and tall palms stood in stoic observation, gently waving their high fronds. Beyond them, the wide sparkling sea.

At a window table looking out on the busy deck, Dulce sat in a flowing tropical print dress as if hidden among leaves and flowers. She was flanked by her sons, who from across the room appeared perfectly normal. One wore a Metallica t-shirt, the other a green polo shirt, and both wore shorts and sandals. They looked alert and fraternal, not identical, with short black hair cut for speed and respectability.

She beamed as he approached, and over the table took his hand in both of hers, acting like an old friend heartened to see him still alive and well. Both boys stood as she introduced them. The Metallica fan was Steven, his golf-shirt brother was Diego, and they shook Sloan's hand in turn.

"You are so punctual," he said to Dulce.

She laughed. "My boys insist on being on time," she said.

They sat and a pitcher of water was refilled. When the waiter arrived, Dulce ordered iced tea and bread for the table. Diego looked around the room and fidgeted with his napkin and sniffed repeatedly as if he were expecting his coke dealer to show up. Steven stared at Sloan with a slight smirk that seemed to signal that he was ready for an interrogation.

"I appreciate your interest in our movie," Sloan said. "And I hope we can all work together productively." Both boys nodded as if they understood what he was saying and Sloan wondered if they had been told to listen and wait for a direct question.

"Let me start by saying," Sloan said, "that I can only offer you an intern position. That means you don't get paid but you learn things you can't learn anywhere else."

He looked from one to the other and waited. Diego's left leg vibrated, hopping up and down, his heel tapping the floor. Steven gave Sloan a thumbs-up.

"I'll ask each of you," Sloan said. The waiter showed up. Dulce ordered a salad, the boys got burgers, and Sloan asked for a fish sandwich.

"Why do you want to work on this movie?" Sloan said. He looked pointedly at Diego.

The boy pressed his hand down on his active knee and rubbed his chin philosophically. "I'm a little nervous," he said, "because I love movies so much and I want to win this great opportunity."

Steven snickered and his mother's mouth formed a sympathetic frown.

"What about you?" Sloan asked the more relaxed brother.

Steven took a sip of his tea and then added a long streaming pour of sugar and stirred it thoroughly, clinking the spoon against the glass like a bell. He sampled the drink for taste and made satisfying smacks with his mouth. "I think," he said, looking Sloan in the eye, "that we should take what is offered."

Sloan smiled and looked at Dulce. "Well, that might be true in some cases," he said. "Probably not if it was your turn in Russian roulette. But it's good that you guys can present yourselves as deliberate thinkers. Here's the thing, though." He put his hands together as if in prayer. "Film is a fast-moving business and the faster you can react and respond, the better you look." He smiled at all of them. "I mean," he said, "assuming it's the correct response. No pressure." He laughed.

"So you need to be fast and correct," Dulce said.

"There you go," Sloan said. "Simple as that."

"We already have a dad," Steven said.

Sloan looked at the kid. "Can you break that down for me, Steven?"

"You're acting like our dad," Steven said.

"But what does that mean, you don't like getting any advice?"

Steven bit into his burger and spent some time chewing the mouthful, finally washing it down with his sweetened tea. "It means—let's get real, okay?—you need us on your team."

Sloan sat back and squinted involuntarily, mentally shaking his head. In one scenario he saw himself laughing and leaving. "Mr Vegas slaps his cards down," he said. "Boom."

Diego tossed his head back and laughed. "He's a

very headstrong young man," he said. When he leaned forward a drop of blood shot from his nose and made a red bullet hole on his napkin.

People at two other tables looked over as his mother fished ice out of the pitcher and wrapped it in her napkin. She handed it to her son and he leaned back and pressed it hard against the recalcitrant nostril. "He gets excited," she said.

Sloan looked out at the beach and thought about taking a long ride on a Jet Ski. With a little luck and some extra gas he might make it to the western shores of Puerto Rico.

When Steven began speaking again, Sloan devoted his energy to finishing his sandwich, occasionally glancing up and tilting his head as if he heard wind seeping in through the windows.

"We are locals," the kid said, "with local knowledge that could be very helpful to our film brothers." He laughed and continued, falling into a plausible Mexican accent, maybe trotting out a sample of the kind of help he could deliver to the crew. "All de foreigner need de goods and services," he said. "Someone got to deliver de big-butt chicas and de bad-boy stimulants, amigo."

"Oh Steven," his mother said. She shook her head and smiled as if he'd farted. "You're so terribly incorrigible."

Diego was laughing, his mouth open as he pressed the lumpy wet napkin to his face.

Sloan swallowed and took a sip of water. "No movie can survive without pimps and dealers," he said, "so if one person can wear both hats..." He raised his fists and extended all of his fingers at once to simulate dual explosions. "Bang!"

"Yeah," Steven said. "Someone got to entertain de troops, man."

"Humor is essential," Sloan said. "When you guys

are done maybe you could go out in the ocean..." He pointed. "Just out beyond that reef line. So your mother and I can talk. Sound good?"

Steven looked out at the water, then over at his brother, making a kind of impish face. "I guess we're about to get hired, bro." He pushed his chair back and stood and patted his mother's shoulder. "Put in a good word for us, Ma," he said. "We got to get off the farm someday."

When the boys had gone, Dulce looked across at Sloan and said, "You know what they say. Boys will definitely be boys."

"Especially one of them," Sloan said.

"Diego was born forty-six minutes later," she said. "He didn't want to come out."

Sloan nodded. "All natural then," he said.

"That's me," she said. "Earth mother. At least back then."

Sloan smiled. "I would have liked to see that."

"What, the births?"

He laughed. "Not especially. Just you in those days."

She pushed her hair behind an ear. "The wilder version," she said.

"Yeah, that one," he said. "Where'd she go?"

"Careful what you wish for," she said.

"I'm already doomed to perdition," he said.

She smiled, her dark eyes swimming. "I'll see you there."

He almost shook her hand on that, feeling slightly off-track, internally heated, externally agitated. Instead, he withdrew the synopsis and handed it across to her. "A brief for Hector," he said. "And also, can you get me a mansion while I'm over here? Like soon."

She put the paper in her purse and took out her phone. She scrolled for a minute, then stood as she placed the call and headed to the patio door. He watched her through the glass as she spoke, her body weaving back and forth in a dance, cobra-like, as she paced and turned at the railing, her dress clinging to hips and chest, a complete volume of Dominican contours, her dark hair hanging over her face as she looked down and laughed, the tip of her tongue touching her top lip. The mother of the devil, he thought. Succubus. Seductress. Temptation beyond all bounds.

The mansion was nearby and much better than the previous one. He spoke briefly on the phone with the homeowner, Mercy Ramirez, and she assured him the gate was open, he could explore the property's exterior for as long as he liked, and they could work out the terms later.

Deals were piling up like tokens without assigned value. He was playing poker with buttons and matchsticks. While receiving weekly funds from Far Cry Productions.

He'd disclosed so much to Sonia, took so much comfort in her company, wanted her skin against his, calming, distracting, soothing, containing him. He drove back wanting to disappear inside of her, knowing she would suffer on the show.

Nico wanted to have a budget meeting in the morning. They needed figures written on paper, entered into a spreadsheet. Smoke signals did not hold together. Numbers on cocktail napkins bled into distortion and forfeited conviction. Symbols in the sand were tracked out by jungle lizards.

At Sonia's he got drunk and stoned and made jokes out of his beach club meeting while they prepared a meal. It was impossible not to talk about the job until the wine was gone and he'd burrowed into her like a mole rat and the eruption of their physical entanglement cast him into unconsciousness.

In the morning he and Nico drank coffee and ate egg sandwiches as they inflated the unknown location fees beyond their best estimates. Sloan informed Nico of the imperative need to put on two summer interns but did not mention that Satan wore short pants and did something of a Cheech and Chong impression while aspiring to be a gangster.

"You seem distracted," Nico said.

"I was thinking about Beatriz," Sloan said. "I told her she could be an extra and she's supposed to come up with another sugar lead."

"I think we have to come up with a political path," Nico said. "We need someone connected to smooth the way into Imperial."

Sloan grimaced. "The thing is delicate," he said. "Trying to go around Dulce would fuck it up."

"I know you're in bed with her, so to speak," Nico said. "But we're getting boxed in. How much confidence do you have in her at this point?"

"She'll do it for her boys," Sloan said.

"What happens in the fall?" Nico said.

"They go away to boarding school," Sloan said. "In the States."

"Okay," Nico said. "So they've had their fun and now it comes time to shoot and what if she decides to back out then?"

"What if a fucking meteor lands on our heads?" Sloan said. "By then she will have signed a contract."

Nico smiled. "Okay, buddy boy, make it happen. And get something from Beatriz so we have a backup to show Napoleon. We will definitely need to scout two locations with Cragmore. There is no fucking way in hell he'll go for one."

Beatriz was out of the office. Sloan left a message and went out for a walk. He headed for the river and managed to find The Black Cat's Mouth. It was closed, not a daytime bar. He stood at the river for a few minutes and then continued his walk. Hazy burning sky, river's shimmering flow, working boats and stationary ships, the far bridge vibrating with vehicular movement, the road full of cars and *motoconchos*, the cheap motorbike taxi service loaded four or five passengers deep. The last in line, hanging off the back above the tire, seemed to hold on by will power. The air was full of exhaust and incessant horns.

It is solved by walking, he remembered.

His phone buzzed. Beatriz.

"I have an old cane farmer for you," she said. "He will talk to you face-to-face but he doesn't speak English."

"Great," Sloan said. "What's his name?"

"Gonzalez," she said.

"With a Z or an S?" he said.

"Z," she said. "They use S in Mexico, and other places."

"What's his first name?"

"I don't know," she said. "Just Gonzalez."

"Maybe it's Rapido," he said. "I'll call him Speedy." There was a pause. "You think he is fast?" she said.

"You're an angel," he said. "Text me the address."

"You will have my mobile," she said.

"I'll give it to Extras Casting when they arrive," he said. "Send a photo too, you in your red party dress."

"Okay," she said.

He called Wilson and instructed him to saddle up. Wilson asked if they would need horses or mules. Sloan explained what he meant and said they should meet in the lobby in thirty minutes.

They drove out north of La Romana and crisscrossed roads between fields and retraced their steps until it seemed the entire world was made of dirt and celadon stalks laid out in a dusty grid.

"Where the fuck is Gonzalez?" Sloan said.

Wilson the copilot read the address again.

"I know the fucking address," Sloan said. "But where is it?"

"If we had a megaphone," Wilson said, "we could drive around calling out his name."

Sloan looked at him. "Why don't you get on the roof and be the megaphone."

Wilson's mouth slid into a frown. "You will have to drive very slow," he said.

"Fuck, Wilson, I'm just kidding."

Up ahead in the road an old truck appeared like a mirage and came into indistinct focus as it got closer. A beat-up Ford the color of wheat and rust, listing to the side as if its payload were uncentered or its frame warped.

Both vehicles slowed and stopped so that their drivers were face-to-face, the old man in the tilted truck made to lean toward Sloan. His wrinkled brown face was weatherbeaten to the extent that he appeared to have used it to shield someone else in a sandstorm.

Studying the gringo's white face, he tipped his straw hat, dirt-stained and sweat-stiffened with decades of use, and peered around him at Wilson and spoke in Spanish. "I saw you drive by twice."

"We're looking for Gonzalez," Wilson said.

"I am Gonzalez," the old man said.

Sloan reached out the window and shook the old man's wiry hand. "I am Sloan," he said.

Wilson explained what they were doing and how they had come to him. Wilson said they would like to see his fields and discuss a rental offer.

Gonzalez did not understand what the Film Office was or why strangers would want his cane.

Sloan told Wilson to say that someone had

suggested him as a man who might be interested in working with a movie company in exchange for money he had not expected.

"Pesos from heaven," Sloan said.

Gonzalez looked at the gringo and asked if he was from Hollywood.

Wilson said Sloan was from Florida but represented Hollywood people.

Eventually Gonzalez was made to understand the basic tenets of their location offer.

They would survey his fields right now and take pictures. They would bring other people to look at his fields later. They would make an agreement that spelled out rental days and times of access and what they would do in the fields and how much money he would make. Plus, he could still harvest most of his fields after the movie company had gone. Some of the cane would be damaged during the course of filming.

Sloan looked at Gonzalez and said, "Twenty thousand dollars. Minimum."

Gonzalez looked at Wilson and the kid repeated the sum.

They followed the truck and circumnavigated his adjoining fields enough to understand their general configuration and size, then drove back to the farm's entrance and parked beside a corrugated tin shack.

Wilson stood discussing more details with Gonzalez while Sloan drove the perimeters and entered the fields at various points to photograph them. There were four distinct fields. When he returned, Gonzalez had made coffee in the shed, propping open the door and the single window with pieces of wood. They sat on homemade wooden stools, simple frames with slats on top, and Sloan showed the old man a few of the photos he'd taken.

When they were ready to go, Sloan asked if Gonzalez had any questions. The old man, who stood about five five, removed his hat and hung it on a nail. He pushed up his sleeves and rubbed his wiry limbs, then ran his hands through his thick gray hair and shuffled his feet as if trying to rub out millipedes.

"What is it?" Sloan said.

"*Una mujer grande*," he said.

Sloan looked at Wilson and upturned his hands for more information.

Wilson said, "A big woman."

Sloan smiled. "I know what the words mean," he said. "What's the question?"

The old man looked at them both and leaned forward and whispered to Wilson.

"He wants a big woman," Wilson said.

Sloan looked through the door to see if one might be walking by, if some big roaming rural woman had somehow caught the eye of Gonzalez.

"When?" Sloan said.

Wilson conferred with the old man, then said, "For during all the time we are working here."

Sloan looked at the old man, whose eyes were averted. "Let me get this straight," he said. "In addition to the location fee, Mr Gonzalez wants to be supplied with a large woman who is amenable to his desires for the whole time that we are working here. Anything else?"

Wilson translated the deal to Gonzalez and the old man added a few more conditions.

"Not young, not old," Wilson said, "with a big ass and big ... uh ... *tetas*." He cupped his hands a foot out in front of his chest.

Sloan started laughing. "Well, fuck yeah, we want our man to be happy."

"He wants a city girl," Wilson said.

"Naturally, a woman of culture," Sloan said. "Maybe a playwright, a cabaret singer, or a curator. And will this helpful hungry guest reside at his house?"

Wilson spoke with the old man and said, "Yes. His wife died two years ago."

Sloan put his hand on the old man's shoulder and shook it gently. "Sorry, my friend," he said, and the old man looked at him, his eyes moist.

They all stood silently, unmoving for a few respectful moments, then Sloan said, "We need his phone number."

Wilson pointed to the corner work table. A battered flip phone lay like a stone among various tools and cups. Sloan picked it up. It was dead. He found the charger and plugged it in and waited until the light came on. He looked at Gonzalez and made the universal phone sign with his hand, holding it to his ear. "*Importante*," he said, and the old man nodded. Sloan flipped the phone open and retrieved the number and then called himself and Wilson.

He thanked Gonzalez and shook his hand and he and Wilson stepped out into the blazing heat, got into the rental, and drove away.

Once they were rolling, Wilson said, "Where will you find a large woman to rent?"

Staring at the road ahead, Sloan said, "Do you have any big older sisters?"

Wilson started to laugh, then stopped. "That's a joke, right boss?"

Sloan glanced over and shrugged. "You know the departmental motto," he said.

Wilson nodded solemnly. "Whatever it takes to lock the location," he said.

"Within reason," Sloan said. "And reason is as wide as the Mississippi."

Late that afternoon they visited the Black Cat's Mouth and found a cleaning crew and a manager who didn't see any problem with filming, especially during the daytime. When the door was closed, the place seemed to be located in a land of eternal night. Wilson held the door open to throw a shaft of light into the main room, and Sloan took long exposures using a stool as a tripod. It was essentially a black box theater, a stage for small anonymous acts. The house lights were put on for additional reference shots, and the cleaners continued. There was a smell of lilac and booze.

As Sloan entered the hotel the desk clerk called his name and waved him over.

"A letter for you," the clerk said, and handed Sloan an envelope.

The front was blank and Sloan used his pen to tear the envelope open along the top. He pulled out a folded piece of newspaper, a cutout piece of the *Caribe Daily*, dated three days prior. He unfolded it and saw an article outlined in red ink.

Dominican Veteran Injured on American Movie Dies Eight Years Later

Sloan looked up to see the clerk looking at him. He folded the page and put it in the envelope. "Was it delivered to you?" he said. "Was there a message with it?"

"I was here," the clerk said. "No message."

"What did the messenger look like? Was he local, foreign—?"

"It was a woman," the clerk said. "A local."

"Can you describe her, please?"

The clerk shrugged, frowned at the desk. "Normal," he said. "Short dark hair." He touched his cheek. "A pretty face."

"How old?" Sloan said.

The clerk lifted his shoulders, looked pained. "Thirty-five?" he said.

"Was she dark, light, medium?" Sloan said.

"Medium," the clerk said, wobbling his hand.

"More or less."

"Thank you," Sloan said.

He got some ice and poured a drink in his room and sat down to read.

Pablo Mateo Cruz, a military veteran and carpenter from San Pedro de Macorís, died yesterday after a long period of suffering. Eight years ago he was injured on the set of an American movie being filmed entirely in the Dominican Republic. At the time he was looking for work and visited the set of the movie. Unfortunately, the set was unsafe and he suffered a head injury that put him in a coma for several months. He was left with substantial brain damage and was unable to work again. This caring young man who had grown up playing baseball and dreaming of business success in his home country had to be cared for by his family and was never able to reach his potential. The cause of death was blunt trauma caused by a fall. The family asks for privacy and prayers for Mr Cruz, who is finally at peace.

At the bottom of the page a single word had been scrawled in red ink. *Consecuencias.*

Consequences. The block letters were childlike and unevenly spaced, as if written left-handed by a right-handed person or vice versa.

Sloan read the obit again, then put the letter away and poured another drink.

A list of new locations was sent by Gene Friedman to Nico and Sloan, who reviewed them at lunch.

Int Airport – Larimore walks through crowd in terminal, notes man following

Int Airport storage – Larimore checks bags

Ext Airport – Larimore exits terminal, gets in taxi

Int Taxi – running shots from airport to rural road

Rural Road – car pursues taxi and runs it off the road, causing it to flip over in a field

Rural Field – armed men converge on taxi, driver is shot as Larimore runs for trees

Edge of Jungle – Larimore escapes into trees as bullets rip through leaves

Jungle – Three armed men enter jungle, Larimore drops from a tree, takes them out by hand

Jungle clearing – radio crackle heard as transmission comes in, armed men get in truck

*Additional Waterfall scene – Larimore seen bleeding from shoulder

Int Batey – Larimore feverish as wound cleaned and stitched by Madame Chery

Ext Batey – brutal assault by Montero, doors kicked in, shacks torched when Larimore not found

Batey montage – residents and Gina's people work together to rebuild houses and add clinic

"His heroics break me into a sweat," Sloan said, sprinkling seeds onto his salad.

"Positively galvanic," Nico said.

"A cryptogenic power source," Sloan said.

"He's wearing colorful tights under his trousers," Nico said.

"Hauling balls bigger than Paul Bunyon's head," Sloan said.

Nico poured himself more iced tea. "Could be worse," he said.

"Sure," Sloan said. "The screenwriter's been kind to us."

"Like anyone gives a flying fuck," Nico said, "about those of us on the ground."

24. The Convergence of Waves and Particles

Gene Friedman's email came in with the latest alarms. Sloan pictured him sitting at his computer, flecks of spittle sticking to the screen and spotting the nearest wall.

Jonathan Cragmore is heading down to scout in THREE days.

Dominic Larue will not be joining due to his DENGUE FEVER. WTF?

The Production Office should be up and running this week.

Cindy Bonnet, the POC, will arrive to assist with the scout.

Office will be set up at Ambassador Santo Domingo.

Your team will need to MOVE.

So there it was, Sloan thought. The Locations Department was being reigned in, made to move in alongside the whole gang, forced into teamsmanship. Phase 2 was kicking in. The initial freedom of scouting, creating your own schedule—unfettered by the proximity of overlords standing on your neck and second guessing your every action—choosing where to go and how to get there, being a savvy navigator of the open road... well, that vehicle was being motioned into the pitstop for a lookover, then into the garage where all the other rental cars parked.

These then were the last days of Phase 1, semi-autonomy, the location scout's innate sense of independence. It was time for full-on Location Management. No more outlier behavior, no more renegade identity. They would be called to task, forced into meetings and group expeditions. They would be coerced into assisting other departments with local knowledge and insider suggestions. They would be made to serve the herd. All for one, and one for all.

Except, nine times out of ten, that was bullshit. It was always every department for itself, every man for himself. Every woman too. Each department cared about the execution of its particular duties, exclusively. Everyone else could be hung out to dry, fail on their own terms, fuck up beyond all measure and create their own level of embarrassment. Every other department could step on their own dick, get their tits caught in a wringer, blame someone else, scream and melt down, fall on a sword, be sent home or into exile.

In a second, in one quick flicker of light, you could be kicked to the curb or thrown under the bus. Or under a train. In a flash, in a day, in a conversation, you could go from hero to goat. You could start crying or slug someone or embrace your inner druggie, quit the show and go into rehab. Once the machine was up and running, once the train of production had left the station, it was all about survival. Getting to the destination.

If everyone did their individual part perfectly, or close to it, and there were no natural disasters, the so-called acts of god, and no serious illnesses or injuries among the above-the-line honchos, no illegal acts resulting in the incarceration of actors, no local insurrections or coups, no major financial or schedule overruns, and if the shot footage looked good enough to match expectations, then hats off to you—a cog in the machine that kept it rolling forward.

Weather the storm, remain cool and professional, maintain your dignity, and do your fucking job, no matter what. Do not be the weak link. Do not let the production down. Make it to the wrap party and laugh the whole thing off. Stress? You've seen worse. This was a fucking walk in the park. Haha.

Except people didn't work in perfect harmony, and you couldn't expect the unexpected or anticipate accidents. And anyone could be replaced. Especially at the beginning.

Sloan answered Nico's call.

"Did you see Sussman's email?"

"Not yet," Sloan said.

"Open it," Nico said. "He sent it to Little Big Man and copied us."

David Sussman was the producer and had until this point been in the background getting the money together, figuring out personnel and budget and dealing with actors' agents. Producer stuff.

Sloan had just returned from an early walk. He toweled off his head and opened his email.

Gene, let's make sure Jonathan gets off to a good start with locations. He has high expectations even if he hasn't said much yet. He will. It's time to tighten this show up. Getting the gang under one roof will help. Call the rogues home. Send me the scout itinerary asap. David

"Call the rogues home?" Sloan said. "How fucked is that?"

"That's what you are, right?" Nico said.

"Well, yeah," Sloan said. "But no one says it to my face."

"The guy is sending us a power statement right off the bat," Nico said.

"If that's what he needs to do, great," Sloan said. "What are you hearing about Cragmore?"

"Not much, just that he's rough on Locations and the art department."

They both laughed.

"We have stunts, guns, and two fires," Nico said. "What could go wrong?"

There was a pause, then Sloan said, "It's the little things that sneak up on you."

"True enough," Nico said, "so let's tighten this fucker up."

"I'll amend our previous itinerary," Sloan said, "and we can fly it up the pole."

"Sounds good," Nico said. "Let's grab a little drink later."

Don't forget the twins, Sloan reminded himself. Where could he take them and suffer the least amount of damage? The resort? The park? Rural roads? Maybe he could send them with Wilson to explore village ideas. Would Satan and Diablo provoke villagers into forming an angry mob? He pictured people shouting and carrying torches, a scene from *Frankenstein*. And what would become of Wilson? Would he start cursing and drinking? Twitching, spitting and starting fires?

Thirty minutes later he was standing in front of Wilson in the meeting room on the second floor that they were using as an office. Sonia was out.

"First off," Sloan said, "we have to move out of here and into the Ambassador by next week. It sucks but we have no choice."

Wilson pointed vaguely to the west. "Over there on the Malecón," he said.

"Yes," Sloan said. "Out of the cool Colonial Zone and into the regular city chaos."

Wilson frowned empathetically.

"But right now," Sloan said, "I have an important,

delicate mission for you. High priority."

Wilson stood up at attention, looking as if he were ready to salute and have an attaché case cuffed to his wrist.

Sloan walked over to the wall where a map of the country, with an enlarged inset of the capital, was taped up. All of the scouted locations were marked by red pins. "Look at this," he said, and Wilson appeared at his side.

"I've hired two young recruits," Sloan said. "They're unofficial interns." He looked Wilson in the eye, holding his gaze to emphasize the importance of the classification. "That means they will help us in a minor capacity but will not get paid. They'll be off the record, so to speak."

Wilson slowly nodded, then looked at the map as if clues about spies were hidden there. "How will they help us?" he said.

Sloan said, "That's classified," and Wilson flinched.

"But since you're in this," Sloan said, "I'm telling you something in the strictest departmental confidence, something which cannot leave this room."

Wilson raised his right hand. Then Sloan raised his in counterpart, a silent pact reached.

"These boys are the sons of the Queen of Big Sugar."

Wilson let out a breath.

"Your mission," Sloan said, "is to pick up these boys in La Romana." He put his finger on the map. "And use their local knowledge of the area." He traced an arc along the coast. "Find some empty spot with an ocean view where a food truck can sit, or a pescado frito stand, probably more toward San Pedro than Punta Cana. This is where Larimore's backstabbing friend Graham Perry meets with Ramon. Understand?"

"Copy that, sir."

"And then, and this is super important," Sloan said. "Look for the border-crossing location, where the Haitian cane-cutter boys are picked up, not far away but not on the coast. Got it? So that these two locations could possibly work together on the same day."

"What does it look like?" Wilson said.

"In the script, it's nothing," Sloan said. "A van loading kids in the back. So we have to make it into something. There has to be a feeling of desolation, right? A place where nothing is going on, where this kind of activity could occur." He walked along the edge of the room and returned. "Maybe a little rise, a hill in the background, with a dirt road for the van." He put his hand on the kid's shoulder. "Pick a spot and stand there and shut out the noise in your mind and try to feel it. Turn yourself in a 360 and visualize the scene. Then shoot it, every angle."

Sloan went to the door and turned back. Wilson was watching him. "Get an image in your mind," Sloan said. "If we were actually shooting this scene at the border we might have an aerial view. Right? In some places you can see a stark indication of the border between the two countries. There's a line between brown and green. You can see the deforestation on one side, the brown, against the jungle on the other, the green. And even though we won't get anything that stark around here, you can use that concept as a blueprint, a way to think about the location. There's a line, or a river, some sort of border. Does that make sense?"

Wilson looked at the map and then leaned closer to it. "I think so," he said.

"You're a natural," Sloan said. "Get ready to go. I'll text you where to pick up the boys. Remember, you're the boss and they are there to observe and learn from you. Don't tell them anything except what you're there for, the mission you're on. Don't discuss the script. You're working together on these two locations. That's all."

"I got it, boss," the kid said.

"Call me if you have any questions or problems," Sloan said. "Good luck."

He called Sonia and put her on villages. They needed more options for the Village Road where Eddie on his moto evades Ramon in his Escalade. There was stunt driving, and a crash.

"Track down some ideas," he said, "that we can shoot tomorrow."

"Like the one we did before?" she said.

"Scratch that," he said. "Let's make a list of villages we can drive the director through. We're going to do some road scouting anyway."

"When is this?" she said.

"He'll arrive in three days. I'm working on the itinerary now."

"Do we need the mules again? she said.

"Unknown," he said. "Standby on that. But let's give Sanchez a heads-up just in case."

Nico was working on the airport. They would scout it regardless of whether or not they were cleared to shoot. Bureaucratic approvals could be long in coming.

During shooting, the eleventh-hour permission scenario was never healthy for the Locations personnel. You might experience heart palpitations, rapid shallow breathing, forehead sweating, a rash or hives, stomach cramps, colon spasms, dizziness, an overwhelming desire to nap, anything to escape the tension. Or your personality might split. You might sit humming and chewing gum while your phone rings. You might laugh like an asylum inmate. You might pretend to be someone waiting for a ride.

While in his room working on the itinerary, Sloan got a call from Nico.

"Amigo, we need to scout more bars," Nico said, with the smallest laugh attached.

"I'm making a list of deficiencies as we speak," Sloan said.

"I just got a call from Cindy Bonnet, the coordinator," Nico said. "She's asking about transportation for the scout, among other things."

"Okay," Sloan said. "What does she need?"

"She wants to know the status of the Ambassador," Nico said. "She arrives tomorrow and wants to make sure there are no issues."

"Like what, bedbugs?" Sloan said.

"She wants us to check it out," Nico said.

"And do what, roll around on some beds?" Sloan said.

"Can you send Sonia over to scope the place out?" Nico said. "We just need a current report."

"Yeah, sure," Sloan said. "She's just sitting around with her thumb up her ass."

"She can leave it in," Nico said, "as long as she puts eyes on the hotel."

"Of course," Sloan said. "We will grant the wishes of Ms Cindy Bonnet."

Nico laughed. "She will no doubt be calling you soon."

Ten minutes later Sloan was typing from his notes when his phone rang.

"Hey Luke. This is Cindy, the POC."

"Well hey there, Cindy," he said.

"I'll be down there tomorrow," she said, "and JC will follow two days later."

"Jesus Christ?" he said.

There was a slight delay. "Jonathan Cragmore, the

director," she said.

"Oh yes, of course," he said. "We are ramping up for the scout."

"Excellent," she said. "David wants this one to go flawlessly."

"Don't we all," Sloan said.

"I suppose we do," she said. "After Dominic's experience... I mean, the man's in bed."

"He did seem to have an unlucky visit," Sloan said.

"He sure did," she said. "He went out scouting and got dengue fever."

"Most people are not hit very hard," Sloan said. "And the odds of getting it are pretty slim."

"How can we minimize the odds?"

"By not getting bitten," he said. "Mosquito repellent, long sleeves."

"We will stock up then," she said. "And am I to understand we need horses?"

"We don't need them," Sloan said. "We got a mule for Dominic because his foot was injured."

"A mule?" she said.

"Yes, they are easier to find than camels or llamas."

"Okay, I assume that's true," she said. "I don't know very much about the country."

"You'll be up to speed in no time," he said. "Can you find out if JC wants a mule?"

"Certainly," she said. "I'll get back to you."

"Thanks," he said. "If you want, you can tell him that Nico and I walk."

"Okay, I will," she said. "Oh, how's the weather?"

"It's raining," he said. "We're in the rainy season."

Clear trails ran and wiggled down the long window surface, liquid invertebrates in waves of precipitation. Translucent vertical streams going nowhere except back to the earth to rise and run again. At the plane of glass the outer world rippled and divided into languid drops condensing and funneling the blue view into reflective fluid prisms. Cycles of life and futility.

Sloan stared into the image, the Caribbean Sea redrawn in sea slugs, versions of himself in elongated orbs, a distorted bed behind him, a drooping desk and lamp, blobs of bathroom sanctum. From the twelfth floor on the Ambassador Hotel's south side, the rain filled the distance and the future. He thought of the lyrics, *From here to Venezuela*. Then thought, from one job to another.

"Will this be fine, sir?"

Jolted out of his reverie, Sloan turned around to face the clerk. He glanced at the furnishings, the muted island photos hung on the walls, the nondescript carpet, the bedside phone, the television cabinet, the coffee maker and ice bucket. He walked to the bathroom and looked at the sink, the shower, the toilet, all there as promised by the standard hotel contract. He looked at the shower head, the unstained porcelain of the tub, the floor tiles, the towels, the mirror. He turned on the water at the sink and waited casually for any unseemly odor to rise. Lastly, he sat on the bed.

"This is fine," he said.

At the front desk he confirmed that long-term guests would be able to self-park and avoid the valet service delays.

He was tempted to call Wilson, make sure he was still alive. But he refrained.

Sonia was on villages and bars and clearing existing locations for the upcoming scout. Nico had an airport meeting.

Sloan worked on a list with a corresponding map of potential roads for driving shots.

Airport
Cane field road day & night

Dirt road with taxi & chase car
Rural, with moto/car chase/stunt into village
Int car, with Gina
Int car, with Ramon
Eddie & Penny on moto x2
Eddie on moto

He called their realtor and left a message. He wanted a mansion outside of Casa de Campo.

He texted Cindy Bonnet and told her the Ambassador checked out and they were expecting her tomorrow.

As a run-up to happy hour, Nico and Sloan took a walk and shared a joint, determined to enjoy the Colonial Zone for as long as possible. The avenues, the parks, the low-rise character, the history, the river, the stone.

Back at the bar, smiling wryly and wearing shades against the fading light of the day, they repeated to each other the words "act natural." And each removed their sunglasses.

"Everyone can see you're ripped, man," Sloan said.

"You're torn, shredded," Nico said. "Blasted out."

"These chairs are wet," Sloan said, lifting up to feel his damp back pocket.

They ordered mojitos and noted that they were the only outside customers, sweating in the glare of string lights. More rain was on the menu, seemingly imminent.

"You're not telling me something," Nico said, squinting down the promenade like he was trying to read a distant eye chart.

"I wasn't saying anything," Sloan said, following the other's squint down the street.

"I mean before," Nico said.

"Before what?"

"Before this conversation even started."

"I don't know where this is going," Sloan said.

"I don't want to be blind-sided," Nico said.

"You look blind right now," Sloan said. "Like a cave-dwelling salamander."

"You look like a secretive person," Nico said. "Keeping secrets."

"That sounds like anybody," Sloan said.

Nico took a huge swallow of his drink and said, "Tell me one thing you're holding."

Sloan drank and ran down the list of omissions in his mind.

Threatening messages related to *TropCav*. Fucking a departmental colleague. Pimping for Gonzalez. Delivering a fake synopsis. Unauthorized interaction with screenwriter. All potential boat-rockers.

"I can't think of anything," he said.

"Bullshit," Nico said.

"Wait, I just thought of something," Sloan said. "I sent Wilson on a secret mission."

Nico smiled. "I fucking knew it," he said. "What kind of mission?"

"Ostensibly looking for the roadside stand and the border crossing," Sloan said, "but mostly babysitting and mentoring Dulce Medina's twin sons."

Nico stared at Sloan while he combed his memory. "Are these the kids Javier warned us about? The spawn of Satan or something."

"Not spawn," Sloan said. "The actual demon."

"Like two actual Satans?" Nico said.

"They're just spoiled brats," Sloan said.

"What does Wilson think?" Nico said. "Is he back?"

Sloan suddenly felt sheepish. "He's probably driving back now," he said.

Nico dug his phone out and called Wilson's number. After a few moments he said, "He's not picking up." Then he left a message. "Wilson, check in asap." And ended the call.

He looked at Sloan. "What the fuck, man?" he said. "He always picks up."

Sloan shrugged. "My guess is he's standing by the road in his underwear while the boys take a joyride and make calls to the States with his phone." He got the waiter's attention and motioned for more drinks.

"What's going on with you?" Nico said. "You're like Jekyll and Hyde."

Sloan looked up at the dark sky and took a deep breath. "Just keeping the plates spinning, brother."

They switched to Brugal on the rocks, ditching the summer frills of sugar, lime, and mint. They waited silently for word from Wilson as revelers passed and the atmospheric moisture lowered like a suffocating velvet curtain.

"You're such a fucking knave," Nico finally said.

"That really stings coming from a lackwit like you," Sloan said.

His phone rang, he saw who it was and answered and put it on speaker. "Hey man, I'm here with Nico. Where are—" He was interrupted by Wilson's tumbling breath-filled words.

"Sorry, I lost my phone for... I hit a dog... oh man... the boys were..."

"Hey, Wilson. Slow down, man," Sloan said. "Slow down. Take a breath."

"Where are you Wilson?" Nico said.

There was a pause full of sharply drawn air. "I'm in my car driving," he said.

"Where are the boys?" Sloan said.

"They're at home." Wilson said. "I dropped them off." He sounded tearful.

"What happened? Sloan said.

"We were scouting—no, we were finished. It was getting late. They started fighting."

"Wilson!" Sloan said. "Slow down so we can understand you."

They waited while his breathing grew steadier.

"Okay," he said. He took a few breaths. "Steven called shotgun and was riding in front. After a while Diego said he wanted to switch but Steven ignored him. Diego flicked his ears and Steven turned around and tried to hit him and the next thing is Diego crawled over the seat and his legs were hitting my head and I was getting pushed and his legs hit the steering wheel and I hit a dog."

No one said anything for a moment. The waiter appeared. Sloan waved him away.

"Then what happened?" Sloan said.

"I stopped the car and went to see the dog."

"Was the dog hurt?" Sloan said.

"He was hurt," Wilson said, his voice rising. "He couldn't walk."

"Fuck," Sloan said. "Where is the dog now?"

"He's here in my car," Wilson said. "He has his eyes shut."

"Goddamn it," Nico said. "Is he bleeding?"

"I don't think so," Wilson said. "Where are you guys?"

"We're near the hotel," Sloan said. "Meet us there. Are the boys okay?"

"Yes, they stopped fighting."

"Hey Wilson," Nico said. "Stay calm and drive safely. We'll see you at the hotel."

"Okay boss," the kid said. "I'm sorry about this."

"Don't worry," Nico said. "Accidents happen."

Sloan ordered a rare hamburger and a bottle of water to go.

With the help of the hotel's desk clerk he located a veterinary clinic across the river that had a 24-hour emergency number.

The hotel was quiet by the time Wilson rolled up in his Corolla. Nico and Sloan were waiting outside and he parked in the street as they came over. The dog was a regular brown mid-sized mutt, short-haired, collarless, with floppy ears and wearing a sheepish face that made him look embarrassed about causing strangers this trouble. The dog lay on the passenger side floor and at first struggled to stand, as if sensing his ride was over. His back legs did not support him and he yelped and lay back down again, breathing heavily. They observed the animal for several minutes, talking quietly and exhibiting a relaxed demeanor.

Sloan slowly offered the back of his hand but the dog turned away. He opened the food box and took out the hamburger patty and held it near the dog and saw its nose quiver. He broke it apart and put a few pieces on the floor mat in reach of the dog's head.

The dog turned its jaws to the side and got a piece in its mouth and wolfed it down. He did the same with the other pieces and with the rest of the patty, the last of which he took from the man's hand. The man poured water into his palm and the dog lapped at it and turned its brown eyes up to the man's face.

The clinic looked like a neighborhood house but with large glass windows bordering a glass door. A light was on inside and the windows were illustrated with large cartoon drawings of a cat and a dog. The parking spaces were empty and the three of them waited in Wilson's car.

A minivan pulled up to the door and a man got out wearing sweatpants and sandals. He was young and had curly black hair and a beard. He took a look at the patient and introduced himself as Dr Sergio Ramos and unlocked the door. More lights came on.

He came out wearing gloves and carrying a blanket. He placed the blanket on the ground beside the open passenger door and they picked up the floor mat and transferred the dog to the blanket. He and Sloan carried the dog inside to a metal table in an exam room. He came back to the front desk and said he would give the dog a sedative and then proceed with X-rays in the morning when his staff was present. He suspected the dog was badly bruised or had a broken hip and maybe spinal damage. He asked for contact info for the dog's owner and a credit card and Sloan complied as he glanced around the front room. Most of it was a store, with an assortment of pet food and toys and collars and leashes and beds. He thanked the doctor for the late service.

Back at the hotel Nico and Sloan got out of Wilson's car and stood by the driver's window as heavy drops began to fall, spotting the pavement and plinking the surface of the car.

"Will you be able to take the dog to your place?" Sloan said.

Wilson shook his head. "My parents have a cat."

Sloan frowned. "Since you found him," he said, "you should name him."

Wilson closed his eyes, wrinkled his nose and looked exhausted.

"Not now," Sloan said. "In the morning."

The kid opened his eyes and placed his hands on the wheel. "Sorry guys," he said. "You're getting wet."

Nico reached in the car and slapped the kid's cheek playfully.

"Don't lose any sleep, kid," Nico said. "We're all in this together."

The rain was hammering on the metal awning as the colleagues entered the lobby. They stood dripping and looking at each other but didn't speak. Nico took the elevator and Sloan took the stairs.

25. The Director's Scout

The production office coordinator was thorough, if not possessed. Even her blonde curly hair was harried, the casual hand-twisted bun constantly coming undone—like her plans. She stood out among the hotel staff and guests as the only one scurrying about, and her falling hair revealed her state of mind. She needed a scrunchie and did not yet have a single underling to go find her one.

The check-in line had been long, the service slow, and her room unready. Her hair seemed as wet as a tropical storm. She saw nothing on the drive from the airport, the wipers on high and unable to stay ahead of the deluge and the taxi seemingly manned by someone auditioning for a stunt-driving position. The weather was an omen of noncooperation and doom.

She needed many rooms, but staggered, as crew members arrived. She needed a meeting room, a smaller one and then later a larger one. Was that so hard to understand? She needed her hair up and off her neck. Was it always this steamy? Was the AC on super high? Did they even have a MAX setting?

The suite reserved for the director was not grand enough. She asked the manager if he'd seen *Mindblown*. He confessed, regrettably, that he had not. Jonathan Cragmore was a VIP, she explained. A bigtime American movie director. The manager nodded sympathetically, as if she had expressed a desire for sheets of a higher thread count.

The man needed a rowing machine in his room. He needed the best ocean view, not a regular one. At least twelve stories up—or more. He liked to see the curvature of the earth when he rowed, as befitted his vision. Was there a penthouse available at a VIP rate? The manager glanced around for his assistant manager, Gloria, so he could sanctify her as his special envoy to handle the obsessive long-range demands of Cindy Bonnet.

Before the dog was released, before his true fate was even known, Wilson, when pressed by Sloan, declared the animal's name to be Pucho. Sloan turned the name over in his mind, rolled it off his tongue a few times, turned away from the phone and shouted the word as if the unfortunate doggie had run too close to the road again, and decided it sounded like a name that could get you into a fight.

"What if I started calling you Pucho?" he said to Wilson.

"That's okay, boss," he said.

"Have you considered Bruno, Benito, Pancho, or Rocco?" Sloan said.

"My mom named him," Wilson said. "I showed her a picture."

"Okay," Sloan said. "This is getting distracting. Let's focus."

He sent Wilson on another mission, back to get the boys with the admonition that they were on probation, that their enlistment in the department depended on the dog's full recovery. They were to accompany Wilson to Altos de Chavón, where he would create a detailed diagram of the amphitheater and adjacent fountain, paying particular attention to areas where the work trucks might park and be out of sight of the camera. The boys could also learn how to conduct a light study.

Also, Gonzalez was not picking up his phone so on the way to La Romana, Wilson should drop by the man's cane fields and locate him and correct the communication problem.

After the chat, Sloan made a note to buy a cheap backup phone for Gonzo, as he had begun to call him. And he had to figure out where to get him a hefty, cooperative woman. Would there be a tryout period? What if the old man rejected her for being only moderately large? Or, more likely, she would take one look at him and realize she needed to negotiate liquor into her deal. Just have faith, Sloan thought, money would smooth it over.

The itinerary passed muster after two revisions, Sussman weighing in to show his proficiency with control and leadership. The Locations Department was reminded to pack up their shit and decamp from the Zone.

After some deliberation it was decided that Nico would pick up Cragmore at the airport and drive him into town. But Cragmore shot this down. He wanted to drive himself in order to start getting the lay of the land. Cindy Bonnet wanted to provide a car and driver but Cragmore only wanted the car. Once the director took possession of the vehicle, the driver would be demoted to delivery man. To cover all options, Nico in his car would follow Sloan in the director's rental, they would meet Cragmore and be prepared either to leave together in Nico's car or drive the director if he changed his mind about self-driving.

The scouts were in the terminal ahead of the flight's arrival time and waited for Cragmore to come through customs. It was a chaotic scene with lots of people moving in all directions. There were loud conversations and shouting and loudspeaker announcements and the rattling wheels of luggage carts. The incessant blaring of car horns ran through the opening doors like the cries of wild animals.

He was easy to spot, a head taller than everyone around him, his large head like a crag itself, his long face an unshaven embankment, thick gray hair close-cropped in a random fashion, with spikes left standing as if a beaver had done the trimming. A military punk style. He wore aviator shades, a black t-shirt and faded camo pants and weathered boots. He looked like a mercenary who had long ago returned from an overseas conflict but maintained his readiness for another one.

"Locations," he said as they approached. He wore a backpack and carried a duffel slung over his shoulder.

"Fit for duty," Sloan said.

Cragmore shook their hands and said, "Gentlemen, let's scout some fucking locations."

Out in the terminal's stream of humanity, he dropped his bags and framed a long shot with his open hands formed into the rectangular facsimile of a camera's view. He began to walk backward with Nico and Sloan running interference, one on each side, to keep him from being jostled. This would be the first look at Larimore as he entered the country, striding into his mission. The camera would back up as the lens zoomed in to frame the solitary figure. As he filled the frame and passed, the camera would pick up the man following the main character.

Cragmore's appearance and actions made him

seem off-kilter and he was given a wide berth. Sloan ran back to retrieve the man's bags before they vanished. He stopped there and took a few photos of the scene, then hustled to catch up with the others.

In the luggage storage room, Cragmore walked around looking at different angles, like a contractor measuring by eye, then stepped behind the counter to see the point of view of the surprised counterman as he might gaze out through the glass into the maelstrom of terminal activity. Nico was hurriedly explaining the purpose of their visit, pointedly mentioning the name of an airport administrator he had met. As the clerk looked on and vaguely protested, Cragmore hand-framed his mental image of Larimore entering the room, with Sloan standing in to play the part of the actor. Then they were gone.

Outside, the director stood in the approach lane and diverted traffic with his imposing height and warzone energy. The increase in the decibel level could hardly be noticed. A frustrated taxi driver got out of his car and shouted "Go Back to Iraq," mistaking the director for an American combat veteran. Nico motioned for calm with his hands, pressing the humid air as drops began to fall. Sloan took photos and they moved toward the parking lot as the clouds opened.

It was quick, the run-and-gun approach. The director seemed confidant, completely sure of himself. Maybe he would shoot that way too, Sloan hoped. Rain or shine, don't fall behind.

Both cars sat on the side of the road a few hundred yards from the terminal as the rain poured upon them. Two food trucks stood like abandoned ghost ships and the sea beyond was a watercolor sketch in the gray air, the whole scene like an underdeveloped image.

In Nico's car, he and Cragmore discussed the

location. The director liked the proximity to the international airport, having the actors talk as planes landed and took off in the background. Nico called Sloan and he got out under an umbrella and struggled to keep his camera dry and find an angle that would encompass the trucks and the ocean and the flightpaths, slopping around in the mud as Cragmore motioned behind the condensation of the car's window like an apparition.

Despite the weather and the capital's afternoon traffic snarl, the director wanted to get familiar with the city and take a cursory look at parks and streets and the exteriors of the scouted bars. They stopped at the hotel only long enough to let Sloan ditch the extra vehicle.

Nico continued to drive so Cragmore could spend his time looking and Sloan could take reference photos on the fly. At certain points, dictated by vision or whim, the director donned a rain jacket and took off on foot into a park or a street. Sloan went with him and Nico followed as best he could with the car. This went on for hours, the director clearly energized and motivated. The car carried water, granola bars, and tangerines, and they made no stops for a meal or coffee or additional supplies, the director the only one of the three who declined sustenance and restroom breaks, prompting the other men to suspect that he possessed the water-conscious biology of a camel.

Thinking ahead, Nico and Sloan knew the itinerary was all but useless, another case of surplus planning and paper. The only time-dependent locations would be apartments, mansions, resorts, and the golf course. And the interiors of bars needed to be scouted during business hours. They would be scouting day and night for the next few days, winging it and changing direction often.

They took a short break for food—the scouts

washed cold chicken sandwiches down their throats with hot coffee as if an air-raid siren was going off— and to allow the director to check in and settle into his room. Nico and Sloan had checked in earlier and they utilized the downtime to plan the next day. Sloan checked in with Sonia and got the update on apartments. Cragmore wanted to scout sugar and waterfalls whenever the weather looked potentially clear so Sloan had asked for some leeway on apartments, if possible.

He did not want to show the best apartment first. Or mansion. Same with bars. Never show the best first. Then there's nowhere to go but down. Deliver it when the poorer choices failed to elicit the required excitement. Then strike the iron. Of course, that was assuming the scout's intuitive process was in line with the director's creative vision, not something that could ever be assumed.

Locations wanted to divide everything into four geographical categories. Easternmost locations in group one—resort, golf, mansion, amphitheater. Group two—cane field, roads, village, border crossing, roadside fish stand or food truck, office exterior. Group three—waterfall, jungle, more roads. Group four—city parks, streets, apartments. Bars were strictly nighttime.

Wilson checked in and said everything was okay. He was heading back. When Sloan asked him to be more specific he said the boys had disappeared for a long time while he was making his diagram but he hadn't panicked and they had returned with wet clothes and dirty skin.

"What do you think happened?" Sloan said.

"I think they climbed down to the river," Wilson said.

"Okay," Sloan said. "No harm done. They probably think they're at summer camp. What about Gonzo?"

"I didn't find him," Wilson said. "The shed was locked and he was not at his house."

"You tried calling him."

"Yes, his mailbox was full."

"Listen, we're about to scout some bars," Sloan said. "Are you past San Pedro yet?"

There was the slightest hesitation, then Wilson said, "No."

"Go back by his house," Sloan said. "If he's still not home, leave a note where he'll see it. Tell him we need to speak with him. Okay? You're the point man on this."

"Okay boss, I understand."

"If you don't hear from him, go back in the early morning on your way to La Romana. Find Mr Gonzalez and make him understand. Then put the boys on the light study we discussed. They have phones and can take a few pics. I want their mom to know they're doing something."

After seeing a couple of textbook tropical dive bars, Cragmore's unease oozed away in the dingy, smoky, languid atmosphere of the Black Cat's Mouth. He stretched out his long legs, one scuffed boot over the other, downed four strong Cuba Libres and finally exhaled. They called it a night.

In the clear light of morning on the open road amid the rows and rows of the tough green stalks of the sugar world, where raindrops full of sun hung sparkling at the tips of leaves as if camera magic lay within, Cragmore sought his dream and began to talk about flying above that farmland.

It sounded more like an aesthetic desire than a practical one. No helicopters or small planes had been mentioned previously. The scouts were trying to figure the man out and give the show what it and he needed to make it as good as possible. Sometimes it was best to make notes and wait for more clarity.

On the outskirts of Batey 108, they parked roadside and waded single file deep into the cane field thicket. The high wet plants, the humidity, the leaf edges slicing across bare skin, the mud sticking underfoot. The sizzle and hum of the tropical sky. They walked without talking, the scrape and rustle of stalks like a soundtrack for refugees. For convicts. For Viet Cong. For tigers.

At some point they stopped and stood there in the maze of silent green. Cragmore closed his eyes and absorbed everything he could.

At the car a philosophical discussion arose. Poverty. Haitian laborers. Unsanitary conditions. The immorality of indentured servitude. Modern slavery. Corporate cover-up. How much of that fit into the story they were telling? In the vast territory of cane lay the hidden stories, the true stories. Where did those overlap with a make-believe story? What kind of film were they making?

The director wanted a fast-moving, entertaining narrative with certain images that would be seared into the viewer's brain. He would like a real batey but could understand that people lived in the shacks and burning them down for a movie scene would not serve those people well. Nor would it be permitted.

"The audience doesn't want to be distracted by the poverty," the director said. "But they will absorb it."

Cragmore called himself a neorealist. He generally shot no more than two angles. He preferred natural lighting and long takes when he could. He did not like studio shooting, favoring the real world, sometimes using nonprofessional actors among the professionals.

They were two hundred yards from the batey but did not visit. Sloan was unequivocal. It was a location deal-breaker.

And they could only hope that their location payment actually ended up helping the batey.

It was an issue they couldn't control, Sloan stated.

Wilson had been unable to reach Gonzalez.

"What the hell?" Sloan said, "Did the man go on a cruise? Move to Hawaii?"

"I left a note," Wilson said.

The kid was back at the amphitheater conducting more busywork with the younger kids. Sloan had instructed him to have the boys take photos of the location every hour to illustrate how the light changed throughout the day, how the shadows moved, and when the place looked best cinematically. Never mind the fact that the scene was scripted for night. In truth, the study could have been done the previous day but Sloan was creating daily tasks for the boys. He imagined they would turn it into a contest. Hopefully one without anger, fighting, or injury to passing animals.

The scout team toured the cane fields of Gonzalez without him and discussed the pre-harvest burning to remove the leaves. The black snow scene. Again, the director mentioned aerials. And again, there was no comment.

"This should be monumental," he said. "Then from the ground we pan up to the apocalyptic sky." He lifted his hands in the air and wiggled his fingers. "We see the ash falling on the workers." He lowered his camera-frame hands toward the earth. "And we find the stricken face of Larimore."

"Great," Nico said.

The director looked at him. "Did Larue talk about building the shantytown here?" he said.

"No," Nico said. "We didn't have this location when he was here."

Cragmore stared at Nico and then scowled. "What

other fields are we seeing?"

"We only have these two," Nico said. "So far."

Cragmore looked at Sloan as if he might have a different response, then imitated a grinning demon and said, "What have you guys been doing, snorting coke and fucking the locals?"

Nico considered resurrecting the difficult sugar-industry argument but just said, "It was on the itinerary."

The director threw his huge head back and laughed like he'd never heard anything funnier. "You think I read that shit?" he said. "That's for the office girls and the producer."

Sloan walked over to the car and got some water bottles out of the cooler. He went back to the others and handed one to the director. Cragmore looked at it for a moment, then took the bottle and opened it and poured the water over his spiky head. "You know what this is?" he said. "A fucking waterfall. Why don't we go see one. Maybe more than one."

Sloan was thinking: Bipolar. Or a childhood trauma involving criminal location scouts.

The ride was quiet. The scouts did not look at the back seat, assuming the director had taken his meds and gone to sleep. The time could have been spent looking at roads and villages as planned but, who knew, maybe he was seeing them in his head. Or running through a list of insults.

As it was, they had time for one waterfall and might run into afternoon visitors. And they were thinking the same thing: Go for the closest one, Bayaguana, the triple, and save Socoa, the designer's favorite, until the morning. New day, fresh start, winner's circle.

Nico pulled over before they arrived and opened the trunk. He put everything in there that wasn't being carried down to the pool. Sloan was taking water and the camera. Nico would take tangerines. Cragmore would take brooding and insolence.

No kind of equine transportation had been requested so none was arranged. The thought from the scouts was to get the harder part done first, the hike down to the pool and back up, then see the falls from the top.

A fair number of cars were still parked in the lot and along the road. At the trailhead they ran into a man charging fifty pesos each and Nico paid it to avoid any sort of hassle either then or later. The team went single file, Nico leading, the director and Sloan following. They soon encountered three guys coming up and after that they seemed to be all alone in the forest.

The silence upheld in the car carried over to the trail. It was as if they were all on separate hikes and just happened to be walking near each other. In Sloan's random estimation, the silence between the men, the lack of energy for conversation, was somewhat proportionate to that of the Batann Death March.

The jungle humidity was significant, the insects annoying but not especially life-threatening, and Cragmore was fit enough for the undertaking, a hiker by nature, though usually in a drier climate. The abundant sweat released appeared to lessen his bile and he became loose-limbed and curious again but not jocular.

The recent rains had fattened up the falls and all three streams added up to an amplified roaring as the men came off the trail and encountered the pool. Cragmore spread his arms and inhaled the mist like a true pilgrim, his face softening as the moisture collected there.

A half dozen people were in the shallows but most of the visitors were in small pools downstream. The director took off his boots and pants and shirt and stood tall and pallid in plaid board shorts, anticipating his impending Dominican baptism.

He waded in and climbed up on a shore rock from which he could see the changing depth. The water's clarity was easily sufficient to reveal unobstructed access and he dove into the pool. He breast-stroked into the middle and treaded water as he looked up at the central cascade, the widest of the three. He swam under the falls and got hammered, then moved to his right over the rocks in search of the best climbing route. At the far edge of the wall he was able to clamber up to a prominent ledge and make his way back toward the middle.

"Are you going to say anything?" Sloan said.

"Not a fucking word," Nico said. "Either he enjoys himself or we get a new director. It's a win-win."

Cragmore got into position, one hand reaching back to stabilize himself at the wall, the other reaching out as he leaned forward to gauge the leap and the depth. He just needed to push off enough to clear the sloping edge of the pool's perimeter. He did not deliberate long.

He leaned back and then leapt forward and launched himself into the air, flailing his arms to gain additional increments of momentum. Without whooping he splashed into the pool and disappeared underwater and popped up shaking his head and grinning.

It wasn't Larimore's leap but it was inspirational for the director. If not exactly a new man, he was now more immersed in the project. He needed something physical and symbolic to dislodge his regular everyday constrictions and release his brain into the story's wilderness.

He climbed out and the scouts applauded. The three white men stood among the darker locals looking as though they were plotting something, figuring a way to work some kind of change at the pool that would impact the enjoyment of others. No matter the year, white men maintained the look of conquerors, of colonial rulers, the offspring of invaders. In the background there was always the hierarchy of color. Of degrees and shades. The spectrum of age-old prejudices. Ask any Black Haitian or the darkest Dominicans.

At the top Cragmore waded into the river and approached the flat area of rock that led to the lip of the central cascade, judging it to be a good platform from which to stage and shoot the leap stunt.

The mood swing was complete and the director sat up front again for the trip home. In the back, Sloan stared out the window and composed his thoughts. He texted with Sonia, giving and getting updates, tweaking the next day's schedule as best he could. He texted Wilson and found him to be unharmed. Wilson said the boys had taken photos, which he called experimental. Sloan leaned back and smiled. On occasion the sinking sun raked through trees or blasted across farmland like warning flashes between towers of cloud.

In the morning they were on the road when Sloan got a call from the vet's office telling him his dog could be picked up. He said he would send someone soon to get Pucho.

It made sense to scout another waterfall, for category continuity, before heading east. It would have been better to hit them on the same day but the schedule was never going to hold and the director's impulses had to be accommodated however they manifested.

Salto Socoa was the designer's top choice and the scouts liked it best as well, though they kept their opinions sequestered. The sun was out, the jungle was steamy and cinematically sinister, bird calls filled the atmosphere rather than people, and the falls fell dreamily into bubbles and mist.

Cragmore had mixed feelings. Which meant he had a choice, welcome news for the scouts.

It seemed that the director was reluctant to go along with the production designer's pick. But he didn't rule it out. He said the injured designer may have been too feeble to make convincing decisions. They'd spoken on the phone after the designer's scouting trip and the director had characterized the other's conclusions as feverish pontifications. This was not unexpected. The director presumably had his own personal vision of what the movie should be, and the production designer wanted to create the look of the show and influence how it was viewed. A certain amount of psychological gamesmanship grew out of this conflict.

The director was the captain of the ship. The designer wanted to build the vessel, create the hull, the galley and the cabins, pick the construction materials, the shape, size and color of the sails, the thickness of the pillows and cushions, the historical style and weight of the anchor.

Creative wrangling rippled down the line and affected the sleep patterns of other departments.

The scouts needed decisions so they could move ahead with contracts and permits and clear the way for the art department to begin its transformative work.

At Punta Cana they had lunch at Mar Caribe and then scouted the grounds, the pool, the beach, and a couple of rooms while clouds gathered over the spine of the island and vacationers filled the air with the frivolity of daytime drinking. The movie group walked around wearing serious expressions instead of bathing suits and appeared to be property inspectors. Afterward, they drove down the road to Casa Seagrape, a similar resort, and passed other similar resorts on the way.

Why was everything coming up in pairs? Sloan texted Sonia and said they needed at least three apartments, but four would be better. She wrote back and said that so far she had two set up for the next day. He said they needed to scrounge up another mansion too.

Scrounge? she replied.

He texted Wilson, who had been instructed to give the twins the day off and was supposed to be getting the golf course ready for their arrival. Wilson said he was there waiting for someone to notice him.

There were no rules, really. They were making a make-believe story in a real world. There were guidelines and expectations and the whole history of filmmaking stacked up behind them. Pushing them into the corridor of the way things had been done before. A producer would tell you the number-one rule was not to go over the money allotted. But that rule could crumble and more money might appear, as if by magic. Many factors could influence the formula. A movie could suffer ill-fated karma and go under, an untold story never to be resurrected by dollars.

They drove into the *Teeth of the Dog* clubhouse lot and parked next to Wilson's Corolla. Inside, Wilson was waiting with Fernando, their assigned contact. He shook everyone's hand and Sloan walked Wilson to the door and told him to pick up Pucho and call Sonia and ask if she could keep him temporarily. Or if not, maybe a friend or relative.

"I'm thinking Gonzo could use a dog," Sloan said. "Until we can get his female friend lined up. After that, he'll probably want to keep the dog anyway. That's what happens with dogs."

"I saw him and took pics of him and his house," Wilson said. "Like you said."

"Excellent, well done," Sloan said, noticing the others watching him. "Okay, gotta go."

As before, Fernando drove them in a four-seater cart over to the eighteenth hole, weaving cross-country to avoid active play on the course. They waited under a tree while a threesome finished putting, then drove closer and walked on the putting surface while the next group was teeing off.

Predictably, the director stood on the green for a moment looking around and then focused on the nearby ocean hole and pointed. "We should be over there," he said.

They followed the seventeenth hole in reverse, pausing on the path or rolling wide to wait between the fairways until balls were hit. At the tee box, Cragmore got out and stood in driving position between the markers and gripped an imaginary club and swung it. On the right side the ocean crashed along the irregular edge of the hole and the jagged rocks that were the namesake teeth of the course. Salt foam sprayed upward and clouds retreated from the sea.

"The dialogue mostly happens on the green," the director said, and looked back at the nearby sixteenth green, another of the three coastline holes on the back nine. Seeing the approaching golfers some distance away, he took off at a quick pace to get a look.

Fernando sat up straight and called out, "*Cuidado! Cuidado!*"

"That's a par three," Sloan said. "They're about to hit."

"He's obviously not a golfer," Nico said, sticking to his hands-off advice style.

As the director stepped up onto the green a ball thudded into the adjacent sand trap. He ignored it or didn't notice, intent as he was on framing the shot in his head. Another ball landed short and rolled to the edge of the green. Cragmore stood on the far edge of the green, facing the pin and the blue band of ocean. He framed the shot with his hands and held it for study. The third tee shot was hit high and wide and exploded off the rocks with a resounding spring that launched it out into the rolling water. Cragmore stood unflinching.

"Fucking Lieutenant Colonel Kilgore," Sloan said, "mentally impervious in his invisible Air Cav hat."

Nico laughed. "I was thinking the same thing."

Apparently satisfied, the director began to walk back to his group on the seventeenth hole as the fourth tee shot was struck behind him. The overhit ball sailed beyond the pin and struck Cragmore's right calf. He cried out and crumpled to the ground and rolled over holding his bent leg in a tight embrace as if he wanted to prevent it from falling off.

"What the fuck is wrong with those guys?" Nico said as Fernando pressed the pedal and wheeled the cart toward the fallen director.

"Everyone is special here," he said.

Cragmore got to his knees and looked back at the golfers heading toward him in two carts. He spotted the offending ball lying in the fringe a few yards from the green. He struggled over to it and from his knees grabbed the ball and looked at it as if searching for a hidden message, then threw it toward the ocean as the cart with his team arrived. They watched the ball hit a rock and bounce sideways and ricochet off another rock and plop into the ocean.

Fernando jumped out and lifted his hand toward the approaching golfers while Nico and Sloan helped the director to his feet. He limped around with a hand on each of their shoulders and flexed his stricken leg.

The golfer who had struck Cragmore got out of his

cart and came across the green toward the other group. "What the hell happened?" he said. The golfers were American, in their thirties, corporate drones in standard golfing attire on a company excursion. "We thought you were off the green." The man wore a stretchy blue polo shirt which would have looked better untucked and less extended at the bottom, as it now brought to mind a long-haul net pulled to the side of a boat.

"Any of you numbnuts heard of the golfing term, FORE?" Sloan said. "Normally shouted."

"What the fuck, man," the man said. "You guys aren't even playing."

Fernando raised his hands. "Just a mistake," he said. "These gentlemen are from the movies."

"The movies?" another man said. "Which movies?"

Cragmore was glaring at the men, too far away for him to launch an attack by limping. He pressed his right foot down and grimaced.

"You guys heard of *Mindblown*?" Nico said.

The blue-shirted man turned to look at his companions, his expression quizzical, then turned back to Nico. "It's only my favorite fucking movie," he said.

"Well," Nico said, "you just hit the director of that film."

There was a long silence with only the sea breeze and the flag flapping and the gasps of the golfers creating the sound of dumbfoundedness. The guilty golfer strode forward with his hand outstretched. "Oh man. Truly sorry, Mr Director. It's an honor to meet you."

Cragmore bent down and pulled up his pants leg to reveal what was troubling him.

The other three golfers were coming forward too, eager to be a part of this.

The first golfer dropped his hand and stared at the

swelling displayed. "Goddamn," he said, and pressed his teeth into his bottom lip. "That's a helluva goose egg, man. So sorry. Really."

The other golfers stood looking at the swollen calf, making faces and muttering.

"We are fans, man," one of them said. "All of us." The others nodded their agreement.

The blue-shirted guy stepped closer and looked up into the director's unsmiling face. "I would consider it an honor to buy you a drink, sir," he said. "If you would meet us at the clubhouse."

Cragmore looked at all of their faces, judging their sincerity. They were not actors. And the adulation was getting to him, bringing back brighter days, the cheers of admiration.

He shook all of their hands and they smiled and thanked him for his understanding and generosity, his humanity, as he'd shown in his work.

Fernando herded his group back into the cart. More golfers were on the sixteenth tee now and play had to continue. The sidetracked golfers on the green refocused on the task of finishing the hole.

Once the director had surveyed the seventeenth fairway and green, he was satisfied with the location and ready to move on. As rain began to fall it made sense to take a break in the clubhouse bar. The admiring golfers, forfeiting their last two holes, joined the other group inside just as the downpour obliterated the outside world and encouraged the bar tab to mount. Fernando was pleased to see the camaraderie between the guests and became more inclined to help the big-spending movie people achieve their goals. As long as no one important was inconvenienced and no damage was done, it would be good public relations for the club.

Cragmore told amusing anecdotes about the actor Tom Flint, whom he had worked with twice already, and the younger men howled and ordered more drinks. Nico kept a sober eye on the situation and Sloan walked around with his phone.

Feeling guilty, he called Sonia and mentioned the homeless dog.

"How many ways can you take advantage of me?" she said.

He was taken aback and couldn't think of anything clever to say except, "What?"

She laughed. "Lighten up, hombre. We're in this together."

"Okay, you got me," he said. "You deserve to be spanked and taken advantage of."

"Oh sure, more easy promises."

This made him start to visualize the act and he lost his train of thought.

"What were we talking about?" he said.

She laughed again. "The dog, man, *el perro*."

"Yes, Pucho, our little cigarette butt."

"That's more South American," she said. "You could call him Puchito, like buddy."

"That's better," he said. "Or Pooch, which just means dog."

"My mom can keep him for a couple of days," she said. "She works close to her home."

"You are unbelievable," he said.

"How's the scout going?" she said.

"Great, the director's getting drunk."

They drove away in a diminished rain, with the director in a diminished cognitive state. Despite his injury, which was nearly forgotten, and quite possibly forgiven, he had promised the three golfers tickets to the premiere of his unmade movie, and Nico had taken down their contact information. These loyal fans also wanted to score *Larimore* t-shirts and shot glasses.

Cragmore was in favor of restarting in the morning

but they were near the mansions and Nico prevailed upon him to undertake at least a pass-by. This was instinct on his part, a desire to utilize the geographical proximity, and to honor the perceived integrity of the schedule—but also demonstratively foolish, since a director who wasn't in a favorable scouting frame of mind would be more likely to shoot a location down.

At the first mansion, suggested by the realtors, the director had one eye closed and the other open about as wide as a paper cut. He waved his hand to continue with barely a glance through the rain-streaked window. They might as well have been looking at the worst unit in a trailer park.

They continued to the property of Mercy Ramirez, the friend of Dulce Medina, and stopped outside the wall. All they could see was the top portion of the house rising in the background. But that was enough for the slouching director, who proclaimed his need for acres and acres of land around the house. Like a zoo. A safari park. Camp David. A winery. A Hawaiian wellness retreat.

Into the western dusk they drove, the steady jagged breathing from the back seat like a peaceful soundtrack for a man resting on distant laurels.

Since the schedule had been gutted, in the morning they drove all the way back where they'd been the day before, this time just to see the amphitheater. It was a key location and the director spent a long time examining the empty place, hobbling up and down the stone steps until his slight limp became a pronounced limp. He checked the climactic fountain's visual relationship to the adjacent amphitheater, trammeling around and nodding as he spoke into a pocket recorder.

From there they spent a long time in the car, cruising roads alongside cane fields, through villages, crisscrossing farmland like members of an agricultural delegation, seeing possibilities and maybes, chatting idly about Buster Keaton and Gary Cooper and open spaces. Their movie seemed to be transforming into a western with Sam Larimore as the sheriff.

In town they ate a late lunch, scouted two apartment interiors and several more exteriors. Cragmore took a break and then they went out to several jazz bar locations, finishing at Sancho P.

Cragmore was in a mellow mood and drank to reflect it. A solo performer sat at the piano, singing in a soft gravely voice and mixing in some instrumental jazz. The night was a good finish to the day and those less jaded might have imagined a cosmic blessing was being bestowed.

26. The Changing Nature of Preparation

Sloan imagined himself in one of those movie scenes where the passage of time is shown by a calendar with its pages flipping by in rapid succession. One day followed by another and another in a blur of movement. Even the shadows of clouds traveled faster over the land. Or his mind was playing games.

Word had come down from David Sussman, the producer, through his ostensible mouthpiece, Gene Friedman, the production manager, regarding the recent director's scout.

Gene, to address where we stand with locations, Jonathan has expressed that he felt himself to be on solid ground that was sinking under his feet. He liked the geography and natural beauty of the country but complained about the rain. He will need to go back with his DP to get a better handle on a shooting schedule. In essence, the scout was scattered and haphazard. One would think the itinerary could be better tailored to the forecast. Locations should be hustling hard to turn up more options. The next scout will be scheduled as soon as possible and will include SPX and Stunts. August is upon us and the clock is ticking. David

In the Diamond Casino, Sloan sat at the bar with Wilson, pretending to be a tourist, as the cacophony of machines and games and the cheap-trinket chimes and bells of the slots swirled around them, the soundtrack of another make-believe world. Daytime, nighttime, your money could evaporate no matter the hour. Sloan was having a drink to blend in, though they were not there to gamble or drink.

The bar girls floated around the perimeter and worked the area, surveying the market in search of the most likely clients. They would smile up to you and lean in to gauge the temperature and casually ask you to buy them a drink as a friendly gesture. The point was not that they were thirsty.

One was eyeing Sloan across the corner of the bar while another sidled up to Wilson. When she casually let her hand drop into his lap and he felt her fingers moving at the exact right spot, he flinched and leaned forward on the bar to grasp his Sprite for comfort.

"Got a room, baby?" she said. He didn't answer and she repeated the question in Spanish. She thought he was the American's tour guide and might be able to use his accommodations.

According to the kid, this was his first time in a casino. Sloan was sure it wouldn't come up at the family dinner table. As it was, Wilson would probably need to schedule an extra session in the confessional booth.

The other girl came over and Sloan soon found himself undergoing the same tactile offer. It was amusing and arousing at the same time. He didn't want Wilson to suffer any psychological confusion about working in the Locations Department. Nor did he want him to fall in love and leave the show.

It was clear that Sloan's desperate idea was a failure. These girls were too young and too underweight to satisfy the needs of the old sugar man

Gonzalez. They were pretty and industrious though. And they had developed a lack of shyness that got your attention. Like heatstroke in the dark.

"Sorry to waste your time," Sloan said after the girls had moved on. "There won't be any complicated deals to translate."

Wilson looked at him. "Maybe you can try the oldest and most heavy."

Sloan shook his head. "I don't know why I said yes," he said. "But I made the fucking deal and now I have to honor it."

"Maybe a different casino," Wilson said, as if he were warming to the dim atmosphere.

Sloan laughed. "You've had enough corruption. Anyway, it would just be more of the same."

"What can you do next?" Wilson said.

Sloan swirled his ice and finished his drink. "I need a mature open-minded housekeeper," he said. "A nice lady who could cook and clean and be a friend to Gonzo and show him some warmth once in a while. For a reasonable fee."

Wilson finished his Sprite. "He said he wants every night."

"He did?" Sloan said. "Damn. I don't know if that will narrow the field or enlarge it."

Later he got a text from Dulce with a thumbs-up. He had asked her how the twins were liking their work in Locations. After their introductory training with Wilson he stopped driving over to pick them up and told them he would text their assignments and they would have to manage their own transportation. Now their mother sent them out with a driver who would wait while they hopped out and acted like location scouts or alley cats. The driver also served as a benefactor if any strong-arm tactics or payments became necessary.

They were now engaged in the search for a village intersection where Eddie's evasion would lead to the crash of the Escalade.

Street / Turn / Side street or alley. Break it down, keep it simple.

Sloan had asked to see their amphitheater light-study photos and Wilson forwarded them.

The photos were not identified with the time they were taken. The viewer could only assume they were taken in order but the time of day would have to be guessed at, not something anyone in the film business ever wants to do. But beyond this very basic problem, the photos themselves rarely showed the subject of the study, the full amphitheater. There were close-ups of the stone's texture that featured ants dragging a grasshopper through the frame. Another showed a young couple kissing against the stone wall and it could be seen that the boy's hand was up under the girl's shirt. Another one showed someone, presumably one of the twins, holding a dog's rear end toward the camera with its tail lifted, presumably by the photographer, to get a medium close-up of the butthole.

Though it had dawned on Sloan that he would need Sonia's help with the female procurement problem, he didn't wish to bring her into it. Eventually he reached a point where he felt he had no other choice. So he explained the situation regarding Gonzalez. In person, in the hotel's garage.

She presented a puzzled expression but he wasn't sure if it was mock indignation or not.

"You want me to find you a fat maid who will fuck an old dirty farmer and clean his house?"

"I wouldn't put it like that," he said.

"Have you seen his house?"

"No."

"Should we advertise in the newspaper?"

"We can't have a paper trail," he said.

"So—we interview women on the street? Maybe you want a department inside the department. A secret 'locate the gordita' division."

"Look, I know it's unusual," he said, "but we need the location."

"It's an insulting request," she said.

"Not really," he said. "It's a job, plain and simple. Everybody wins."

She turned up her hands. "What do you expect me to do?"

"Just give it some thought," he said.

She stared at him and then stepped closer and looked into his eyes. "Are you okay?" she said.

He smiled. "I'm fine," he said. "I just didn't think this through."

She smiled too. "Can you find some time to relax?"

"I'll make time," he said.

In the first dream he was drinking with Nico, who had his phone on speaker, and the producer was saying that the locations they had already scouted were merely placeholders.

Nico looked shocked to hear this and Sloan mouthed "What the fuck?"

The producer said they should start over and fill those spots with new locations.

Sloan was shaking his head while Nico flipped birds at the phone with both hands.

In the second dream Sloan was alone at a casino bar, absorbed in his thoughts, not making eye contact or encouraging solicitation. When he looked up to reach for his drink, a woman appeared at his side and he was shocked to see Dulce Medina in a dark low-cut dress. For a moment he wondered if he'd forgotten a meeting and then had the wild thought that she was there to take the Gonzalez caretaker job. As she smiled at him and he fell into the depths of her dark eyes, he forgot every previous thought and was suddenly aware of her hand resting in his lap. Even without her moving or applying pressure his excitement grew so elevated that he went into a frantic mental search for the words with which to excuse himself before the unstoppable eruption occurred.

When he awoke, both dreams retained the unsettling discomfort of nightmares.

The Locations Department brainstormed about public green spaces or gardens that might serve as the grounds of the mansion location. They would need to find a way to cheat the connection, by way of a constructed gate and a road that could conceivably lead to a house in the distance.

And, of course, any such options would have to be sanctioned by the production designer.

Sonia mentioned the Botanical Garden and everyone jumped at the idea.

"Scout it," Nico said to Sloan, "and make it look too good to pass up."

"I'll go with you," Sonia said, "in case there are any language issues."

"Early light," Sloan said. "So we need to arrange an early entry."

Nico waited for other suggestions. "What else you got, Sonia?"

"I think maybe Mirador National Park," she said. "Not too far from the garden."

"Anything else?" He looked at Wilson.

Nothing more was offered.

Nico nodded. "Great. This keeps us securely on the two-choice track."

Sometimes the benefits felt miraculous. With a few

emails to the Events Division and a phone call and a discussion of generous funds to help sustain the vast Botanical Garden, they were in. Two guards met them at dawn and they were given a golf cart to use before the property opened to the public at nine.

The vegetation was dense, as befits a tropical garden. The early sunlight steamed through trees and touched the wet grass in shimmering stripes. Birdcalls announced the day. In an area so large and devoid of people in this bustling city, the atmosphere was otherworldly, and with its stone walls and gravel trails it resembled the well-kept ruins of some former kingdom. Flamboyants flared in scarlet bloom, stately palms stood watch, gumbo limbo grew in smooth-skinned arcs. There were hardwoods, lagoons, fruit trees, bromeliads and bamboo.

They explored the garden through its existing pathways, sought out a sense of immense private property, the impossible grounds of super affluency. Within this great expanse they needed an imaginary driveway to the imaginary house somewhere out there. They had to suggest, to point the production designer in a direction so that the connection to a mansion located elsewhere could be seen. With his camera, Sloan carved the place into pieces, isolated landscapes of natural wonder that could fit the narrative. The portrayed property would not feel like an African savannah, endless open country that might be viewed from a wide front porch, but rather a dense private forest estate that serenely proclaimed fictional wealth and privilege.

Finally, as they became drenched in sweat and labor, Sloan stopped the cart and they sat in silence and let the place exist around them and seep into them, fill their lungs with the rarefied air of this escape from the city's discordant energy and chaos and, for a short time, from the job they were actually embarked upon. It was necessary to recognize moments of beauty and peace and seize them when they occurred. To pause and let them wash over and nourish you.

Sonia had not been there since she was a teenager. They languished in the moment, clothes damp, skin flushed, and drank water, finished with the task, away from everything that had brought them together. They never showed affection in public, not since that first inebriated night when they had fallen into each other. They were colleagues on a mission, sharing an unusual job, enjoying a botanical environment, forgetting everything outside of this moment. His arm slid from the seatback to her shoulders and she leaned into him and he pulled her closer so her head rested against his chest.

But being in the moment was unsustainable. It seemed as temporary and make-believe as the movie, he thought, even as she kissed his cheek. It was all illusory, blending into flickering images.

Was *Larimore* real? What was the point? Aside from a job that had unexpected adventures and a look at places one might never have gone. What about *Tropical Cavalcade*? As real as a poster hanging in an office and a film anyone could watch. And Pablo Cruz, now deceased if the story was to be believed. Wasn't he real? A footnote now, a story among many stories, an endless stream of stories true and made up every day, day after day, flowing throughout time from the first story, about food or a dangerous animal, until mankind's journey reached its natural or unnatural conclusion. If it happened, though, wasn't it natural? Sprung from nature, from the cosmos.

"Are we working on a good movie?" she said.

He kissed the top of her head. "We're working on a movie," he said. "That's enough."

At the front gate the street was loud and busy, the sidewalk active, the vendors in place. No rain yet. As they walked toward the car he saw a woman in the shade of an umbrella selling sliced fruit—pineapple and papaya chunks on a stick. He stopped walking and stopped Sonia.

"What do you think about her?"

"I'm hungry," she said. "Let's get some fruit."

They stood before the vendor's cart and Sonia smiled and made small talk as they bought two fruit sticks. The woman was in her forties and heavyset, wore tight elastic purple pants down to her calves, a tight pink t-shirt, and sandals. A stretchy red headband pushed her medium-length brown hair up into a clump. When she took the cash from Sloan her plump cheeks lifted with a warm smile. He was pleased to see that she had plenty of teeth.

She asked if they'd been in the garden and Sloan showed her a few images in his camera.

"But none of you two together?" she said in Spanish with a mocking frown of concern.

"Tell her what we were doing," Sloan said, and bit off a piece of papaya.

Sonia went into an explanation of their work and when she said the word movie—*pelicula*—the vendor appraised them in greater detail. She didn't understand why they were spending so much time with her and then began to imagine that a crowd of movie people, sort of like a circus in her mind, would be stopping by to purchase fruit.

Sonia paused while the vendor sold three sticks to a woman with two children.

When they were alone again Sonia introduced herself and the woman said her name was Maridalia. It was explained to her that they needed to hire someone to stay with and assist the elderly owner of a cane field, a man who was a farmer. Maridalia was puzzled and suspicious. Sonia told her it was a job but not a regular job and would only last a couple of weeks. The making of a movie had lots of unusual jobs that did not last a long time but usually paid well.

Maridalia asked what assistance the old man needed.

"He needs some cooking and cleaning," Sonia said. "His wife died a couple of years ago."

"Who does it now?" Maridalia said.

"No one," Sonia said.

The vendor frowned, imagining a pigpen. "Where does he live?"

"Over near San Pedro," Sonia said.

"What about the nighttime?" Maridalia said, eyebrows raised.

Sonia shrugged. "Whatever you wish," she said. "By agreement."

The vendor shook her head, made a face like she'd just caught a whiff of a sewer leak.

Sonia said the job paid one hundred American dollars per day in cash. Then asked if the vendor wanted to see photos of the old man and his house.

Without much hesitation, she said she did.

While Sloan consulted his phone, Maridalia asked about food.

"The man will buy what you need," Sonia said.

The first photo showed the old man without his hat, his hair combed straight back and either wet or slick from a product, wearing a clean blue shirt and with a kind of reluctant half-smile on his face, which looked pleasant, notwithstanding his weather-beaten skin. No doubt Wilson had a hand in the hair and the wardrobe, as if he were practicing for work in other departments.

Maridalia wobbled her head a bit, noncommittal.

His house from the outside looked like an old wooden shack but there was no junk around it. Wilson must have cleaned that up too. The living room was sufficient in furniture, with two chairs, a couch, and a small home-crafted table, plus a television, not large but not small either. The kitchen had the basics, sink and fridge and stove, with shelves for the dishes. It needed cleaning. The only bedroom photo showed two single beds. At least they had sheets and covers.

Maridalia was trying to picture herself there, a prisoner of the old man. It was a lot of money.

Sensing her misgivings, Sonia said, "Are you married?"

The vendor's answer was yes and no, perhaps indicating a separation.

"He comes around sometimes," she said, turning herself sideways, "to get back here." She smacked her bulbous bottom and the flesh shook like it had been awakened from sleep. Sloan watched it move, counting the seconds. One, one thousand...

"Jesus," he said under his breath, reflexively calculating the possibility of a side deal.

She saw him looking and laughed, knowing what she had and how men operated.

"I have to think about it," she said. "I have a friend who might be better for this." She was thinking that her friend needed the money badly and would do it for fifty, leaving her with a nice commission and no physical work. "Of course I would take my cut. For making arrangements."

"Naturally," Sonia said. "Do you have a picture of your friend?"

She began to scroll through her phone as Sloan casually moved around and snapped a waist-level shot of her entire full-figured frame. She glanced up at him and stuck out her tongue.

She showed Sonia a photo of two women so badly backlit that they could have been cartoon representatives of an inflatable toy company.

"We need a better photo than that," Sonia said. "How soon can you see her and get a new picture?"

She shrugged. "Maybe this week."

"She looks like the same height as you," Sonia said. "Same size too?"

Maridalia cocked her head and then nodded. "More or less," she said.

"Same age?"

"More or less," she said. "A little older."

"We want you," Sloan said, smiling at her. "If possible."

"Let's exchange numbers," Sonia said. "We'll stay in touch but let us know soon before we find someone else."

Maridalia put out her bottom lip like she was offended but said she understood. She took Sonia's phone and called herself. Then she answered the call and they both entered the name of the other.

"What's your friend's name?" Sonia said.

"Carmen," she said.

"Call her," Sonia said as they turned to leave.

"Thank you," Sloan said, and after a few steps turned to see Maridalia watching them go. He pointed at her, poked his finger to make his point, and smiled. She smiled back.

At the curb beside his car, Sloan noticed an arrangement of stones near the back tire. As Sonia opened the passenger door he stood staring at the stones. It seemed to him that the white stones created a drawing of a section of railroad track. Two lines connected at regular intervals by a couple of stones placed between them.

"What is it?" Sonia said. "Looks like a ladder."

"A ladder," he said as two boys raced by on bikes. Other pedestrians glanced at him as they passed. He was taking a picture of stones on the sidewalk.

"Just kids playing," she said.

"Yeah," he said. "It just caught my eye. Nothing really."

She looked at him as he went around the car. She started to pursue it but then let it go.

The hotel meeting room, now the production office, was staffed by the POC, Cindy Bonnet. Locations had some table desks in a corner but rarely used them.

Nico and Sloan preferred their debriefings at the terrace bar of a different hotel. Surprisingly, some locations were being chosen and the location contracts would be sent out in a day or two.

"Well goddamn," Nico said. "I thought everything was still unsettled."

"Someone is talking to the director," Sloan said. "Pushing him."

"The next scout is gathering steam," Nico said. "And before they arrive we need the bits and pieces— the border, Ramon's office, the roads, the village—all strung together cohesively."

"For the sake of argument, and to move ahead with an updated focus," Sloan said, "let's say we have the airport, the food truck, the amphitheater, the golf course, the waterfall and jungle, the cane field, the resort, the jazz bar, and the dive bar. Am I missing anything?"

"The airport wants script pages," Nico said.

"Fine," Sloan said. "There's nothing controversial there."

"There's a ton of running shots with dialogue that won't be picked by photos," Nico said.

"We have to map out some good options," Sloan said. "The other main focus has to be the mansion and the apartment. The park and the city streets will fall into place once we have a schedule and a shot list."

"So the village is swinging in the wind," Nico said.

"That's wide open."

"The taxi stunt happens next to jungle," Sloan said. "And Eddie and the Escalade start out beside a cane field."

"Right," Nico said, nodding. "I think I'm at that point where I need to reread the whole script."

"What?" Sloan said.

The place was getting louder and they had to speak up. It was Friday night and craziness was in the air. They could smell the sea blowing in from across George Washington Avenue and along the waterfront merengue blasted from portable players and people drank cold Presidentes and straight rum from plastic cups and danced acrobatically in a way that simulated fornicating while fully clothed. There was a stream of blinking brake lights as the traffic ran east and west and a purple sheen on the ocean as it spit the white froth of its waves at the city.

"I said I miss the Zone," Nico shouted.

"Fuck it," Sloan shouted back. "Let's go."

Officially, they were off for the weekend. The production did not pay for extra days or overtime at this stage, a stage without a crisis. The crises would come later, along with whatever measures were needed to negate them. But Locations was never really off. Even during downtime the pressure to move the ball forward was felt. It never went away. All you could do was numb it.

The days rolled into each other, with new developments arising and old ones getting reworked. Sloan roamed the countryside, logging miles and racking up images, coordinating with Sonia and Wilson, who followed up on local info and district government contacts for various villages.

The dog, Pucho, needed a permanent home. He spent too much time alone and being back to full mobility had begun to develop bad habits. Like an apartment vandal, he would roll all the paper off the bathroom roll and made a regular game of hiding shoes in difficult-to-find places.

Maridalia, after considering the net loss to her pocketbook if she split the money with her friend Carmen, called Sonia to claim the job. She did not bother to send a photo of Carmen, essentially squelching the competition. There were now plans to introduce her to Gonzo and clinch the deal. Sloan would have preferred to have the info on Carmen in case a backup plan became necessary, in the event that Maridalia bailed out partway through. But he felt she would likely hold steady while the money was coming in.

Dulce said everything was fine, that her brother was reviewing the deal to come up with a suitable figure. This made Sloan nervous. She kept pushing their next meeting into the future and he felt he was being strung along. At the same time he felt boxed in. Any other sugar company inquiries to partners of Imperial or to subsidiaries could get back to Dulce and backfire, blow up in his face. Aside from the Gonzalez wild card, all his sugar eggs were in one basket.

More apartments were scouted. Some owners were extremely slow to respond to letters of request, as if they had until the day before shooting to confirm their interest.

The mansion idea had taken a turn into the rare world of the double cheat. Now the front acreage and the rear ocean view were being considered as individual locations separate from the house. The team was scouting for a hilltop overlooking the sea, a piece of land from which to create the mansion's incredible view. Something that did not actually exist in the region they were scouting. There were some stunning modern villas overlooking golf courses.

There was also a very expensive villa up north in Las Terranas that Locations was working on. They saw pictures and learned the net worth and their common consensus was that they would never in this lifetime get a reply from the owner. Or, if they did, the price would be far out of range of this movie's budget. Still, it was pursued, fool's errand or not.

The trickster twins submitted numerous village photos and apparently expected the Locations team to guess where they had been taken. They also positioned themselves as distracting elements within their compositions, impersonating signposts, vagrants, and roadkill. This was a source of amusement only the first time.

27. The Tech Scout

The production office staff increased in increments. First was Sheila Mulready, the assistant production office coordinator, who joined Cindy Bonnet, the production office coordinator, and took up residence at a table opposite her immediate boss so that they faced each other and could communicate with facial expressions and hand signals as well as words. They had a well-established working rhythm and used a shared body language, often with eyes, nose, and lips, to convey mockery, disgust, incredulity, or impatience, especially when one or both were on the phone. Since they had quit smoking, their combined consumption of diet sodas required a stack of cases in its own corner like a monolith.

Along one wall of the room two folding tables were outfitted with a coffee maker, creamer pods, sugar packets, boxes of pastries, a basket of chips, cookies, and gum. A small fridge held water, sodas, and individual yogurt containers, the last added as a concession to gastro health.

Three young local production assistants, Ana,

Rafael, and Maria, were added as more crew members arrived and the pace ramped up for the technical scout.

The aural texture of the room became a buzz of conversation against the background hum of printers and low volume reggae punctuated by snorts and cursing and the popping belch of carbonated cans.

The rains would peak in September and October, which coincided with the shooting schedule. October was the sugarcane burn and harvest season. Everything would collide and blossom then. And out of the black dirt and burnt leaves would be born the story of their labors.

Now was the time to delineate the burn area and mark the blueprint of the batey set to be built. Nico and Sloan needed to steer as much sugar work as conceivable to the Gonzalez property, the safer, more dependable of the two sugarcane locations.

The old man had been smitten with disbelief and gratitude at the sight of Maridalia. So much so that he cried and then told her and Sloan that he'd gotten dirt in his eyes earlier in the day. She sized up the house and deemed it serviceable. And she liked the fact that the old man looked up to her, both literally and figuratively. She was already counting the money and said she would be ready to move to the house whenever the schedule was confirmed. Payment would be weekly.

Location agreements were under review at the resort, the airport, the golf course, and the amphitheater. Others were so far verbal in nature. In Santo Domingo, Municipal Services and the Parks Department were working with Locations on the control of street parking, to be confirmed after the tech scout. Maps and diagrams were being utilized and updated periodically. The Film Office was organizing meetings and assisting with the navigation of red tape.

Representatives of various departments began to drift through the production office to see what was happening, get any paperwork they might need, grab a cup of coffee or a bottle of water. It was a hub and a place to go if you didn't know where else to go.

It was also a place to complain—about power outages, internet disruptions, the hotel's staff, the rain, the heat, the humidity. Or the food. Some crew members were at first inclined to compare everything to California but as professionals they knew that failure to adapt would sink them.

They came through like a parade of masqueraders. Dominic Larue, the production designer, returned in a triumphant show of normalcy, without crutches, neck boils, rashes or mysterious secretions. From his department there was also the art director, by all appearances healthy and precise.

Others coming aboard for the scout were the property master, the set decorator, the leadman, the gaffer, the best boy electric, the key grip, the best boy grip, the key rigging gaffer, the key rigging grip, the best boy rigging gaffer, the best boy rigging grip, the sound technician, the construction coordinator, the greensman, the special effects coordinator, the transportation coordinator, the transportation captain, the picture car coordinator, the stunt coordinator, the first assistant director, the second assistant director, the second second assistant director, the key set production assistant, and the unit production manager.

Metaphorically holding the director's hand would be the director of photography, also known as the cinematographer, an avuncular confidante, a guiding force in the look of the film, a master of light, shot blocking, camera movement, and timely reassurances.

A bus was chartered. In brokering the rental, a great deal of emphasis was placed on the state of the vehicle's air-conditioning system, its reliability and deep chill factor. It was assumed that inquiries about the engine would be perfunctory.

Small umbrellas were purchased by the production office to be handed out before the scout to those who wished to carry them. Likewise, cartons of insect repellent were made available. In an emailed memo the attendees were warned to be wary of contracting dengue fever, however small that likelihood actually was, and also to be aware of the presence of drug dealers, instances of petty theft, sexual assault—the same kinds of risks as most places—and people driving vehicles without the use of proper safety features, including headlights. Horns, however, were continually, insistently, proven to be in reliable working order.

Of course most of these potential dangers had to be expected, nearly taken for granted, but they needed to be expressed in writing. Otherwise, one was bound to crash head-on into the common producer's rebuke: Why is this the first time I'm hearing about this?

The itinerary was hammered out by Locations, based on weather forecasts and the availability of certain locations. And common sense, geographically speaking.

Per the director's request, though the word insistence would be more accurate, he and the DP were to scout several locations with Nico ahead of the group. Meanwhile the scout attendees were allowed time to settle in, get acclimated, organize their affairs, explore the area, and use the hotel's pool.

Several men took advantage of the downtime to make a beeline to a casino. The reliable instigator of this party-time attitude was Reggie Sordom, the AD, a hard-charging bulldog whose energy for his nocturnal appetites rivaled his professional zeal. Early on he'd characterized himself with the catchphrase "Knock 'em down and Reggie will Sordom out." Another one, often shouted in a noisy atmosphere or after an elevated level of inebriation had been attained, was "Sordom and Gomorrah!" Other crew members who had partied with Sord, as he was called, swore that if you looked up the word *excess* in the dictionary you would find the flushed and grinning face of the assistant director, his spiked blond hair sticking skyward like he'd been up all night running his restless hands through it as he ground his teeth and flexed his jaw, chewing the nightlife to pieces.

The greensman and the rigging grip went with him and they all sat together at the bar having drinks and encouraging the night girls to continue breathing suggestions in their ears and using their discreet hand manipulations to directly emphasize their offers while the men engaged in conversation and laughter.

Two of the girls, coquettish in their underage appearance and almost look-alikes, dressed as bad Catholic schoolgirls out for a club night and were rewarded by the benevolent Sord. He inquired about a special powered additive to the festivities, procured a packet in the parking lot, then crossed over to the hotel side and got a room key and returned to the bar to stock up. Each of the girls carried two shots of his choosing and he brought a cold beer as a chaser that wouldn't make it to the tenth floor.

The threesome left for the elevators while Sord's tamer associates remained at the bar and the third girl sat waiting dejectedly beside them for a sign of meaningful erotic indulgence. A new girl took up the slack and tried her luck with the Americans. Almost immediately the rigging grip regretted his hesitation, passing up the AD's invitation to a free rumpus room. He couldn't at that moment imagine knocking on the door of 1004 and interrupting whatever was taking place inside.

The new girl wormed into him and mentioned what she'd like to do with her mouth and he looked into her eyes and said, "Fuck it." He finished his drink and stood and rearranged the crotch of his pants.

At the elevators he pushed the button and waited with the girl gripping his arm, playing the sweetheart role. Nearby stood a silent security man in a black suit holding his hands together at his waist. The doors opened and the grip stepped inside with his friend. He pushed the button for the tenth floor and kept pushing as the door failed to close and the button failed to light up. He locked eyes with the impassive guard. Finally the grip pointed upward and said, "My friend is on ten."

Remaining motionless, the guard said, "You need a key."

The grip started to say something, but then just looked at the girl. They stepped out of the elevator and he reached for his phone and realized he didn't have the AD's number. He had a crew list back in his hotel room. They walked back to the bar and she expected him to go over to the hotel and check in and get a key while she waited there with plain water and justifiable doubts. He nodded at her, glanced around for the missing greensman, then walked toward the hotel side. He passed out of sight, crossed to the main entrance and went out to the street.

The greensman idly played a few slots and wandered around absorbing the jangly blinking atmosphere while finishing his drink, thinking about starting his research into nurseries and other plant sources so he'd feel more confident on the tech scout. On the walk home he called his wife.

Up in 1004 the assistant director crouched naked but for his leopard-print thong, tapping out a line of cocaine onto one of the four breasts exposed to him on the bed. He'd sampled the drug and found what he expected under the circumstances, a weak mix sold to tourist suckers. Still, he could do it all and get an adulterated kick. He rolled a twenty into a tube and downed a shot of vodka and snorted the line across a raised nipple. The girl giggled and he tilted his head back and pinched his nose and then inhaled sharply with a forceful shake of his head. He tugged the obliging nipple and both girls rose to their knees and grabbed at his tiny jungle garment as he extended his offering and raised his arms overhead, hollering like Johnny Weissmuller's *Tarzan of the Apes.*

The director wanted the cinematographer's input on the waterfall action, the most dramatic way to shoot the jump to shock the audience, knock them out of their seats with a surprising, propulsive and frightening scene. The DP, Nigel Waverly, was English and understated and strictly factual, unlikely to show empathetic emotion or jump headlong into the director's pyretic dream.

His expertise, however, his analytical assessment of the location and the natural elements at play, balancing the camera angles with the shot sequence, reportedly put most directors at ease.

"We stay with the mathematics," Waverly said, gazing up at the falls. "Where you get into trouble is in trying to reinvent the wheel." He was a world traveler with long brown hair and a close speckled beard. He wore a broad safari hat to protect his pale skin and a long-sleeve tan sun shirt. Around his neck, as a practical tool and a symbol of his profession, hung a dark viewing glass on a black leather cord.

Cragmore stepped closer to the man's face. "This is the moment that defines Sam Larimore," he said, almost playing the general to his new colonel.

"We have a vertical shot," Nigel said, "from up there and from down here. It could be very straightforward and effective." He paused, using his viewing glass to look at the sun passing behind clouds. "And also boring. To prevent that we can use the golden ratio, a Fibonacci spiral, to shoot the character away from the center and show the magnitude of his surroundings, the ballsy nature of his physical risk."

Cragmore looked up and pictured the man leaping out, falling, the cascade and the jungle and the sky containing him until he dropped into the pool and plunged out of sight, escaping his tormenters—and the camera, briefly—at once. He wasn't hearing anything new. Perhaps it wasn't possible to reinvent the wheel. Maybe it was possible to reinvent the cinematographer.

Cragmore was known for long takes. The prevailing style was faster now, jumpier, with many more cuts, jarring in the effort to inject more speed into the pace. It could throw you into a seizure.

He'd be back here soon with the whole tech-scout crew. And everyone would want to know what to expect on the day of filming. He noticed Nico standing over at the sandy edge of the pool, giving them space to tackle the problems. At least he wasn't pointing at his watch.

Sandwiches from the hotel had been brought along and they sat in the air-conditioned SUV on the road beside the Gonzalez cane field chewing on damp bread and chicken as they watched the dusty grass waving against the darkening sky beyond.

"Are you thinking elevated shot here?" Waverly said.

"I'm thinking of three crane shots," Cragmore said. "The first is on the road, the motorbike and the Escalade heading toward each other. The second one is Gina's Suburban arriving at the batey at night. The third is later when we really see the scale of the batey."

"You mean when he's recuperating there?"

"Yes, revealing the whole batey in the midst of all this cane and then moving in to find him embedded and living within this squalid environment."

"That's very good," Waverly said. "But don't we see it when he's dropped off there?"

"We don't really know where he is," Cragmore said. "It's dark, with firelight, a mysterious place where he disappears into the night."

Nico made a note about constructing a plywood path through the field to allow the crane to reach the camera position from the road.

The director and the cinematographer got out to discuss the action following the discovery of Larimore crawling out of the field. Penny and Eddie on his motorbike. The approach of Ramon in the Escalade. Eddie's confrontation, his distraction. The arrival of Gina in her Suburban.

Nico met them as they returned to the car.

"Where to?" Cragmore said.

"We have another cane field not too far away," Nico said.

"Another one?" Waverly said. "Which one is the location?"

"They're both under review," Nico said.

"What does that mean?" Waverly said.

"It means nothing is easy with sugar," Nico said. "We need a backup."

Waverly looked at the director for comment but none came. They all got into the car.

They were on a road perpendicular to the entrance to Batey 108 when the sky opened. Nico drove slowly with the wipers on high while they circumnavigated the expanse of cane, getting a sense of the contiguous fields and the overall footprint.

"Much bigger world, this one," Waverly said from the backseat.

Very astute observation, Nico wanted to say.

"We get it," Cragmore said. "Let's head back."

In the office, the rest of the Locations team worked on clearances and maps for each day of the tech scout. One map showed all of the locations in relation to each other, an area comprised of a good portion of the eastern third of the country, from Santo Domingo to Punta Cana.

Other crew members would drift over to interrupt the work with questions about ethnic restaurants, particular kinds of stores, or a cheaper laundry service than the hotel offered. Some asked if they would get the chance to ride a horse.

Sloan looked up to see a man assessing at him with crossed arms and a tight mouth like he might have been constipated. Sloan judged him to be nearly Sonia's height if he were wearing boots.

"Gene Friedman," the man said.

"Oh hey," Sloan said, standing to shake hands. "Luke Sloan. Welcome to the DR."

"Good to be here," Gene said. "Let's hope we're all accounted for at the end."

"Should be," Sloan said. "Did you hire any clowns or rule benders?"

"Just you guys," Gene said. "I want to meet with your security options as soon as possible."

"How about right after the scout?"

"That would be optimal." He looked at Sonia and Wilson, introduced himself again and added his title, unit production manager, each time he shook hands.

As he walked away, the younger team members looked at Sloan.

"Don't worry," Sloan said. "He just has a stick up his ass."

In the morning the group loaded up in the bus in front of the hotel with Nico standing by the driver, a dark middle-aged man with square Dior sunglasses resting on his head, wearing a dapper brown dress shirt, black trousers, tan loafers, and several gold chains. His name was Leonidas.

With the bus idling and cooling the air inside, the assistant director conducted a safety meeting, speaking from the front of the vehicle in general terms about the need for a heads-up attitude, the need for traffic awareness, the prevalence of crime and drugs, a warning that together they would be seen as a bloated, oblivious blob of distracted travelers easily targeted by opportunists. He spoke audibly but looked as if he'd arrived from the luggage compartment after a long trip, his clothes disheveled, his face blotchy, seemingly beaten by heavy bags, his eyes in need of Visine.

Sloan drove his own car, as did Sonia. Wilson stayed in the office, holding down the fort.

The bus parked alongside Duarte Park and the crew disembarked like a tour group and stood milling around the director as he spoke. The gang looked to some passersby like a religious assembly who did not adhere to the usual dress code for public gatherings. These people wore shorts and running shoes and carried folders and notebooks instead of bibles. But the congregation followed their prophet all around as he gestured this way and that. He entered the street, where he stood with his hands formed into an open rectangle and moved it from one direction to another as horns blared and vehicles gave way.

While Sonia took notes and Nico kept an eye on the group's perimeter, Sloan redirected traffic away from the director. After a few minutes of chaos, the leader returned to the sidewalk and fielded questions.

The best boy electric, standing next to the gaffer, said, "Why doesn't he use a viewfinder like other directors?"

"Force of habit, I guess," the gaffer said. "He's old-school. One less thing to carry around."

As the meeting concluded, Sloan discussed the generator position with Electric, and then, with the transportation captain, the preferred placement of equipment trucks, making a quick sketch in his notebook.

From the Colonial Zone they traveled to Piantini, a neighborhood in the heart of the city, and stopped among rows of condo blocks. It was a busy, upscale area, and the modern building that the production had picked reflected the social status of Manny La Vega, Gina's helpful brother, whose unit would house Larimore while he stayed out of sight.

After several elevator trips, the whole group assembled in the seventh-floor unit and met the owner, Julieta Morales, who insisted, in keeping with her deep respect for decorum, on shaking everyone's hand. She was an elegant woman in her forties, dressed impeccably in an iridescent blue-green pantsuit the color of a quetzal's tail feathers, her dark hair in a glossy cascading ponytail, her makeup invisibly perfect, her smile genuine, her teeth whiter than the backlit curtains. She could hardly believe that her rather ordinary apartment had been chosen over all the other units they'd seen. And she was excited to know that the handsome movie star Tom Flint would be there, sitting on her couch or at her kitchen table, exuding his limitless charm. Her husband was at work, basically indifferent to the project, but he'd given his approval. She could earn the extra money and enjoy her good fortune among their neighbors, some of whom had already let their celebrity envy slip out into the open. Anyway, her husband was on the board, if anyone tried to cause trouble.

The condo was open and spacious, mostly white and gray, with light wood floors, speckled quartz counters, and contemporary light fixtures. The long balcony looked out on an assortment of buildings of varying heights, and down upon the tops of royal palms and other tropical trees.

The designer wanted to change the furniture and paint the walls to make the place more island colorful, which made the director roll his eyes. He held up his hand to pause the designer's pitch, then talked about injecting more action, either by having a gunshot taken at Larimore on the balcony or having a fight in the hallway right outside the door, neither of which was in the current script. The owner listened with a dazed smile on her face.

Sloan was on the balcony when the rigging grip came out, and he did not like the strained look on the man's face. "Hey brother," the grip said. "Do you think I can use the bathroom?"

Sloan exhaled and braced himself. "Can you be more explicit?" he said.

"I need to take a fucking dump," the grip said.

"Do you really want to perpetuate the basic grip stereotype?"

"What's that supposed to mean?"

"It means can you possibly wait until we get out of the nice lady's apartment?"

"Look, I'm serious. I overslept and ate a bunch of leftover beans and goat stew."

Sloan grimaced. "Jesus," he said. "I can see the walls and the plumber's invoice already."

"That's not funny, man. I mean, don't we have the location by now?"

"Presumably, yeah. I just didn't want to destroy the

place this soon."

"You're a fucking riot." The grip shifted from foot to foot and Sloan heard rumbling, possibly from a nearby construction site. "Can you get permission right now?" the grip said.

"Follow me," Sloan said. They went back inside and through the crowd over to the kitchen where the owner stood.

"Julieta," Sloan said. "Would you mind if this fine gentleman used your bathroom?"

She smiled at them. "Of course not," she said. "You are welcome. Just down the hallway there."

"Thank you ma'am," the grip said, dipping his head slightly and stepping away exuberantly.

"I think he has to blow his nose," Sloan said.

They watched as the director and the gaffer spoke about lighting the space. Sloan noticed the liberated grip reemerging just over five minutes later. He closed the bathroom door but failed to seal it with gaffer's tape or any kind of industrial adhesive. The malodorous fumes crept outward and claimed the kitchen and living room and then the airspace of the entire unit. The survey was brought to a close. The crew filed into the hallway, thanking the owner as they passed. Sloan said he would be in touch, and the offending grip pointed at the balcony as he left, blending into the crowd and suggesting that the sliding door be closed, a feeble attempt at misdirection.

The plan was to scout the Botanical Garden, not far from the condo, then have a late lunch in Piantini before returning to the Colonial Zone to scout streets and bars. Though some streets would play with the park and others with the apartment, the director would cheat the physical relationships in order to shoot streets he felt had a better look. While they scouted the Botanical Garden, Sonia would jump ahead to the restaurant to submit the orders—derived from printed menus distributed on the bus so crew members could select their meal—and make sure the table was ready with water and bread when the group arrived.

Likewise, she would leave the street scout early to confirm that the dive bar, The Black Cat's Mouth, was open and prepared for the group's arrival. From there she would move to the jazz bar, Sancho P, and do the same.

By special permission, and with a representative of the Garden escorting them in a motorized cart, the bus was allowed to drive beyond the parking lot to an area of interest featured in the location photos. This area was contained in a loop of road that could be closed to regular visitor traffic and was thus favorable to the control needed for prep and shooting. The surface of the road was paved and covered in leaves and dappled light. It looked established and authentic as a driveway to a distant mansion. The director stood alone in the road staring into its depth and sunlit beauty as it stretched away into a manicured forest dreamland. The group was gathered silently behind him, captured in his spell, waiting for a signal.

He walked into the undulating pattern of light on the road, wavering into fiction as the distance grew between him and the others. He stopped again and came to his senses and looked back. He waved them forward and the group walked to join him. He wasn't exactly smiling, they saw, but seemed lost in thought. He looked directly at Sloan for a moment.

Cragmore took the production designer aside to discuss the need for an outer property gate, one that would lead the scene to the gate of the actual house. There would need to be a transition point, a smooth joining of the Garden road to the real driveway.

"Two gates would be strange," the director said.

"These people are so rich," Larue said, "and have so much property that they want an inner security apparatus closer to the house."

"Two gates would look fucking stupid," the director said.

"There is a great distance between them," Larue said.

"You drive through a gate and then come to a gate," Cragmore said. "Why don't we put a third one on the front steps?"

The designer looked down at the road and thought about the scene. "For you to have a reverse from the front porch I'll need to build the porch here," he said. "Otherwise, there's no forest depth."

"How will it match?"

"Inside the mansion's gate I'll plant a small forest to match this."

"So we'll come out of the forest and boom, there's the house," the director said.

"That's how we transition," Larue said. "We don't see the wall or the gate at the house. We hide them or take them down."

"It's a night scene," Cragmore said. "We'll establish the mansion, then pick up Ramon making the long drive to it."

Next, he talked with the cinematographer and the gaffer about lighting the road to simulate moonlight. The cinematographer suggested the use of white helium weather balloons suspended overhead. They could be hit with spot lights that would reflect uniformly and cast a general glow over the area. A light breeze would even create a movement of light and shadow like the moon filtered through branches.

The restaurant was Italian and the long table for thirty-one had been set up along the back wall. Sonia had already placed the orders and she took the bus driver's meal out to him as soon as the crew offloaded. Sloan followed her out to the street.

"How did it go at the Garden?" she said.

"It was a hit," Sloan said. "You made me look good."

"Our team looked good," she said.

He checked in with Leonidas and checked the drink cooler and the snacks, and then went inside to eat.

Some of the crew had salads and appetizers and were lighter on their feet. The pasta and pizza eaters grew groggy and longed to fall into comas in their bus seats. Dessert was not offered but quite a few coffees were consumed.

In the Colonial Zone the group wandered the streets behind the director like a troupe seeking a stage. It was hot and steamy, rain was threatening, and the key set PA made regular runs to the bus to bring bottles of water back to the wilting followers.

Between the streets that connected to different locations—the jazz club, the apartment, the dive bar, the park—some of the crew, those who had not finished or read the latest version or read the script at all, became confused and unable to align characters with locations, taking notes and looking at others' faces to see if confusion was possibly the norm in this instance, if the problem wasn't perhaps the script. Who the fuck was Graham Perry? How many brothers did Gina have? Did Montero have a first name? If Larimore was so smart why did he return?

The Black Cat's Mouth. The simplest of bars, darkness its primary quality. The river, the reflections, the ominous atmosphere. Since it rained while they were crowded inside, the street when they emerged shone with greater color and richness. The director called for a wet-down and wanted to shoot day into night. Special Effects would hire a water truck on the night of filming to hose down the area. Locations would have to secure the bar for night work. They would need to restructure the deal and buy out the business.

The first day of the tech scout concluded at Sancho P. A good omen for those in the mood to toast a good day. The bus left them behind to find their own way home. Those who wanted to display their work ethic and get to their private space took the provided ride back to the hotel. Those who had already been through rehab did the same. The after-hours players—Props, Stunts, Rigging Grip, Sound, Greens, Picture Cars, First AD—chose to decompress and compare notes. Praise or castigate the director. Make bets on the show's success or failure. Celebrate their freelance employment. Alleviate uncertainty with alcohol.

In the morning the hotel had a buffet set up for those who made the time to eat before the bus pulled out. A bilingual article in the *Free Daily* was passed around at the same time as the coffee.

Dear Amigos: Make Way for Hollywood—the big flashy spenders

A movie group was seen in Santo Domingo yesterday flexing their American muscles.

A gang of conquerors claimed Duarte Park and rode a bus into the Botanical Garden.

The movie is called *Larimore*, the perfect name for a first world invader.

You may benefit in some way. You may also be run over by a bus.

It is said that many locals will be employed by this movie. So far one driver was hired.

The movie's villains are Dominicans. We understand that this will be a comedy.

Or propaganda. Or a negative portrayal of island life. More to come.

"What kind of fucking bullshit is this?" Gene Friedman said. "And how did they know where we were?"

Nico spooned some yogurt and fruit onto his plate. "You didn't think anyone would notice us? It's just a cultural humor piece."

"I want security with us from now on," Gene Friedman said.

"Did you pick a company yet?"

"Sloan hasn't given me the fucking information," he said.

"Inexcusable," Nico said. "I'll definitely speak to him."

This turned out to be a warmup for Gene Friedman's view of the day.

At Socoa Falls Sonia got a call from the man who was trailering three all-terrain vehicles. He had broken down on the outskirts of the capital. When asked how long it would take to repair his vehicle he said he couldn't say until he knew what the problem was but he thought it was the carburetor or the engine itself so either a day or three days.

The bus was already en route. Nico relayed the report from Sonia and the director weighed in immediately, saying they would stay on course, that he'd already made the hike and any film professional could do it.

Some of the crew felt a walk in the woods would be fun and healthy. Others took a dimmer view. Several wondered if they'd even be missed down at the pool. The second assistant director, Cecilia Wilkins, who in the course of her work had to scurry around and expend enormous amounts of energy all the time, made a comment to Sonia to the effect that she should have vetted the vendor more carefully and had a backup plan in place.

Sonia said, "Next time we'll insist on work-history documentation and hire a second vendor to follow the first one."

Cecilia was tying a wet bandana around her neck and pulling her hair up as she watched Sonia walk away.

Water was handed out and the long staggering expedition proceeded downhill. The chorus of coarse language conjured up images of the French Foreign Legion—minus the cigarettes, sand, and khaki. The slick trail caused frequent slips and falls and soon the mud mixed with perspiration on faces and arms and legs created an organic camouflaged appearance.

The director was standing in the pool as the last stragglers filed into the clearing. In this natural setting he spoke over the roar of the falls about the jump, the angles of the action, and Larimore's commitment. People squatted and washed their arms and faces. Others removed their shoes and emulated the director. The few outside visitors steered clear of the larger group, which to non-English speakers seemed to be preparing for a baptism.

Afterward, the crew trailed into the trees with less clothing, becoming more liberated in their scouting, a group transforming with each scratch, stain and insect surprise, wearing headbands and fogged glasses, dripping their inhibitions into the ground. They pushed through branches, breathing heavily and growing more focused, hearing the director's rendition of the Spanish shouts of jungle pursuers. As intended, when they emerged into the open again, many had been initiated into the cult of Cragmore.

Sordom, the 1st AD, unleashed his Tarzan yell and the stunned silence was followed by rolling laughter.

Back at the top, the group scouted more jungle, the director insisting that the waterfall sequence would require a full day, the jungle work another day. Following this, a smaller group of personnel approached the falls to discuss the stunt and the equipment required. The rest waited in the bus and took in the cool air and the water and snacks onboard. There was a subdued current of communal energy.

They scouted the general vicinity for pieces of road for the airport-taxi chase, for a crash site off the road, where the driver is executed, which physically linked to Larimore's jungle entry and subsequent escape from armed pursuit. When the director got out of the bus everyone followed and Sloan took photos and made notes. Only one jungle shot was needed, Larimore running into the trees. Afterward, the scene could cut to the waterfall jungle they had just left.

Complaints of hunger-induced headaches rose and spread and the bus headed east to Bayaguana where there was one restaurant equipped to handle a group of their size. It offered typical Dominican food and that was made clear by Locations. Their travels did not put them in a city and everyone needed to roll with the plan. Understandably, the restaurant did not take reservations or prepare any food before the party's arrival or even have the staff to efficiently manage such a large group. Regardless of the reality of the situation, the day's geographical route, and their actual location, the stop took too long and certain people grew fidgety and then agitated and then unpleasant. The food was heavy and this basic fact added to the weight of the atmosphere at the table. The tech scout's prescribed hallmark was efficiency, organized motion meant to propel the project forward into concrete, real-life progress. The food, the *mofongo*, the *sancocho*, and the *pollo guisado*, however tasty, all dragged the production down. The bus may as well have been stuck in a mudhole.

Some people got the wrong order or didn't understand what they were looking at. Some shuffled off to the bus, a familiar environment with snacks. The director stood outside staring into the uncertain future like a king awaiting his retinue. Gene Friedman paced around the table poking metaphorically at Nico and Sloan, who were standing together, with hand gestures and muttered words of criticism. To the other patrons and the staff he appeared to be rehearsing his part in a play in which the other cast members were mute.

Everyone knew you could go from hero to fool in an instant, then back again, over and over in an infinite loop.

Nico stood glacier-faced, signaling for the check by intermittently writing in the air. Sloan sipped his coffee and stared into the middle distance as if afflicted by deafness as well.

More roads, a geographical survey of the region skirting the basin of agriculture to the south. Then down into the village of Los Llanos, the first one Sloan had scouted. There were several options there and they spent two hours figuring out the mechanics of the chase, the stunt, the crash. Having just seen the market area of Bayaguana on the way out of town, the production designer now wanted to add several rustic wooden market stalls to the village crash scene instead of having a single cart of fruit. The director liked the original idea of having smashed papayas all over the Escalade when it arrived at the mansion. So the main target stall had to have fruit in order to deliver that indignity to Ramon. Whether it made sense or not to have market stalls in an alley between houses did not enter the discussion. In movie logic, anyone in this story could conceivably have a handy market stall a short walk from their door. Maybe this would start a trend, Sloan thought, and market stalls would no longer be confined to markets. Free the stalls.

They attracted a neighborhood crowd and Sonia collected loads of useful information and made a few friends. The locals were excited to have a movie invade their unvarnished lives.

The ride home featured a buzz of chatter and the thuds of heads slumping against windows.

The third day's first stop was the airport. Wilson had been able to enlist the services of a company called Triangle Security and a guard followed the bus in an aging Monte Carlo that emitted oil smoke and sent a negative signal to those crew members who happened to look behind them.

"We're a socially responsible production," Gene Friedman said to Nico. "He's back there flying a banner that says Ugly Americans."

"Do you want me to cut him loose," Nico said, "or just change vehicles tomorrow?"

"Fuck," Gene Friedman said, turning away.

"Option number three," Nico said.

At Las Américas International, the bus pulled up alongside the cantilevered overhang on the upper level. The crew offloaded like tourists who had lost their luggage. Sloan parked below in Short Term and came up the stairs. He saw the guard parking behind the bus and directed him to park below before his car's fumes asphyxiated innocent travelers in the area.

Their administrative contact Eduardo met the group and led them inside the terminal where they stood in a herd in the middle of the concourse discussing the action. Sloan went back outside and found the guard standing beside the bus. He wore a generic tan uniform with a silver badge attached to his shirt pocket. The butt of a pistol could be seen sticking out of his pants pocket.

Sloan called Sonia as he approached the guard.

"Our guard has a firearm," he said to her.

"A what?" she said.

"He's got a fucking gun in his pocket. Tell him to wait in his car until we need him." He handed his phone to the guard and the man listened and handed the phone back and shrugged. Sloan nodded and pointed to the parking area. When he'd gone, Sloan called Wilson.

"We have to change security companies," he said. "Tomorrow's guard should have a car that does not burn oil and he should not carry a weapon. Okay?"

"Copy you, boss," Wilson said.

Across Route 66, the approach to the airport, the sea was a band of blue stretching across the open southern horizon. Along the view's righthand side the coast formed the long cove bordering the capital. Further on, the westernmost appendage of the republic jutted out into a point aiming south. On the other side of that was Haiti.

Sloan drove over to the vacant rocky land where they had seen the food trucks. The area was empty now and the rough track led to the concrete foundation of some former enterprise. Beyond that was a smaller cove and a marine park known for its coral reefs.

Sonia led the bus to Sloan and the spot for the roadside fish stand—or possibly a food truck—was pinpointed. The guard did not appear and Sloan assumed he had been withdrawn from duty.

It was as if the cane had always existed. An expanse of duplicate stalks like the cornfields of the Midwest. The breadbasket was in decline, fallen behind tourism, but that was not obvious at ground level.

The bus followed Sloan's SUV in circumnavigation. On a paved road near Batey 108 a spot was picked for the discovery of Larimore crawling out of the field. And for Penny and Eddie's intervention by motorbike.

The cinematographer Nigel Waverly studied the sun and the gaffer took notes and the picture car coordinator walked down the road examining the striated surface.

No one was around. No one showed up to meet them. They walked into the field and out again and it seemed that Locations had struck such a deal that they were now entitled to carte blanche.

Hats and sunscreen came out. Notebooks were used as fans. The sun beat down as if to murder the cane, burn it early. Some stood in a slot of bus shade, lined up like prisoners out for roadwork.

The cutters came to mind, swinging their machetes for hours.

A motoconcho came by and the sight was startling, a break in the crew's solitude. A man drove the small high-pitched motorbike with a woman and four children of differing sizes somehow balanced on the machine behind him. They passed slowly, six dark faces staring at the bus and all the pale people on this desolate back road. The crew stared back at them, each group seeing the other as a sideshow.

It was a twenty-five-minute drive to the Gonzalez farm. Between the two sugar locations was a village called Ruben Milagro, where a river crossing with a low, flat concrete bridge had been scouted for the Haitian border crossing. The day's itinerary had included Ramon's office exterior in La Romana but that was rolled over to the following day so they could devote more time to sugar and the border location. They would be traveling east tomorrow and the itinerary change made sense.

When they drove through the town and passed the yellow-painted curbs, the central park with its orange gazebo and white benches, the concrete-block houses—some painted and some raw—and the blue cock-fighting club, the director called for a stop. He wanted to explore the place as an option for the chase scene between the motorbike and the Escalade.

They found a pale aqua house with a dirt yard and an unpaved alley beside it. There was laundry draped over a wall and strung to a wooden power pole. The bus stopped and the group descended on the location and spread out like locusts. An old woman came out clutching the waist of her dress in one hand and her throat in the other. Sonia moved in to ease her mind.

The previous day's village location was scrapped, or held in check as a backup, and this new village location was upgraded to the top tier. The director and the stunt coordinator worked out the mechanics of the action. Lighting, art direction, and parking were discussed, and they moved on to the next stop.

The humble inhabitants of yesterday's village location, who had begun to believe they were about to have unexpected money bestowed upon them, would soon find that their winning lotto ticket had been rescinded. The director, however, was quite pleased, having found the new location himself, shortcutting the interpretations of the middlemen, and feeling his vision transferred directly from his brain to the real world. Like most directors, he relished an accidental bullseye.

The border-crossing location was audibly endorsed as cool. The bridge was rudimentary and narrow, without any railings, built barely above the surface of the Rio Soco. While the opposing banks did not give the impression of belonging to a separate nation, the thick vegetation and slow-moving water delivered a realistically remote feeling. Several young men were in the shallows washing their mopeds and motorbikes. Drawn by curiosity, they engaged the crew in conversation and it became known that the river sometimes overflowed the bridge, which did not normally make it impassable but did markedly enhance the visual drama.

Neither Gonzalez nor his truck were in evidence. Under a darkening afternoon sky, the crew waded single file into the heart of the cane like disoriented explorers hoping to establish dominion, which, in a sense, they were. Some regretted their choice of clothing. Since there was no clearing or place to convene, they marched back out and stood in the road.

"So you know the feeling of being in there like the cutters," Cragmore said.

It became apparent that the batey would need to be built in the road itself and extend into the field on one side. That way it would be surrounded by cane and have a road leading to it. The backside could be closed in by adding planters of cane mixed with structures of some kind.

The special effects coordinator cut a bundle of cane stalks to conduct a burn test elsewhere. He would use smoke machines to add more smoke to the fire scene. The art department took photos and measured the road and began to sketch the set.

Lightning flashed across the sky and forced everyone into the bus. Water bottles were passed around. Sloan sat in his car as the rain arrived, making notes on the road closure and the production parking problems.

Day four encompassed the eastern locations. Resort, amphitheater and adjacent fountain at Altos de Chavón, golf course, and mansion.

They started at the furthest point and worked their way back. The resort was a standard, straightforward, beautiful, relatable location, one that could anchor many variations on the lustful reconnection between Larimore and Gina. Given as they were to cinematic shorthand, certain crew members nicknamed the location Fuckfest.

Security was a no-show, perhaps due to the travel distances of the day or the relatively short notice. But no one cared or possibly even noticed. The day's locations were in the high-roller category. And the mood was good.

The amphitheater was being set up for a concert. Workmen and technicians were moving around and it was assumed that the movie group had something to do with the evening's event or an upcoming one. Or they may have been seen as tourists walking off their lunch.

The production designer, Dominic Larue, was fixated on the Ferris wheel scene from *The Third Man*, even going so far as to characterize the semicircular shape of the amphitheater as a broken wheel. Cragmore had little patience for this sort of digging through the past for thin analogies.

"There's been a thousand betrayals in movies," the director said. "We're not in Vienna in black and white."

"I'm referencing the nature of the conversation between Welles and Cotton," the designer said. "Their characters' divergent views of the value of an individual life. Just as Graham Perry can easily throw Sam Larimore to the wolves."

"For fuck's sake," Cragmore said. "Should I shoot this scene in sepia tones? Should I ask wardrobe to put our guys in fedoras like Harry Lime and Holly Martins?"

"I'm brainstorming, searching for another layer,

more subliminal menace," Larue said.

Cragmore looked around for Gene Friedman, who was fading back into the crowd and making himself smaller. "Friedman," the director said. "Did we bring a medic? Do we have something for the designer's recurring fever?"

The questions were clearly rhetorical and no one spoke as the director walked down to the stage.

He turned to the approaching crew and spoke as an orator, his arms extended upward.

"We'll need at least two hundred extras," he said. "And we have to make them look like two thousand. Bus them in, just like a real concert. Which is what we're staging here." He went on to demonstrate a low camera angle, as if from the point of view of an amplifier behind the singer. He explained how he would weave into the crowd with a Steadicam to find Larimore and Perry and overhear their conversation. He would cut to Gina watching, a lone anxious figure hidden among the dancing, raving, ecstatic revelers.

They followed him to the fountain where he enlisted Reggie Sordom to play Ramon, Cecilia Wilkins to play Gina, Sloan to play Montero, and Nico to play Graham Perry while the director played his hero, and they acted out the climactic fight scene. A carefully choreographed sequence of movements, a ballet of life and death as upbeat music laced the night.

"You've all seen the schedule," he said. "We have a full night in the amphitheater and another one here."

Altos de Chavón seemed a perfect place to have lunch. Open, airy, lively. The restaurants were accustomed to large groups, just not those in a great hurry. Locations had selected a tapas bar with the idea that many small dishes would move quickly. In reality, nothing was ever fast enough.

For the *Teeth of the Dog* establishing shot,

Cragmore liked the tee box on the seventeenth hole. For the dialogue on the green he could just turn around and slide back to the sixteenth. This time nobody hit him, his large entourage as unmissable as a herd of wildebeests in thrall to the ocean.

The scale and value of the mansion would be partly obscured by the darkness, thus representing a shadow empire whose operating details were not entirely clear. The son would arrive at night to see the powerful father. The mansion itself was not as powerful as its location and the surroundings were meant to be within the scope of the story. It would be made to differ from its real-life neighbors by the illusions the movie created. They would cheat the front and the back of the property.

Sloan spoke with the caretaker inside the front gate. The art department and the greensman worked on the plan to connect the long drive inside the National Botanical Garden to the mansion's driveway. They would need to return on their own for follow-up planning.

In the scene, Ramon would leave his car and go through the front door. The camera would pick him up on the back patio where his father, Luis La Vega, would be smoking a cigar and drinking rum. Instead of the view across the inlet to other houses the production would cheat the reverse and insert an unobstructed view of water. At the appropriate location the art department would build a replica of the patio where the father and the son could stand before the open nocturnal sea. It would become a matter of editing.

Though it had not been officially scouted, Sloan knew of a nearby beach he thought they should look at right then, while they were close and the mansion was fresh in everyone's mind. The beach was a cove wrapped in the arms of twin elevated ridges of rock and palm. It was as yet undeveloped and reeked of exclusivity. In the story, a private beach, a private cove. With an ocean majestic.

To the south the blue Caribbean Sea stretched away to South America. Shooting during a full moon was suggested. Though they still had to scout the exterior office on the way back through La Romana, that location was a no-brainer and the day, the whole technical scout, was essentially over. There was a sense of accomplishment, a fortified feeling of elation spreading through the crew. This show was going to happen. It was real.

A few curious beachgoers strolled by, others were camped out on towels and two vendors were still operating. Cragmore walked over and purchased a beer. Others followed. Bottles of cold Presidente were raised. Someone toasted Sam Larimore. Then Graham Perry, the betrayer.

The designer and the art director were talking at the water's edge, out of earshot.

"Here's to Harry Lime," the prop master said. Laughter erupted. And the theme was batted around like a beachball.

To the Black Knight. To Colonel Kurtz. Nurse Ratched. Rolo Tamassi. Little Bill.

28. Gods of Misrule

With the framework in place, each department buckled down to work.

The director, the AD, and the cinematographer holed up to nail down a shooting schedule. Room service, hallway walks, personal time, more food, cocktails, brainstorming, out to dinner.

The art department had major construction to get started on. Foremost, and most time-consuming: the batey, an entire ramshackle village that would eventually burn. Or get damaged by fire. Then the two pieces connected to the mansion. The Botanical Garden's woodland road needed a gate to mark the mansion's entrance point. The mansion needed vegetation to match the Garden's tree-lined drive. The cove needed a patio constructed to match the mansion's actual patio. The village needed a constructed residential addition to be demolished by the sliding Escalade.

Locations had successfully persuaded Production to build the batey on the Gonzalez property, using the burn as the principal driving factor. The larger cane fields belonging to Imperial Sugar were also desired by the director and the cinematographer for certain scenes. Paying for two sugar locations was driving the producer into a monetary meltdown and he was pushing to drop Imperial and do everything at one location. The producer indirectly held the purse strings and had to justify financial decisions to the investors. Though the film was technically independent, several companies were putting up money and in the end a studio would distribute the movie.

Meanwhile Locations did not have signed contracts with either sugar location. Dulce Medina was in the States, getting her boys into prep school and spending some family time with them. Gonzalez was missing in action and Sloan began to suspect that he had a secret life somewhere else.

On top of unsigned contracts, other things were pressing down on the Locations Department. The condo owner, after their tech scout visit, now thought the location fee should be increased. She phoned Sloan and claimed that too many neighbors were complaining and making her life difficult. And the intrusion of people into their unit would be larger than she had imagined.

"Julieta," he said. "We already have an approved agreement. The production is coming down on us about our budget and we can't spend any more. I'm sorry but we will have to pick another unit."

There was a moment of silence before she said, "I'm sorry too."

"Think it over," he said. "We can speak again. Meanwhile, I have to present another option."

"What happens then?" she said.

"Well, if everyone likes it, then we have a new winner. You'll be out."

"I'll talk to my husband," she said.

The cove beach was under the management of a neighborhood association. Their next meeting, three weeks away, would need to be attended by Nico and Sloan so they could make their pitch. The start of principal photography was scheduled for September 7, two weeks out. The interruption of normal rejuvenating sleep patterns had already started.

Sloan could not figure out how to pay Maridalia for her time with Gonzalez. He had promised cash, so easy to say during a conversation in the service of a persuasive deal. The accounting department, and by extension the money overseers Gene Friedman and David Sussman, did not like cash arrangements. They also did not like slippery side deals or transactions without a clear paper trail. Sloan was waking up at three in the morning trying to convert the money into payments that did not lead to a failure of reimbursement. The smarter and simpler move would have been to increase the location payment to Gonzo and pay her out of that. But that method wouldn't be quick cash in her hand, as he had promised, and without Gonzo knowing the terms.

Maybe he could turn her into a nurse without a bank account. A skilled health professional keeping Gonzalez in shape for the shoot—making sure he got his insulin shots, let's say, or his heart meds—while harboring a lifelong fear of banks. But then, Accounting wouldn't pay for labor with cash. They would insist on a timecard, forms filled out, taxes withheld. Which would leave Maridalia with a check. And kill the deal.

He would have to pay her cash himself and find a way to get reimbursed. He would have to submit receipts for believable additional fees. Like what, crop dusting?

Gene Friedman told Nico to find a warehouse to use for Construction's workshop and for the building of cover sets, a place where the company could move to on short notice for ready-to-go interiors in the event of bad weather. It would contain the resort guestroom and a batey shack. It had to have a fenced lot to hold the work trucks. And not be near the airport's flight noise.

"He said ASAP," Nico said. "Like they haven't known for weeks that this was needed."

"Yeah, it's like the tech scout solidifies the rumor of a job," Sloan said.

They had walked out to the pool deck to talk privately. There was no one in the pool and they wouldn't have cared if there were, as long as they weren't from the production. And anyone from the movie in the pool during the day at this point would be a person who already had a flight out.

"Two weeks," Nico said, bringing his right index and middle fingers up to his lips as if they held a cigarette. He drew in a sharp hit of air and released it in a stream like smoke. His cheeks puffed out like part of the relaxation technique. He looked over at Sloan standing against the wall in the shade. "Where are the sugar contracts?" he said, waving his imaginary cigarette around.

"We have verbal deals at least," Sloan said. "Dulce is out of town and Gonzalez is around."

"What the fuck is his full name?" Nico said. "Even Jesus Christ had two names."

"When he signs he'll enter his full name," Sloan said.

"Goddamn it," Nico said. "This is dragging out too fucking long."

"Looks like you picked the wrong week to quit smoking," Sloan said.

"I don't need movie lines," Nico said. "I need signed fucking agreements."

"If you lose your humor," Sloan said, "you're dead

in the water. You're a crab shell lying on the bottom."

"I haven't lost anything," Nico said. "There's a time and place."

"Yeah, no time like the present," Sloan said. "I'll work on the warehouse." He pushed himself off the wall and crossed into the blazing tropical sun. The pool looked inviting.

That afternoon a memo was issued by the producer.

DATE: August 24
TO: All Departments
FROM: David Sussman
RE: Budget

Thank you all for an excellent tech scout. It's exciting to be a part of this project and to see more crew coming in every day. This will be a challenging 28-day shoot in a foreign country. Never forget that we are guests of this nation and need to be mindful of the laws and customs at all times. Please be respectful of your fellow crew members and be polite and helpful while staying in your own lane, meaning the lane of your department. We are all professionals who pride ourselves on professional work at all times. We are also professional in our attitudes and decorum. The schedule and the environments will test us but we will move ahead to our goal one day at a time. We will have to shoot some nights and probably some six-day weeks. In fact, I'm fairly sure this will be necessary to accomplish our goals on time and on budget. Which brings me to the subject of this memo. We have got to work together and get our costs down. This cuts across the board. Locations, Art, Grip & Electric, Transpo, Local Hire, Rentals. If you can wear two hats, grab them and put them on. We need to sacrifice for the common good. We are all in this together. We can make a movie we will all be proud of. I'm counting on all of you to lower your departmental budgets and pitch in with all you've got. David

This produced some feedback in the production

office.

"Sure, what about actors? Are they wearing two hats?"

"Maybe Tom Flint can play Larimore and Ramon."

"Maybe Margaret Nogales can play Gina and Madame Chery."

"Surely Wardrobe could do Hair & Makeup." This got laughs too, partly because those departments had their own separate rooms. You couldn't have all those racks of clothes or all the cosmetics and hair dryers and curling irons in the production office. Likewise the assistant director department with its one-line schedules, revelatory shot lists, and private meetings with the director. The art department had a sizeable meeting room of its own so they could stretch out with their vision boards and props. Extras Casting had their own room to conduct interviews and record video. Accounting, of course. They needed privacy and quiet for their computing of figures, their forms, their locked-up stacks of cash.

Since they did not have a workshop yet, the art department wanted to start building the batey set on site as soon as possible and Dominic Larue began to breathe down the neck of the locations department by sending group emails and texts asking when they could enter the property and copying Friedman and Sussman. Nico started eating Tums like candy.

Sloan and Sonia broke down the locations into two categories: viable or squirrelly. When asked, Sloan defined squirrelly as unpredictable. Then he changed that delineation to nervous.

They made a location list and put V or N next to each entry. The N group contained the condo, both sugar locations, and the cove beach that would connect to the mansion.

A commercial realtor set up two warehouses to be viewed the next morning. Before he left Sloan put a note in front of Sonia with the addresses and the words I Need Your Help. When she looked up at him he raised his eyebrows and made a face that may have conveyed doubt or despair or pleading. When he pictured the face he'd made, he saw the central character Pasqualino in the Italian film *Seven Beauties*, trying to survive in a Nazi prison. Sonia palmed the note and put it in her pocket.

He was supposed to take Gene Friedman with him but he left alone. The first warehouse was less than ten thousand square feet and looked too small and too shabby. Sonia did not show up.

The next one was fifteen thousand square feet, with a ceiling height of twenty-one feet. There was one bathroom with multiple stalls and sinks, and the building came with electricity, water and internet. It had a fenced lot and was located in a free zone with exterior security. The airport was twenty minutes away. Sloan thought the price sounded fine but the decision would be made by Gene Friedman, who would want to see it the next day after he got Sloan's recommendation. The realtor said he understood. As they stood outside talking, Sonia drove up. Sloan introduced her as a Cooling Consultant and said they needed to discuss portable AC units and fans. He asked the realtor to give them a few minutes alone inside.

In the bare open space there were echoes and no privacy except the bathroom.

He took her hand and led her there and closed the door. "I've missed you so much," he said.

She did not respond but let him kiss her and kissed him back as he lifted her up onto the sink counter. She responded physically, wordlessly, and pulled up her skirt and helped him pull her panties aside and enter her. The close walls resounded with the dull slapping of her exposed bottom on the counter as she hung onto him and he bounced her up and down, rasping like a choking dog.

Afterward, they wiped themselves off. "You didn't sound normal," she said. "Are you okay?"

"More or less," he said.

As they left the bathroom together, the outer door opened and the realtor stuck his head inside.

"Everything fine?" he said.

Sloan gave him a thumbs-up. "One bathroom for all," he said.

They moved their cars outside the fence and the realtor locked the gate.

Sloan stood beside Sonia's car as the realtor drove away. She was seated behind the wheel.

"I'm sorry that was so rushed and unromantic," he said.

She looked up at him, squinting into the brightness. "If I didn't want to fuck you, I wouldn't."

He looked away, tracking a passing car. "You know I hate to neglect your beautiful breasts," he said. "It actually pains me."

"I understand you," she said.

"Your job is secure," he said, "no matter what you do with me."

"I never thought differently," she said.

"Since you're here," he said, "what do you think of this place?"

She smiled. "The bathroom might be awkward for some women, if any will be working here."

"Yeah," he said. "One or two might, but they'll be pretty tough. And they could hang up a sign. Occupied. Fuck off."

"Not my problem," she said. "But I don't want anything bad to happen to you."

He leaned down closer to the window. "I hope we get some quality detox time after this is over," he said. "I don't plan to get the first flight out."

She smiled again. "I hope so too. Just be careful."

He felt her sincerity expanding in his chest. "Don't take any shit," he said.

He sent Wilson to stake out Gonzo's house.

"Go to the field, go to the house. Look for the truck. Talk to the neighbors. Find him," Sloan said. "Check the windows and see if there's a way inside."

Wilson looked stunned. "That's illegal," he said.

"He might be incapacitated in there," Sloan said. "Heart attack or stroke."

Wilson slowly nodded, seeing the humanitarian angle.

Sloan reported to Friedman's office and closed the door behind him.

Friedman was typing at his computer. "So I go all the way over to East Santo Domingo and find that you already made a deal on a warehouse that costs more than I want to pay," he said.

"The guy is bullshitting you," Sloan said. "I told him you would be making the decision."

"Why the fuck didn't you tell me you were going?" Friedman said, looking up.

"The realtor told me he had a narrow window and I bolted over there," Sloan said. "If it was any good I wanted to at least get a foot in the door."

"Oh you got your whole body in the door and now I'm squeezed in too."

"What's that mean?" Sloan said.

"It means he won't come down on the price now."

"Maybe there was never any negotiating room," Sloan said.

"Is that the conclusion your associate came up with too?" Friedman said. "What's her name?"

"Sonia."

"You must have a fat department if you can both take the time to go."

"I value her opinion," Sloan said.

"What was her opinion on the unisex bathroom?" Friedman said.

"She was cool with it."

"Do you think HR would be cool with it?"

"It's big enough that construction could rig up a partition for the last two stalls."

"I see. With a door and a sign. Only Females Beyond This Point."

Sloan shrugged.

Friedman tapped his fingers on his desk. Then pointed to the laminated erasable wall calendar.

"Where are we with the sugar contracts? The guys need to start building ASAP."

"It's under control," Sloan said. "I feel good about the verbal arrangements."

"Why aren't they signed?"

"One out of town and the other a possible medical delay."

Friedman looked at his desk and pinched the skin of his forehead into a ridge at the middle.

"Sussman is chewing my ass on this," he said. "We cannot have any spikes in the numbers."

"Understood," Sloan said.

Friedman looked him in eyes. "About that newspaper article the other day. That harassment."

"What about it?"

The production manager squinted and his eyes seemed to move closer together. "I was thinking maybe it had something to do with your cinematic notoriety around here."

Sloan made a face he hoped looked seraphic. "Long time ago," he said. "Ancient history."

"Nobody's reached out to remind you or fuck with you?"

"That article just seemed like some joker trying to be funny," Sloan said.

"That doesn't answer my question."

"No, I don't think that was aimed at me," Sloan said. "And no one else has taken aim."

Friedman stared at him for what seemed a long time. "Get those contracts," he said.

As Sloan turned to leave, Friedman spoke again.

"Oh, I was just about to send you and Nico the latest from the director."

Sloan felt a weight appear in his chest. "Yeah, what's that?"

"I hesitate to call it a wish list," Friedman said. "That sounds too flexible." He made a sort of sarcastic smile. "He wants hand-to-hand combat at the condo. Larimore's cover is blown, he has to move on."

"Where?" Sloan said. "A new location?"

"Most likely," Friedman said. "We'll figure it out."

"Is that it?" Sloan said.

"No, that's not it. He wants a boat, a fishing boat, a sailboat, something, anchored off the resort."

"Who's going to show him samples?" Sloan said. "You need a marine coordinator."

"We don't have a marine department," Friedman said. "I need you guys to do it."

"We're not boat guys," Sloan said. "We don't have time for that shit."

The production manager's face collapsed into mock pain. "How fucking hard can it be? Find a cool boat, show him a photo, and get an incredible rental price."

A headache and a stomachache blossomed like algae in Sloan's body. "That is totally fucking background," Sloan said. "Talk to Set Decoration."

"Set Dec is swamped," Friedman said.

"What, with lounge chair cushions?" Sloan was being fucked with and he knew it.

"Don't forget who put you on this movie," Friedman said.

"Yeah, thanks," Sloan said.

"One more thing," Friedman said. "Cragmore wants a donkey at the batey. And you guys already have an animal wrangler, the mule guy. Get a couple of donkeys so the director has a choice."

"Sure," Sloan said, opening the door. "We'll toss in an armadillo as the donkey's little buddy."

A memo went out announcing the Production Meeting at 3:00pm in the breakfast room opposite the pool. The tables were arranged in a large square with white tablecloths and pitchers of water. A hotel notepad and pen were placed at each setting, along with a drinking glass. Attendees arrived early and stood around joking and comparing notes on their experience thus far. Outside the windows a lone dark-skinned female swimmer in a neon pink bathing cap performed laps, the back-and-forth seen by Sloan as a rhythmic countdown to disaster.

Last to arrive were the director and the AD, who took their seats side by side. The meeting was conducted by the AD, with many clarifications inserted by the director. The initial focus was on the schedule. After that, various concerns and problems were addressed.

Due to the amount of preparation needed, and the number of days of night photography, the batey fell at the end of the shooting schedule. Because of the turnaround time needed between work days, the day shoots and night shoots had to be separated to allow for sensible, efficient scheduling, either by placing nights at the end of a week or by stringing many nights together in a row. Some weeks, the work would start later and later as the week wore on. At the batey, all-nighters would be bunched together at the end of filming. By that time, everyone would be turned into zombies.

Other night scenes included the amphitheater concert, the adjacent fountain showdown, the mansion, the Botanical Garden, the cove, some of the streets and roads, and some of the resort. The condo was split between day and night.

Sussman shifted the spotlight to Locations and questions were applied to Nico and Sloan as cloud cover reduced the natural light coming from the windows and the room's recessed bulbs gave it more of the character of an interrogation chamber with all parties focused on the two figures sitting together in a heated glare of incrimination.

"Maybe you can explain the sugar story?" the producer said. "Maybe not."

It was impossible to discern who exactly was being addressed so Nico extended his open hand in Sloan's direction, deferring to the other man as being the much more likely to have an answer to such an unusual question, as if they were barely acquainted and mere chance had placed them together at the table.

Sloan drank some water and refilled his glass and launched into the same "difficult to penetrate the sugar industry" explanation he'd been giving since what now seemed like his infancy. Then he said, "But I actually feel confident enough in the current situation ..." He paused to watch the swimmer leave the pool and pull off her cap and stand facing him. She wore a one-piece blue bathing suit and he took a moment to examine the extent to which she filled it out. She tilted her head to one side and begin bouncing up and down on her toes, her hair jumping in loose ringlets, her right ear apparently in need of draining, her breasts rising and falling in concert.

"He's suddenly got stiff person syndrome," Cragmore said. A mass of chuckles rippled out.

Sloan looked down at his notepad and saw the

long-faced donkey he'd sketched. "As I was saying before the outside world interrupted," he said, "I think we can start building as needed."

"You mean like today?" Sussman said.

"Like yesterday," Sloan said.

"With no contract," the producer said. "What supreme faith. You feel the same, Nico?"

Nico's face had become the same shade as his blank notepad. He gestured at Sloan with his thumb, subliminally dreaming of hitchhiking out of town.

"Speak up man," Sussman said.

"We have every reason," Nico mumbled. He scratched his neck and said, "Sound methods."

There was silence at the table.

"Okay," Sussman said. "We'll move on to the next issue."

The AD, Sordom, said, "Let's go over the waterfall jump."

The producer interjected. "Before that I want to state that our firearm scenes will feature real firearms, so Bruce Ludski, our armorer, will handle those exclusively. We will have no live ammunition on our show, zero, none whatsoever, but no one else but Bruce should ever touch any of the guns aside from actors on set who need them for the scene and who will receive them directly from Bruce. The 1st AD will reiterate this, but it cannot be stated enough. Also, in the climax we will see a real shuriken in Larimore's hand but the one he throws will be fake. No one gets their eye stabbed."

"Yes. Thank you David," Sordom said. "Bruce will be arriving next week and he will conduct a firearm safety meeting before any weapons are used on set. But again, NO ONE on the crew except Bruce will ever pick up a firearm. They are not toys or fun props to play around with. Our prop master, Rob Fenton ..." he gestured at Rob, who lifted his hand, "will handle all other props but only Bruce will handle weapons. That means firearms, knives, and the shuriken."

He let that sink in, then said, "Let's move on to stunts then, shall we?"

When Sloan called Wilson, the kid was sitting in his car in front of Gonzo's house. He had not been able to enter the house, he said, but he had looked into the living room through a gap in the curtains and seen no evidence of anyone being inside. He could not see into any other rooms.

"Wait there until nightfall," Sloan said. "Don't leave without calling me first."

"*Claro, jefe,*" the kid said.

With Sonia, Sloan consulted a list of other residents of the Piantini condo where they planned to shoot. They narrowed the list to a couple of people who had sounded enthusiastic about the project and were willing to rent their units for production support such as a holding space for actors or a place to set up hair and makeup.

"Let's call both of these," Sloan said, "and tell them we might be changing the shooting location and want to know if they're interested in being the new hero unit."

Sonia made the calls and received a positive response from each.

"Great," Sloan said. "We'll let that news settle in the building for a day or two and see what happens."

Sonia's mother had stopped complaining about the dog, Pucho.

In response to the approximately fifteen texts Sloan had sent her over the last ten days, Dulce's reply finally came back in the form of a smiling devil face. Sloan stared at this for a while, eventually taking some comfort in the smile.

He sent Wilson back to Gonzo's house and told him to contact a neighbor and get some information even if he had to use a rubber hose to get it.

Wilson asked why he would need a hose and said he would try asking nicely.

Late at night Sloan went out to the malecón and walked west for a couple of miles, gulping down the sea breeze, tired but not tired enough to sleep. He reached Hispaniola Park and turned around. Under the fluttering palms he saw a few couples talking and laughing, barely glancing his way. Out on the boulevard cars rumbled by, their fading sounds enveloped by waves sloshing and groping into the rocky hollows and crevices under the coastal ledge. He tried several times to light a joint, finally squatting with his back to the sea. He stood smoking from his cupped hand, staring back at the cluster of high-rise lights to the east. He walked and smoked, eyes lifting to the stars, dropping to the dark horizon, periodically checking his surroundings. To the south a ship was passing and he tracked its lights moving slowly through the world. His phone buzzed.

He looked at the text, arriving so late, and found a bench. He felt spasms in his legs.

We nearly met eight years ago. I kept all the articles about that incident and the resulting inquiries so I know you more than you know me.

He read it again. He looked around to see if anyone was near him. He had the feeling a car would stop along the curb at any moment and someone would get out and approach him.

His thumbs wavered over the phone, his lungs expanding into the night. He wrote back.

I heard about you.

He saw a distant figure shambling toward him from the direction he was heading. He looked down at the next message.

We are connected. It cannot be otherwise.

He pictured the sister—short hair, a stocky, a take-charge kind of girl, younger than him but older than her brother. Indistinct features. He was sure he heard a feminine voice in the words. Had he read a description of her back then?

Why are you contacting me?

After a few minutes the reply came. *Maybe I'm obsessed. And here you are, back again.*

He wrote: *You believe in coincidence, but not accidents. Nothing I can do about that.*

The lone figure was getting nearer. An odd animated gait, with twitching movements, possibly indicating drink or drugs. Sloan kept smoking and stretched out his legs like he didn't give a fuck.

You're an educated man. You know what a monkey wrench gang does.

I do know. Property damage. I'm glad you're reaching out. I feel closer now.

You guys think you're gods. You probably want to meet me. Hear my voice.

As the passing man looked at him, Sloan stood up to face him, the stub of the joint in his mouth, the phone held down at his left side, his right arm also down, his body in a state of readiness.

The man watched him as he passed, quivering along the esplanade, rubbing the top of his head, his hand running back and forth over stubble.

Funny you should say that. I like both ideas.

I'll be seeing you. You probably won't see me.

Let's not rule it out. You're entitled to your hobby. I don't fault you for it.

It's not that, it's not closure either. I don't believe in that shit.

I don't either. Do what you have to do.

I will. Goodnight.

Let's talk. Call me.

She did not reply or call. He gave her more time. But he did not call her.

What could be said about time? About reality? Time moving forward, not backward. The universe expanding, not contracting, not staying still. Everything moving outward from the Big Bang. Nothing could be undone, taken back, retracted. Eight years ago they almost met. If they were ever going to meet could not at this moment in time be known. It remained to be known, no matter how much it was dreaded or desired. The future was speculation.

Reality could be broken down into elementary particles, which were not even particles in the way we conceived of particles. They were points in space-time. They were comprised of three things: mass, charge, and spin. So from the bottom up, the very bottom, everything was in motion, all the time. The so-called particles had velocity and a position, which was ever-changing. The position held true only for that infinitesimal fraction of time when it was measured. Then, it was gone.

Like Pablo Cruz. Never to be seen there again.

And so it was with us all.

29. The Carnival Life

The ranks swelled with carpenters, mostly local. A local medic was hired, along with a relief medic. Local drivers were hired. Two local PAs were hired for the Locations Department.

Sanchez brought two donkeys to the hotel in his trailer. Cragmore went down to inspect the animals and determine which one would be the better actor. He had Sanchez parade them out into the grass bordering the drive-up, where one of them, the smaller one, a female, deposited a load of equine biscuits just as Sloan joined the group to mitigate any negative publicity that might tarnish the production's standing with the hotel.

Cragmore judged the larger donkey the more likely to remain donkey-like under pressure, such as the hotel-lawn audition, and picked him. When asked the animal's name, Sanchez said he didn't know. Sloan named him Emile, gave him the remains of the apple he'd brought down, and repeated the name as he stroked the donkey's head and scratched behind his ears. He guessed the animal only understood Spanish but what if his actual name were Angel or Julio and he got confused by the new name and become stubborn. As the animals munched on the lawn, Sloan was bothered by the fact that he hadn't saved part of the apple for the other donkey, the loser, who kept looking at him.

Julieta Morales called Sloan and asked about the rumor of another unit in her building being selected.

"We need to move ahead," he said, "and you indicated that you'd lost interest."

"I certainly did not lose interest," she said. "I was simply going over all the details."

"Okay, my mistake. Since you didn't call me, I assumed—"

"Lucas," she said. "I thought we had an understanding."

"We do," he said. "But we need a signed agreement."

"I will send it over," she said, "and we'll make it official."

With each passing day Sloan wished he'd planted a tracking device on Gonzo's truck. He vaguely wondered if Transpo carried that kind of item in their gear and made a note to ask.

Nico had some kind of family illness back home in California and turned dark and withdrawn and mostly silent. He mentioned that he might need to leave for a short trip and Sloan did not reply at first. He thought of a standard platitude—it is what it is—but couldn't get it out.

Finally he said, "That's totally fine, amigo. Do what you gotta do."

The workshop was up and running. Equipment trucks were based and loaded there. Camera, Grip & Electric, Props, Greens, Special Effects, Set Dec. A multi-room trailer was rented for Hair & Makeup,

Wardrobe, Production Office, and second-tier actors. Motorhomes for the biggest stars, Tom and Margaret.

The batey shacks were being built. The monumental gate for the mansion was being designed, the materials sourced.

In Locations, the new production assistants were Santo Castillo and Belkis Santana. Sonia brought them up to speed and explained the most urgent issues. While they completed their paperwork, Sonia made inquiries at area hospitals. Wilson had met one of Gonzo's neighbors who said she thought he had not been feeling well. She knew him as Maximo.

At a regional hospital in San Pedro there was a patient named Maximo Gonzalez. Sonia was unable to get him on the phone so she called Wilson and had him leave his post to check on the patient. Within the hour Wilson stood at the foot of the sick man's bed and was able to confirm his identity. He called Sloan to report.

"What's wrong with him?" Sloan said.

"Chest pains," Wilson said. "He's under observation, getting tested."

"He's probably thinking about Maridalia," Sloan said. "We should get her over for a visit."

"What if it kills him? Wilson said.

"Talk to him," Sloan said. "Make sure he remembers you. Ask him if he'd like to see her."

The shooting schedule was divided into west and east. Since the cane fields worked at the end of the schedule and were located in the eastern section, the company would start with its base in the capital and then move east to La Romana and base there for the second half of filming. That half would include the Punta Cana resort, an hour further east of La Romana. Separate west and east diagrams made by Locations provided the crew with geographical overviews showing where locations were in relation to others.

The schedule would start with scenes of Larimore without his romantic co-star. The airport, the park, the condo, the jazz bar. Then the taxi crash, the waterfall, the jungle work.

With the additional Locations personnel the department worked on securing parking for Duarte Park for the first day of shooting, including a nearby basecamp. The work trucks had to be close to the location for equipment access. The caterer and nonessential, nonworking vehicles such as trailers, the crew bus and incidental crew cars would be at basecamp, ideally a short walk away, but if logistically unavoidable then within a reasonable shuttle distance. The complaints would come no matter how ideal the set-up. It was the nature of people.

With a representative from Municipal Services to guide and assist them, the team used barricades and cones and caution tape to mark the curbside spaces needed. Notices had been handed out to area businesses to explain the temporary inconvenience and thank them for supporting the film, whether or not they cared about movies or planned to see it or resented that their help was involuntary.

To top it off, parking guards were employed to prevent regular citizens, called civilians in the parlance of film language, from moving whatever obstacle they wanted in order to park wherever they wanted. The parking guards were instructed to be unarmed to prevent an altercation that might get out of hand and lead to an overly dramatic conflict. This precarious situation, balancing the needs of the filmmakers against the daily functioning of locals going about their lives, produced anxiety and insomnia within the Locations Department. Sloan had tried different tactics over the years, from downing shots to deep breathing to relaxation recordings of crashing waves, white noise, and whale songs.

Call time was 5:30am. The caterer would set up at 4:00am, with breakfast ready to eat at 5:00am. Locations would be on location at 3:00am, checking the parking, the basecamp, the park itself, seeking out anything unexpected that might impede or negatively impact the day's filming schedule. On Day One, it was all hands—except Nico—on deck, flooding the field with enough bodies to deliver the location and the basecamp as intended so the show would get moving and the first day would be accomplished successfully. This was important for morale, for setting the tone of the show, for good luck, for the enjoyment of the fact that after months of preparation and uncertainty and the sheer unreality of making a movie, the train had indeed left the station.

The first early rising was surreal, actual sleep time unknown, whatever nocturnal state of mind had been achieved was blasted away by the array of alarms—phone, room clock, hotel wakeup call—all intended as an absolute failsafe. Then room coffee and a hot shower to the head.

Once Sloan was there, in the dark, he felt a sense of peace, a calm before the storm. Pre-chaos. The quiet of the resting city. The parking guards were mostly awake and the reserved spaces were mostly intact, good enough to get the job done since they had overkilled the parking requirements to be on the safe side on the first day. The only denizens of the park were a stumbling old man with hair like Einstein's and a slinking ribcage dog.

He rousted the guards into a renewed state of attention, had them patrol actively, issued instructions to the team, left Sonia and Santo Castillo at the park, then took Wilson and Belkis Santana to the basecamp to meet the caterer. Using a printed diagram, they went over the vehicle parking plan by flashlight. Then the catering truck and support van arrived.

Sloan went back to the location. The trucks began to roll in, rumbling loudly and hissing into position with assistance from the transportation captain, who shouted up and down the streets as if everyone in the area were already awake.

With the trucks in position the drivers were shuttled over to the basecamp for breakfast. Vans were making their first runs. Sloan patrolled the location as signs of daily life began to appear. Delivery trucks, doorstep sweepers, circling pigeon flocks, the curious and the motley ambling into the coming dawn.

The pale sky, the AD department, the two picture cars. Walkie-talkies handed out. *Testing, testing. Radio check. Good check. Good check.* Then "The eagle has landed" as Cragmore arrived.

Rehearsal commenced with camera setup. The choreography of the cars amid the actual traffic, the city awakening as the actor's stand-in exited the vehicle, walked through a miscellany of extras in the art-directed park. There were invented vendors of balloons and food. There were nuns and skateboarders and musicians. The movie carnival turned the park into a carnival, compressing its life into a single day.

For Sloan, the day fragmented. Time grew slippery. He could feel the trance coming on. The crew was established, the situation under control. The park's perimeter was patrolled by set PAs, a zone of filming surrounded the camera team and the director. Real life passed by on the periphery. People stopped to observe, then moved on. Cars came and went. Horns blew. People shouted, laughed, sang out. Extras were positioned by the 2nd 2nd AD. The background was constantly being tweaked.

There was no dialogue. The actor, Tom Flint, walked on set as Larimore, having gone, story-wise, through his jungle trials and subsequent recovery already, chiseled lean and hard and wary. Cragmore took him aside to tone down his swagger, to temper his performance with jaguar savvy, as he called it.

Sloan walked to basecamp, another park with old stonework as pavement. He had texted Wilson to put a breakfast aside for him. Within the sonic strata of general urban traffic he could hear the disturbance of port trucks across the boulevard, and the periodic blast of a ship's horn. As usual, a great weight had lifted after the working trucks were in position and the crew was able to maneuver, all the pieces of moviemaking beginning to work together as a whole. A machine.

He sat under a tree on a plastic chair with a plate of eggs, toast, potatoes, and beans and a cup of hot coffee. He also had a vanilla yogurt. His walkie kept him updated, crackling but audible at this distance from the set. Though it was only 9:00am his body was telling him it must be 5:00pm.

He sipped his coffee and zoned out. They would be here all day and they were entrenched now. It would take an earthquake or a military invasion to get them out before they were done.

He walked back to the set, his mind elastic, his walkie catching the eye of certain pedestrians. The task now was to prevent external slowdowns, to make sure Locations wasn't responsible for the day attaining the dreaded classification of Unfinished.

As he got close he heard "Lock it up!" from the AD. Sloan was careful to determine the shot's direction by watching the PAs and the camera. Larimore was in position, a Steadicam operator behind him. Then came "Rolling!" and then "Speed!" and then "Action!" and Larimore began walking, the camera moving around him as he strode ahead, moving quickly and purposefully, seemingly a busy man crossing a park, keeping an eye on those around him.

The background noise was ambient. The star attracted attention and a crowd formed in his sightline. When the scene was cut, the crowd yelled out and waved. He waved back.

Security was visible in their dark uniforms, but lowkey, using hand signals and civility to keep people from getting too close. Behind them, a couple of stationery off-duty undercover police officers added a layer of seriousness. Their weapons were concealed under plainclothes but no one mistook their manner or purpose. When actual police officers were hired, they came armed. No discussion.

Sloan scrutinized the area, looking for trouble. He avoided looking at his watch, not wanting to bring the slowness of the day to his mind's forefront. The trance, the slog, the tedium, the boredom of the actual shoot. After all the work of preparation, of trying to turn words on a page into real places, this part dragged him down. If all was going well on location, the shoot was mind-numbing in its repetitive crawl.

The director mixed his shots, going wide and low as Montero arrived and stepped out of his car like a lethal giant in pursuit of his quarry. Then a long lens on Montero following among the citizens, capturing him in a narrow angle of view, the background blurred, the emphasis on Montero's face, his murderous eyes and large, stone-shaped head. After that, reaction shots, people scared of the man passing.

Sloan stood way back under some trees among the locals, arms folded, mind blank. He noticed that Sonia had appeared next to him.

She gave him a smile. "Twenty-seven days to go," she said.

"Lunch in an hour," he said. "I feel like I'm in

quicksand."

"I'll cover the set with Santo," she said.

"Keep half the guards with you, send the rest for lunch," he said. "Then switch them. The AD will probably do the same with the PAs."

"Okay," she said.

"Our new PAs seem pretty good," he said. He was thinking about a leak in the crew—thinking it had to be a local, but then not necessarily—and that the leaks predated the newest personnel.

"They don't know much," she said. "But they're smart and eager."

"Good," he said. Then, after a minute, "Did you ever research that other movie I did here?"

She looked up at him over her sunglasses. "Yes," she said. "I was curious about it."

Instinctively he scanned the faces he could see, not knowing who to look for. "And?" he said.

"It was mainly just old articles from that time," she said. "The sister was mentioned. Her name is Beca Cruz. Rebecca, I guess."

He nodded. "Was there a photo of her?"

"No," she said. "It must be her who contacted you."

"I would assume," he said. Across the park the next shot was being set up. After that, lunch.

"Did you hear from her again?"

"She texted me a few nights ago."

Sonia turned to face him. "Really? Did she threaten you?"

"No," he said. "She said she was obsessed."

"About what?"

"Her brother recently died," he said. "So I guess she was triggered by that."

"Where is she getting your info?" she said.

"I think someone on the crew is tipping her off," he said.

"Oh wow. That would make sense."

"I'm not doing anything about it," he said. "I just want you to be extra vigilant."

"I will," she said. "It just makes me a little nervous."

"Me too," he said. "I'm hoping it might help me to stay awake."

She laughed. "It looks like you need help."

He smiled and his eyes closed. "I'm going to speak to the cops and go grab an early lunch," he said. "Then I'll need a bucket of ice water to stick my head in. Maybe I'll just kneel in front of a cooler."

Film crews disrupted the natural order. Because of that, having cops on set could be beneficial. Uprisings had been quelled. Riots, robberies, and mayhem were averted by the presence of police. The only problem was, no matter the size of the set, no matter how vast a region was being protected from potential incursions or threats, no matter how many law enforcement officers were employed by the production, they tended to mass together in one place, congealed like a clump of frog eggs, typically where the craft service table was located. Endless snacks and drinks.

The two off-duty cops were an unbudgeted expense, an exception sanctioned for the start of filming. Everyone wanted the first day to go off without a hitch. And if everything went well, the cops would be seen as an unnecessary line item that Locations had wasted money on. Conversely, if any criminal activity disrupted a subsequent unpoliced set, Locations could be blamed for failing to provide adequate security. It was advisable to walk a thin line and be prepared to deflect whatever complaints came your way. Because complaints came with the territory.

He greeted the officers cheerfully and mentioned the lunch schedule, then courteously requested that they move around once in a while to make their presence more widely felt. As he spoke he made a swirling motion with his fingers, intending to support his suggestion of a perimeter patrol but possibly suggesting either a helicopter or a scalp massage. They smiled and nodded and he wondered if he might personally need their assistance in the near future.

As he walked to basecamp he was glad to feel the edginess, the uncertainty. It gave him an invisible companion on the long road to wrap. Otherwise, there were just all these filming days ahead. One after the other. The paychecks would keep coming, sure, racking up money, and with it, time. Freelance time to take as needed. All you had to do was say no to a job and do whatever else you had in mind. What kind of freelance idiot did that?

How could he be so ambivalent after all this time? He was living the carnival life.

At the airport the regular taxis, those who were not enlisted as picture car taxis in the scene, revolted against their exclusion by sounding their horns like a bunch of bleating sheep as close to the entrance as they were allowed to get. This took an intervention by airport security and Locations to bring the noise down to a normal airport level. Here was another scene with no dialogue but plenty of authentic ambient sound.

Locations discreetly paid meal money to some drivers, buying them off for the inconvenience and the loss of working hours. When word of this got out, all manner of "taxi" drivers were approaching them for payoffs, including people in beat-up cars and pickup trucks who had never charged a fare in their lives.

By the time Larimore exited the terminal a solid rain was falling and this dampened the demands of the imposter taxis. The director loved seeing the main character's weather introduction and an atmospheric start to the taxi chase. He felt he had merely thought about a rain effect and it had come to pass. The script supervisor made a continuity note to wet down the hero taxi—unless it was determined that it would be wind-dried—when the chase resumed on a different day at a different location.

Wilson needed to be in the office, stationary and resolute in his duties. There were maps to make, certificates of insurance to be requested, location agreements to be processed, check requests to be submitted. Nico had gone home to be with his ailing mother. This left the other four—Sloan, Sonia, Belkis, and Santo—to manage the set, opening it for the caterer and closing it when the last of the gear was loaded out.

Sloan took on the position of opener, showing up at the ungodly hour of zero-dark-thirty, so-called no matter the actual predawn time, to make sure the caterer got in position to start cooking. Santo was trained to be the closer, the last man out, to handle directly or take note of any lingering location issue, such as damage, and to make sure no company property was left behind.

All this would change when the company switched to nights. The opener would show up before dusk. On split days, the scenes would slide from day into night, the timetable adjusted accordingly. Certain scenes called to be shot at "magic hour" when the day began to change to night and the colors in the sky were often the most dramatic. The light was called golden.

Sancho P looked about the same as usual. Since the scenes were being shot "day for night" while the club was closed during the day, the windows had been blacked out to eliminate any trace of natural light. Some blue lighting had been added to enhance the coolness of the place, and posters of the Dada period had been hung on the walls. In the relative gloom their details were not particularly clear but Sloan recognized a Picabia painting and a Man Ray photograph. He imagined they were intended to add an antiestablishment vibe that aligned with the character of Larimore.

Meanwhile, the condo was being prepped by the art department. He left Sonia at the club and headed over to the next location. With Nico gone, they were understaffed. Whenever Belkis or Santo was left alone at a location they would call him with questions. Before he could get there, Santo called from the condo.

"The lady wants to know why we are painting the walls the same color," he said.

"Tell her I'll be there in a few minutes," Sloan said.

Dominic Larue wished he were on a different movie, one with more need for his creative vision. In the narrow confines of his hampered role on this one, he struggled to contribute anything of substance to the look. He had the paint in his budget and wanted to use it to make the condo color his choice, regardless of the fact that the director was pleased with the location as it was.

So he picked a color that, when the color chart was fanned open, was two shades away from the current color, which meant, no matter how close it was to the existing shade, it was in fact different. And which gave the owner the option of having it painted back to the original, which would entail more labor and cost and inconvenience and follow-up by Locations. Unless she chose to keep the new color. It was a costly gamble built on ego and wounded pride.

Lately, Larue dreamed of building sets for a grand period piece or an extraterrestrial world, something like the interior of the Moskovsky train station, the futuristic architecture of an alien city, an underground sporting arena, or a red-light district that would make Tokyo look like a slum.

As it was, he had the batey. He had an encampment of cane field shacks as his greatest achievement, the pinnacle of his creative impact on *Larimore*. He might become known as a master of the rundown, the industry's emperor of the impoverished.

When Sloan saw the color change he had to strain to keep a straight face and explain the situation to Julieta Morales, the condo's owner.

"Look," he said. "This might seem crazy to normal people like us. But production designers concern themselves with tiny details that no one watching the movie will ever notice except them and other production designers. They live in an insular world of design. In this case you might call it Design Without Reason. They see minuscule differences in color as contributing to the texture of the film and sending subliminal messages to the audience." Sloan knew he sounded crazy himself. "People will feel a certain way after being exposed to certain colors and shapes."

She stared at the painter rolling out the new light gray over the old slightly lighter gray.

"This is so mysterious," she said. "I will just tell my husband we needed a new coat of paint."

"That would be the best thing," Sloan said.

As he was driving back to the Colonial Zone, Sloan got a call from Wilson, who had been sent to the hospital with a contract for Maximo Gonzalez to sign.

"He went into surgery," Wilson said.

"Did he sign first?"

"No, boss, he was unconscious."

"You could have put a pen in his hand and helped him sign," Sloan said.

Wilson was quiet while he tried to imagine himself doing such a thing.

"Wait there a while," Sloan said. "Keep me posted and get the map done."

He texted Dulce. *Hi. Hope you had a great trip. We are shooting and time is short. How soon can we meet and solidify?*

She wrote back about ten minutes later. *Hola mi papi chulo. Sorry to neglect you for so long. We could meet tonight if you can.*

Sloan stared at the screen. She'd gone off the radar and now she was calling him cute daddy. Was it good news or bad news? He doubted he could make the two-hour drive there and spend some time and then drive back again without falling asleep at the wheel and dying in a fiery crash.

I'd love to but the weekend would be better.

Oh papi, she wrote back, *tonight would be a good time to solidify.*

What the fuck? he thought. Did she want him to die in a fiery crash? All solidified.

He waited a minute, mentally flipping a coin that wouldn't land. Thinking "a bird in the hand" type reasoning, with her as the bird. A delay might roll into untold days. He'd emailed her the agreement and he kept a hard copy with him in case of a scenario just like this. Was she actually ready to sign or was she just in a mood to jack him around? There was no way in hell he could tell.

She sent him her preferred time, 7:00 to 8:00pm, and her address. He hadn't been to her house before.

Then he sent Sonia an update, saying he was off to get a contract signed and wouldn't be back to the set. He asked how Vuk was handling the shoot. She said he was a perfect Serbian gentleman. Sloan said cleavage was both a stimulant and a sedative.

He went to his hotel room and showered and tried unsuccessfully to take a nap.

The mansion looked modest from the front, fit for a lowkey queen on a Casa de Campo cul-de-sac, but it sat directly on the ocean. He would have considered it for the mansion location but hadn't wanted to risk anything that might upset the sugar deal. Now he second-guessed himself.

She opened the gate and greeted him at the door in a flowing aqua leaf-print gauze kaftan that left her body free to oscillate and appeared to be the sole garment clinging to her person. She hugged him, breathed alcohol into his face and ear, and he followed her bare feet across the white marble through the modern living room and out to the terrace.

Moonlight glinted off the ocean and the horizontal stripe of blue pool out past the lawn. No neighbors could be seen and there was no evidence of staff at home. The devilish twins had left the nest, possibly never to return except for holidays, and the lady of the house had entered a new phase.

On the patio table sat a sweating, half-gone pitcher of mojitos, glasses and flutes, and a bottle of champagne chilling in its own ice bucket. A tray of cheeses, a glass bowl of olives, a stack of cloth napkins. Also, Sloan noticed, there was a round ashtray in which a ceramic pipe nested in the shape of a bird. Beside it, a lighter and an embroidered silk pouch.

Presumably there was, and would be, a lot to celebrate.

"You look well," he said. "I mean great, actually. Happy."

She laughed. "I've been enjoying myself."

"Is it your birthday?" he said.

"No, it's yours. Sit, sit," she said, motioning with her hand. "Can I pour you a mojito?"

"By all means."

She stood and poured and served him. He was so thirsty he downed most of the glass in the first taste. She refilled him, letting him catch up to her.

He let the rum sink in and said nothing, feeling the night and her presence. His mind floating.

She filled and lit the pipe and handed it to him. He took it and smoked, relaxed into the present moment, knowing he would never make it back to the capital tonight. He would be lucky to get to the set in time to set up crew signs and meet the caterer.

She was standing behind him, unable to sit still. She rubbed his shoulders, her fingers digging into his muscles. He felt a loosening, ripples cascading through his body.

"I've been unfair to you," she said. "I thought about that while I was gone."

"Why is that?" he said.

"You've been straight with me," she said. "I know that."

Her fingers crept up his neck, massaging both sides, and worked into his scalp, lifting his hair. She tilted his head back against her breasts, pillows of solace, he thought, as she gently pulled him deeper and pressed her soft flesh against the sides of his face. He imagined his head engulfed.

When he opened his eyes she was sitting in his lap, facing him, straddling him. He felt like a gap in time had opened.

"Do you want to talk about the contract?" she said.

"Not at this exact moment."

"Things are solid between us," she said, settling her thighs, squeezing her bottom.

She reached over and lifted his glass, downed a swallow, then shared it with him.

She leaned wide to the table and he cupped her breasts, lifted them in their gauze covering.

She brought her mouth to his and rutted in his lap as they kissed. Rum and mint mixing.

She floated upward. He watched her hands at his pants, pulling them down, his knees pushed apart, her body sliding between them, her hair against his thighs, her mouth taking him in.

He heard his groans as if from a mountain. Her steady suction drawing him empty. He shuddered, finally stood, wobbling, drank, poured more, smoked and blew everything into the sky. She was still down there, on her back, her kaftan pulled up to her waist, legs drawn up, her bare wetness lifting, offered on a tray of stone.

He stepped free of his fallen pants, knelt at her glistening lips and lapped, stretched out and buried his face there, licking her and gripping her heavy bottom to anchor himself. Digging deeper.

Maybe he wasn't breathing correctly, healthily, not receiving sufficient oxygen, seeing flares and hearing a neighbor's yelping animal, hallucinating about oysters, the fresh brine and slippery elastic texture, the liquid dish. She scooted back in audible increments. He rolled over, his back to the cool stone, his wet face to the sky.

He heard a shot, awoke to the moon, the only witness, and heard the cork thud nearby. Dulce rustled and billowed overhead, white foam spilling over her fist. She stared down at him, smiled and gestured upward with the bottle.

They sat and sipped vessels of turbulent bubbles in the silver moonlight.

He saw the pages of the agreement fluttering, held down by the olive bowl. He broke off a chunk of cheese and ate. He plucked olives with his fingers, dripped oily spots across the paper.

"I like what you said about the donation," she said. "It helps the right people."

"Yeah," he said. "I need to put a batey in the area. Then burn some of it."

"You said you had another option."

"I did," he said. "But the owner is unhealthy now."

She looked out at the ocean, the breeze stirring her loose hair, then back at Sloan.

"I won't quibble," she said. "I'll name my fee and handle it without my brother's involvement. It will finance my personal project without going through the corporation."

"Makes sense to me," he said, and continued to feast. "As long as you're a corporate officer."

"We all are," she said.

"Did you show him the synopsis?" he said.

She shook her head. "I decided against it. Either he wouldn't read it or he'd ask too many questions and turn it into something."

"Okay," he said. "What's your number?"

"One twenty."

Sloan smiled but did not laugh. He could still taste her.

"That's a big jump," he said.

"You've added the batey," she said. "And the money for the other place is floating now."

"The total was one hundred."

She lifted her head and her dark eyes caught the moon. "Everything is on me now."

"Can we do one ten?" he said.

It was her turn to smile. "Only because I like you," she said. She stepped inside and returned quickly and set a tiny glass bottle on the table. "You can take this if you want to stay awake," she said. "I don't want to hear about you turning into a fireball on the side of the road."

Jacked up on coke, he drove the nearly-empty highway like a man in a tunnel, a pipeline. Darkness wrapped around the headlight beams and he burrowed on into the remainder of his life. Possessed of a document, which he held up to examine when a car approached, water circles and translucent cheese stains making it an artifact, her signature something a child might make, a doodle symbol that would be different the next time. A one-off signature. An escape hatch.

She'd made him coffee too, a full curvaceous caretaker, and scanned herself a copy of the agreement, and then hugged and kissed him goodbye, friendly partners in this deal, so long in making, so long in the coming. He had wanted to fuck her right then, and pictured her now crashed out and splayed open in her kaftan. He'd taken the time to fondle her breasts, large and heavy, swaying freely before him under their thin cover, then pressed into him, joining them together in softness.

This specific attention had made her giggle, high as she was, and she'd said she had him figured for a breast lover from the very first moment. She knew. And he knew the batey was last in the schedule. And that he would be seeing her again.

The streets were calm. He was early. Was there a split call? What day was it? It was Thursday. Street work, day and dusk. Tomorrow was Friday, the condo. Split call. End of the week. Late work in a residence with weekend leniency. Hoped for and expected. He was out of his head. He could use a shower. No need for a nap. Not now.

In the darkness of his car he snorted more coke. Get through the day. Level out tomorrow. Get it done. Crystalline particles of light. Night dust. Streetlamps of different hues, luminosities. Random night dwellers on the predawn hunt. Or lost. But not him. He had a car. Locked.

He closed his eyes for a second.

Bam! Fuck! Transpo pounding on the window. Truck idling.

He changed into a clean t-shirt. No toothbrush. He rinsed his mouth with water, spit in the gutter. He gargled. Where were the guards?

At 10:14am he got a call from Wilson.

"Morning boss. I'm at the hospital."

After a long pause, Sloan said, "Okay."

"Maximo died," Wilson said. "About five minutes ago."

"Are you sure it was him?" Sloan said. "Mistakes are made every day."

"Are you okay, *jefe*?"

"I'm fine," Sloan said. "That just fucking sucks, that's all. He was a good man."

"What about the agreement?" Wilson said. "Who will sign it now?"

"Forget it," Sloan said. "The location died with him."

"Does that mean ..." Wilson hesitated. "The queen of ..."

"The queen smiles upon us," Sloan said.

Sonia did not smile upon him. He slunk around the set's perimeter like a leper. He avoided small talk, strolled around making lists in his head that had to be redone a little while later.

He heard a walkie squawk. "Locations!"

He wasn't planning to stay long and hadn't bothered to pick his up. He heard Sonia take the call.

"Go for Locations," she said.

"This is Sord. We have a noisy crowd near camera."

"I'm on it," she said.

Sloan got a coffee from craft service and waited on the sidewalk. It was full daylight and the camera team was down the street, apparently ready to get the first shot off. Which would be Larimore walking. Traffic was being held intermittently for rehearsal. He listened to the horns and regular morning street noise. Sonia was calling.

"There's a group of guys shouting out comments and laughing loudly," she said.

"Did security confront them?" Sloan said.

"Yes. They got quiet for a minute, until he left."

"How old are they?"

"They're twenty-something."

"Okay, let's make friends," Sloan said. "Get Santo to bring them a case of beer and tell them they need to move further away to drink it. A block away."

"Really?"

"Yes. Make sure he gets a receipt. I'll buy it from him and deal with the fallout."

After a while the radio complaints dropped off and he heard the call for action.

He texted Sonia. *I have to go to the office, be back later.*

Ok, she said.

From the garage he made it up to his room unseen. Showered, brushed his teeth well.

In the office Cindy Bonnet asked how things were going on the set. He said, "Fine. Good."

She told him Stunts and Rigging wanted to visit the waterfall the day before shooting to rig a jib arm at the top. This was so the camera could swing out and look straight down to capture the jump. After the top shots were done, while the team was moving down, the jib would be removed.

"I'm meeting someone from the Ministry of the Environment there on Monday," he said, delivering info that she didn't need to know.

"Bet you'll be glad to get Nico back," she said.

He paused on the way to his desk and looked back. "Definitely. When is that?"

"This weekend," she said. "He'll be ready for Monday."

At lunch he got a call from Sonia. She was sitting

on an apple box next to the camera with a plate on her knees. Guard duty on set with some PAs and security. Under a wide-brimmed Bahamian straw hat she'd gotten on another show. He pictured her as he'd seen her earlier—damp v-neck t-shirt, deep cleavage, hair falling on her neck, shorts, brown arms and legs, running shoes, walkie-talkie riding low on her hip.

"The beer boys went away," she said. "But they must have drunk their beers fast because in a while we could hear them from their new position, even louder."

"The old booze backfire," Sloan said. He was trying to squelch his sniffling. He wasn't used to cocaine and his nose was running.

"I was sending security over there again but the AD got pissed off and got in my face."

"Sord the Norseman," Sloan said. "Ready to plunder."

"He asked me if I got the job because of my tits," she said.

"I hope you told him the truth," Sloan said.

"I said 'Absolutely, that's how I get all my jobs.'"

Sloan smiled. "What did he say?"

"He asked me if I wanted to get a drink after wrap."

In his slightly paranoid state, Sloan wondered if she thought he'd be jealous of that. "Did he say where?"

"I said I couldn't because I already had a date with my boss," she said.

"No you didn't."

"No I didn't."

Between his sniffles, he heard her sniffling. Then gasping squeaks, not sounds he had ever heard from her. She was crying.

"What's the matter, Sonia?"

She sobbed into the phone. "He yelled at me in front of the crew, told me I was an amateur and an island idiot."

"What'd you do?" Sloan said.

"I walked away," she said.

"Did he see you cry?" Sloan said. "Did anyone?"

"No," she said. "I'm just crying now. With you."

"That's great, baby," he said. "Listen to me. Don't ever let them see you cry. Okay? Never. Sord will kick you if you're down. Cry alone or cry with me."

"Okay," she said, sniffing her remaining sadness, her embarrassment, inside.

"Let's meet this weekend," he said.

He called Wilson, who he'd expected to see in the office.

"What are you doing, making funeral arrangements?"

"Hey boss. I was waiting to see if any family showed up. Maybe the location is still …"

"That's a nice thought," Sloan said. "But we don't have time to wait for legal matters to be resolved."

"Maybe Maximo had a partner," Wilson said.

"Just get back to the office," Sloan said. "I'm texting you Maridalia's number. She was going to help us with Maximo. Call her and please explain why we won't need her anymore. And thank her very much for her willingness to help us."

He left the office and went up to his room. He snorted another line and pulled up some history of the island. He opened his notebook and made notes with a pen. He wrote fast, intending to put down the gist of the problem, if not its absolute accuracy. Recorded history, after all, was incomplete and interpretive.

Two New World colonies, one Spanish and one French, shared the same island, Hispaniola, the western third having been ceded to France after Spain's defeat in a European war. It was split into separate colonies in 1697. A defining cultural distinction between the two began during settlement. Spain promoted an influx of settlers while France brought in great masses of African slaves to create a plantation economy.

Beginning in 1791, Haiti's sugar-producing slaves revolted to break away from French domination, leading to the first Black-led nation in the western hemisphere. In their 1803 revolution the Haitians defeated the French Army, declaring independence in January 1804. In the next few months most of the remaining European population were massacred, thus ridding the Haitians of their oppressors. Haitian soldiers took inspiration from the French Revolution as a justification for their genocide, a revolt against French atrocities and slavery.

In 1805 Haitian forces entered Santo Domingo to lay siege to the Dominican capital. The attempt was unsuccessful but on their return journey to Haiti these forces burned towns and slaughtered thousands of Dominicans. Many prisoners were marched to Haiti and massacred there or forced to work as slaves. This brutal invasion claimed the lives of nearly half of the Spanish side of the island.

In 1822, Haiti invaded Santo Domingo and took over the entire island for twenty-two years. This occupation led to a Dominican economic decline and a resentment of Haiti by Dominicans.

In 1844, the Dominican Republic regained its freedom, fueled by a rebellion led by Juan Pablo Duarte, known as the father of Dominican independence. In contrast to other Latin American countries, the Dominican Independence Day commemorates freedom from Haiti, not Spain.

The two countries warred again in 1849, 1854, and 1859. The unending conflict with Haiti led the Dominican Republic to enlist the support of Spain, who made their former colony an overseas province. This led to a guerilla war between pro-Dominican forces and Spanish troops. After huge financial losses, along with a staggering human toll, especially from yellow fever, Spain withdrew in 1865. Haiti finally recognized Dominican independence in 1867.

In the twentieth century, the Dominican Republic prospered from its sugar industry, and throughout this time many thousands of Haitians were brought in to work the cane fields.

In 1930, Rafael Trujillo rose to power in the Dominican Republic and ruled with an iron fist. In 1937 he ordered the Dominican military to slaughter thousands of Haitians near the border in an effort to rid the country of its neighbors. This episode of genocide was called the Parsley Massacre because soldiers would carry a spring of parsley and use the pronunciation of the word in Spanish—perejil—to determine if people suspected of being Haitian would mispronounce the word because of their Creole language. This method of locating victims illustrated the difficulty of a visual identification of the targeted ethnicity within the border region.

In 1961, as Trujillo was being driven in his 1957 Chevrolet Bel Air on a road outside the capital, he was ambushed and shot dead by assassins, some of whom were members of his armed forces.

Present-day tensions remained hostile due to the shared and tangled history of invasions, territorial disputes, exploitations, and mistreatment perpetrated and endured by the neighboring nations.

Aside from the economics of the sugar industry, Sloan started to see the bateyes as a kind of ongoing payback for historical animosities. A perpetual reminder.

He texted Nico. *Hey man, I hear you're coming*

back. I hope your mom is doing better now.

The reply came within five minutes.

She has breast cancer. Treatment has started. Let's meet Sun night for new game plan.

Sloan replied. *So sorry brother. Safe travels. See you Sunday.*

He thought of his own mother. She'd remarried and moved to North Carolina. He hadn't seen her in eighteen months, hadn't seen his sister in New Mexico in two and a half years. His father lived in Japan. He realized they weren't the tightest of families. But he was a loner, always had been. Even if he were reborn as an affluent polygamist with a harem of wives and concubines and belonged to the Elks, Rotary, Lions, and Toastmasters clubs, he would still be a loner.

They got through the condo without much incident, no one except the above-the-lines using the in-house toilet. The working crew went down to the street where the portable units were parked.

After dark a fight was staged in the open-air hallway near the elevators. Larimore's cover was blown. The scene was lit just well enough to see that Larimore was fighting for his life against a knife-wielding, would-be assassin who was actually a stuntman whose prone body would be dragged into the condo unit before the elevator door opened or anyone stuck their head out of another condo on the seventh floor to see what all the commotion was about. Who was this nameless, stick-on character—presumably hired by Montero—who was able to follow Larimore from bar to building despite the fact that on a previous occasion a follower had been sensed on the street? Why did the shadow stake out that bar? Did Montero have a league of shadowy associates staking out many bars in their maniacal effort to stumble upon their prey?

Sloan felt embarrassed for Duncan Barlow, the

screenwriter. Was he being coerced into adding scenes for the director? Would Cragmore get a screenwriting credit too? What was the point of adding this sloppy scene? Was the audience imagined to be nodding off at this point in the story?

In the course of his faked death, the stuntman suffered a dislocated shoulder.

On Sunday Sloan spent the afternoon at Sonia's apartment, engaged in erotic frolicking and luxurious napping in her bed. He disclosed that he'd secured a signed sugar contract from Imperial but did not elaborate and she did not inquire about details.

He met Nico at a Zone bar at dusk. Things had changed, as they do. Nico would meet with Gene Friedman in the morning and propose that he leave the show early, as soon as they started the batey work. Sloan said he totally understood, of course. They toasted their collaboration but it was half-hearted by now.

The Ministry of the Environment official, Fausto Guzman, met Sloan at the top of Socoa Falls on Monday at ten thirty, more or less, as agreed. The waterfall fell under the Natural Resources division and the Film Office had recommended that they be involved, in essence to cover their government asses. Sloan figured it was a perfunctory meeting and would have bet a paycheck that they would not be going to the bottom.

They walked on the riverside trail to within sight of the cliff edge, water flowing steadily before them and tumbling away into mist and open space. Sloan explained that they would secure the top and bottom for safety and film from both vantage points. A professional stuntman would leap out and fall down into the pool.

Guzman pondered the idea. He said his main

concern was for the preservation of the natural beauty of the country. He did not mention a concern for the preservation of human life, so obvious it could go unspoken. He specifically did not want any equipment secured by drilling into the riverine boulders or trees. Sloan assured him the camera arm could be held in place by ropes and nylon straps staked into the ground or tied to trees. He made this promise on the spot.

When he was informed of the proposed date of filming, a darkness fell over the face of the government man, much like the shadow of the cloud sliding over the men as they spoke. He told Sloan the permit could take six weeks. The men looked at the cloud, as if seeking a solution from above. When none came, Sloan asked if there was a way to expedite the permit, perhaps in the form of a "rapid processing" payment. After a brief pause, Guzman said that this was possible.

Sloan asked him the amount of the permit and was told it was one hundred US dollars. He produced two one-hundred-dollar bills and handed them over, saying he could use the permit itself as the receipt, no rush.

They shook hands and walked back to the parking area.

Despite his displeasure, Gene Friedman remained sitting at his desk, acknowledging the fact that his standing posture would not lend enough gravitas to his anger to warrant the extra energy.

He slapped an envelope with Sloan's name on it and his petty cash receipts sticking out.

"Nico passed this along to me," Friedman said, "because he doesn't know what you've been doing in his absence. You expect Accounting to pay these vague 'location expense' charges like 'beer' and 'permit gratuity? What do I look like, your fraternity brother?"

"I don't have any fraternity brothers," Sloan said.

"And what is this?" Friedman said, lifting the stained and wrinkled pages of the sugar agreement. "A placemat or a contract? Did you sign it yourself? Did you make up a number that sounded impressive?"

"That's a valid contract," Sloan said.

"Who signed it?" Friedman said.

"Dulce Medina," Sloan said.

"Do you see a D or an M here?" Friedman said.

"I know it looks like a Stone Age infant signed it but she's an officer of the company who happened to be slightly inebriated at the time," Sloan said.

The production manager stared at him with a suspicious expression. "I'm not quite sure what to make of that," he said. "It's been said that you worked to capitalize on a personal relationship."

Sloan nearly laughed. "Who the fuck cares how the agreement was completed," he said. "There it is on your desk."

Friedman pursed his lips sourly, like he had a wedge of lime between them and his teeth. "Don't take this the wrong way, because it's my job to question everything," he said. "But it could appear that this fee is structured to include a kickback."

"Wow," Sloan said. "Now I see why you're so often compared to Sherlock Holmes. Except you either have a shit memory, or you enjoy acting like you do."

"What am I forgetting?"

"We had two locations and now we have one. Consequently, the price is consolidated."

"What happened to the other location?"

"Are you serious?" Sloan said. "The man fucking died."

"Really?" Friedman said. "Do we have a death certificate?"

"We can get one," Sloan said. "As it is, our

coordinator, Wilson Diaz, was at the hospital."

Friedman drummed his fingers on the desk and looked at the wall calendar, then waved the agreement. "So all this money goes to ..." He stirred his other hand in the air like he was thinking of saying "Abracadabra" or "Open sesame."

"It will be used as a donation," Sloan said, "for the benefit of the cane cutters."

Friedman seemed lost in thought. "There is something funny about all this."

"Okay," Sloan said. "You got me. You wore me down with your penetrating inquiry. I had the other guy killed by heart attack so I could orchestrate a lucrative deal for myself."

"Get out of here," Friedman said.

With Nico able to cover some of the time on set, Sloan scouted a new location, a place for Larimore to go after the condo no longer worked as a hideout. Larimore would now spend daytime hours at an athletic club, swimming, working out, drinking blended health drinks, using the bathroom and showering. He would keep his valuables in a locker and sleep in a rental car he parked in different places. Even after Sloan read the new scene a second time, he still laughed.

While he was out roaming the city, he stopped by the Botanical Garden to see how the art department's prep was going. When he saw the monumental gate being erected as the entrance to the vast grounds of the mansion belonging to Luis La Vega, his first thought was *The Hound of the Baskervilles*. He couldn't actually picture any gates related to that story but the overwrought macabre metalwork brought it to mind.

Was this monstrosity related to a portrayal of Big Sugar? Wasn't the show preposterous, humorously excessive, over the top? Was the director secretly subversive, reinventing himself in plain sight, making a comedy out of a romantic adventure? Maybe Sloan would nod knowingly at Cragmore like a fellow puzzle-solver. A silent observer who was in on the joke.

As if the collective wishes of the crew propelled their forward motion, the days fell by the wayside. The location list grew smaller as places faded away in a cinematic rearview window. Everyone wanted to get through, reach the finish line, succeed, as if better things awaited them, a vacation or the next job, the promise of future glory and more paychecks. It was like being on a carousel, moving up and down and around like children fluctuating between moments of squealing and tension and giddiness and terror and dizziness and disorienting music—getting you nowhere except older and more experienced.

Sometimes a thin line existed between authorization and a can of worms you wish you'd never opened. Once the taxi crash site had been selected Wilson was sent over to a local title registry office to ascertain the property's ownership. The information was indecipherable and he was advised to return with a real estate attorney. At that point, Locations backed away from the legal route.

There were three requirements for the crash location: a desolate stretch of curved road, a forest near the road, and unfenced land between the road and the trees.

In the bed of a rented pickup truck the grips rigged a framework of steel piping so that the vehicle could function as a camera car and track the motion and drama of the taxi carrying Larimore as it was pursued by the other car. The camera was mounted to a base that was clamped to stacked boxes strapped and winched in place. The scene was meant to be frenetic and frightening as the camera led the taxi around the curve and the pursuers pulled abreast of the taxi to force it off the road.

The production had one taxi and needed to get the shot of the crash—the taxi going off-road—in one take in the event that the car got damaged and then no longer matched the previous view of the car leaving the airport. Prior to the stunt, reaction shots of Larimore and the driver had to be taken inside the taxi as the men watched the other vehicle gaining on them.

The lead-up to the stunt was rehearsed several times and each time the director called for more speed. As the camera rolled and the taxi was being overtaken, the director called for more speed and the AD shouted the order into his radio. Without reducing the camera truck's speed, the director wanted the taxi closer to the camera. Inside the taxi now were two stuntmen buckled in under a roll bar, prepared to crash.

The taxi hit a small plywood ramp hidden in the roadside weeds. The car lifted up on two wheels, careened into the adjacent grass, fell onto its passenger side, and slid about ten yards. The director jumped down from the truck and shook his hands in the air, yelling at the AD and everyone else that the taxi had not rolled over.

The taxi was righted and inspected for damage. The side mirror had broken off and the right side was dented and scratched. The entire car was wiped down, then road dust was reapplied, spread over the surface in naturalistically appropriate handfuls of dirt by the prop master. They would shoot the scene again and they would not see much of the right side. If necessary, they could cut some of the first take into the scene during the editing.

Sloan's stomach felt as bound up as a rubber band ball. He was afraid someone—random official or cop or landowner—would come along and shut them down. At home, that would have been much more likely. Here, he was getting away with it. His rental car was angled into the road, flashers on. Base camp was back around the curve, two miles away, on a derelict piece of land with vine-covered sheds and an abandoned tractor.

During rehearsal, or when the camera was rolling, traffic had to be held. Santo had one end of the stretch of road, Sloan the other. They would step out and raise a hand and speak to the drivers. They explained that a movie was being filmed and the wait would be short. People were generally curious and respectful. If this spectacle was occurring on a country road, it must've been approved by the government, if not by the creator himself.

From inside his car Sloan watched the taxi roll over twice and wobble to a stop. The back seat stuntman, dressed as Larimore, crawled out of a window and ran toward the trees, the gunmen from the other vehicle firing at him as they approached the taxi. The scene was cut and the camera repositioned for a closer look at the gunmen shooting into the driver-side window, then taking off after Larimore.

"Okay," Sloan said to himself. "The driver has been executed. Let's wrap it."

No permit, no contract, no location fee—a completely stolen location. With various frayed nerves dangling in the summer air.

When questioned by the producer on this point, Sloan had said that the Film Office told him they'd be fine. Which, from a certain angle, could be interpreted as the truth. Nico backed him up. What choice did he have?

To the delight of many, the actor playing Graham Perry arrived to shoot the first two of his scenes—the dive bar and the food truck. He was a popular B movie star with a cult following who would need to come back and die during the finale outside the amphitheater.

At the waterfall's pre-shoot rigging, Sloan monitored the installation of the jib arm and posted two guards overnight. One was meant to keep the other awake. And vice versa.

In the morning's predawn darkness he met the guards in the parking area as they stretched and walked around like they'd been immobile for a while.

He walked the trail by flashlight, hearing the roar of water getting louder. He shone his light on the yellow straps lying on the ground and waving like grass in the river's current. The jib arm was gone. He searched around, his light jerking in all directions. He walked farther away from the edge and still came up with nothing. The arm had either been stolen or sent tumbling over the cliff.

The AD was furious, torn between yelling at the guards or blaming the grips. He stormed over to the falls to check the evidence, searching the ground for footprints and other clues as the sky was just beginning to lighten. He wanted to believe that the pressure of the river had loosened the straps and steadily pushed the steel arm sitting on its steel baseplate inch by inch to the edge.

He sent the riggers to the bottom, telling them to retrieve the arm and bring it back up ASAP. Sloan stood aside, thinking the river could never have pushed such weight, that it defied logic. He thought someone local had known another way in, had untethered the arm and pushed it over.

Crew members gathered by the bus and filled the air with the sharp slapping of exposed skin and the nose-wrinkling citrus of insect spray. The caterer was soon serving coffee and breakfast.

Cragmore took the news in stride, declaring that he would shoot the bottom first and then move up. They would waste some time waiting for light at the pool. With the shooting sequence reversed, lunch would be ferried down by production assistants. There would be some jungle work at the bottom with Larimore alone. The jungle scenes with the soldiers would be done at the top the following day.

When there was enough light to see into the pool, the grips located the submerged arm, stuck in the sand like a sunken oil derrick. By then, a PA had showed up with diving masks. It took them several underwater trips to dig out and dislodge the arm, which was now bent to the point of being unusable. The info was relayed by radio and a man was immediately dispatched to the capital to get a replacement arm.

Larimore was mostly wet in the pool area and barely needed Hair & Makeup. The few civilian pool visitors who hadn't seen the closure notice or who had circumvented the main trail were politely informed of the pool's status and invited to watch quietly from a distance. This proved to be uneventful while the camera was being rigged in the water but paid off when stones were dropped as missiles from above, crashing into the pool in a blind attempt to kill the hero, all of which turned out to be a warmup for the guy leaping from the top as shouts and gunshots were heard. After the cut, clapping broke out from every vantage point. Cragmore wanted another take. The AD yelled, "Quiet on the set" and a second stuntman dressed as Larimore made the leap.

After the meal break the jungle escape and trekking shots were completed and the crew and the actor hiked back to the top. In the morning they would start with the leap from the top and the downward point of view.

At the end of the day the medic had dispensed adhesive bandages, vitamin C, aspirin, gauze wraps, aloe, antiseptic gel, rubbing alcohol, and treated nothing alarming. It seemed miraculous.

The trucks were left overnight. With extra security.

On the way back to the location in the morning dark, one of the passenger vans was struck by a car encroaching into their lane. Both vehicles were disabled but no one suffered more than bruises and shock. Although the day started with a delay, the sky was clear and the stunt looked good. Ramon's militia were suitably menacing. Gunshots upset the birdlife and rattled the nerves of several locals. One of the soldiers suffered a puncture wound in his thigh from a broken branch and had to be driven to a hospital. A dehydrated makeup assistant fainted and spent time recovering in Sonia's car.

The completion of the waterfall was seen as a turning point, with an over-the-hump inflection. The company prepared to move to the eastern portion of the shoot. Packing up, changing hotels, moving to La Romana. Travel day.

Due to Nico's absence, the neighborhood association meeting regarding permission to shoot at the cove beach had been postponed. Sloan had emailed a proposal and now the meeting had been reconvened with a few board members, and Nico said he would attend without Sloan.

Another pointed, accusatory bilingual article came out in the *Free Daily*.

Dear amigos: Hollywood continues to roll like conquistadors among us—
You may have heard of the two plots that serve all movies:

Someone goes on a journey. A stranger comes to town.

In our case, a carnival of strangers came to town. Again.

They trapse across the land like a motley tribe of Fortunados.

They cruise the roads and roam the jungles. They jump from waterfalls.

In their brazen occupation they mock the locals and trample our island culture.

In their gringo affectation they churn out trash while stomping on guavas and mangoes.

This latest reckless colonial enterprise will want you to buy a ticket and get taken for a ride.

So far no one has been maimed or killed. But the show ain't over folks.

Stay tuned as we prepare to celebrate their finish.

Word got around the set that two crew members had been on that "other show." There was talk of an implicit threat to the production and fingers were pointed. The fallen jib arm was mentioned, how it easily could have killed someone, though no one mentioned just who might have been in the pool in the middle of the night, maybe some noctivagant swimmer practicing their backstroke without critical onlookers.

Gene Friedman confronted Nico and Sloan at basecamp in the village and demanded an explanation. They stood next to the catering truck in a dusty parking area. Nearby, the silver Escalade was being dressed by a prop assistant with an appropriate amount of mud to match the car's action on roads leading to this point. After today's fruit-stall collision, the car would be seen again at the mansion with papaya stains on its hood and windshield, as it had been already at the Botanical Garden's "gate" to the mansion.

"Look at the content," Sloan said. "It's got a

nationalist viewpoint or it's a leftist diatribe. Or maybe it's from some wannabe anti-imperialist clown. A prankster anarchist."

"Or someone on the crew with an axe to grind." Nico said. "Trying to make waves."

"So we just ignore it?" Friedman said. "Is that your recommendation?"

"They're like vandals having a laugh," Sloan said. "They might spray-paint a slogan next."

"They mention the other show by inference," Friedman said. "Don't say it's not connected."

"Suppose it is," Sloan said. "Do you want to shut the production down? Call in the Seals?"

Friedman looked at each of them and showed his teeth. "I want you guys to keep your fucking eyes open and tighten up the security. Let's get through this thing without any more problems."

Later in the day some wardrobe was stolen from a rack left outside the truck while the guards were watching the Escalade fishtailing down the street.

A short and slight local rider had been found to play Eddie Perez during the motorbike stunts. He wasn't a professional stuntman but he showed his riding skills to the stunt coordinator and after some specific instructions was ready to ride as the best friend of Penny La Vega, Gina's headstrong daughter.

The primary Dominican parts, aside from Gina, played by the Mexican actor Margaret Nogales, were cast out of New York, including the two underage principals. These parts were all being played by lighter-skinned actors, as a contrast to the darker Haitian characters. Dominican skin color ran the gamut from Spanish to West African, with every shade between. Extras Casting got the Dominican extras locally. The main Haitian roles, those of Madam Chery and the young girl, Fabienne, were cast in Miami. The other Haitian parts were filled by a mix of local

Haitians, who could contribute to the Creole language heard at the batey, and dark Dominicans.

Whenever the young actors playing Penny and Eddie were on set they had a tutor, by contract, so some time could be devoted to middle school lessons when they were not on camera. And at least one of their parents had to be present with them on set, as also stated in their contracts.

After his compadre moment of TropCav unity with Sloan, Nico took off for the cove association meeting, which he later termed a success, though more expensive than his estimate.

Within two days he broke out in shingles, an angry band of blisters that wrapped around his torso like a cephalopod's knobby gripping arm. He drove himself to a La Romana Hospital Emergency Room and waited in agony on a hall gurney until a doctor looked at the rash and prescribed an antiviral medication. Nico spent the next several days in his room wearing boxers and a loose t-shirt, pacing, napping, eating, applying calamine lotion, and following up on random location details. He took this ordeal as an omen and called his ailing mother. Within the week he was on a plane and gone for good.

Besides Far Cry Productions, there were four other companies who had invested in *Larimore*. Two of these were European, one based in Stockholm. Their Swedish representative, one of the many executive producers on the show, arrived on location to meet with David Sussman and Gene Friedman and attack the spiraling costs. The man's name was Thor Lundqvist.

When the crew heard about this, some of them asked if the man had brought his hammer.

And Friedman invariably said, "Yes, and he's

applying it to the budget."

Since they were understaffed, Sloan spent more time complimenting his team, often pointing out, in the middle of a pep talk, little ways to improve.

After meeting with Thor, Gene Friedman killed the search for any new locations. And if a place for Larimore to hide out after the condo was gone, so was the need to vacate the condo. Consequently, the hallway fight scene would be cut. Slashed. Excised. Scrapped. Killed.

At the border-crossing location, on the grassy bank of the Rio Soco, Sloan shared this good news with Santo and Belkis. They were assistants, not location scouts, and consequently didn't honestly feel his jubilant relief. His laughter seemed delirious to them. He asked if they knew of Chief Inspector Dreyfuss and they both smiled politely and said they did not know the name. "What about Clouseau?" he said, and got the same reaction.

The production appeared to be running like a well-oiled machine. Nothing seemed likely to derail Cragmore from his mission. His wish for an offshore picture boat at the resort—something slick, a luxury speed boat or a yacht—was nixed along with the condo fight scene and he barely acknowledged it. He was admittedly in the zone, staging his comeback, and the crew felt it too.

In the new office, Wilson asked Sloan how Belkis was doing on set. Sloan said she was very nice, very polite to the crew, could be a little firmer in her location directives, but was a fast learner. When he realized Wilson wanted to hear more about her, he added that she probably had a wild side just below the surface. Wilson didn't respond to this but made a mental note to look for signs.

Since the batey location had changed from the cane field already tech-scouted, a new mini-scout was added to a day when running shots were being filmed at the edge of the field.

The same needs were transferred to the new cane-field location. A plywood path to deliver the crane into the field. A stretch of road to assemble the pieces of shacks already built and being built at the warehouse. A village would be installed. A fake batey not far from Batey 108. A parallel village of actors and filmmakers.

As the harvest season grew closer, the population at Batey 108 was increasing. Vans could be seen coming and going. Haitian men were out on the perimeter roads, watching, and the work trucks of the production were observed. This was a strange occurrence. A water truck was spotted. At 108 there was one water spigot for the entire village. Naturally, the men wondered if the facilities at the new batey would be better.

The golf course morning was breezy with a blue sky. Little white caps rolled continuously toward the green. The actor playing Luis La Vega hit a slice on every take but the shot was not seen on camera. The ball strike made an authoritative ping as Larimore and Gina approached.

Tom Flint and Margaret Nogales had met the club manager and taken selfies with him. He had been given autographed headshots, which would go up in the clubhouse in a row of celebrity photos.

The resort was an hour away and the forecast was rain. In a cost-cutting move, a new directive, yet another consequence of Thor's visit, axed the use of the cover sets—a resort guestroom and a batey shack interior—both ready at the warehouse, due to the travel time required from the eastern base of the show, even further away than the actual location. Thor's remark on the subject was now quoted: "Rain or shine, make it work." He chastised Sussman, the producer, in earshot of the greensman, for wasting money on the cover sets, and it was clear who the heavy hitter was and which company had to most to lose should *Larimore* underperform. Sussman defended himself by saying he had based his decision on information he got from the Locations Department.

Word got around the set and the key set PA said if Thor yelled at him he would walk.

"I don't fucking care," he said. Which was bullshit because the AD yelled at him all the time.

"That's a moot point," Cecilia Wilkins, the 2nd AD said, "Thor has absolutely no reason to talk to you or even look at you, ever."

Besides the guestroom, Tom and Margaret had love scenes in the pool and on the beach, moving from a lounge chair that collapses in the sand to the sand itself, and in the surf, either as a tribute to, or in imitation of *From Here to Eternity*. Resort guests followed the action as closely as they could, taking photos from balconies and from under dripping umbrellas from distances that would make it hard to identify the actors. Except with a serious telephoto lens.

The most intense love scene, in the privacy of the guestroom, was a closed set, wherein only the camera operator and the sound man were allowed in the room. The action grew quite physical and Tom Flint fell off the bed and injured his upright penis by bending it against an overturned chair. For the rest of the day he did not stand up entirely straight and wore an expression that made him look like he had just tasted liverwurst for the first time. He refused the medic's attention, though the medic had not offered any.

When the two stars walked hand in hand on the

beach after dark, with the rain gone and the moon rising, it appeared that Larimore was bending closer to his lover or willing himself to be nearer to her stature.

Cragmore was unhappy with the day's work. He disliked both the rain footage and Tom Flint's hunchback appearance after his injury. In a private meeting with Sussman, he hatched a plan to return on Saturday, after Thor's departure, and reshoot some scenes. Tom Flint would regain his normal sexiness by then, he said. Sussman convened an emergency meeting with Locations and told Sloan to make it happen for Saturday.

As the company headed into nightwork, and into the final scenes, there was talk of internal logic, of a story coming together with all the elements assembling like a puzzle. Drama, romance, comedy, adventure, morality tale, the triumph of good over evil.

At the mansion, once the correct amount of papaya had been applied to the grill and hood of the Escalade, closely matching the amount in the photos of the car taken at the gate to the property some days ago, they were ready to shoot.

The actual entrance to the property was a forest now, through which the car proceeded to a revealing view of the well-lit house. Once Ramon had parked and exited the vehicle in a foul mood, he and the car both being noted with silent amusement by his father's guards, he proceeded up the front steps. A butler let him in and he passed through the house to the back patio.

The company moved to the cove, where Luis La Vega was smoking a cigar on his patio when he greeted his son. The ocean waves, lit by hidden lights up on the ridge, rolled in as the men drank rum, smoked formidably, and discussed the problem of Larimore. The dialogue was steely and intense. A death sentence in the dead of night.

Up on the road a production truck was partially blocking a neighbor's driveway. Though it was the middle of the night and no one needed to leave the house, the owner stood outside shouting so loudly about being disturbed, insulted, and mistreated that Locations had to get the truck moved immediately so that the only sounds would be the actors and the ocean.

The amphitheater/fountain set felt something like a pre-wrap party. The climax of the story and the last location before the batey work, which would include the final scene with Gina, Fabienne, and Larimore in the car at night, riding beside the endless cane fields.

But this was live music. This was Tootski Root in the flesh.

Some of the crew snorted coke to assist with the all-nighter, and the smell of weed wafted among the trucks—all part of the party atmosphere involving a reggaeton star known to be an advocate. And with the end of the show nearly in sight, and with the musicians and all the extras, no one could really point to where the weed was coming from. That shit came from everywhere.

Once the sound checks were satisfactory, and Tootski had achieved the proper elevation, the music got underway. In the background some crew members were dancing.

This was a diegetic event, a concert within the story, the music heard by the characters and the filmmakers alike. Between songs, audio playback at a lower volume kept the groove going. A voice came out of the flashing lights and assaulted Sloan with excitement. It was Beatriz Fernandez in her red dress, but he was buzzed and so much time had passed since he'd seen her at the Film Office.

She shrieked and hugged him and he remembered.

She kissed his cheeks, one after the other, and her vertiginous perfume encircled his head as powerfully as her arms did his torso.

"Hello Luke," she said. "The day finally came. I took your advice on the wardrobe."

He laughed and kissed her cheeks, one after the other. "You look fantastic," he said.

People were jostling them around and he thought they might be lifted into a crowd-surf when she began to dance up against him like he was a favored extra. The music blasted out again and she shouted in his ear. "I have to get back to my position." She pointed. "Close to the camera."

He watched her blend into the crowd and disappear, and he stayed among the extras until his erection calmed down.

Though the ADs and the PAs issued constant warnings, the stone steps were treacherous and high-heeled extras stumbled and fell like dominoes during the course of the night. The medic kept busy attending to sprained ankles and contusions of varying degrees of severity.

The music continued as background playback on the second night. The fountain shoot-out was choreographed in lengthy detailed pieces so the nearby restaurants were long closed before the gunfire occurred. The scenes were shot in a sequence of bloody ballet moves. Graham Perry, the charismatic traitor, was once again a crowd-pleaser, dying majestically. After they wrapped, he put on a t-shirt that said *Not In The Sequel*, which cracked up the crew and presented a startling new concept.

30. Praise is the Sound of Silence

The donkey Emile was delivered by Sanchez and left on location for the duration, along with several bales of hay. He would be needed in ways yet to be determined. He could stand around as a handsome prop. Or a Haitian boy could ride him into the field to deliver something. He might be a pet for the recovering Larimore. He was a relaxed animal and seemed like he'd be fine with improvisation.

Sonia took it upon herself to look out for Emile. His initial water bowl was a plastic bucket, but this was too small and unstable. She wrangled a metal tub from Greens and bought a supply of five-gallon water jugs. Then she purchased an equine vitamin and mineral supplement and a metal brush to keep his coat smooth and clear of debris. He used his tail to combat flies and followed the shade as it rotated around a construction shed at the rear of the set. When Emile saw Sonia coming he kicked out his hind legs, brayed, and tossed his head around.

There wasn't much shade for the crew other than that cast by trucks, the portable toilets, and the batey shacks on set. They needed the sun but prayed for rain. They had days to go, and would follow a sequence from Larimore's life at the batey to the burning of the cane and the falling of the infamous "black snow," to the kidnapping of Fabienne, the torching of some of the shacks by Ramon's goons, led by Montero, finishing with a scene of rebuilding. A fire department official from La Romana inspected the water truck, spoke to the special effects coordinator, and signed off on the shoot.

The batey was constructed close to a T-junction, so that work trucks and catering could wrap around the corners and be close but also far enough away from the set to preclude visual interference. At each end of the intersecting road, barricades were set up to dissuade random vehicles from proceeding. Guards were posted at the vehicles on both sides of the T.

On the first batey shoot day, the crew bus broke down enroute to the set. The crew napped in their seats or stood around in the dark beside an alien cane field and then began grabbing every caffeinated drink available from the coolers. Sodas, mostly, and a few cold coffee drinks. There was no hot coffee. An emergency call was placed to craft service as the sun was rising.

Meanwhile, a passenger van was dispatched to provide multiple shuttle trips. Leonidas lifted the hood on the bus and searched for a remedy by peering around and moving his hand from one spot to another as if the defective part might levitate into his grasp. He made a call for a replacement bus but couldn't say exactly when that maneuver would happen.

A half day was lost and it was lunchtime when everyone was accounted for on set. Many of the crew were overheated and in a bad mood. After all this time the menu choices had begun to seem fewer and fewer when in reality the people were just tired of the same items being served so many times. When Ronny Sanderson, the key set PA, spoke up, he was speaking for many.

"I'm just about rice and beaned out, man."

Tables and chairs had been set up on the dirt road with white popup tents over them. Beside the catering truck, the salad bar tables were getting an overlay of dust and flies. Some of the flies may have come directly from Emile's eyes or the corners of his mouth. No one was thinking about arthropodal travel patterns.

"Fuck this," one of the grips said. "How about some potatoes once in a while."

"How about some tots," Ronny said. "How about some mashed, some baked, some hash browns."

Half-eaten meals were dumped in the trash. Oily paper plates blew down the road, symbols of protest that would have to be collected by Locations personnel. The basic rule was universal: Leave a place as you found it. Excluding, of course, the scripted and agreed upon damage.

Normally, the caterers were the only part of the production who were reliably thanked, typically after every meal. For everyone else, feedback came by way of complaints. If you fucked up, you definitely heard about it. If you were doing your job just right, silence confirmed it.

Faces and necks were burnt, as if even the idea of sunscreen had fallen out of favor.

The one-line schedule was modified. The wide establishing crane shot—sweeping overhead from the midst of the cane field and down to the batey—was pushed to the next day, deemed to be too time-consuming for what was left of this day, linked as it was to a Steadicam that would move through the village at ground level in one continuous track.

Most of the day's shots revolved around a sickly

Larimore inside a sweltering airless shack, sweating and ashen, lying on a damp bed or staggering to a window to push aside a rough curtain and wonder who the passing people were. Makeup & Hair, and Wardrobe hovered right outside.

The following day a different bus showed up. It was older, the cloth seats worn threadbare in spots and in retention of an ancient smell no one appreciated. One of the wardrobe assistants felt ill but couldn't get her window open and vomited in the aisle. This led to an exodus toward the front of the bus and more bodies than usual sharing the same seats. At the location, the medic ascertained that the sick woman had a fever and a PA drove her back to the hotel.

Everyone started saying they were beaned out.

On the road beyond the catering vehicles, two figures emerged from the cane field. The guard called Sonia and together they walked to intercept the intruders. They were two young Haitian men in their twenties, one tall and thin, the other not as tall but just as thin. Sonia spoke to them in bits of the French she knew, with Spanish and sign language. A trail through the cane was visible behind them, which to her looked recently cut. Both men wore old polo shirts, shorts, and sandals and carried machetes as if they were seeking work or carried them as a matter of course.

They were from Batey 108. The taller one called himself Evens, the shorter one, Daniel. Sonia told them there was no work at the moment but they could check back another day. They casually inspected the radio on her hip as strange sounds and words flowed forth. Daniel put the gathered fingertips of one hand to his lips in a question about food. She had them follow her to the shade of the caterer's van and wait. She went around to the front of the food truck and collected cold sodas and plates of tostones, red beans, and rolls. When she came back to the van the guard was attempting to converse with the Haitians.

After they departed by the same route, Sonia marked the entrance to the trail with an orange traffic cone. As she passed his truck the caterer came out and took issue with her liberties and said the crew came first. She apologized and said she knew that but had noticed that less food was being consumed lately. He took that as an insult and said he would continue to prepare the usual number of meals.

The next day he served a seafood stew made with shrimp and conch. By early afternoon some of the crew were keeled over and heaving in the cane. There was a mutiny and people vowed to bring meals from the hotel and charge them to their rooms. Gene Friedman spoke to the caterer about the food poisoning and was assured the conch source had been a mistake that would never happen again. Friedman told him to cut back on all seafood and serve more pasta and bananas.

More Haitians showed up and Sonia received permission from the caterer to make use of the food rather than see it thrown out. Friedman looked at the table of Haitians eating and told Sonia they were not running a daycare center. Sloan interjected and said part of their agreement, the verbal part, included maintaining good relations with the neighboring "real" batey. Friedman thought this sounded like a Locations bullshit story but had too many other problems and simply walked away. Sloan had only been eating peanut butter sandwiches, yogurt, and fruit, and felt either light-headed or fine.

A girl name Judeline spoke enough Spanish to communicate with Sonia and become the 108 spokesperson. She was thirteen, wore a clean purple dress and her hair in three braids, one on each side and one at the back of her head, all adorned on the end by a baby blue plastic barrette.

Judeline told Sonia they had ducks and chickens at 108 and took trips on Sunday to a river for bathing. Very soon oxcarts would be arriving to carry the bunches of cut cane to trucks to deliver to rail cars to transport to the mill. A Dominican with a Haitian father used his pickup truck to bring them scraps of wood and sheet metal to repair houses and make new buildings. They had a schoolroom for learning Spanish and at night the men used it to play dominoes. She said they needed a clinic because blade cuts led to infections. It was her third year there.

More of the crew dropped out with fever. No one wanted to catch or pass along whatever was going around. Mosquitoes outnumbered the flies on set, day or night, and the scent of repellent was ubiquitous. People wore straw hats like campesinos but the facial shade didn't prevent the bumps on their faces and necks from being noticeable and frightening. On location, the fear of dengue spread like a separate fever.

The stars of the show, Margaret and Tom, each had a motorhome. A trailer between them housed Hair & Makeup, and Wardrobe. Another motorhome was available for the other principal actors—Madame Chery, Fabienne, Ramon and Montero—to relax in and stay cool. An SUV and driver were stationed nearby to ferry actors to the set.

The batey set looked like a smaller, skinnier version of 108, on which it had been modeled. It was a patchwork of multicolored sheets of rusted and painted corrugated tin. It was impossibly downtrodden and hopeful at once, glorious and eye-catching in its unabashed poverty. A parallel section of cane had been cut to expand the village and to provide room for an emergency lane.

Wilson visited the set as often as possible, his office workload having significantly lightened. Now that he was sending out releases to the applicable locations, letters to be signed that stated that everything had been returned to normal and any damages had been satisfactorily repaired, he was able to focus on Belkis and lend his assistance.

Until she was called before the camera, Margaret Nogales wore a wide-brim brown gaucho hat outside, with a brown bandanna tied around her face that gave her the look of a female Zorro. Even with her face mostly masked, her eyes drew people's gaze, possibly in anticipation of the unveiling, when her beauty bolted loose. You could understand Larimore's galvanization.

When they were not needed on set, the extras, mostly Haitian, sat under a tent on folding chairs and made trips to the craft service tables for snacks even though they had their own supply in the tent. People needed to walk around and see other things. They would sometimes see the other Haitians, the local Haitians, the hungrier Haitians who were not allowed beyond the catering area. The extras saw only the fake batey and the actual batey dwellers were not allowed to visit the nearby replication. It seemed possible the two groups could have switched places.

Once the daylight roadwork was done—Larimore being found by Penny and Eddie, the game of chicken between Eddie and Ramon, Gina's retrieval of the injured hero—and the quiet, touching scenes of Fabienne caring for the white man in their midst had all been shot, it was time for the burning of the cane and the trashing of the village. Then the nightwork could begin.

Real sugarcane burning was done to eliminate the bulk of the leaf trash, reduce the weight of the product, and make it easier for the cutters to harvest the bare stalks. Predetermined sections of acreage were control-burned. The burning turned the Black workers blacker, stained their skin and clothes with charcoal flakes, and gave the cutters, returning to their families at the end of the day, an apocalyptic look of ragged, dirt-streaked survivors of a respiratory torment.

With the camera low to the ground, the special effects crew ignited one section of cane and the flames were seen leaping from stalk to stalk. A wider field-level shot caught flames rising from multiple places, the result of propane being fed through gas lines to flame bars. Smoke machines were aimed into the scene and a gray fog billowed through the cane. A "foreman" ran through the scene as smoke and ash lifted and swirled. The special effects crew used portable electric blowers powered by the generator to spray cellulose "ash" out over the cane, a dark insulation material made from ground newspaper. From inside a shack, another camera caught the ash raining down, a confetti of the damned fluttering before a hazy sun. In the foreground, "workers" coughed as they passed, and from off-camera, the sound of a crying baby was heard.

The soundman gripped his headphones and bowed his head in concentration. He lifted his hand and then looked around. Something was troubling him. Soon everyone heard the engine. The AD called the cut and everyone scanned the sky as a helicopter approached from the southeast. The reverberations increased until a wobbling staccato penetrated the set and the entire crew was looking up at the black aircraft hovering straight above them.

At the edge of the road Sloan heard his walkie squawking but there was no sense in screaming into the radio. He saw Friedman running toward him, weaving between the shacks as he kept looking up to see if anything in the sky had changed.

He pointed up as if Sloan had not noticed anything out of the ordinary.

"What the fuck is this?" he yelled.

"A chopper," Sloan said.

Friedman face was red and his words sputtered out. "Get rid of it," he shouted.

Sloan raised his hand and waved the chopper away but it failed to change position.

Cragmore and Sordom were charging over to add their consternation to the inquisition.

"Are you guys handling this?" Sordom shouted.

Sloan nodded as they leaned in and completed the circle. "We're on it," he said.

"What does that mean?" the director said.

"We're trying to figure out who's up there so we can report it."

"Report it to who?"

"The airports in La Romana and the capital."

They all looked up and stared at the stationary airship.

"Get the tail number," Cragmore said, and read the sequence as Sloan wrote it down in his notebook. "It's a Bell 429," the director said. "Probably taking pictures."

"Or fucking with us," Friedman said.

The director reached overhead and waved his arms in parallel like he'd worked on an active runway in his earlier days. Like he'd be familiar with those red-cone flashlight extensions. When nothing resulted from his motions he turned both hands into middle finger extensions.

"Is it those anarchists?" Friedman said, and everyone looked at Sloan.

His face compressed into a doubtful smirk. "Those newspaper clowns? They couldn't afford a stunt like this."

"So what then?" Sordom said. "Sightseers, film junkies, Tom Flint fans?"

"The goddamn property owners," Cragmore said, and they all looked up again.

Sloan pulled out his phone and walked away, calling Dulce. It went to voicemail and he called again. Another voicemail. He texted a string of exclamation points.

He kept the phone to his ear and kept walking. She called back four minutes later.

"Hey," she said.

"Hey," he said. "Do you guys have a black helicopter? A Bell 429."

She paused. "The company has three."

"Listen," he said, and held the phone overhead. "Hear that?"

"Where are you?" she said.

"We're in the cane," he said. "The chopper is sitting right on top of us."

Crew members and extras were taking photos of the aerial disturbance. The smoke had dissipated.

"Is it bothering you?" she said.

"Are you joking? We can't work with the noise," Sloan said. "Is that your brother up there?"

She paused again. "He might be gathering documentation," she said.

"Can you ask him to stop?" Sloan said.

"No, I can't do that," she said. "He'll leave when he's finished."

He turned around on the road and headed toward the village, leaving her words hovering. Ahead he saw Sonia tending to Emile, brushing the movie ash out of his coat, soothing him as he shifted and tilted his head and ears in response to the bothersome vibrations in the air.

"Being harassed wasn't part of the deal," Sloan said.

"Interruptions happen all the time," Dulce said. "Like rain and riots."

He passed Sonia, who was watching him, and kept walking. "Dulce," he said. And as he glanced up the chopper rose quickly, tipped sideways and droned away over the fields.

In the ensuing silence, like waking from a bad dream, he said, "We have money for you."

"I've been busy with house guests," she said, "but I'll respond to your message soon."

The burn scene was reset and filmed two more times.

At dusk, with the sky still fulgent in its colors, terrified Haitians ran screaming from their cookfires as Montero and his thugs fired shots in the air and tossed torches into shacks whose windows erupted in leaping flames, most of the damage simulated by the use of propane. As soon as the cut was called, Special Effects jumped in with fire extinguishers to suppress the incidental burning. After some discussion with the director while they watched the video replay on the monitor, the AD—to reset the action—called out "Back to one."

The next night barrel fires danced in place around the village, a donkey stood in view at the side of a foreground shack, ghostly figures rustled in doorways, and the adjacent cane tips waved languidly in a moon-dusting of movie lights. Madame Chery came forth in her headscarf, her skin dark and deeply cross-hatched, as car beams raked over her.

A black Suburban parked, cut its lights. Gina stepped out and approached the village elder.

The two women shook hands warmly but the scene was marked by a menacing portent.

As Gina began to speak, a distant whistling drew

the soundman's concern, and a moment later a thunderous starburst exploded and hissing twinkles of incandescence showered down over the cane field. Another boom and a riot of cascading sparks followed. Then another.

The crew stood in awe, their faces turned to the light like heliotropic flowers, aglow in the wash of each burst.

"What the fuck now?" the director shouted between the sonic detonations. He looked in the direction of their hidden neighbors. "Is that the batey? What do they have to be celebrating about?"

Sloan was already heading for his car when Friedman shouted after him. "Do something, Locations."

Trotting along the road past the caterer he tried to keep track of the number of fireworks sent up. Ahead, another one lifted off as a screaming tracer, angled over the road and the set, then exploded, illuminating the sky in a white and rosy glow, smoke trails falling from a flower of light. He knew who it was. And they would be leaving very soon. He got in his car, started it, turned it around, estimating the launch location. Probably on the next intersecting road.

He turned right, darkness swallowing all but his headlight beams. Then he saw taillights in the distance, tiny red dots running between the stalks. Turning left, then they were gone.

He stopped to examine the debris in the road. Spilled and spent matches, burn marks in the dirt, burns on a plywood stand with slots aimed toward the production. A dud rocket on its side. Evidence no one would investigate. Was that it? A celebratory disruption by anarchists? Did they laugh and have fun?

"Beca," he said to the cane, raising his hands as if she were lying in wait. "You got me."

His walkie was squawking, fading in and out of range. He thought he heard the word *clear.* Then again. It was a question. The AD asking if they were clear. Then Sonia saying, *Standby.*

He texted her. *All clear.* And she responded to the AD.

Sloan was in no hurry to get back. He looked at the swarm of insects swirling through the light of his car's beams, connecting the twin shafts with moths, mosquitoes, and flies, like erratic electrons of various sizes. A frenzy of visual chaos. He killed his engine and killed the lights and stood in the road under the vast field of impartial stars. Over the cane he could see the radiating glow of the lights up on the crane.

How long could he stay away? Would they imagine he got kidnapped by the anarchists? Now it suddenly sounded appealing.

He looked at his watch. 1:29am.

The Batey 108 Haitians who had been asleep in their shacks were probably awake now. Maybe wondering if the movie would actually bring the rumored improvements.

As he returned to the set, lunch was being served. The crew sat under tents with fans blowing through. He wasn't sure but thought maybe the volume, the chatter of breaktime, diminished as he passed. Beyond the fan vibrations, he kept thinking he heard helicopters approaching. He would eat later.

Craft service had saved the day with empanadas and grilled cheese sandwiches, substituting substantial snacks for some of the endless bags of crunchy junk. Sloan grabbed a couple of empanadas on his way out. Dawn was nowhere near and he texted Sonia to say goodnight.

Getting in his car—the sky dark, the wind in the bending cane all around, the set behind him, the granular light indicating some alien landing base, the indistinct pulsing sounds of the generator like aural hallucinations, the whole thing almost in the permanent rearview—he felt disoriented. The shift was beginning. The next big change. Job status. The moving on. The next thing, whatever it was.

He drove down the road, a vibrating night tunnel, his car wobbly, his mind wobbly. At the intersection he cleared himself and accelerated onto the pavement, windows half-down, wind blowing through the car. The vibrations increased. He shook his head and saw his hands shaking on the steering wheel. The car slammed down on the left side. His face hit the edge of the window glass and his foot hit the brake. The vehicle ground to a stop, biting into the road's surface. He saw a wheel rolling ahead of him. His wheel. He touched the side of his face, looked at his hand. Threw the door open. Stepped out and looked around. Felt the tender spot again as he stared into the light of his beams. His tire was still rolling down the road. Escaping.

He looked around again, making sure this was real. That he hadn't been driving through his own head. Mosquitoes whined in his ear. He reached inside the car and turned it off and grabbed his flashlight. The empanadas were on the floor.

The right front tire was missing two lug nuts and the other three were loose. He tightened them by hand. The back tires had all their nuts. He searched behind the car for about fifty feet and found one silver nut glinting in the light. He put it in his pocket. In the other direction he located the missing wheel and rolled it back to the car, hunched over in the glare of his headlights. He leaned the tire against the fender and stood breathing, looking back the way he'd come.

In the distance headlights were approaching. Sloan wondered if he should run into the cane and lie down. This—getting gunned down—must be the next step in the execution. He waited.

The vehicle was moving slowly, engine rumbling, its lights imperfectly aligned, one brighter, like the other one had a cataract. It stopped behind his car and he saw that the vehicle was an old truck. A man got out and walked toward him. The man was short. He stood before Sloan and looked up into his face in the light. He reached up with gnarled fingers and lightly touched Sloan's swollen cheekbone. He glanced at the loose tire, then moved around the rental car looking at the other tires. He was an old man in an old straw hat. A farmer, Sloan thought.

He watched the old man walking back to his truck and suddenly thought that he knew him from somewhere. The man came back carrying a jack and a lug wrench. He dropped the jack beside the loose tire, squatted at the nearest rear wheel and removed two nuts, then took two from the other side.

Sloan felt unsteady. He watched the old man jack up the car and secure the errant wheel, then go around snugging up the remaining lug nuts. The man gave Sloan a fresh look and patted his shoulder and said, "*Con cuidado*," and turned to leave with his tools.

"Gonzo?" Sloan said.

The old man stopped and looked back at him. Then he set the tools in the bed of his truck, got in, and started the engine. As he passed the bewildered Sloan, he raised his hand.

"*Muchas gracias*," Sloan said, remembering the lug nut in his pocket.

Thinking the payment for the sugar location would be in two parts, the down payment and the balance, and then following that with the fantasy of delivering checks to Dulce on two separate occasions, at night, as before, he was stunned to read that she had sent him her bank information and requested a wire transfer.

As far as he knew, she had not visited the set. Now he imagined she was having an internecine conflict with her brother Frank and they were letting the scenes play out in the cane field.

He passed the banking info along to Gene Friedman and Accounting.

In his room with the curtains drawn, he dreamt that he did deliver a check and was greeted by a tipsy Dulce in a teddy. She wasted no time in her manner and bearing stating her eagerness for sex and her preference for it, telling him she wanted him up against her big soft side, turning around to display the fullness of her lower half, then lying down on the rug and offering it. Looking up at him, she said she favored the position because of the angle and the increased depth.

He said she already knew his depth and it hadn't changed. She laughed, validating, he thought, the fact that humor generally made women feel generous.

He stood by the coffee table relishing the sight of her, self-satisfied that he had known this was going to happen. He sipped his cocktail and noticed the condom packets on the table. I'm such a romantic, she said.

When he was finally inside her, riding with her rocking motions, the sounds of pleasure filling the room, his personal tide rising and his right hand forcing her to lift up so he could grasp her breasts, briefly, before pivoting back to the rug and bracing himself to achieve greater depth, his release just around the bend, a sudden noise broke the spell.

He awoke, saw his hotel room, and was struck by tremendous regret. There was more shouting. He bolted out of bed and stuck his head in the hall. A guy was pounding on a door.

"Motherfucker," Sloan said.

The guy down the hall looked at him and said, "What'd you say?"

Sloan shut his door and sat on the bed. That was as close as he'd get to fucking Dulce Medina.

He opened the set before dark and saw that nothing appeared to be destroyed or stolen. The trucks remained where they had been parked, and the guards were accounted for. In the catering truck, breakfast was being prepared, the first meal, no matter the time of day. No rain was seen on the horizon. Nor were there any helicopters coming in low over the fields blasting *The Ride of the Valkyries*.

He was called to a meeting with the director, the producer, and the UPM. Cragmore was making a case for two more days. He said he got fucked by the chopper and fucked by fireworks. He was about to shoot the abduction of Fabienne, a cornerstone of the movie. But he needed more batey life. This was the real fabric of the movie, he insisted. The heart. The meat.

Thor was gone and Sussman relented. They could wrap early tonight and then have enough turnaround for the crew to shoot two more split days. The question to Sloan was about securing the location for the extra days, without additional costs being incurred, and he assured them they could proceed because the harvest was still a week or two away.

"Just like that?" Sussman said. "On your say-so."

"Go for it," Sloan said.

Cragmore said, "With friends like this, who needs saboteurs."

Sloan may as well have been wearing a scarlet letter on his shirt. He slunk like a pariah through his remaining time on location. He texted Dulce and said the money was being wired and they would be finished shooting in two days. And would then dismantle the set. She replied with a heart, nothing more.

The extra footage consisted of workers in the field, stained machete blades swinging, dark faces and arms soaked in sweat, drops falling in slow motion, the tears of the working man, the labor of slaves. In one field scene, the director included Evens and Daniel, the two young Haitians who had first visited from 108. There were cookfires at dusk, the shelling of beans in a tub, old people and young, women gathered in standing water at a spigot, taking turns and sharing tales.

An old woman's face as she lay on her bed, the skin of her cheekbones burnished golden in the candlelight, the drape at the window barely stirring, her eyes staring into the camera as if friend or family or spirit had entered her room. A close-up of a child chewing a piece of cane, the exposed fibrous pulp as white as his teeth.

By the end, many in the crew showed some degree of weight loss. Not exactly a skeleton crew but some had departed early, haggard with the leftover fatigue of fever, too many cane field days, listlessness.

Normally the wrap days—the post-shooting period of cleanup, making sure no loose ends were left dangling—were a beautiful ending to a long project. Following up on the closure of locations did not prevent long torpid lunches and the recounting of dramatic and humorous moments along the way. Coinciding with this was the unavoidable letdown, that lost feeling of dissatisfaction that inevitably occurred following the termination of the unusual, always-changing life of the preceding weeks or months. In part, because the paychecks were ending.

Wrap time was considered gravy, or ice cream, after the stomach-churning meal of the show.

Friedman told Sloan he didn't need to stay. Sonia and Wilson could handle the wrap, at a much lower cost. Sloan should wrap out his paperwork, his petty cash, and check out of his hotel room. It was a bland dismissal. Devoid of the customary salutation: Great working with you.

A final statement came out in the *Free Daily*, the third from the Anarchists, which Sloan now capitalized in his notes, like an official name.

Goodbye goodbye investors in image
All pillaging tricksters please leave our shores
Go home simplistic saviors of the downtrodden
The fakery is done, the story burned out
RIP Pablo

He went up to Altos de Chavón for a last night, to a relatively high-end restaurant. In the bar's mirror he looked like a castaway. Despite everything he felt fine. The job was done. The TropCav curse might finally fade away.

He'd invited his team for drinks and dinner. Sonia was the first to join him.

"Are you going to shave?" she said.

He shrugged. "Sometime."

"What happened to your face?" she said.

He shook his head. "Bumped into a door," he said. "Tired, clumsy."

She had a mojito. He had Brugal on the rocks.

"To the finish line," she said, lifting her glass.

"Here's to us," he said, clinking her glass with his. They watched each other in the mirror.

"What's next?" she said.

"Taking a break," he said.

"Where are you going?"

"Dominica," he said. "Tomorrow."

She smiled. "Sounds good. I've never been."

"Neither have I," he said. "But they call it The Nature Island. And I'm halfway there already." He turned to face her. "You're welcome to join me."

"Oh, would you allow that?" She laughed.

"You know what I mean," he said. "It would be fun if you did."

"I know what you mean," she said. "But I have to wrap for a few days. And I have to find a good home for Emile. And I need to save some money."

"Sure," he said. "I had to ask. But the movie's over. Things change."

He ordered another drink. She put her hand on his arm.

"I enjoyed it," she said. "And I learned a lot from you. Thank you for hiring me."

He laughed. He felt like kissing her. "There was no way I wasn't going to hire you. Your first impression skills are off the charts."

In the mirror he saw Wilson approaching and turned to greet him.

"My man," he said, and gripped the kid by the shoulders.

"Hey boss," Wilson said. "Hey Sonia."

"I'm just a regular civilian now," Sloan said. "We all go our separate ways."

Wilson grimaced. "It's sort of sad," he said.

A club soda was ordered for him and he remained standing to face the others.

"It's a weird feeling," Sonia said. "The life we had together suddenly ending."

Sloan drank and felt the welcome burn. The dependable numbing. The melancholy.

"During the production we live in a vacuum," he said. "A fictional world within the world. When it ends we don't know where we are. We're lost, temporarily."

"That's true," Sonia said. "You must be used to it by now."

"Not really," he said. "It's always a strange sensation even though I know it's coming."

They sipped silently for a moment, surrounded by

the sounds of communal pleasure.

Wilson told them he'd sent the departmental thank-you letters to all the locations, plus the Parks Department, Municipal Services, and the Film Office. "Hey," he said. "How's Nico doing?"

"Good question," Sloan said. "I need to give him a call."

"We had a good team," Wilson said.

Sloan raised his glass. "You guys were amazing," he said. "I really would like to thank you and say that you totally fucking nailed it but I can't, because, you know, technically, praise is the sound of silence. So let's have a moment of silence."

They laughed, clinked their glasses, drank, and held the moment.

Within fifteen minutes Belkis and Santo had shown up—separately, much to Wilson's relief—and they got a table in the open courtyard, sequestered from the evening's stream of humanity.

The gathering was memorable, and probably would be for a while. He had wanted to take them someplace they didn't frequent, being far removed from the capital where they all lived and not much on the radar for locals of their age. The fact that the production had shot there made it special in another way.

Afterward, there were sincere hugs of gratitude and comradery forged in the trenches of film.

Like Sloan, the assistants Santo and Belkis were now unemployed and would disappear back into the freelance world of waiting. Or at this early stage, they might choose a more dependable path to steady work.

At the parking area, Sonia and Sloan lingered, talking while the others left. She said she had a present for him and they walked together to her car. She opened the door, withdrew a small gift-wrapped box, and handed it to him. He shook it gently and it rattled.

Inside, on a little square of cotton, lay a pale blue stone, irregular but smooth, as if tumbled, and he held it in his palm. It was either a piece waiting to become jewelry or a piece by itself.

"Do you know what it is?" she said, smiling.

He vaguely remembered a kind of gemstone that was found nowhere else in the world but he couldn't think of the name. It was blue, marbled with milky white patterns, like a portable glimpse into the Caribbean Sea.

"It's beautiful," he said.

"It's larimar," she said, and laughed. "Only found in the DR, in only one place."

"Larimar," he said. "Ah, I get it." He laughed too.

"In case you start to forget the movie," she said. "Or me."

He shook his head. "One is a lot more likely than the other." He put the stone in its box and slid it into his pocket. "Thank you," he said.

"What'd you get me?" she said.

"I accidentally left it at the hotel," he said. "Just spaced out."

"You could bring it by my room," she said, shrugging.

"I will do that," he said.

He looked around the parking lot, the stone streets and buildings, the strolling figures, the open night above the river, the stars over the distant sea. He held her and she put her arms around his neck and their eyes locked. The kiss started as light as air, lips brushing, tongue tips teasing—their former secrecy released in a public arena—and then became flushed and frenetic in a force akin to uncaged carnivores.

Epilogue

He flew to San Juan and took a regional flight on a Twin Otter to Dominica, declared himself a tourist, and cleared customs. Outside, he took a photo of the Canefield Airport sign, thinking it would be a good intro in his text to Nico.

The small island airport, the lack of development, the informality of a rugged mountainous landscape, the three miles to the capital, Roseau, itself a quaint township compared to the Dominican capital. He had scaled down significantly. Something about the similarity in the names appealed to him, made sense in some abstract way, gave him a feeling that a random decision was the right one.

He had no plan except to unplug, disengage, hike, breathe clean air, explore, let the greater world fall away in layers. To be nobody, an anonymous lizard shedding its skin. A student.

And that's what he wrote—for occupation—with a ballpoint pen in the guesthouse ledger.

The next day he made a list of places and activities. He walked around the capital fluctuating between relaxed and the opposite of relaxed. The people were friendly but not overly so. Wood was a basic resource on the heavily forested island and the colorful buildings were low and mostly timber. There were chickens and goats in town. English was the official language, left over from the Brits, but a French-laced patois was also spoken and reminded him of the Haitians. Kids wore school uniforms. Mist rolled off the hills and mountains to the north, east, and south. Offshore to the west, sperm whales lived, the only place they resided year-round. They slept vertically in groups, heads upward, suspended in communal meditation. Rainfall in the Caribbean was the highest here. Tropical rainforests, thermal springs, jungle waterfalls, a boiling lake.

He rented a small four-wheel-drive pickup and plotted his route. He reminded himself that he was just a tourist in search of natural beauty. Or filling the time between jobs. He wasn't scouting.

And yet, he was always scouting. It was in his blood. He saw everything in terms of filming. Camera angles, light direction, time of day. Basecamp. Catering. Where would the crew park? Could a ten-ton grip truck make the turn into that lot?

He drove down to Scotts Head to snorkel. He wanted to clear his own head.

The water was outstanding. Maybe the best he'd ever seen. The narrow strip of land leading to the elevated peninsula was rocky. The island was rocky, of volcanic origin, its beaches made of black sand.

He swam with squid, a pair whose huge, curious eyes followed him in effortless locomotion. It was like they had nothing better to do. As he watched them watching him, he thought he might have to delete calamari from his diet.

He saw an octopus wrapped around a rock, nearly invisible in its camouflage, and had the same thought.

Too smart, too fluid, too impossible to be real. A fellow alien on earth.

A turtle crossed his field of vision, a strange brown being flapping its shell through the blue.

Further out there in the depths were the sperm whales, living their large deep-diving lives. Would he swim with them? Would he hear them click-speaking?

The next day he drove north to Laudat, near Morne Trois Pitons National Park, so he could hike to Boiling Lake, through the Valley of Desolation. Which sounded about right. He'd been keeping to himself. Did he have to share it with someone special? He'd tried that. Then the work killed it. Or he killed it. Or she killed it. Or they both killed it. Did a photo have any meaning if no one else saw it?

He stayed at Mountain House Lodge in the tiny village. Found a guide named Charles and took off early the next morning. The hike was arduous, up and down, but did not appear to be any kind of strain for Charles, who carried a machete to nick thin limbs out of the way or tap low hanging branches in warning. The guide wore rubber boots suitable for mud puddles and never appeared to be short of breath. He didn't speak much but he kept an eye on Sloan and made sure he was okay.

The Valley of Desolation was aptly named. Sulfurous fumaroles, the odor of poisonous steam, mist swirling around menacing yellow holes. Low cloud ceiling. A parched, desiccated, scaly landscape. Gases escaping from molten magma below ground. Poor light for filming. Difficult access for a crew. A producer would label it dangerous, excessive. Off-limits. Not to be scouted.

The lake itself a great bowl of steam, a flooded fumarole, clearing at times to reveal gray bubbling water. The rim uninviting for close inspection. The area full of cracks, holes, hot vents.

Seven hours there and back. In the misty village the night cool came early. A hammock on the porch, the quiet black sky, a constant chorus of tree frogs. Callaloo soup and cassava bread well earned. Along with the rum.

Sloan realized he had to mix it up. He would continue north, check out Portsmouth, the second town. Stores, internet, rustic civilization.

Driving on the left kept him vigilant. The narrow road consisted of wild blind turns which prompted regular horn blowing to announce a vehicle's presence in its lane. There were frequent steep drop-offs as the road wove through mountainous terrain.

He took a beachfront cottage. He wanted to relax but felt like he was rushing. To what? There was no one paying him to scout. No clock was ticking. Except the one marking his life. Let us not forget the big picture. We are all rushing headlong to our deaths.

He sat outside on his porch drinking coffee in the morning light, the sun still behind the mountains, the calm, open bay before him.

In a few weeks he'd have forgotten the names of half the crew he just worked with. Not that he was the greatest of minglers. In fact, he was a lousy mingler. What was he, then? A guy who reflected on his lack of mingling. Waiting for the next mission.

Meanwhile, he would climb Morne Diablotin, the highest peak on the island, the culminant position for this trip, an expedition and a challenge. He could do it without a guide. There was a trail. He could figure it out because there was no reason not to.

Feminine French voices in conversation found him and he realized he had neighbors in the cottage to the north. He saw two women on their porch and then saw them leave a little later. When they got to the beach they glanced behind. One of them waved and he waved back. She looked like Jane Birkin. He decided to stick around.

After a restorative swim he walked north along the sweeping curve of the beach. The sand was gray, the bay fringed with coconut palms and a few small establishments. At the far end of the bay the curve extended into a promontory with two hills and he decided to walk there. There was an old fort and a wide view back at Portsmouth, the irregular land rising behind it, the clouds riding the land.

He emailed Nico the photo of the Canefield Airport sign. And wrote:

I moved on but can't get away from this. Hope you and your mom are doing ok.

He was slicing a papaya when he got the reply.

Damn, you're being followed. Mom is ok, doing treatments.

A few minutes later Nico called.

"Hey man, where are you?"

"Dominica," Sloan said.

"Scouting again already?" Nico said.

"Not for money."

"Ahh, you've lowered your rate," Nico said.

"Temporary civilian," Sloan said. "When you don't make it, you spend it."

"How'd the show end up?" Nico said.

"It got done," Sloan said. "I skipped the wrap. Sonia and Wilson are handling it."

"And everyone was happy?" Nico said.

Sloan wasn't sure it was a serious inquiry but refrained from laughing. "That's a complicated question," he said. "Cragmore got into batey life at the end and added more scenes. He used some people from the real batey as extras so they got a little money. We fed some of the neighbors a few times. Then there was the rebuilding scene so I guess it ended with a message of hope."

"So what's the verdict?" Nico said.

"There's talk of multiple Oscars," Sloan said.

Nico laughed. "You lying snout-fair."

"You distant nebulon," Sloan said.

The laughter was like old times for a minute.

"What are you doing there?" Nico said.

"I'm about to eat a papaya," Sloan said. "Then read a book and plan a mountain hike. What about you? How are those blisters?"

"Mostly dried up," Nico said. "As soon as I can put on a wetsuit I'm going surfing. Like next week."

"That's cool," Sloan said. "Take care of yourself."

"Likewise amigo. Be well."

He'd barely read on the show. He didn't count screenplays as reading. He'd carried Chandler and Portis with him all this way. *The Long Goodbye* and *Gringos*, respectively.

After a papaya and cheese-toast lunch, he settled into the languid heat of the porch and opened *Gringos*, which felt appropriate.

In the afternoon his neighbors appeared between the cottages carrying bags as they returned from town. Their hands were full but the Jane Birkin girl nodded and Sloan said hello. He could not think of anyone the other girl looked like. Maybe Simone Signoret.

They set the bags on their porch and walked back over.

"You are alone?" the Birkin girl said. She seemed like the leader.

"I am," Sloan said. "My name's Luke."

"I'm Emilie," she said, "and she is Justine."

"It's a pleasure to meet you," Sloan said.

Justine looked at him but seemed like she'd be more comfortable in black and white, wearing a scarf and smoking unfiltered cigarettes.

"You just arrived?" Emilie said. Her questions

doubled as statements.

"A few days ago," Sloan said. "I went snorkeling, went to the Boiling Lake, did not snorkel there, then came here. What have you done?"

She smiled and glanced at her friend. "We are lazy," she said.

Sloan laughed. "That's so funny," he said. "You mean you haven't done anything?"

She laughed too. "We took a boat tour on the Indian River." She pointed vaguely.

"How was that?" he said. "What kind of boat?"

"A small one," she said, moving her arms in sync. "No motor."

Sloan nodded. "A rowboat."

"Yes, that one," she said, looking at her friend, who did not elaborate.

"What did you see?" Sloan said.

Emilie lifted her palms. "It was a lazy river," she said, smiling dimples into her cheeks. "Just some birds and *crabe*." She added a syllable to crab and made pinching motions with her fingers.

Justine jumped in. "At the end was a jungle bar. With rum."

The story seemed to end there. A local guide rowed them up a lazy river the Indians once used to reach the sea. Capped off with punch.

"We will make vegetable pasta for dinner," Emilie said. "Callaloo, dasheen, fresh local."

"We invite you," Justine said.

"Super," Sloan said. "I will completely clear my schedule."

Emilie laughed. "Come at seven," she said. "Or we can shout for you."

He received an excessive emergency email full of caps checking his immediate availability.

The producer, someone he didn't quite remember,

hoped he was doing well, attached the brief and expressed his apology, concern, and irritation regarding the short turnaround time. It was a holiday commercial scheduled to be on the air in four weeks. He needed scouting in Miami ASAP.

The title of the ad was: Jump into the Holidays with Brighter Teeth.

Sloan immediately thought of a better title: Bite into the Holidays with Brighter Teeth.

The first mockup illustration showed a desk with a standing sign beside it that read: *Patient Check-in.* Behind the desk sat a prim, well-dressed woman whose nameplate read: *Director of First Impressions.* Her horrified expression, as she faced a patient that the viewer could only see from the rear, conveyed the kind of distaste she might feel if she discovered a cigarette butt in her salad.

Sloan was left to wonder if the tooth color was yellow, gray, green, or some combination.

Other illustrations showed the patient in an examination room, outside a modern office building shaking hands with a man in a white coat, at an outdoor restaurant, at the beach holding a beach ball, walking along a vibrant street with an attractive woman, getting out of a car in front of a decorated house, sitting at a festive table laughing heartily with other holiday guests. The message was clear. A bright-toothed person could be proud and happy to go anywhere.

A few replies came to Sloan's mind.

I wish I could help but I'm focused on vomiting.

I'm currently supporting a moratorium on dental promotions.

I'd rather be dropped in chains into a boiling lake.

Instead, he wrote back saying he was out of the country but sent his thanks. He recommended a couple of Miami scouts and provided their contact info.

He didn't need to be shouted over. But he miscalculated the walking distance between the two cottages, or the speed of his saunter, and arrived for dinner a minute early, darkness already fallen.

He brought a bottle of rum and was greeted warmly by his French neighbors. The cottage was identical to his, but messier, as befitted the housing of twice as many occupants. The place smelled of fruit and lotions and candles. The girls said they were hungry.

There were books and clothes scattered around, and sand on the floor, and it looked as if they had made a home. Emilie was tossing a salad while Justine chopped the vegetables. A large pot sat on the stove. They were vegetarians and presumably shared the bedroom, as friends or more.

Sloan got out glasses and ice and poured.

The girls were lithe, with similar straight brown hair, and of nearly the same height and age, perhaps five or ten years younger than him. They were from Lyon, not Paris, and met at university. Emilie had studied Ecology and Justine was an Event Manager. They asked Sloan about his work and grew more interested as he spoke about it.

He tried to explain the freelance aspect, how the vacation concept could be unreliable and cancelled at any moment. How predicting his future, or even anticipating it and making long-range plans, didn't work. This seemed like the main downside to outsiders.

He wanted to say that each job was its own little story and that he lived a string of stories within the wider story of his life. A catalog of experiences, places, and people. But this sounded commonplace and trite. And where did it lead?

It was a kind of hamster wheel, he said, but the

changes between day and night—what the hamster operated by—in his case were marked by job and no-job, spread out and more varied.

"Hamster," he said, pronouncing it slowly. "How do you say it in French?"

"*Am-ster*," Emilie said. "*Le am-ster.*"

"Yes," he said. "They like to run on a little spinning wheel at night and sleep during the day."

"We understand," Justine said. "France has many *am-ster*."

They finally sat down to eat. A lamp and candles were lit but the AC was off. The sound of surf poured into the room through open windows, along with salt air. Sloan made a third drink for all of them. His skin was slick. He outweighed either of them by forty or fifty pounds but they held their liquor. The French constitution. He was calculating their fitness for strenuous hiking. Since they claimed to be lazy.

He found the meal to be delicious, the dasheen cooked soft, with a nutty sweet-potato taste. Butter and lemon in the pasta, the callaloo like spinach among the noodles.

"Day after tomorrow," he said, "I'm planning to hike up Diablotin, the highest peak here."

He got up to make another round of drinks. The girls watched him with shining eyes.

"How long will it take?" Emilie said.

"I think about eight hours, up and down," he said.

"What will you see?" Justine said.

He smiled and said, "The world."

They laughed. And he set their drinks on the table.

"What do we need?" Emilie said.

"She means what do *you* need," Justine said.

"Shoes and water," Sloan said. "A snack. Shorts and a t-shirt."

They sat looking at him, drinking as the idea fermented.

"Are you strong?" he said.

Emilie showed her thin bicep muscle and strained to make it bigger.

"We can do it," she said. She glanced at Justine, who smiled close-mouthed.

"What do you have? Boots, running shoes? Something besides sandals?"

"We have tennis," Emilie said.

"Great," he said. "It will be muddy." He made a slope with his hand. "And steep sometimes."

Justine looked dubious.

"Think about it tomorrow," he said. "If you want to go we'll leave early the next day."

He raised his glass. "To our adventure," he said, and they all clinked.

Speaking like it was a done deal, he said, "We'll come back here at the end of the day. Then, the next day we can go down south and swim with the sperm whales. I'll drive. After that I'll bring you back up here if that's what you want."

"Like a taxi," Emilie said.

"A free taxi," he said.

They drank more and he said sperm whales were the largest toothed animal alive, with the largest brain on the planet, who dove to great depths to prey on the elusive giant squid. But they were docile with divers as long as their calves were not approached. The famous white whale in *Moby-Dick* was another story because men were trying to kill him and he sought revenge. Then Sloan said he wasn't sure, but he might want to skip the whale watching and not intrude on them.

They killed the bottle and he thanked them. They hugged as a sloppy group. On the porch they kissed each of his cheeks in the French fashion and it seemed funny. He stumbled home.

Sloan slept like a possum in an extended state of

thanatosis and then shuffled into another dormant state on the porch and sipped coffee, holding the cup so that the heat rose into his nose and invaded the slits of his eyes. He contemplated his situation on the shore of Prince Rupert Bay.

He had a plan for a couple of days and maybe that was enough for the moment. But his life was always waiting for the next unknown, unseen thing to present itself. He wasn't controlling the narrative. He passed from one stage to the next, but there was no transformation taking place. The liminality was missing.

He waded into the bay and swam without a mask or fins, gliding along the sandy bottom, feeling his way through a blurry world. The clear, clean water provided him with a minor transformation. The fish were indistinct, flashes of fluid color like prism shards. He longed to see something startling, a platypus, some chimeric creature that would shake his perceptions and defy his experience.

He stood in the shallows looking up and down the beach. A few walkers, a few porch dwellers, coconuts scattered like brown rocks, clouds piling up over the central heights. No sign of the lazy French girls yet.

He poured another cup of coffee and called Sonia.

Her voice lifted him skyward. "Good morning Lucas."

"Good morning my dear," he said. "What's happening there?"

"We're almost finished wrapping the batey," she said. "All the wood and stuff was given to 108. The planters, the barrels, some of the furniture. The carpenters helped build some new dwellings. They have all the tools and work fast."

"That's great," he said. "It's not like they need any permits out there."

"What are you doing?" she said.

"I just took a swim. Tomorrow I'm hiking up to the highest point."

"*Chévere*," she said.

"How's Emile?" he said.

"He's still here," she said. "Our little friend, Judeline, loves to ride him." She paused. "We are kind of making him a donation." She laughed. "We have to pay Sanchez though."

"You have to hide it from Friedman," he said.

"I know," she said.

"How's Wilson?"

"He's good. In the office today."

"How's your mom doing?" he said. "And Pucho?"

"She's fine. She loves Pucho and he loves her."

He laughed. "That's the way it goes with dogs."

"When are you going home?" she said.

"In about a week."

There was a moment of wind rustling through the cane. "The Medina lady came by," she said.

"Did you talk to her?" he said.

"Yes. She was checking the cleanup. And she asked about you."

"That's nice. I really hope she spends the money on the batey," he said. "But who knows."

"*Quién sabe*," Sonia said.

He pictured her standing in the dusty road in her broad field hat, her beautiful face shaded from a blazing sun. "Was there a wrap party?" he said.

She laughed. "If you can call it that. Friedman paid for everyone to have one drink at the hotel bar."

"That cheap little bastard," Sloan said. "No food?"

"Oh yes," she said. "Little bowls of mixed nuts."

"Symbolizing the crew," he said. "How clever."

"But then the AD bought a lot of drinks," she said. "And the director thanked everyone. That was nice."

"All is forgiven in victory," he said. He took a breath. "Did you ever spend any time in Miami?"

There was a pause. "I went shopping with my mom when I was a kid," she said. "And I've been to the airport to connect."

"When I get back," he said, "I want to buy you a ticket to come visit me. If you want."

"Really?" she said. "Okay, cool."

"I was thinking we could go somewhere else too," he said.

"Sure, I would love that," she said.

"Me too," he said. His chest felt full and he thought he might take a nap.

"How do you like it there?" she said.

"I like it," he said. "It's peaceful. Except for the driving."

She laughed. "Nothing's worse than our driving over here."

They wished each other well, encompassing the avoidance of injury or intestinal issues.

Sloan saw nothing concrete on the horizon but this woman occupying his mind.

He went out to get some groceries and a few supplies for the hike, which he knew would be a slog. Mud, bruises, and not losing the route. If he could recall it, he'd sing a chant the Fortunados sang as they journeyed into the unknown, the world itself, up and over mountains and hills to the lethal sea where the enigmatic enemy waited. He opened his notebook and wrote.

hay hom hay hom, all de good rider now dey com
charlie mike charlie mike, de wild dog he gonna bite
capibara capibara, bird on de head, all de bad mon
soon to be ded

www.ingramcontent.com/pod-product-compliance
Lightning Source LLC
Chambersburg PA
CBHW030546020726
47494CB00005B/1502